DEATH AND VENGEANCE

SEELEY JAMES

Published by
Machined Media
12402 N 68th St
Scottsdale, AZ 85254

DEATH AND VENGEANCE released May 14th, 2019
Print ISBN: 978-1-7322388-6-2
ePub ISBN: 978-1-7322388-5-5
Distribution Print ISBN: 978-1-7322388-7-9
Sabel Security #6 version 2.23

Formatting: BB eBooks
Cover Design: Jeroen ten berge

SEE THE SEELEY JAMES COLLECTION

SEELEYJAMES.COM/BOOKS

FOR MY DAUGHTER
and our future president
Amelia

CHAPTER 1

ADMIRAL ANNIE WILKES HAD BEEN expecting to spend the rest of the day handling emergency calls about the bombing. That changed when she stepped out of the ladies' room. A pistol peeked from under a jacket draped over a stranger's arm. She scanned the Mumbai Hilton's hallway for her security detail. Five yards away, her lieutenant lay face down on the floor. Farther away, her chief of staff struggled against restraints and a gag, his arms held in check by two men in business suits.

"I don't have time for this." She turned her angry gaze to the man with the gun. "We're on the verge of a world war. There's been an attack—"

"Change of plans, Admiral," the man hissed. "You're coming with me."

He opened his suit coat to flash a red silk square sewn on the inside. Three stars were bleached into the material, two small ones with a larger one above them. The symbol of a high-ranking Redjacket.

Her anger flared. "If you're one of Roche's toadies, you're already in more trouble than you know. Now get out of here."

"It's pronounced, Row-SHAY," he snarled.

"I don't care. You're obstructing an admiral of the US—"

"You've been summoned to a special briefing." He shoved the weapon into her ribs. "We need to get our stories straight about the Saudis."

Admiral Wilkes felt her anger explode. She knew President Chuck Roche was a double-crossing bastard, but the events of the day were rapidly spiraling beyond her expectations. A quick glance around the hall gave her no hope. Five men watched her without concern. None were in

Navy uniform. More Redjackets. The hotel employees were nowhere in sight.

"A hundred twenty-five dead sailors are my priority." She glared at him. "I'm on my way to conduct a full investigation of the incident. If you have any relevant information about—"

He smirked. "Before the investigation, we need to have a little talk. Like I said, you're coming with me."

Wilkes found ten eyes impatiently awaiting her compliance. She considered screaming for help, but the meeting room was around the corner at the far end of the hall. Too far to be heard. She pulled herself up to her full five foot four and tugged her uniform straight. She looked him in the eye. "In that case, I need to get my purse."

"You don't need a purse."

She leaned to him. "Once a month, a woman needs her purse if she's going somewhere for more than an hour. Are we going to be away for more than an hour?"

"Fine." His gaze dropped to the floor. "Where's the purse?"

"In my room. Fourth floor." She stared him down.

"We'll hold the meeting there." He pushed her toward the elevator and nodded to his associates. They dispersed around the room, covering the exits and securing the perimeter. From the bulges in their jackets, she figured they were all armed.

Wilkes prayed one of her procurement officers would step out of what had been the Fifth Fleet Suppliers Conference to rescue her. Maybe they could overwhelm her abductors. After a little thought, she realized that would turn out badly for her unarmed people. It was supposed to be three days of brown-nosing suppliers to ensure the best prices for food and fuel for the Navy. Not a venue that called for a heavily armed security detail. Besides, her people were busy. Minutes earlier, the meeting room had been turned into an emergency command center for NAVCENT after the news broke that her flagship had been sunk in the Red Sea. Everyone was calling someone, getting facts, determining casualties, assessing threats, investigating—doing their jobs.

She could handle Redjackets. She'd have to.

The Redjacket pushed the elevator button. They rode in silence to her floor. She checked the man's reflection in the polished metal. Twenty-plus years younger than her sixty-three, and presumably stronger. She would need to be clever.

She marched down the hall. She swept her keycard across the lock. It clacked open. She stepped inside, eyes looking for weapons, advantage, anything. She walked straight to the bathroom. He followed a step behind, his onion-breath on her neck.

Opening the bathroom door with one hand, she spun around behind it, waited until he committed to following her in, then kicked it closed with all her strength. The door banged his head into the metal frame.

Momentarily stunned, he staggered back a step. His right arm remained extended, the pistol reaching into the bathroom. Admiral Wilkes grabbed his wrist and pulled it hard against the door. Slamming her bodyweight into the wood, she closed it on his arm. Leveraging the barrel, Wilkes pried the weapon from his slackened grip and, as his hand dropped, slammed the door on his fingers.

The man let out a howl and pushed back. He charged at her full force. He clutched desperately for the pistol. Soap dishes and lotions and makeup clattered to the floor. Some part of her uniform ripped.

Still holding the pistol by the barrel, she hammered the butt into his forehead as hard as she could. He staggered backward out of the bathroom and fell on the bed. She leapt on him, hammering a second and third blow. He spasmed with a concussion.

She said, "Menopause was ten years ago, moron."

His eyes rolled up, then back. He struggled beneath her.

She pressed the pistol to his forehead. "Before I blow your brains out, tell me what you thought was going to happen."

He gurgled. His eyes rolled forward and focused for a second on her. "Suicide."

She pushed the barrel harder into his skin. "You want suicide? Fine with me."

She started to squeeze the trigger, then stopped. The pearl grip felt familiar. It had her initials engraved on it. It was her pistol. A gift from her daughter. She'd left it behind so as not to scare the civilians. A quick scan of the room revealed her open suitcase, her belongings shoved unceremoniously into a pile on the floor. She'd left the place ship shape five hours earlier. Only an hour after the sinking of her flagship, someone wanted to fake her suicide?

Her ship at the bottom of the Red Sea, a recent run-in with President Roche, her ship's intelligence report, followed by this Redjacket attack told her all she needed to know about the enemy she faced. Of course, they wanted her to commit suicide. Bastards. She shuddered and brought the pistol down with all her might on her would-be killer's forehead. He spasmed again. Dead or severely concussed, she didn't care.

Voices called out from the hall. Most likely the other Redjackets. President Roche's paramilitary volunteers viciously attacked the press, anti-Roche protestors, and anything else that bothered them. For the past year, in every company and government agency, people had been secretly joining the Redjackets to do President Roche's bidding. Some were true believers in the Roche agenda—whatever that was. Others joined to bolster their careers. She had hated them from the moment they first cropped up in her command.

Wilkes pressed her ear to the door. The voices receded.

She dared a peek. Two men put their ears to doors at the opposite end of the hall with Berettas held at their thighs. Trying to locate their boss' voice, she presumed. They planned to help him stage her suicide.

If she could reach the meeting room, fifty officers would shield her with their lives. But how to get off the floor? She ruled out the elevator and calculated the steps to the stairwell.

At the end of the hall, the Redjackets were listening at the last door. They would be turning around and trying the other direction. It was now or never. She ran for the stairwell.

Bangs of pistol shots reverberated in the narrow space. Plaster burst in front of her, showering her in dust. She threw open the door and turned up one flight of steps. Her hand banged against the railing. The pistol fell from her grip. It cartwheeled down two floors. She cursed and kept going. Higher up, she heard the Redjackets entering the stairwell below her. They headed downward, misdirected by the echoes of her falling weapon.

She exited onto the eleventh floor and heard the service elevator open behind her. A surprised maid stood with her cart, half in and half out of the compartment. The admiral gave both the woman and her cart a shove and pushed the button for the ground floor.

Running to her people for cover was no longer an option. If the Redjackets would fire on an admiral, they would turn the meeting into a blood bath. She had to lead the danger away from her staff and let them run with the bombing investigation. Her top priority was to get back to NAVCENT headquarters in Bahrain. Her chief of staff had been working on her travel but hadn't updated her on the status. The airport was physically a quarter mile away, getting around the runway to the terminal was three miles, but it may as well be a hundred when you're outnumbered four to one.

Who could she turn to? How deep could the Redjackets reach? Who could she trust to help her get back to Bahrain?

Was Bahrain even safe?

The elevator door opened to a bustling staging area. On her right, a room service waiter stood ready to push a rolling table with lunch for two onto the elevator behind her. On her left, piles of laundry in rolling hampers waited for sorting. In the near distance, she heard a voice speaking English, "You cover the restaurant exits. I've got housekeeping."

She fled for the nearest door.

Outside, she stopped for a breath behind bushes meant to obscure the hotel's service bay from arriving guests. Wilkes put her hand in her jacket pocket for her phone. She found only torn fabric. Fearing the worst, she checked her medals. The special one was still there looking like a riflery ribbon.

Two men in chef's white rounded the bush. One lit a cigarette. The other texted on his phone.

She grabbed the phone out of his hand and punched in the US country code and number for Bobby Jenkins. She thumbed out a text. "It's me, Annie. In danger. Get that friend of yours, the guy with the security company to send help. Armed help. Trust no one. Borrowed phone. Leaving Mumbai Hilton. Will contact you when I can. HELP!"

She pressed send and waited until it read, "delivered." She handed back the phone and ran down the alley.

CHAPTER 2

MIGUEL AND I WERE PICKING off targets in the shooting range in my basement when Tania smacked me on the butt. I secured my Glock. Miguel did the same after a side glance and raised eyebrows. Tania's wild hair shook while she said something that wasn't registering; partially because I still had my earmuffs on and partially because Mercury, winged messenger of the Roman gods, was shouting over her.

Mercury said, *Check the Screaming Eaglet Tania's pimping.*

Mercury and his friends had fallen on hard times about fifteen hundred years ago. They've been getting by on handouts and hope ever since. He found me a split second before an Iraqi sniper's bullet plowed a furrow through my skull. He insisted I return the favor by evangelizing for him. He and his pals dream of returning Western Civilization to its former glory. A state in which all surrounding lands are conquered, all possessions seized, and all survivors paraded down the Appian Way. He wears a skimpy toga, a helmet with bronze wings and sandals. Oh, and he's black. He insists the Roman artists decided against realism in favor of fashioning marble and bronze that let the white population see what they wanted.

Mercury pointed. *Bro, you listening to me? 101*st *survivor over there. Tell him about me. Give him your whole Jupiter-saved-me-from-a-life-of-sin schtick.*

As the god of eloquence, Mercury decided to talk like a rapper because they represent the future of American culture. At least, he thinks he talks like a rapper. He comes off like my grandfather at Christmas dinner saying, "Let's get this party lit!" But Mercury was right about one thing. There was a new guy in the room.

Three feet behind Tania stood a young man at parade rest, his alert, penetrating eyes fixed on me. Short and built like a bantam weight fighter, he seemed calm, relaxed, unconcerned. And yet his peripheral vision roved over everything in the room from the light switch on the wall behind him to the dead cockroach under the paper target on the left, eighty feet downrange.

There's no mistaking a soldier who's fought for his life. The experience leaves an indelible mark. The US Army is the best trained, best equipped, most invincible fighting force in the history of civilization. No one on Earth can survive its unleashed wrath. It's a smooth machine that never fails to achieve its objectives. But—every now and then—a guy radios in "left" when he means right, "northeast" when he means "north," or "kilometers" when he means "meters." One little mistake can leave a squad exposed to enemy fire. Plans evaporate, people make wrong turns, the whole machine breaks down. An unbeatable soldier loses his advantage over the ragtag locals. He reverts to caveman instincts for survival. The world around him becomes a universe of death. His eyes take in every object for miles around, evaluates it as friend or foe, threat or benign, useful or useless. He makes instant decisions that—if right—will keep him alive for one more second so he can take another step without dying.

The man I'd locked gazes with had just gotten home from the war. By my guess, he'd been separated from his unit in a nasty firefight. Might have taken some friendly fire before getting back. At one point in his recent past, he'd been convinced he was going to die and managed to survive on his wits alone. A day like that makes a man swear on his family Bible to never lose situational awareness again. Not for a second.

A knife stabbed through my heart. My worst deployments cascaded over my soul in a tsunami of fear and desperation. My skyrocketing heartrate pounded in my ears, and adrenaline coursed through my veins like ice water, as if it were yesterday. In my peripheral vision, I saw Miguel—my fellow Ranger through five of my eight deployments— making the same calculation and coming to the same conclusion with the same reaction.

"What the hell are you doing?" Tania's hand gripped my bicep and yanked me to face her. "Is that a man?"

She pointed at the body we'd tied to a post between the targets at the far end of the space.

"No," I stated the obvious. "That's Yuri Belenov."

Mercury said, *Shoulda shot him like I told you, homie. Now, she's going to make you explain stuff like why you let Belenov play with your laptop.*

I said, *I had to sleep sooner or later.*

Mercury said, *Sleep it off, you mean.*

"Did you kill him?" As the words left Tania's lips, Yuri raised his head and pleaded for salvation with his bloodshot eyes.

She pushed the table up and marched down the range. The accents of her multiracial heritage shifted from Asian to African to Latin as she moved through the stark lighting.

"Jacob Stearne." I stuck my hand out toward the new kid.

His eyes were still on Tania but snapped to me quickly. He checked my hand for weapons, then checked that my pistol was still stowed, before shaking hands. "Cody Jefferson."

Miguel stuck his hand out for his turn. "Did you say Cody?"

Cody glared up at the big guy. "We're not all DeShawns, Darnells, and Trevons."

"And we're not all Two Feathers." Miguel laughed and slapped Cody's shoulder. When a six four, two hundred thirty-pound Navajo laughs, everyone breathes easier. "Chill, you'll be fine here."

"What the hell were you thinking?" Tania pushed the Russian at me. "He's a human being. You could've killed him."

"He hacked my car and won't reset it."

"I don't give a damn about your car." Tania looked back and forth at us. "Get packed and get over to Sabel Gardens. You've got a mission. You're leaving on the hour."

"It's my day off."

Mercury leaned over Tania's shoulder. *Hey now, brutha, when Pia-Caesar-Sabel sends you on a mission, you warm up your Veni, Vidi, Vici speech—none of this day-off bullshit.*

I said, *I'm not going on any more of Ms. Sabel's spur-of-the-moment, unplanned missions. Too many people get killed doing that.*

Mercury said, *That's what mortals are for, fool—dying at Caesar's whim. Quit thinking you have a right to the pursuit of happiness and grab your gear.*

Cody's eyes took in the Russian's cuffed hands and shackled feet without betraying his thoughts on kidnapping. He said, "Yo. A firing range in your basement?"

I turned to Tania. "Your kid's sharp."

"I mean, is that legal?" he asked.

I looked him over. "Probably."

Tania set to work untying the gag in Belenov's mouth. "You can goof off later. Ms. Sabel wants you there now."

"I broke up with you because you're a terrible liar."

She left the gag halfway down and faced me. "You broke up with ME?"

Miguel laughed.

"Stay out of this, Two Feathers." She spun to him and stuck her chin out. "You're going with him."

"This your first day, Cody?" I gave the new guy a smile.

Mercury waved his arms. *Hey, dawg. I think Cody can see me. Can he see me? Ask him.*

I said, *No one can see a figment of my imagination. PTSD-induced schizophrenia, the doctors said. I'm insane, you don't exist. Deal with it.*

"Yes, sir." Cody straightened up.

"101st Airborne?" I asked.

"Yes, sir." He did a doubletake, unsure how I knew. "Screaming Eagles."

"Good outfit. Two tours?"

"Yes, sir."

Mercury acted like a drill sergeant. He prowled around the young man. *Got into a jam in Somalia. They ran from Al-Shabaab fighters only to fall into friendly fire. He left some friends back there. But he fought with honor and distinction.*

"Somalia?" I asked. "Lose some guys?"

He tried to suppress his curiosity as he nodded. "You?"

I pointed at myself and Miguel. "75th Rangers."

He dipped his head half a millimeter out of respect. Which was a lot for Airborne.

I asked, "Did you hear President Roche wants Congress to declare war on Saudi Arabia?"

"Yes, sir."

"You OK with that?"

"Circumstances be a bit suspicious, sir. Can't see Saudis pulling off sinking a ship. But. Not my call, sir."

"Going to re-enlist if they approve his declaration?" I asked.

"Lotsa good people could go down in that." He shook his head as if he already felt the pain of losing brothers still in the service.

Exactly how I felt. Not that any of us could stop it.

"Hey," Tania stepped between us. "Don't be ignoring the topic. I gave you an order. Get moving, soldier."

Cody's gaze never wavered from mine. I asked over Tania's head, "Are you on Ms. Sabel's personal detail now?"

"Yes, sir."

"What's your impression of the boss?"

He looked at the three of us, wondering how to give an honest answer without sounding like a brown-noser. "She's yoked, sir. Never seen a woman that big before."

"Tall," I said. "Never call a woman big. Especially one who could rip your arm off."

"Yes, sir." He glanced at Tania with an expression that said, will never happen again.

"Were you there when Ms. Sabel asked Tania to go on whatever mission she's trying to dump on me?"

His gaze slid to the back of Tania's head before coming back to me. "Yes, sir."

Tania slinked into the corner.

I asked, "What was the mission?"

"Ms. Sabel ask Agent Tania to get busy finding someone named Admiral Wilkes in Mumbai."

We all turned to Tania, even Belenov.

"Can't face going back to Mumbai?" I asked her.

"Did you mess with his car?" she asked Belenov.

"We were negotiating," the Russian said with his light accent. "I've been pardoned, but Jacob does not care—"

"I don't care about your pardon either," she snapped. "Get his car going again."

Belenov wiggled his zip-tied wrists behind his back. "I need a laptop."

Tania made a beeline for the stairs to get cutters.

"You can send Dhanpal," I said to her back.

She stopped in her tracks three steps up. "He's covering a shortage in Vancouver."

"His grandparents live in Mumbai. He speaks the language. And, Vancouver's closer."

I thought the ethnic advantage would tip the scales. No one cared about having a second generation Mumbaikar—who also happened to be a decorated Navy SEAL—on staff. People want quantifiable data. Everyone in the room whipped out their phones to check my math. A few begrudging grunts of admiration escaped my doubters.

"Not as dumb as you look," Tania said. "Closer by three hundred something miles."

Cody asked, "How did you get that?"

"He gets messages from god," Miguel said.

Cody did another doubletake. I frowned at Miguel. Whiplash would claim the kid if we kept telling him things he wasn't ready to hear.

"Teamwork," Tania said. "Pia's all pissed off about the country getting polarized. She doesn't want that happening in her company. I could sell it to her as teamwork. Dhanpal's the best on the team for the job."

"And—bonus—it's actually true." I nodded at Tania. "But you'll have to go back to Mumbai sooner or later."

"Not today." She blushed and looked away. With a touch of pride, she added, "Jaz is taking me to the Inn at Little Washington tonight."

I wondered if her boyfriend understood what dinner at the fanciest restaurant in DC did for her expectations. He was a rich kid from the best side of town. She escaped the street gangs of Brooklyn by joining the Army. Jaz Jenkins, son of pharmaceutical king Bobby Jenkins, was a prize catch. For a second, I considered calling Jaz and telling him to bring a ring or change the destination to a place with plastic-coated menus, but it wasn't any of my business.

"Make you a deal." Tania thumbed at Cody. "I'll dump this mission on Dhanpal if you take numb-nuts here."

Cody took the insult without showing any emotion. He glanced at me and said, "I can un-hack a car."

Tania didn't make deals that easily. Maybe there was something wrong with the new kid. If it were just back-from-battle adjustment issues, she would've been there for him like a mother hen. She could've told him about coming home after I pulled her out of a burning Humvee. She wouldn't dump the kid on me for anything simple.

Mercury said, *Betcha Cody's got dirt on Tania, my brutha. Dirt on Tania could come in handy in the event of any future negotiations.*

My used god was right, there had to be a story in there somewhere. New guys were assigned as tag-alongs until they were ready for going alone. Tagging behind Tania, who had no boundaries, probably led to dirt of some kind. Maybe he witnessed something embarrassing to my lovely and constant ex. And Cody was green enough to talk about it.

I turned to Tania. "Deal."

CHAPTER 3

Pia Sabel nodded and Maria, the upstairs maid, grabbed the stack of sports bras. Pia nodded again, and Maria added racerback shirts. The maid then scurried out of the closet to the suitcase on the bed and carefully packed the clothes. She trotted back to the expansive walk-in closet. Pia pointed at a stack of leggings.

Having spotted something, Maria stopped in her tracks. She went to the far corner of the room. She pushed back a chair and pulled something from behind it. She held it up with a smile. "You remember, Señorita?"

Pia moved closer. The black jersey of her first soccer team. Before kindergarten. It was tiny. She took it from Maria. Memories flooded in with her first touch of the fabric. Her father telling her why the game was a valuable life-lesson. Teamwork built the nation, teamwork built Sabel Industries, nothing in life could be achieved without it. She remembered the oath she swore on that jersey. She had promised her teammates they would win the championship. Then she had to badger her father and the coach into creating one.

Her phone rang. Veronica Hunter. Pia had a million unanswered questions from their last conversation. *How could you do that to your daughter?* first among them. She wondered what she wanted from Hunter. A healthy relationship? Impossible. To witness the woman's death? No, that was too harsh. Imprisonment might soothe Pia's need for vengeance. For Roche, on the other hand, death. Pia felt a chill thinking such severe thoughts. What was worse than death? For Roche, whose ego was monumental: public humiliation.

She let Hunter's call go to voice mail. She didn't want to have that conversation in front of Maria.

She handed the child-sized jersey back to Maria. "Keep it."

"Somewhere special, señorita?"

Pia looked around then shrugged. "I don't know. Let's just hang on to it."

"What the hell is this?" Jonelle Jackson, otherwise known as the Major, called from the far end of Pia's bedroom. She wore a tailored suit with her afro pulled back in a tight, gelled bun at the nape of her neck.

Pia strode out and faced the CEO of Sabel Industries. "I'm meeting Dhanpal in Mumbai. Bobby Jenkins asked me to find his second wife. I'll send you an email explaining my whole itin—"

"Oh no you won't." The Major marched across the room, fisted her hips, and looked up at Pia. "You have a video call with managers across the company tomorrow."

Pia glanced at Maria. "Give us a minute, please."

Maria bolted through the sitting room and out to the hall beyond.

"You get this corporate stuff." Pia tossed her hands up. "I hate it. Suits, asset leverage, value propositions, headcount, liability, depreciation—I don't know what they're talking about. I like to be out in the field, engaging with people."

"Doesn't matter what you like. You have responsibilities. These people work for you. You owe them a future, a secure job, a happy work place. They need to see you taking this seriously, Pia."

"I take it seriously." Pia flopped on the bed. "You're doing a great job. Everyone respects you. That's why I put you in charge."

The Major moved into Pia's line of sight and crossed her arms. "I appreciate the trust you've shown in me. But forty thousand employees need motivation. No one joined Sabel Technologies or Satellites or Security or Capital because they wanted a paycheck. They joined because they wanted to change the world. And so far, they've been changing the world. Eventually, employees start polarizing over petty office politics. Someone wants it this way, and someone else wants it that way. They need a strong leader to keep them working like a team. Alan kept them together and focused on the goal."

"Teamwork," Pia said. "I'm all about teamwork. You're the coach, they're the team. You can take them to the Olympics and win gold."

The Major's gaze shot to Pia's gold medal in its display case. It needed dusting.

Pia sat up and watched the carpet, waiting for the Major's guilt trip to pass.

The Major sat near her. "They miss your dad. He constantly walked the halls in all the divisions. He knew everyone. He knew every project. Not because he had a magic, eidetic memory but because he had a staffer who made copious notes before he visited an office. He prepared because he cared."

They sat in silence, breathing and remembering the gregarious man's incessant celebrations of everyone around him. After a long time, the Major smoothed the bedspread. "They need to see you. In the division offices, in the meetings, on the production floor. They need to know who they're working for and that she's worth it."

Pia stood up and paced away. "I'm not Dad."

The Major didn't respond.

Pia looked out the window. A tinge of resentment tweaked her nerves. She said, "They don't miss me. They miss Dad. So do I. But I'm not him. I can't yell at people one minute then tell them they're the greatest thing that ever happened to the company the next. I'm not a coach, I'm a player. I need to be in the field."

The Major thumbed a handful of things in the suitcase. "What's in Mumbai?"

"Remember Bobby Jenkins' second wife? The admiral? She's gone missing."

"Annie Wilkes?" The Major's surprise echoed off the walls. "Isn't she the admiral the administration said disappeared after the bombing? Did Bobby tell you how to find her? If he did, you need to report that to the authorities, not go off on one some spur-of-the-moment mission."

"He doesn't have a clue other than she left the Mumbai Hilton on foot a few hours ago. He's desperate. He's an old friend of Dad's. I can't say—"

"Yes, you can say no." The Major squinted. "You know damn well you could send a team out there who're better than you at finding AWOL admirals. What's this about? You think she knows something. You think she can stop this crazy war Roche is calling for? Hold on, now. Are you trying to take down Roche?"

Pia looked over her shoulder. "What? No. It's a favor for Bobby."

"Don't give me that." The Major crossed to Pia. "We had an agreement. You're staying out of politics. Damn near got that poor French girl killed. And that old man Willy-Mac too. Not to mention—"

The Major wisely stopped short of blaming Pia for Alan Sabel's death. Everyone in Pia's immediate circle felt guilt about the horrific death of Pia's beloved father. Pia felt the Major's unspoken words anyway. Her spiteful glare filled with tears. She turned back to the window.

"Look." The Major stroked Pia's shoulder but kept a stern tone. "—Losing him was tough on us all. But right after, you ghosted on the employees when they needed you most. It's been a year. You've had time to deal with it and move on. Everyone's been patient with you so far. Now it's time for you to change. It's time to become the rock your employees can cling to in a storm. And Roche has created a lot of storms for us. This is no time to be running around India looking for ghosts. Your responsibilities are here. It's not my name at the top of Sabel Towers."

Pia's phone rang. It lay face-up on the bed. The caller ID read, Veronica Hunter. They stared at it.

It rang again.

"She's a former president and the current vice president," the Major said. "Don't send her to voice mail. Answer it. Say no to whatever she's planning, and let's prepare for your video conference."

Pia frowned as the phone rang twice more. She fidgeted her fingers. "She told me something last night."

The phone stopped ringing. They stared at it in silence as if expecting it to animate and run away.

"OK, I'll bite," the Major said with a suspicious glance, her voice slowing as she spoke. "What did she tell you?"

The phone rang again. Hunter.

"Did you know?" Pia asked.

"Know what?" The Major backed up as if Pia might hit her.

They faced each other. The phone rang. Their hearts beat and their gazes met and each measured the other.

"Don't equivocate," Pia said.

The phone continued ringing. "Veronica Hunter" prominently on display.

"Suspected," the Major said. "When the President of the United States gives her personal cell number to a young soccer star, it raises questions."

"That was years ago," Pia said over the ringing phone.

"But she kept taking your calls. And you've never been her biggest fan. That could've spelled trouble in many different ways."

Pia nodded. "True."

The phone kept ringing.

"I asked Alan about it." The Major sighed. "He was evasive. Which made it more suspicious."

"Ours is the best spy company in the world." Pia twisted into the Major's line of sight. "And it's all under your leadership. Did you use our resources? Did you satisfy your curiosity?"

"Yes."

The phone stopped ringing.

Pia wondered if it would be wise to ask her next question. She did anyway. "What did you find out?"

"Hunter is your birth mother." The Major tried to relax as if it were no big deal. "Meaning Sandra Velocitane was your first adopted parent. And Alan adopted you when Sandra was murdered."

"Who else knows?" Pia's voice rose to near-shriek.

"Bianca." The Major grabbed both Pia's arms. "It's OK. Someone had to do the research. I needed someone I could trust. You kept her secret when she asked you to—she'll keep yours."

"When was this?"

"Over a year ago. Just before Alan was killed. I never had a chance to ask his side of the story."

"What else did you find out?"

"Everything."

Pia squeezed her eyes shut and willed the world to go away.

"How do you feel about your relationship with her?" the Major asked.

"Sickened. Hopeful. Proud. Disgusted. I don't know. Why didn't she want me? Why did she hand me off to strangers? But, she was the President of the United States of America once. That's an accomplishment even if you don't like her politics. Or her family planning."

"Are you reconciling with her?" The Major nosed toward the phone.

"The mother who was too busy to raise me?" Pia scoffed. "Abandonment, the pinnacle of motherhood."

The Major's line of questioning took her out of the moment and into her long-tangled relationship with Veronica Hunter. A spiritual umbilical cord connects mother and child regardless of any other circumstance. Their cord was unforgivably tangled. Sometimes tangled around Pia's neck. She wondered what relationship, if any, she wanted to have with a woman who had allowed her to be tortured by rogue agents. Pia convinced herself Hunter was her door to revenge. That was as far as it would go.

When she looked up, the Major's eyes were on her, waiting for a direct answer. Pia said, "I don't see reconciliation as a possibility."

"Have you restarted your sessions with Dr. Harrison?"

"I'm never taking his pharma-solutions again."

"There are other psychiatrists."

Pia paced the room, her arms crossed tight across her chest. Therapy had been a good idea for dealing with her most recent bombshell. She had been seeing therapists most of her life. They served a purpose up to a point. Now, she was done with them.

"Whatever you do with that duplicitous egg-donor, you need to leave the political side alone." The Major stood still while Pia paced the room. "I know what you're thinking. You have plenty of reason to destroy Hunter, Roche, the whole lot of them. Vengeance is a false god. Revenge brings nothing but remorse. Think about the cost, Pia. Think about what we've lost already. What we stand to lose. Roche owns you. He controls our biggest customer. He has the Justice Department stacked with political sycophants. He has the most powerful army in the world at his fingertips. He's politicized the FBI and the CIA and all the special ops branches. Don't even get me started on the Redjackets. He's finally figured out how much power he has and now he's ready to use it. Don't give him reason to use it against you. Don't you go getting involved with either of them."

"I won't."

"You have tons of experience on a soccer field. You have zero experience in the political field."

"I get it."

"You have responsibilities to forty thousand employees. We need you. Here. Now."

"I know."

"You can't think about what you want. Think about the rest of us."

"I will."

"Then unpack this bag and meet me at the office. We'll plan out how to get the troops reenergized."

"OK." Pia tugged some leggings out of the suitcase.

"Leave the spandex for the gym. Or Luon or Nulux, whatever you call them these days." The Major waved in the direction of the second walk-in closet. "Put on one of those nice suits you never wear."

"Give me half an hour."

Pia watched the Major walk out.

When she heard her CEO's heels hit the marble hallway, she picked up her phone and called back.

Hunter answered.

Pia said, "I'm not going to Mumbai." She paused, knowing she shouldn't say what came next. "I can join that meeting you wanted to set up."

CHAPTER 4

President Chuck Roche let Texas Senator Hartwell Thomas wait outside the Oval Office while Roche read the reports on the man. An aide had typed up strategies about how to get people to do things they didn't want to do. He didn't need to read someone else's strategy. Roche always went with his gut. It always worked. He tossed the strategy papers and told his secretary to let Thomas in.

Roche rounded the desk and stood with his left hand on his silver-handled cane. The big Texan strode in like he owned the place. At five eight, one hundred forty-five pounds, Roche never feared the big guys. He knew they were lambs. Thomas's weathered face was an obvious spray tan, his boots never slotted into a stirrup, his hat wasn't even waterproof.

Roche waited while Thomas remembered protocol and approached. The man took a knee and kept his head down. A good sign of an obedient servant. Roche extended his hand. Thomas kissed the proffered fingers. It was the most satisfying thing Roche ever felt. He said, "Rise, Senator. You're a good man."

"It is truly an honor to serve a man of your magnitude, sir." Thomas stood and opened his palms. "Your administration will go down in history as the greatest era in all of civilization. Why, the Pax Romana was never as great an age as you've given this nation. Being in your presence reminds me of how blessed I am to offer my help and services. You are indeed the man of the century, Mr. President."

"Is that it?" Roche asked. It didn't matter. He didn't have time for the full list. "I'm glad you're happy, Hartwell. The Redjackets were a brilliant idea."

"Thank you, sir." Thomas smiled. "When I first saw the need for a secret society of like-minded people in every company and every branch of government and the military, I got busy. I patterned them after the pre-depression Italian *squadristi*. We've been waiting for a leader of your stature. It is an honor—"

"Congress won't take up my war declaration until the investigation concludes. They're all talking about doing what their constituents want instead of what I told them."

"The problem is asking for a declaration. If you just do what every president since Truman's done, why you'll have that war started—"

His veins pulsed with anger beneath Roche's translucent skin. "Just because those wimps wormed their way into unpopular wars that ruined their reputations doesn't mean I'm going that route. Hell no. That defeats the purpose. I'm going to have a popular war. Like FDR did. Everyone pulls together in a declared war. You can ration supplies, draft young men, have martial law, hate the common enemy—and everyone goes along for the war effort. I told them that's what I want. Why haven't they done it yet?"

"That's on account of how a republic works. See, the co-equal branches—"

Roche slammed his cane on a nearby table. "I need a leader who can corral these morons and get them to march to my drummer."

Thomas looked around the room. "Sorry, sir. I don't follow you."

"You're going to be my next chief of staff."

Thomas choked. "Beg your pardon?"

"You heard me. I need you as my chief of staff. I'm done asking people. That never goes well. I want that war declaration rammed through right now. I'm ordering you to take the job." Roche leaned back against his desk and crossed his arms. "Any questions?"

Thomas stuttered and stammered and wiped his brow. "Sir, I'm a United States Senator. I serve the great State of Texas in the—"

"I know that. Did I mention I'm not asking?"

"Well, um, it's just that … I'm working hard for you in the Senate. I chair the Intelligence Committee. From there, I can tell when certain agencies might be getting a tad too close to the Redjackets. It's a very important—"

"Remember back when this country was on the right track? You could go to your neighborhood school without being bussed anywhere. People respected their elders—" Roche shook his cane in Thomas's face "—because we made children pray every morning. Everyone called me Row-SHAY, none of this disrespectful crap."

"People just don't move from the Senate to chief of staff. It just isn't done. I mean, it's not exactly a lateral move. Besides. Uhm. It would leave my constituents without proper representation."

"Coal miners got to live in homes provided by the coal companies. You could get gas for twenty-five cents. Women wore hats. Men wore hats, too. That way they could tip their hats as a sign of respect. And decent college kids never had tattoos." Roche shuddered as if he'd drunk gasoline. "A college education was a special thing for special people. These days they let all kinds of people go."

"Like I said, without me on the Intelligence Committee," Thomas said, "we wouldn't get any advance warning about investigations into the Redjackets. The leadership could be in a heap of trouble, and we'd never see it coming."

"Women wore dresses." Roche looked to the ceiling with a smile. "Remember that scene with Marilyn Monroe standing on the subway grate? That kind of thing never happens anymore because they're all wearing pants. When did women start thinking it was OK to dress like a man?"

"Begging your pardon, but it's just too risky. I spent years building the Redjackets—for you. That should earn me this one indulgence. I'm sorry, sir, I must turn down the offer."

"Imagine the future we're building, Hartwell." Roche put his arm around the larger man and turned him to the open area of the Oval Office. "Imagine a country that offers exclusive privileges for the deserving. Imagine restaurants with separate sections for successful people. You won't have to eat next to some lowlife listening to hip hop. Imagine public schools chartered for just the smart kids. That way your kids don't have to sit next to someone 'axing' questions instead of asking them. Imagine going to the bathroom and never getting harassed by gender-confused predators again." Roche squeezed Thomas's shoulder. "That's the goal, Hartwell. That's what we're doing here. Making a future that looks like the good old days."

"And I want that good old future, sir." Thomas wiped his brow. "But I insist, I can serve you better from the Senate."

"Which one of us is the commander in chief?"

"Ah, well, that would be—"

Roche smacked Thomas's shoulder with his cane. "Texas was going to get the next drone base, but I've decided on Nevada."

"Sir! You just can't do that. The award has already been announced and—"

"There are $3 billion in grants going to studies conducted at Texas universities, Hartwell. Were you aware of that?"

Senator Hartwell Thomas stammered, seeking words that wouldn't come. After a long time, he finally spat it out. "My son is the leading researcher of oil deposits in the Gulf. You can't just halt the funding."

"Can, Hartwell. Can and will yank those funds." Roche gave a laugh. "Alabama's on the Gulf. They're itching to grow their oil business."

"They could never replicate … Holy mother of God, Mr. President."

Roche walked around his desk and found a folder. "Then there's this."

Thomas squinted as he read the papers. "How did you get this? You don't have a search warrant. This is an encrypted email between a lobbyist and me."

"And a bank." Roche grabbed Thomas's right hand and pumped it. "Let's not forget the bank. By the way, I don't need a search warrant unless I let the FBI go ahead and press charges. So, here's the deal, Hartwell. You start tomorrow. Write up a big press release. This is great news. You get to work with me every day. Congratulations."

Thomas stood stock still as Chuck Roche shook his hand. For the first time in the man's career, he was speechless.

Roche loved those special moments. It was an important, transitional moment in the lives of the people who worked for him. He'd witnessed it many times. It happened when they quit pretending to have independence and dedicated their lives to helping him do what he needed done.

Roche leaned back and waited for the second stage of the moment. The one in which they realized what a great opportunity lay before them. They would obey him from that moment forward, and their lives would be fantastic. There would be no more discussion. He could tweet a command from a thousand miles away, and Thomas would jump to his assigned tasks. He saw the transformation in Hartwell Thomas complete its cycle.

The Texan dropped to one knee and pulled Roche's hand to his lips. He kissed it repeatedly. "Thank you, sir. Thank you. Thank you. I cannot thank you enough for your generous benevolence. You are a magnificent man. I will endeavor to be the best chief of staff you've ever had."

"First order of business." Roche smiled and motioned for Thomas to rise. "We need to drive a wedge into the opposition party. If they come together, they'll bring down this administration. That future you just imagined goes out the window. We don't want to worry about them closing down the Redjackets either. That's what the war is all about. We need to get that war declaration out of Congress. Then we'll be home free. The citizens always pull together for a war effort. Think about that future, Hartwell." Roche spread his hand across the heavens. "You and me, bravely defending America from the evil Muslim terrorists. I'll silence the opposition with my courage. No one can speak against me. I'll be everyone's hero."

"Absolute brilliance, sir."

"I've got plenty more brilliance, Hartwell. But it can wait. You asked for this meeting. What was it you wanted to see me about?"

"Ah. Well." Thomas lowered his head. "Wilkes. She's not dead."

CHAPTER 5

IT WAS A BEAUTIFUL CINCO de Mayo when I answered my front door. The cops wanted Belenov and had a bag full of personal effects from his recent stay at the White House. They had orders to put him on a flight to Toronto because he owned a pretty good likeness of a Canadian passport. When I cut him loose, he had the audacity to ask for $200 in cash. On top of that, he wanted me to burn the bag the cops claimed held his clothes.

Mercury peered between the two men in blue. *Give him up, homie. They also have orders to arrest you for kidnapping if they don't get the Russkie.*

I said, *Why do they want him so bad?*

Mercury said, *Yours is not to question why, my brutha. Just give him up.*

I said, *He hasn't told me his secrets yet.*

Mercury walked away. *Your opportunity is lost. Go with what your favorite god tells you.*

The hard part about having a personal relationship with a god is knowing when to listen and when to ignore. Sometimes he's testing me to see if I'll keep the faith. Kinda like what the Judeo-Christian God did with Job. Sometimes it's easy, like when Mercury tells me to rape and pillage—cuz that is so 500 BCE. Other times it's not so clear, like the time he told me to rescue the damsel in distress who turned out to be a heroin-addict-serial-killer. Later, I discovered Jupiter had bet him a hundred aureus I'd leave her to die. Free will sucks.

It's natural to have trust-issues with a god who thinks the Super Bowl can't hold a candle to Christians versus lions in a real death match. But he was on to something, the cops appeared to be itching for trouble.

I gave Belenov the money. "You better make good on your promise."

"Have faith, my friend." He held up his hands. "I always deliver."

Miguel and Tania left me with Cody. I never know what to do with new guys. Back in the trenches, we avoided getting to know them because they had a tendency to die. Taliban snipers always picked off the inexperienced guys first. But it was down to the two of us and, after all, he did un-hack my car. We did the get-to-know you stuff. Now that he was out of the army, he was dreaming about growing some dreadlocks like Larry Fitzgerald or Richard Sherman, although he was leaning toward the ancient Maasai warriors' red locs. I too once had visions of post-army life that didn't work out. Buzzcuts are easy. But I saw no reason to bring him down. I said, "You'll look epic in locs, bro."

"You gonna explain about your Russian hostage?" Cody asked.

I held my finger to my lips for silence. Cody nodded.

I called Anoshni. Miguel had brought the dog home from the reservation about a year ago and named him after the Navajo word for love. But the mostly-Anglo neighbors in Miguel's condo clamped down on dogs without pedigrees, so Miguel gave him to me. I grabbed his leash but didn't put it on him because he was well behaved most of the time. I carried it in case a neighbor gave me a hard time.

We headed out for a walk around the block. I searched through Belenov's belongings. Dime-sized listening devices had been sewn into the seams of all his clothes. His iPhone had been split open, and a thick piece of technology had been sandwiched in. The CIA thinks they're oh-so clever.

Cody tried to change the subject. "What about this war, think it's legit?"

"Nah," I said into one of the bugs. "Just Roche trying to cover up his inadequacies."

"'At's about how they all start, right?"

We walked two blocks before I found a landscaper tossing big limbs into a shredder. He charged me fifty bucks to mince Belenov's goods. A second later, the CIA's beautiful plan was reduced to shreds of metal and cloth no bigger than a grain of rice and buried in a pile of sawdust.

That's when I felt it was safe to tell Cody about Yuri Belenov. "The

Russian government disavowed his citizenship after Miguel and I caught him and his crew of hackers. We snagged proof they had crashed two American airliners to support Chuck Roche's campaign claim that then-President Hunter had mismanaged the FAA. After winning the election, Roche managed to shelve our evidence and grant pardons to Belenov and his boys. But then Roche kidnapped the Russian and forced him to create deepfakes and plant emails. Belenov escaped Roche's clutches and asked me for sanctuary. He made promises about new evidence that would expose Roche. But he didn't come through. Which was why we were using him as target practice. Now that he's been saved by the cops, it's anyone's guess if we'll ever hear from him again."

Mercury walked alongside us trying to look like a professor, scratching his chin and acting serious. *Ask him the deep question.*

I said, *What question?*

Mercury did an eye roll. *The one that's burning in your soul.*

"My turn to ask you something," I said to Cody. "How did you piss off Tania?"

Cody stared at me sideways as we walked. We went a block before he spoke. "What's the 4-1-1 with Ms. Sabel? Word is she be sleeping three hours a night and screams and shit."

"Answer my question."

"All due respect, sir—" he stammered a bit "—I chose serving up at Sabel Gardens. Don't I get in on what's going down with the boss-lady?"

Couldn't argue that. People tend to get edgy closer they get to her personal problems.

My gaze swung over his head. The average Ranger, SEAL, and the other special ops guys tend to be short, compact men. Miguel and I always stood a head taller than the others. I brought my eyes down to Cody.

"When she was four," I said, "two off-duty CIA operatives broke into her home and killed her parents. A guy named Leroy Johnson strangled her mother while little Pia stabbed at Leroy with a kitchen knife. After fifty or something stabs, one of them hit his femoral artery. He bled out in seconds. Unfortunately, her mother was already dead. At least that was the woman she thought was her mother. As it turns out, Ms. Sabel was adopted. But she didn't learn that until a few days ago."

We walked in silence for a long time. Finally, he said, "There'd be more to that story?"

"When I know what kind of guy you are, I'll tell you the bad parts."

That got a raised eyebrow out of the guy. "That wasn't the bad part?"

I stayed quiet.

"Aight," Cody said. "My turn then."

"Right."

"I said something that set off Ms. Cooper."

"That's not hard with Tania. What was it?"

"Not sure." He shook his head. "I done tried to apologize—"

"That only makes it worse with her." We rounded a corner and Anoshni took a twenty-yard lead. "Did you ask her an insensitive question, like how she got shot in the head?"

"She got shot in the head?"

"We'll come back to that." The pup disappeared around the corner. I asked, "What were you talking about before she turned into the ice princess?"

My phone rang.

Cody said, "May have said she was beautiful."

"Dude. She's got nearly ten years on you," I said. "Never say that to a woman unless you're going to ask her out."

He looked off into the distance.

"Oh, no. Really?" I genuinely felt sorry for the poor bastard and answered the call.

Dhanpal's voice was backed by airport noises. "Thanks for giving me the lead on this mission. I love going to back to the country my parents couldn't wait to get out of. But I need you on this one."

"I like sleeping in a bed, having home cooked meals, scratching my dog's ear, waking up alive, stuff like that." I looked around for my dog. I spotted him and started catching up.

"Jacob, you're the gung-ho-est guy I've ever known. When Pia says let's do this, you're out in front, leading the rest of us by a mile." There was a pause. "Oh. Too soon to bring up Pia? Sorry."

"Forget it."

"I mean, if the boss shot me," Dhanpal said, "I'd have some issues too."

"SAY WHAT?" Cody nearly broke his neck whipping around to look at me.

I glanced at the screen on my phone. Speakerphone mode. The cartilage in my ear keeps clicking that button. Damn.

I shook my head at Cody. "Long story."

"C'mon, Jacob," Dhanpal said. "Pia won't even be on this trip."

"Since when does a SEAL need a Ranger to hold his hand?"

Mercury started laughing. *Brutha, I swear. After all the times I saved your miserable life in the wars, now you're going to die over dog shit?*

I never know what he's talking about half the time, but I scanned the area while I kept talking to Dhanpal.

"I'd love to help you out, but I'm gonna…" my voice trailed off when I saw Anoshni taking a dump on a perfectly manicured lawn.

An old guy stared at my puppy out his front window. From the look on his face, I would be dead in ten seconds if I didn't act fast. I looked around for a bag to use as a scoop. Nothing. An oak tree offered the largest leaf in the neighborhood. I pulled one down, covered Anoshni's small log, scooped it up, nodded at the old man, rubbed the leftovers with my boot, and walked away.

The whole time, Dhanpal was going on about the importance of the mission. Redjackets had something to do with it, he said. I wasn't too keen on fighting other Americans. I joined the military to protect citizens. Even the ones dumb enough to join the Redjackets.

"Buddy, save your breath." I found a trash can and tossed the oak leaf. "I'm not going to hunt for somebody's ex-wife."

"Dude. That is not what this is about." Dhanpal dropped into his dead-serious voice. "The *USS Caine* was not sunk by the Saudis."

"Whatever." I checked my hand. Poop smears on three fingers. I looked around for a paper towel, tissue, rag. Nothing.

"This is going to be huge," Dhanpal said. "This is a Jacob Stearne-sized mission if there ever was one. I need your help."

Cody was looking the other way. I pulled his shirttail out and cleaned my fingers on it.

Better his shirt than mine.

"Hey!" Cody gave me a nasty glare. "What the hell you doing?"

"Someone with you?" Dhanpal asked.

"New guy. No sense of humor." I started walking. Anoshni fell in. Cody trailed behind muttering to himself about whether it would be bad manners to kill a co-worker on his first day.

Mercury walked ahead of us and talked over his shoulder. *You should be listening to Gunga Din, dawg. He just told you something of international importance.*

I said, *So?*

Mercury said, *If you could solve an international situation, you could get on TV. Then you could finally tell the world that the real road to salvation is called the Via Cassia, which once had twenty-eight shrines along it that were all dedicated to me—your personal god!*

I said, *I'm not going to…*

I started to take the phone off speaker then decided I didn't want to touch it if any molecules of dog doodoo remained on my fingers. I held the possibly-still-disgusting digits away from my body.

"Think about it, Jacob." Dhanpal's serious voice went to DEFCON 1. "The US Navy is invincible. No one can sneak up on us without sonar seeing them miles away. No one can fire a missile without radar picking it up. The last damage-sustaining attack on an American ship was the *USS Cole* almost twenty years ago."

He left a long silence. I looked at Cody. He looked at me. He was still pissed about the shirt.

He'd get over it.

"I'm going to grill some salmon for the new guy," I said. "I kinda owe him now. So. Have fun in Mumbai."

"You're not hearing me."

"The Saudis didn't do it. Heard you. Don't care. Not my problem."

"No one could sink the ship," Dhanpal said. "So who did?"

Mercury leaned on Cody's shoulder. *Say what, bro? Who sank the ship? Now there's an interesting question.*

I said, *If the Saudis didn't … I don't know. It was someone else. OK? Hey. I don't care.*

Mercury said, *You mean you don't want to care. But deep down, you do.*

My used god was right, it was an interesting question. An unthinkable answer came to mind.

It couldn't be.

Dhanpal sensed my thinking process. "You see? Get it? This is big. You gotta help me. It's your duty to your country."

"Duty?" It always pisses me off when someone pushes that button. "I've got a dinner plate full of Purple Hearts for doing my duty. And a handful of Bronze Stars to go around the edge. Don't give me that 'duty' crap. Where does it get you? Gut shot by your boss, that's where. No thank you."

I clicked off.

Cody was staring at me, looking disgusted. "A brother calls for help—and that's how you answer?"

CHAPTER 6

PIA WONDERED WHY SHE WAS doing this. Because it was as close to field work as she could get and still be back in time to please the Major? Or because she held out hope that Hunter's promise was genuine? Both, she decided. There could be a handful of other reasons if she gave it more thought.

The closer they came to their destination the more Pia's anger rose. She never hated anyone as much as the man she was about to face. And yet she found herself marching into a meeting with him to please a woman she hated almost as much.

"Do you always wear those athletic outfits?" Vice President Hunter asked as they crossed the Eisenhower Executive Office Building's lobby.

Pia didn't answer.

They took the stairs down two levels, heels echoing on the marble. Hunter said, "Who did you send to Mumbai?

"No one." Pia tensed. "It was a personal favor for Bobby. But I just don't have the time. I have a video call with a couple hundred Sabel execs in an hour."

"One of your agents landed there this morning."

Pia felt an invisible shiver go down her spine. A former President who had once run the CIA, Hunter could watch every move she made. That creepiness could weigh on their budding relationship.

"We have offices there." Pia gave her a conversation-ending glance.

Hunter nodded. "Did you tell Jonelle about today's visit?"

"We call her the Major." Pia walked ten yards before answering the question. "Not exactly."

"Ah." Hunter lifted her chin with undisguised pride. "She told you to stay away from me."

"I determine my day." They walked another ten yards before Pia said, "I still don't see what I have to gain from meeting the bastard. He tried to shoot me."

"That was days ago." Hunter waved it away. "Keep focused on the future. The nation needs you."

Pia faced forward and kept walking.

Hunter couldn't handle the silence. "There's a lot at stake here. He thinks a war with the Saudis will be contained. You and I know it'll escalate. He's the most powerful man in the world, Pia. He doesn't listen to reason. He only listens to people he trusts."

"You know I'm going to tell him to resign," Pia said.

Hunter smiled at security people as they wound through the underground toward the West Wing. "When men meet adversaries, they fight. When they hear wisdom from an inside source, they listen. I want you near him. Near enough for him to trust you. You can't get revenge from a distance."

Striding through a labyrinth of corridors and offices, Pia noticed they shared a quick and confident pace. It made her wonder about nature versus nurture. Did it mean she had the same personality as Veronica Lodge Hunter? Was she capable of making the same heartless decisions? Would she abandon a child for her career? On the other hand, could she have faced down the myriad aggressive men Veronica must have vanquished?

They made their way to the West Wing and up the back stairs to the living quarters. A Secret Service agent showed them to the Treaty Room. Pia paced the large room. An oversized desk took up half of one wall with antique chairs and tables scattered around the edges. The space could host a dance contest. Then Pia realized it allowed the press to witness the signing of treaties. Photo op central.

Hunter examined the sidebar. "You know he's trying to destroy Sabel Industries, cancel all the government contracts, things like that. He's doing it as a preemptive strike. He's convinced you want to destroy him."

"Not as dumb as they say, then."

"I convinced him—" Hunter caught her gaze "—that if you're an ally, you won't touch him."

"And he bought it?"

"You don't owe me anything, I get that." Hunter stood near the entry. "But I need you to hear him out and make peace with him. Otherwise, this whole thing could blow up in my face at any minute. Surely you don't want to watch Chuck destroy me." She paused. "You know he's threatened me with the Attu Island cover up. I don't want to do time, Pia."

Pia glanced at her. Hunter bit her knuckle and looked away. Pia turned her gaze to the South Lawn and the Washington Memorial shining in the bright spring day.

"You made promises," Pia said, "gave me hope. Is this about you—or us?"

"Did Veronica tell you her secret?" Chuck Roche's voice made Pia's skin crawl from clear across the room.

"I'm calling her mom now." Pia tried not to sneer over her shoulder and failed.

"Show some respect or I'll…" Roche snarled. "I'm the President of the United States and you're one of my subjects, so sit down and shut up."

Pia felt herself turn red with anger as her fists balled up.

"C'mon, you two." Hunter stepped between them with her hands up, ignoring the prohibitive distance between them. "It's time to put away acrimony and work together. Pia can bring the youth vote in, Chuck. She's appealing and has no political past to dredge up."

"It's become a custom for people to kneel and kiss my ring." Roche leaned his cane forward. No rings adorned his fingers. He tapped his silver handled cane on the floor and waited. "Like they do for the Pope."

"She's not aware of the new protocols," Hunter said. "You need to give her good reason to join us."

"I have a great reason." Roche scowled at Pia. "I've seen the video from Attu. You pulled the trigger nine times, putting nine bullets into Viktor Popov."

"I don't miss." Pia turned to Hunter. "I'm outta here."

She stormed toward the door.

"If you care about your employees," Hunter caught Pia's arm as she passed, "they need you to listen."

Hunter turned to Roche. "If you care about the balance of evidence, she has more on you than you have on her. Make nice."

Pia felt her muscles tightening. Every fight she got into on the soccer field started with her muscles tightening and ended with a red card. Fights never benefitted the team. She willed herself to chill. She squeezed two words out through her clenched teeth. "Five minutes."

No one spoke for eight breaths, but each was a progressively calmer breath.

Hunter said, "I'll leave you two alone to work it out." She left.

"Drink?" Roche asked.

Pia shook her head. "What's so important that you needed this meeting?"

"The Saudi's attacked an American battleship—"

"We don't have battleships."

Roche waved her off. "Warship, destroyer, whatever it was. You're missing the point. We've been attacked, and Congress wants to wait for the investigation to conclude before giving me a declaration of war. That's outrageous. The country needs influential people like you to stand up and demand a war."

"You're so far out of your league, you don't even know what the game is. You should resign."

Pia looked at the service tray full of alcohol and mixers. Though she rarely drank, she felt a sudden urge to grab the tequila and slug back a shot. Instead, she poured herself a glass of orange juice.

"War is good for everyone." He tipped his cane toward her. "Especially you. Sabel Technology stands to make billions on the increased intelligence contracts. That's good money for a girl like you."

Pia crossed her arms and kept her mouth shut, hard as it was.

"Sabel Satellites just might get some new contracts too."

"They'll catch up with you eventually." She sighed. "You'll resign either way. Do it now and spare yourself the shame of being dragged out."

Roche laughed and pulled a glass from the bar. He looked at the options and opened a Red Bull. "We're very much alike, you know." He cut off her outburst before she started. "Don't argue. Listen. We're both strong willed, powerful leaders. You're young and naïve. You don't see it yet, but I'm a very wise man. That's how I got so rich and powerful. I am the ultimate in what men strive to achieve. The summit of mankind. You should listen to me. I'm telling you, it's because we're alike that we don't get along."

"What are you going to do when the Redjackets start testifying against you?" Pia turned her back on him and faced the South Lawn.

"Leaders have to be ruthless." He gulped his Red Bull and let out a satisfied sigh. "You know, Pia, mankind has always looked to the strongest leaders to make the hard decisions. In ancient times when the tribe was in danger, someone had to decide who should be terminated. While the rest of the tribe cowered in angst and fear, people like you and me took care of the problems." He waved his glass at her. "Like you did with Popov."

"Those Redjackets are the cowering guys." She kept her back to him. "When they get tossed in jail, they'll give you up before breakfast."

"People worry about stress. You know where stress comes from? Worrying about things out of your control. That's why seven of the ten most populated countries in the world are run by absolute rulers. The people don't worry because they have Putin or Xi or Bolsonaro to make decisions for them. In America, the little people wonder every day if they're doing the right thing. If they're making the right decision. How can they make their contribution to society? Every day, thousands of Sabel employees expect you to tell them when to show up for work, what to do when they get there, when to go home, what days to take off. Without you, those people would starve to death. They know it. They choose to work for you. They know you're worth following. They rely on your leadership."

That responsibility felt like an anvil on her chest. Roche was doing his best to produce that effect. A sip of orange juice stilled her nerves. Though, not as well as a shot of tequila.

"Look beyond your company, Pia." He crossed the room to stand next to her. "There's a nation full of those peons out there. They need direction from a man like me. For years, they've been like lost sheep." His voice rose with anger. "Congress and other presidents have led them astray, turned them away from manufacturing jobs with promises of free education. Those people will never engineer anything. They're not smart enough and never will be. Can't fix stupid, they say. And the politicians aren't real leaders, they're dreamers who forgot what sheep are good for. Sheep are good for shearing. Right now, the sheep are being devoured by foreign wolves."

Roche's voice had risen so loud he had to stop to take a breath.

"I'm going to use our military to settle those wrongs. I'm going to line up our forces against the Saudis and slam down my wrath. Don't think for a minute the Chinese and Koreans and French won't get that message."

Neither of them spoke. They sipped their drinks and stood alongside each other and watched the throngs of tourists on the National Mall.

"Look at them," Roche said. "They're wandering in the wilderness. Lost. They do what their leaders tell them. I'm a great leader. All I have to do is dream up a good idea, and Fuchs News puts the message out. A million people signed up to be Redjackets after the first public announcements. We have Redjackets in Sabel Industries, Pia." He faced her with a thin smile. "Who do you think they're going to testify against, me—or you?"

Pia held his gaze.

"You're wondering why I need the Redjackets?" He turned back to the view. "Bureaucracy, that's why. When I told the FBI to investigate you, they demanded a basis. They wanted a formal request with reasons and evidence. A paper trail. The Redjackets came down on your little parade of communists an hour after the call—"

"The Women's March is not communist."

"Whatever. You're getting hung up on the details. You'll never be successful if you get bogged down in who's a communist and who's a troublemaker. It doesn't matter." Roche swept his hand across the window. "They're lost sheep, Pia. They search for meaning in their lives. They need purpose. My leadership gives them purpose and meaning.

You need a purpose, Pia."

A hundred responses flooded her head. Most of them inflammatory. She sipped her OJ and sorted her thoughts. She remembered how her father always told her, "Make no enemies." Where did that leave her? She finished her drink and looked at the empty glass.

Pia warmed her voice. "What's your plan?"

A smile crept across his face. He turned to her. "Your generation has known nothing but success. They've never suffered. They've been lazy and overfed. These kids need to suffer to become great. They need this war, Pia. They need something to rally around. The press keeps them worried about which campaign manager is rotting in jail. Congress has them worried about whose attorney pled guilty to felonies. Some state prosecutor wants them to worry about where some charity funds went. The people don't care about any of that. They're mad because the Saudis sank our ship—and they want vengeance." He lowered his voice to a growl. "They want this war."

Pia watched his eyes.

"The country needs you on board. You can join me and rally the people around our battle cry. You can wave the flag and lead the charge against those damn towel heads. Or you can oppose me. And if you think that's going to work, there's something you should know. I wasn't kidding about that video from Attu Island. Veronica thinks her friends at the CIA buried it." He stepped close and looked up at her. "I put one of my people in charge of the CIA. They're loyal to me now. I have a video of you committing the cold-blooded murder of a Russian diplomat. So think about it. Join me or go to jail. What's it going to be, Pia?"

CHAPTER 7

President Roche slammed the Oval Office door behind him. His cane swept across the Resolute Desk, sending knickknacks and papers and the phone to the floor. "THAT BITCH!"

"Who?" Hunter's voice.

Roche spun around to see Hunter and his new chief of staff, Hartwell Thomas, sitting on the couches. The latter looked surprised and a little scared.

"You said that little shit would be an asset." He slammed his cane on the desk. "She said, 'fuck you!' to the President of the United States. You think that's an asset?"

"That's great," Hunter said. "It's the second step—anger. She was in denial last time, that's the first step. She couldn't believe people voted for you. Now she's angry. Next time, she'll bargain."

"What're you talking about?" Roche tapped his cane on the floor and pushed the handle away from him. "That death-thing?"

Thomas stared at Roche for a moment before remembering his duty. He scrambled to the commander in chief and dropped to one knee and kissed Roche's fingers. "Working for you is the greatest honor imaginable, sir. Thank you for this blessed opportunity to serve in your administration. I never imagined—"

"Kubler-Ross stages of grief," Hunter said with a disgusted glance at Thomas. "It's not just a common response to grief, it's primarily how we handle every change in our lives: denial, anger, bargaining, depression, and finally, acceptance."

"Let me know when we get to acceptance. Talking to her is like talking to a tiger. All that muscle and sinew rippling under her skin just waiting for a chance to shred you into bite-sized pieces. I'm ready to send the Redjackets after her. She's better off dead."

Thomas rose and backed up two yards.

"And how did that work last time?" Hunter asked. "Backfired. You almost got impeached. Give me a little time. I'll bring her around."

"What did she tell you about Mumbai?"

"She lied. But that's OK. I'll take her shopping." She saw the confusion his face. "It's amazing what a daughter will tell her mother over a shoe rack."

"Three days." Roche punctuated his statement by slamming his cane on the desk. "That's all you get. Then I send the Redjackets to eliminate her and that pack of losers she uses for bulletproofing."

"You throw them around as if you could order them to commit murder." Hunter tilted her head in question. "I'm going to assume you're exaggerating. Tell me you're exaggerating."

"I'm exaggerating." Roche bristled at the way she treated him. "I don't have anything to do with them."

All three were silent a moment. Hunter tossed a glance to Thomas. Roche noted the two had some prearranged signals. He would keep an eye on them, keep them from ganging up on him. Maybe it was time for another purge.

"I'm not sure Sabel is such a good idea," Thomas said. "We still have some Redjackets in jail from the last go-round. They're hankering to cut a deal with the prosecutors."

Roche stepped close to the big Texan and pushed up to his face and shook his cane. "Sounds like candidates for a shiv. Start with the weakest guy. It'll send a message. Make it happen."

"I was thinking along the lines of pardon." Thomas managed a disarming smile.

"Pardons don't work." Roche spat his words. "I called Wilkes and offered one for her daughter. Some people would rather rot in jail than do what I need done."

"If you're going to talk about Wilkes," Hunter grabbed her purse, "I'm leaving. I can't be party to any conspiracy. You might need me to pardon you someday. And quit talking about that video from Attu Island.

Believe me, it'll get us in more trouble than you realize."

Roche watched her saunter out. When the door closed, he said, "I want that war, damn it. Is the Wilkes problem resolved?"

"We're not talking about the streets of New York here," Thomas replied. "There have been a few complications."

"How did they let her get away? You really botched that one. You and your Redjackets are useless."

"No one expected a woman of her age to put up a fight like that. Unheard of." Thomas tossed his hands in the air. "She pistol-whipped our man."

"Why haven't they tracked her down yet?" Roche smacked the desk with his cane and circled around to the chair. "What good are these people? You told me we could count on them."

"Mumbai is a big city, sir. Twenty million with the mightiest slums in Asia."

"Then double the crew. Triple it. Make it a competition."

"An American admiral killed in the streets of Mumbai? The Indian government would whip up an investigation using every officer in India."

"Make sure your guys do it neatly then. Make it look like the Saudis did it." Roche relaxed a little. "Yeah, the Saudis double-crossed her. What about her aides? Are they onboard?"

"Well now," the Texan said, "they bought the story about the intelligence operation, but a killing might blow our facts sky-high."

"So?" Roche grabbed the back of his executive chair. "Eliminate them."

"We would be making a big ol' pile of naval officers."

They stared at each other while Roche wondered if he'd made a bad pick. Thomas seemed to be loyal to those military whiners instead of his president.

"The men have a heap of concerns." Thomas wiped his face with his palm. "If the Indians find them, they won't have any US Constitution or US President to back them up. They want assurances."

"Assure them I'll have them dropped from a helicopter—"

"With all due respect, sir, they want lawyers standing by." Thomas shrugged. "It's not a bad demand. The lawyers we provide would protect us too. Not just from conspiracy charges, but from the chances of someone brewing up a wider investigation."

"Yeah, why not?" Roche dropped in his chair and put his feet on the desk. "Send Mike and Rod."

"They're American lawyers. We'll need whatever they call good ol' boys in Mumbai."

Roche smelled a rat but didn't have any alternatives. "You have someone in mind?"

"Indeed," Thomas smiled. "And we could fund it from the Inaugural fund. There's still a few million stashed away in there."

"Do it." Roche pointed his cane at the Texan. "But if you ever use my money to pay off some crony of yours again, I'll can your ass on national television."

"I swear," Thomas held up his hands, "I had no idea—"

"Don't lie about it. Just get on with killing Wilkes."

"How about a different approach, sir?" Thomas asked.

Roche raised his brows. "I'm listening."

"The suicide was a no-brainer if we could've pulled it off as planned. But killing a flag officer is going to bring in the Navy, the Joint Chiefs, everyone. Especially if we made it look like a Saudi did it. It would bring down the brightest spotlight you've ever seen. And if you think cops stick together, wait til you see the ticked off Joint Chiefs. The risk is too great."

"Then what do you propose?"

"Character assassination."

Roche smiled. "Nobody beats me at that game."

"I'd appreciate it if you would let me do the honors, sir." Thomas closed his eyes. "As high profile as she is, this could use something less overt and more nuanced in the approach."

"You think I'll screw it up?" Roche smacked the desk with his cane and looked the man over. "My thing. I'll do it. But if it doesn't work, you go kill her yourself."

"Watching you perform would be terrific. I've seen you do this so many times—and do it so well … I just want to give it a try. Want to see if I'd learned as much from you as I hoped. That way I can catch the blowback if it goes south. Be the fall guy. Keep you in the clear. That's all. I meant no disrespect."

Roche got out of his chair and clasped his hands behind his back. "You know, I was thinking. It might be time to have a chief of staff who is a laser gun like me, zapping the rodents of this filthy country. That would put fear into our enemies, right? Yeah, maybe we could get Nora in on it too. Three of us zapping anyone—"

"I'm not so sure we want to bring the Secretary of State in … just yet. Too early."

"Fine." Roche turned to look at the Rose Garden. "Run with it, Hartwell. But keep my Redjackets going after her and anyone who goes looking for her. Have them bring her in, dead or alive. Make them the heroes on this. We need heroes."

CHAPTER 8

Two days after Dhanpal asked me to lead his mission Cody was still assigned to me. I had assigned myself to my kitchen. He'd become a fixture at my house since I served him my trademark grilled salmon. Even though neither of us is gay, he proposed marriage over my cooking. I politely declined.

One day I hoped to find a woman who might appreciate my culinary skills enough to marry me and start working on populating the nation in our image. My hunt for true love was not going well. The last woman my spatula won over was currently fighting extradition to France over a multi-million-euro art fraud. You win some, you lose some to Interpol.

Our phones buzzed with an incoming text. Cody gave me the summary. It came from Bianca Dominguez, head of Sabel Technology. The short version: Our internal communications systems were considered compromised by Redjackets within Sabel Industries. A review of critical personnel was underway. Until further notice, all important communications were to be conducted face-to-face.

"That's bad, right?" Cody asked.

"You know what binary means in the digital world?" When he nodded, I continued. "Everything is binary, ones and zeros, on or off, except Sabel Technologies. Alan Sabel pioneered a ternary system. It uses on/off/maybe. It's one step shy of quantum computing. That's why the NSA, DIA, CIA and every other something-A in the government uses Bianca's systems to crack codes and read Putin's emails. Nothing in the binary world can hide from Bianca and her people. Our phones are … were the most secure system on the planet."

Cody whistled. "Good thing we be guarding your kitchen, not

sneaking into North Korea."

I shook the kitchen knife at him. "I said no more veiled references to the Mumbai mission."

"Hey now," Cody leaned back, his eyes focused on the tip of the knife. "I didn't mean to throw shade—"

"You haven't been on Ms. Sabel's crazy missions." I set the knife down and leaned over the counter. "She gets some wild idea that she can change a world-gone-mad and runs straight into danger without a plan."

"Word is, you have issues with the woman. You should work that shit out."

Mercury leaned around Cody's shoulder and waved his hand in front of the kid's face. *I think he can see me, dawg. We may have us a new disciple. Tell him about me. Tell him how I saved your life from fifty-two Iraqi Republican Guards in the battle of—*

I said, *Leave him alone. If I tell him about the Roman Pantheon, he'll re-up for another four years in the 101ˢᵗ.*

"Why you looking at me like that?" Cody had a sour look on his face.

"I worked things out with Ms. Sabel. She said I don't have to go on poorly planned missions if I don't want to. And guess what?"

Someone pounded on my door. Anoshni started barking. I looked at my greasy fingers, then at my braised pork cannelloni with apples and brie. A culinary masterpiece in progress. Stuffing cannelloni with pork is not as easy as they make it sound on the James Beard website. I looked at Cody and tilted my head to the door. He pushed off and went to get his very own copy of *Watchtower*.

Cody returned with a concerned look on his face and thumbed behind him. "That billionaire guy who be all up on TV is out there with a big-ass general behind him."

Bobby Jenkins was two steps behind the kid and shoved him aside. "Jacob, you have to find Annie."

"Hi there, Bobby, I—"

"My daughter's in jail because … you know about that. Annie was in the process of resurrecting the talks to get Jenny a presidential pardon. She wouldn't just run away. You have to find her."

Before I could wipe the pork off my hands, General Thompson

pushed both Bobby and Cody aside. "What the hell is this I hear about you turning down the Wilkes mission?"

"General, I just, ah …" I grabbed a wad of paper towels while Bobby and the general spotted my disembodied meat pile with a mixture of surprise and disgust. Great dishes don't look all that great until final assembly. Presentation is everything.

Mercury leaned his elbow on the general's shoulder. *Yeah, home boy, you just 'ah …' what? Lost your nerve? Chickened out? Ran away? Decided honor and glory mean nothing anymore?*

I said, *Decided one dead Sabel agent is better than two.*

Mercury said, *Thompson-boy here saved you from a straight-jacket in the Army insane asylum. You're gonna tell him you're a coward?*

A straight-jacket because of you, I said. *A god who wants more followers might try a more positive approach.*

I gotcha bro. Mercury produced a six-foot golden trophy out of thin air, *Here's your very own award. Izzat positive enough for you?*

A statue of a man shrugging his shoulders with his palms out, standing on a tower of marble columns. At the bottom was a plaque inscribed, *Jacob Stearne, Bystander in Life, Participant Award.*

The trophy evaporated when Tania pushed between Thompson and Bobby. Miguel towered over the crowd. He dropped a bag on the floor that landed with the unmistakable clank of gun barrels. Many gun barrels. Probably enough steel to rebuild the Titanic. Everyone flinched.

I said, "What is this, Grand Central Station?"

"Dhanpal's gone missing." Tania glared an accusation at me. "He reported in when he landed in Mumbai. He went to the Dharavi slums. His video feed went dark just before gunfire broke out. Pretty sure there were Redjackets involved. Last thing he said was, 'Congress Jacob would never go.' What's that about?"

There was that word again, Redjackets. Americans shouldn't be hunting down other Americans. Especially Sabel Security, we're the good guys. But Dhanpal? Missing? That part had my gut flipping over. We'd been to Avernus and back together. He didn't just disappear.

Mercury leaned over my kitchen counter and turned his grin into a scowl. *You let him go alone. You could've been the hero, on the news, saved the admiral, saved your teammates, done—*

I said, *Yeah, fine. I get it.*

"Get what?" General Thompson asked.

"That you guys think I perform miracles." I looked at five expectant faces waiting for me to produce answers. "Why does everyone want me to solve their problems?"

General Thompson said, "I've seen you perform miracles."

Miguel said, "Me too."

Cody's gaze whipped back and forth from the general to the big guy. Two people from opposite ends of cultural, social, and professional spectrums agreeing on the reality of miracles must've troubled him.

Tania leaned over the counter. "Are you trying to weasel out of this?"

Mercury crossed his arms. *You know why they're heating up like that, my brutha? Because cowardice is punished by decimatio. That's the root word for decimation. It's the sentence for the spineless: the killing of every tenth man in the cohort. The death-sentence is carried out by the man's squad mates. Your friends have chosen you to be the decimatio who will suffer the fustuarium.*

I once read about fustuarium, Latin for clubbing a guy to death. Very intimate. The decimatio has been replaced in the modern era with a choice between transcendental meditation and group hugs. But—given the mood of the crowd—neither of those options would fly.

"No, no, you got me all wrong." I wiped my hands and looked at everyone. "I was, um, forming a team. Cody here's all over it. Right, Cody? And we're leaving in … an hour. Probably."

Miguel leaned over the general with a menacing glare. Tania narrowed her eyes to downright beady.

"Don't go making fun of us now," Thompson said. "Pia said you refused to take the mission."

I raised my palms and tried to think up an excuse. All I wanted out of life was to cook interesting dishes, find a nice girl who liked me, walk the dog, like normal, boring people. But Dhanpal was missing. That was not good. Navy SEALs don't go missing. And talk about peer pressure, everyone wants me to get my head blown off on ill-conceived missions.

Mercury said, *Nothing new there.*

I stood there with my mouth opening and closing and nothing coming out.

Bobby Jenkins leaned in. "Well?"

"Relax," I said in a voice that would've made my mother worry. "I've got this."

"I owe you my life." The general saved me from lying in detail. "I did my best to pay you back. Still, I think I've earned the right to say, GET YOUR HEAD IN THIS MISSION AND GET MARCHING, SOLDIER!"

Army training never leaves you. I snapped to attention and saluted. "Yes, sir."

All options were exhausted. All hope of that normal life shelved for the foreseeable future. Apparently, I was leading a mission to Mumbai.

"Sorry." Thompson winced at his own outburst. "Annie and I served on the staff at the Joint Chiefs years ago. We were very close. She's one helluva woman, Jacob. She deserves better than running blind all over India. Get out there and find her."

"Wait a second." Bobby Jenkins snapped a look at his friend. "She was married to me when she served at the JCS."

General Thompson continued to face me as his eyes slid to the side to check out Bobby. His gaze came back to me. "Get moving, Jacob."

"Hold on," Bobby said, facing the general. "How close were you?"

"Let's just focus on the reason we came here." Thompson grabbed Bobby's shoulder and spun him around to leave.

"I'll do my best." I mustered all my confidence and fell short.

"It's a big city, twenty million." Thompson said as he navigated around Miguel. "You need to do better than your best. Do you have a plan?"

"Absolutely," I squeaked.

Before they got outside, we could hear Bobby asking, "Do you think he can do it?"

Thompson answered, "Better'n anyone else. He gets messages from this long forgotten … Just put your faith in Jacob."

When the front door closed, Cody looked at me. "Zat true? You saved the general's life?"

"Long story," Miguel said.

I returned to stuffing my cannelloni.

"You're cooking?" Miguel looked angry. He never got angry. "You should be packing."

Mercury leaned his elbows on the table and twisted his head to catch my gaze. *Forget the food, homes, you need to be having Cousin Elmer get the jet ready, grabbing your armor and rifles. Get fucking moving!*

I said, *You shouldn't swear like that. The other gods don't swear.*

Oh really? Mercury stood straight up. *Dude, you should've heard Jesus screaming at Pope Pius XII during the Holocaust.*

"You playing with us?" Cody watched me work for a few seconds.

"Not exactly."

"Do you really have a plan?" Tania asked with an edge in her voice that could snip sheet metal.

"Sorta." I fidgeted the meat. "I'll think of something."

"Are we down for Wilkes or not?" Cody asked.

"Screw Wilkes." I shook a fistful of pork at him before tossing it back in the pan. Braised pork doesn't have as much dramatic effect as a knife. "We're going after Dhanpal."

"We?" Cody looked excited. "I'm in. What's the plan?"

"I've got plenty of plans—in my head." I stared at the cannelloni. It looked nice. It would've been a great lunch. I sighed, dumped the tray in the trash, and washed my hands.

"Where was his last known position?" I asked.

"Dharavi," Tania said, "three miles south of Chhatrapati Shivaji Maharaj International Airport."

She made it sound easy to pronounce. Her ordeal in Mumbai must've been longer than I thought. "Let's just call it 'south of the airport.'"

She shrugged.

"You OK going back?" I asked.

"No choice." She tightened up. "Annie Wilkes is Jaz Jenkins's mother."

"Make the call," I said. "We need Sabel One fully fueled and a double crew for international. Wheels up in an hour."

"Cousin Elmer had it fueled and waiting twenty minutes ago." She kept her skeptical gaze on me. "No one but the pilots know about it, and they think we're going to Stockholm."

Cody looked confused. "Cousin Elmer? Sweden? Wazzat?"

"Ms. Sabel's cousin is in charge of company vehicles," I said. "Stockholm is halfway. Gotta refuel."

Tania said, "What does 'Congress Jacob would never go' mean?"

"Dunno."

The buzz of four phones filled the room. Notifications from Bianca about a press conference regarding Wilkes was in progress at the White House. Cody pulled it up first. We crowded around his phone.

Hartwell Thomas, chief-of-staff-of-the-week, stepped to the podium in the White House briefing room.

"I know that guy." Cody pointed at Thomas. "He talked at my platoon in Mogadishu. Wanted people to join on up with the Redjackets about a year ago. Only he didn't call 'em that."

On TV, Thomas quieted the crowd. "Sadly, we must report the results of a preliminary investigation into the disappearance of Admiral Wilkes. After some kind of altercation at her hotel, it appears she has fled the area and abandoned her command. We do not yet know the full circumstances. We do not want people speculating that she had something to do with the sinking of her ship. We want everyone to wait for the results of the full investigation. If she was involved, if she conspired with others, that'll all come to light. There is no reason to think the fact that she ran from the hotel on foot means she has something to hide. Her staff was in the midst of compiling reports and activating protocols to investigate the bombing. They had not yet found anything implicating her. Her decision to leave—taking only a pistol and not her phone—is not an indication that she feared the investigation. We hold Admiral Wilkes in our thoughts and prayers. We are also praying for her daughter, currently serving time in Leavenworth. Thank you."

We looked at each other as he walked away from the reporters' shouted questions.

"That guy must've been in the military," Tania said, "cuz he's got the throw-someone-under-the-bus-before-the-investigation-starts down like a pro."

We climbed in Miguel's SUV and drove to the executive terminal at Dulles, where Ms. Sabel keeps the company jets.

Mercury squeezed into the space between Cody and me while Tania railed about how men are all losers, incapable of making even the simplest commitments in life.

Mercury said, *You should've called Jaz Jenkins and told him she's needing an engagement ring.*

I waved him off. *Not my problem.*

No, your problem is information, Mercury said. *Twenty million Indians, dawg. Miguel speaks French, Tania speaks males-suck, you speak Pashto and Arabic, Cody speaks English. If you're going to get anywhere, you need to find a way to communicate.*

I said, *I'm working on a plan.*

Mercury said, *Zat right? Tell me about it.*

I said, *It's a sixteen-hour flight. You're gonna figure out what 'Congress Jacob would never go' means by the time we land or I'm converting to Judaism.*

CHAPTER 9

PIA WATCHED THE VIDEO SESSION shut down. Tapping her pencil on the pad in front of her, she wondered if her notes would make sense tomorrow. The Major sat quietly, appraising her. Which felt worse than having the Major let loose with a tirade or a list of improvements or any feedback at all. Pia missed her father at times like these. There were no moments of uncertainty in his presence. Everyone knew exactly where they stood with him before, during, and after every interaction.

"Happy?" Pia asked.

"Quite." The Major leaned back. "You have improved tremendously since yesterday's session. Going over your notes instead of going to the White House makes a big difference. So does the suit. You look more professional. We used to have a saying in the military, 'Look sharp, feel sharp, be sharp.'"

The suit felt more like a straight-jacket. The boardroom a padded cell. And Sabel Industries' tower, a prison. Her gaze swept to the window and the city of Bethesda, eighteen floors below. Some people relished the view from on top. It gave them a sense of accomplishment. Pia knew the reality: no matter how accomplished one becomes, everyone is one bullet away from going home forever.

"How many more of these?" Pia asked.

"Two more with the division executives, then we'll be ready for the board. You don't want to talk to them until—"

"Why the hell did Dad do that?"

"You know why." The Major closed her laptop and rose.

"If he put all the shares that make money in my name, why did he give you and the others the 'voting' shares? He didn't trust me."

"He wanted to protect the employees." She put her hand on Pia's shoulder to comfort her.

"From me." Pia crossed her arms.

"Or anyone who may seek to unduly influence—"

"Which reflects on me, doesn't it? Makes it seem like I'm incompetent. Unstable." As soon as Pia said the last word, she regretted it.

She had been unstable. She had let everyone down since her father's death. Maybe he was right to protect the company. That didn't make it feel any better to have eight other people voting on whether she could run her own company, choose her own executives, and reject customers like Chuck Roche as she deemed necessary.

Then there was Roche's threat. It had bounced around inside her headache for the last twenty-four hours. The board would kick her out the minute the video from Attu Island came to light.

That day on the island came back to her in a rush. The biting wind, snowflakes that felt like glass shards, and Viktor Popov grinning as they faced off a mile from their respective bodyguards. The old Russian had smuggled a pistol and made the mistake of pulling it on her. He paid the price. But, just as Jacob had predicted, every bullet she drilled into the mastermind of evil replayed in her head at the slightest provocation. Nine bullets, each carefully placed to cause the most pain before killing him. He'd pleaded for his life. A coward in the end. Pia took a deep breath and refocused on the present.

Warning the Major about Roche's threat crossed her mind. But it would wait. Pia had a couple options left that might derail Roche before her crimes became public knowledge.

The silence stretched to the point Pia no longer knew how to restart the conversation. She longed to start over with a gentler tone of voice. Yet, anger over voting shares still heated her veins.

The Major said, "He was thinking of Veronica Hunter. Not you."

"I can handle that old witch." Pia got up and slammed her chair back under the massive table.

"She's more cunning than you can imagine. Alan knew firsthand how duplicitous she can be."

"Did you forget all she's done to me?" Pia scowled at the memories. "Not to mention what she's tried to do."

"Then why the hell did you run off with her yesterday?"

"To get Roche under control."

"I don't think so. I think you did it because you wanted to please your birth-mother."

"Jealous?"

"With a right. She could easily go down in history as the worst mother of all time. You owe her nothing. You owe your employees a stable company. You owe your customers a reliable partner. You owe—"

"YOU?" Pia tried to calm herself. "Is that it? It's all about you?"

"Well, I certainly deserve better than this." The Major pushed her smaller frame closer to Pia and raised up on her tiptoes. "I've been to all your birthday parties since you were sixteen. I didn't see her there. She didn't even send a card. Christmas? Olympics? World Cup?"

Pia turned away and walked to the window. "What do you want from me?"

"For you to stop being selfish. Look around you. Start thinking about the company and everyone in it."

"Selfish? I fund ten charities in Bethesda alone. I took over Dad's scholarship fund for—"

"Charities make rich people feel better about being rich. That doesn't mean you're not selfish."

"Then what do I have to do to please YOU?"

"Nothing's changed. I want all your attention where it belongs. Let's give everyone confidence in you. The board, the employees, the clients—all of them. Let them see the caring Pia, the involved Pia, the Pia I know, at the helm."

Pia sniffled and breathed and knew the Major was right. One day, Pia would avenge her father's death by destroying the complicit. Until then, she owed his legacy her full attention. On top of that, she owed everything to the Major, Jonelle Jackson, the quiet woman who kept her father's legacy growing. She owed her friend and mentor better than the venom she'd been dishing out. In that moment, she resolved to do what the Major asked.

That meant giving up her pursuit of the guilty. That meant leaving the deaths of her loved ones unresolved. The thought curled her tongue like tainted milk. Bile rose in her throat. She could not give up that driving force in her life. The list was down to the last two names. The last two participants in the murders that reached deep into her childhood. As ugly and consuming as revenge always is, it drove her life from one minute to the next.

In that second, while the Major watched her think, she came to the only answer available to her. She would juggle both the Major and Hunter. An easy thing for an insomniac.

Nonetheless, it would be a lie. A painful but necessary lie. The Major deserved better. Maybe one day the woman would forgive her. Maybe not.

"OK," Pia said without looking at her. "You win. I'm in. What's my afternoon look like?"

"You and Bianca are visiting the Technologies campus in Columbia."

"Not in these shoes." Pia turned her foot.

"I wondered why you chose pumps. I wouldn't own any if I didn't need the height. And you don't need more height."

"They went with the suit." Pia exhaled. "I'm going to pop over to Nieman's before I head out."

The Major picked up her things. "I've got to fix our supply chain in Greenville, then you and I have a working dinner with the phone consortium. They're planning a lot of satellites. We need that business."

"Right. I can do this." Pia picked up her laptop and pad.

They went their separate ways. Pia left her McLaren in the garage and took an Uber to the Mazza Gallerie.

PIA STRODE INTO NIEMAN'S SHOE department. She pushed a Secret Service agent aside and marched straight to Hunter, who was engrossed in a pair of Golden Goose sneakers on a low pedestal.

Without looking up, Hunter said, "These are perfect for you."

Pia glanced at the shoe. "Seventeen hundred for a pair of beat up sneakers covered in rhinestones? Pass."

"Think of the children in Bangladesh working twelve-hour days to make these for you." Hunter rose. "Does Jonelle know you're here?"

"If you want to talk to me, I'd prefer she doesn't know about it." Pia picked up the sneaker. "Says made in Italy."

"Tsk. Tsk. Those poor Bangladeshi kids, out of work for the season then."

"What did you want?"

"Someone who won't lose control and throw f-bombs at the President of the United States."

"Good thing you're concerned about Bangladesh, that's how far you'll have to go to find someone like that."

Hunter smiled. "Who did you send after Wilkes?"

"I gave Bobby some referrals. I'm not in the ex-wife business."

"I thought I was tall at five-ten." Hunter looked Pia over from head to toe. "How did you get such a great fitting suit?"

"Tailors on staff." Pia crossed her arms. "Are you going to answer me?"

"You were supposed to win over the man." Hunter pulled a Manolo flat off the shelf. "He's going to wreck my career, you know."

"He'll have to share the credit." Pia took the shoe and slapped it back in place. "He'd only be capping the damage you've already done."

"You should be nice to me," Hunter gave her a cold glance. "I talked him down from releasing your video."

"Thanks." Pia crossed her arms and checked the shoe displays.

"Think about the country," Hunter said. "If we can stop his vainglorious war, he'll never make it full-term. He'll be out before the election. He could resign in shame. He could be impeached for any number of crimes. He could get bored and walk away. Think about who that leaves in his wake."

"You."

"He doesn't trust me."

"Imagine that."

"He's trying to force me out." Hunter picked up a Jimmy Choo skimmer. "It takes a congressional vote to dump a vice president. He's been working on it since the day he gave me the job. If he succeeds,

Hartwell Thomas is in as VP."

"He was a decent politician." Pia spied a black Zadig & Voltaire high-top boot.

"Thomas built the Redjacket organization."

That information took Pia by surprise. Her people had been tracking the secret society for months. They couldn't find the communication network, much less an org chart. With no discernible hierarchy and no traceable chain of command, it was the most frightening extrajudicial paramilitary group imaginable. No legal accountability. Which made Pia wonder why Hunter had offered up the founder. No doubt, a political rival.

"You have to help me," Hunter said. "Thomas has been asking questions about everything I do. He's been getting security clearances for his Redjackets so he can replace the Secret Service. They're planning more Redjacket attacks on newspapers and TV stations. You don't want me to be removed from office, do you?"

Pia bit her tongue to keep the obvious answer from echoing through the store. The picture Hunter painted about Thomas's plans made Hunter look like the lesser of two evils. If it was true.

Hunter held the skimmer up to Pia. "You'd look good in these."

"Walking into retirement, maybe."

Hunter looked at the boot in Pia's hand. "Those are perfect—if you're going to pour concrete."

Pia put the boot back. Hunter put the skimmer back. They wandered to the next pedestal of shoes.

"I need help too," Pia said. "Roche told me he has Redjackets in Sabel Industries."

Hunter looked at her with genuine concern. Pia tried to determine if Hunter's interest was because her company had been infiltrated or because Roche had told her about it.

"You made promises." Pia closed in on Hunter.

"I know." Hunter backed up. "We're getting there."

Pia said, "Is there really a video from Attu Island?"

"Drone feed." Hunter gasped. "He shouldn't even know how to find it. Wait. Nora Ratched. That slut. We can't let that get out. We'll have to cut a deal with him. Negotiate something."

"What's Ratched's deal?"

"The former CIA Director who wormed her way into Secretary of State without regard to optics? She's ingratiating herself to Chuck. And showing him how to access that video is definitely her style."

"The way he was talking, I expected him to release it right after our meeting."

"I buried it under security designations a mile deep before my term expired." Hunter bit her thumbnail. "He can override those but doing it would leave a paper trail proving he already knew it existed, making him complicit in a coverup. Damn. That means he's getting smarter. It'll take time, but Nora will find a way out for him. He'll put it out there sooner or later. And that's bad for both of us. Your crime is obvious enough. He'll make my part look like a coverup for my daughter."

Pia checked Hunter's expression. The woman obviously expected some gratitude for helping Pia. Pia felt nothing but manipulation. She picked up a Givenchy ankle boot with three silver buckles. She tossed it to the nearby attendant and called out her size. The attendant ran in the back.

"You're going with those?" Hunter shook her head.

The bargain was apparent: they could help each other. Time and again, Hunter had proven herself a slippery partner. Yet Pia needed Hunter's help before Roche ruined her. Once more, Alan Sabel's legacy weighed on her like an anchor. As much as she owed the Major, that world would soon come crashing down on them both if she didn't act.

"What can I do about it?" Pia asked.

"We need each other," Hunter said. "You can help me stay in office. I can keep you free of murder charges. You'll need to learn how to sway public opinion. I'm not talking about rallying fans before a big match. I'm talking about tough political reporters who've been tearing apart public figures for decades. That takes practice. Can you make the governor's speech tomorrow?"

The decision twisted her intestines like writhing vipers. She loathed the boardroom, and soon they would loathe her. She loved field work. The type of field work she was about to dive into was new to her. Hunter knew that world better than anyone. And Hunter needed help in return. Helping Hunter was an unselfish act, she told herself. The Major would approve. And the Major was right, she felt an urge to help her biological mother. Sick as that idea was.

Pia said, "Have an intern pick me up at the Starbucks across from Sabel Towers."

Hunter smirked. "Don't want Jonelle to know?"

Pia grabbed the vice president's arm roughly. "You use her given name in a pathetic effort to stir up whatever racism might lurk in someone nearby. You can't help it, dividing your perceived enemies is in your nature. But from now on, call her the Major—like those of us who respect her—or you and I are done."

CHAPTER 10

PRESIDENT CHUCK ROCHE SAT IN the Oval Office watching the news when his secretary buzzed him on the intercom. Again. He muted the TV and pressed the button.

The secretary skipped formalities. "Senator Krueger on line three for you, sir."

"Send him to Hartwell." Roche hated being interrupted with all these calls. "That's what the chief of staff is for."

"Mr. Thomas specifically requested this call be sent to you, sir."

"Fine." Roche resisted slamming his cane into the phone. "I'll take the call. But tell Hartwell to get his ass in here right away."

He stabbed the button for line three. "Fred, what's new?"

"What the hell are you doing with the Redjackets?" Senator Krueger's tone of voice pissed off the president. "We had a deal. You were to stay away from them. Distance yourself—particularly after that last fiasco with the Sabel girl. We have the vote on your war with the Saudis coming up. This is no time for some nosy reporter to link you directly to the Redjackets."

"I don't know what you're talking about, Fred."

"The Intelligence Committee got hold of reports, Chuck. Rumor has it there were Redjackets in the hotel lobby moments before Annie Wilkes disappeared. You better not have fingerprints on this whole Saudi business. And you sure as hell better not have anything to do with Annie's disappearance."

"Are you threatening me?" Roche stood up, shouting into the speakerphone and fondling his cane. If they were in the same room, Fred would get a taste of the silver handle. "Don't you dare try to intimidate me, motherfucker. Don't think for a minute I can't halt the highway construction going on in your state. Did we do all the environmental impact studies required? Have the anthropologists found remains of ancient graves?"

"Hold on, now." Krueger's voice folded like origami. "I'm just telling you what I've learned over many successful years in politics. And that is, if the Redjackets are involved, and the opposition can tie them to you, you can kiss your Saudi war goodbye. There's nothing I—or anyone else—can do to stop it."

"Redjackets are American patriots, damn it!" Roche's shout echoed through the room. "They have the right to freely assemble. No one, especially you, should stand in their way. As for Wilkes, I only know what I read in the daily briefings. She met with some unidentified men in the lobby then she left the building. Maybe they were CIA guys. Maybe they were coconspirators with her and the Saudis. Maybe she's gone bad like her daughter. We just don't know yet. But one thing I do know, if you start leaking information to the press, your state won't get another federal dollar spent until they elect a leader who knows what loyalty means. Am I making myself clear?"

Krueger stayed silent.

"I expect your loyalty on this one, Fred." Roche looked up to see Thomas peering around the door. He waved the man in. "You know what loyalty means? You tell everyone what you know about Annie Wilkes. What you know is she's disappeared with shadowy men. That doesn't look good, does it?"

"Annie wouldn't do that," Fred whimpered. "She was liaison for the JCS back in the day. She's a fine officer and a dedicated public servant."

"Get your head out of your ass and prepare the public for the other Wilkes. The one who might be in league with terrorists. Do it before lunch. I can hear the bulldozers going silent as we speak. Who's the president?"

"You are, sir." Krueger's voice had an edge Roche didn't care for.

"Which is better, to run off on your own whim like a teenager or to do what the President of the United States tells you?" Roche didn't wait for an answer, he clicked off.

Thomas dropped to one knee and kissed the president's fingers. "Every day is a new and refreshing honor to serve you, our invincible leader, and this great administration—"

"What the hell is going on with those fags in the Senate?" Roche pushed him away. "That press conference you held didn't do the trick."

"Well, that would be a long game, sir." Thomas backed up and stood at the front of the desk. "We've planted the seed. When it germinates, we'll add to it."

"Takes too long, damn it." Roche paced behind the desk. "She could surface at any minute, and God only knows what lies she'll tell."

"Two more seeds planted and we're home free." Thomas held his hands out. "Today, we're leaking that she left with five unknown operatives. Tomorrow, we'll leak that the operatives may have ties to the Saudi royal family. After that, we can tell every red-blooded American to report her whereabouts. Anyone traveling anywhere in the world will become our eyes and ears. Then, if she's found, and there should be an old fashioned shoot-out, why, we have—"

"If, if, if … I don't like it." Roche stopped pacing and pointed his cane at Thomas. "You're a failure. Your plan has already failed. Her staffers are asking questions about the 'intel officers' who showed up. They'll expose that cover story by this afternoon. And what about the senators? If Krueger is questioning me, the rest will be in revolt by tomorrow. We should've sent more Redjackets, then used your story after the shoot out."

"Begging your indulgence, sir." Thomas shook his head. "It needs another twenty-four hours. Then we're free to operate—"

Roche walked up close to his chief of staff. The man certainly didn't appreciate the urgency of the situation. He could do things the Thomas way and fail or take control of the situation and win. Easy decision. "I think you're cracking. It's the stress."

"Sir." Thomas drooped. "I spent years drafting qualified people into the Redjackets. We have to keep their operations cloaked in secrecy. We can't let them be exposed to public scrutiny. They can do your bidding— but they can only operate with impunity if no one knows when they're coming. Think of what we can accomplish. The drug dealers we can eliminate in their home countries. The terrorists we can slaughter before they cross the border. The radicals right here at home who want to undermine our patriotic values. We can stop them before they get any momentum. The newspapers and TV outlets that think they can print lies without suffering any consequences must be shut down. We can keep this country on the right path, Mr. President. But to do that, we need our little group to have a free hand. They need to work quietly on your behalf. They see you as their great leader. They look to you to protect their identities."

Roche thought about this and turned to the window. The South Lawn looked green, the sun was bright, spring was in full bloom. "Maybe you're right."

"It's your choice, sir." Thomas straightened up. "We can keep a covert profile or go forward in full public view. We tried that a couple weeks ago with the kidnapping. The public didn't like that at all. They were—"

"Those were my orders!" Roche spun to face his accuser. "Are you saying I made a bad decision?"

"Oh no, sir. I meant only that—"

"You are under a lot of stress, aren't you?"

"I, ah, this is a much different job than the Senate. I've not yet—"

Roche squeezed the man's arm in sympathy. "Why don't you take the day off, Hartwell? Go home, hug your wife, think things over."

Thomas checked his commander in chief's eyes.

"I mean it, Hartwell." Roche stepped away. "Take a personal day. You deserve it. You're right about your plan. Keeping the Redjackets under the radar is a much better strategy than my idea. You go ahead and take the day off. Go to the park. Smell the roses."

"Are you certain about that, sir?"

"Absolutely." Roche smiled at him and pointed to the window. "Look out there. See all the tourists frolicking on the National Mall? Join them. Have some fun. I can handle a bunch of whiny senators for one day. You deserve it. Really."

Thomas stammered a bit and Roche reassured him and walked him to the door and told his secretary what a great man was Hartwell Thomas.

Then Thomas went home to his wife and children.

Roche went to Thomas's office and opened every drawer. He ran his hand under the drawers and under the desktop. He looked around at the cabinets and pulled books off the shelves. He ran his hand over every surface of the credenza. Nothing. Anywhere.

That pissed him off. Using his cane like a baseball bat, he slammed the desk lamp into the near wall. He splintered a picture of some goofy looking kids. Then frustration overcame him. He started whacking the chair as hard as he could. After the fifth smash, the chair fell sideways. On the underside was a slit in the fabric.

"Come to Papa." Roche dropped to his knees and pushed his hand inside. He swiped left and right until he felt something. He pulled out a little black book and opened it. What he was looking for stared back at him on page one. Redjackets. Generals and captains. Each name had a phone number.

Roche wasted no time. He dialed three of them in quick succession. "This is a competition. Get your best squad out to Mumbai. Bring back Wilkes. Dead or alive."

CHAPTER 11

THE CONTROL TOWER NOSED US into a corner of Mumbai's unpronounceable airport, where we couldn't avoid going through customs. Sometimes wealthy people park at the far end of an airfield, walk away, and send their pilots and crew through official channels. Saves on bag searches. Mumbai wasn't allowing those privileges. Not even at four in the morning, usually the best hour for getting away with privileges. Since we were eligible for searches, we opted to leave the machine guns in the jet's hold. The pilots would figure out a way around customs and meet us later. The line at passport control was miles long.

I had settled in for a long wait when an attractive young woman caught my eye. She patrolled the roped-off Disney-line of travelers, giving each one full study.

Mercury leaned over my shoulder. *Don't look now, homie, but the woman you're ogling is full-on IB.*

I said, *I don't ogle.*

Mercury said, *Then wipe the drool off your chin, dawg. She's IB.*

The subject of our discussion wore a dark jacket with a blue, open-collared business shirt. An unusually professional outfit for the predawn hours. Her skirt was tastefully short. Her heels showed off calves of steel. If the last woman I'd fallen for hadn't shoved my heart in the kitchen blender and pulsed the puree button for a week, I might have fallen for this one. The old Jacob fell for anyone in a skirt. But the new Jacob was done with such foolishness. I had resolved never to fall in love again. Until next time.

Mercury said, *She's looking for you. Why else would an IB officer be scanning this crowd?*

I said, *What's IB mean?*

Mercury looked at me as if he could still smell dog shit on me. *Do you ever do research before you fly around the world? IB, India's Intelligence Bureau, the oldest intelligence organization in the world. Oh, that's what stopped you from reading any further—intelligence. I know how it is, mortal. You see words with lots of syllables and no pictures, and you're—*

I said, *Why would I worry about IB officers?*

Mercury said, *The question, young blood, is why is the IB looking for you?*

Her yellow bindi turned to me. Her head tilted a few degrees off center. "Who are you then?"

I might've been staring. I said, "Uh."

Answers like that always make me question why, if Mercury is the god of eloquence, I always choke when a beautiful woman asks me a simple question.

"Welcome to India, Uh," she said with the hint of an English accent. She stuck out a hand and smiled. "Have you a surname to go with that?"

I felt Miguel and Tania and Cody pretending they didn't know me by turning away and texting each other.

"Sorry." I shook her hand. "Jacob Stearne."

"Jacob." She frowned playfully. "They said you were handsome."

Tania couldn't help herself and snorted a burbled laugh.

"Who is they?" I asked. "Your overlords at IB?"

Her frown turned real. She unhooked the ribbon from the lane. "You and your mates will follow me."

I followed her long, black braid through a labyrinth of corridors and offices in the terminal until we reached an all-white room with no furniture. She left us with two tough looking cops who went through our pockets, checked our passports and visas. They considered giving us cavity searches until they tried to maintain eye contact with Miguel. They settled for extended pat-downs. Tania slapped one guy's hand away. Once satisfied, the cops opened an almost-invisible side door. We went through to a room with ten chairs lined up against one wall and a desk and chair opposite. After what felt like an hour but was most likely five minutes, our IB officer joined us carrying a serious stack of folders under her arm. She took the desk and motioned us to the chairs. We sat.

"Your visas claim you are tourists." She stared at me. "You look like a bunch of skivers faffing about to me."

"I'm leading them on a spiritual quest." Tania took the first one. "These guys never meditated at the Vipassana pagoda before."

Our interrogator gave Tania a cold stare. She opened the first on a stack of folders and had Miguel step forward. She gave him the third degree about his heritage, military service, current employer, and so on.

I turned to Mercury who was enjoying the grilling. *What's the yellow bindi mean?*

Research, brutha, try it sometime. Mercury shook his head with disappointment. *If she's a southern Indian, probably not much. It's gonna be like makeup to them. If she's more traditional, it could mean she's from the prosperous or trader classes. Whatever, she's not thirsty for you.*

I said, *All I care about is if she can help us find Dhanpal.*

Mercury said, *Dude, you do come up with great ideas sometimes. I told Jupiter we shouldn't let a sniper blow your brains out tomorrow, but he never listens to me.*

What? I snapped to face him. *You're going to let me die tomorrow?*

Mercury slapped a hand over my mouth. *Keep your voice down. We're not supposed to tell you about the future. It's off limits, we can't tell you about—*

I said, *Lottery tickets, stock picks, I know the drill. But you guys decided I'm not worth saving from a sniper?*

Mercury said, *If you only knew how many times I talked Jupiter out of smiting you! Remember that time in high school when you were drunk-driving Ashley home and y'all spun out on the ice? Ever wonder how you managed to stay on that tiny bridge, homie? No? Not even a dim recollection? Shoulda left you to Jesus that night, he's a big fan of Darwin.*

I said, *You always say that. You can say anything was your work after the fact. I don't believe you.*

Mercury said, *Nature of faith, my brutha. Your tireless deities are painfully aware of your lack of devotion.*

I said, *What about the lady here, can she help us?*

Mercury got up and walked away. *Dawg, the real question is, why are you asking me?*

Tania was halfway through her background check. I raised my hand. "Ma'am, if you don't mind, can we cut the crap and talk?"

She pondered my question while Tania shot me a nasty look over her shoulder. "A proper chinwag, is it? What about?"

"We could start with your name and what you're looking for."

"Radhika Chopra." She held me with what she thought was a tough gaze. Radhika never tried lying to Pia Sabel. I had plenty of experience staring down tough gazes.

"Any relation to Priyanka?" I asked. "I mean, striking resemblance."

I have no idea where that came from. Sometimes Mercury injects stuff into my brain before I can think it through. I just go with it. Guessing from her reaction, Priyanka Chopra was a model or an actress or Miss India, maybe all of the above.

Radhika all but blushed and shook her head and leaned over to look at the floor to her left.

While she composed herself, I dove in. "As you're already aware, our friend came here a couple days ago. Dhanpal Singh." I let her expression give her away. "We think he's in trouble. We came here to get him out of it. Will you help us?"

She took a deep breath and waved Tania away from the desk. "Since you're being honest, which I appreciate, I can tell you ..." She twisted her mouth while she thought, then pushed away from the desk. "I must consult my superiors before—"

"I'm showing you all my cards. Don't disappoint me by dragging your boss into it. You're smart and capable and can help us with some simple concepts. First, what does the IB want? Let's cut through an hour of bureaucracy and make a deal."

She considered my offer for a few beats. "Me? Trust you?"

"Why not?" My humiliation tweaked my voice. "We're trustworthy."

"Sabel Security has a questionable reputation from Vienna to Riga."

I have no idea how she picked the cities where we most recently burned bridges. Literally in some cases. I said, "Well. You can trust me."

"That's not what I hear from Bucharest to Monaco."

Mercury said, *You're cooked, dude. Time to fall back on Monster Slayer here.*

My delinquent god liked referring to Miguel as the ancient and revered god of his tribe.

"Ouch. OK, you got me. But you can trust him." I pointed at our stoic Navajo. Something about his high cheek bones and nerves of steel instills trust in strangers.

Chopra looked at Miguel. "We want Wilkes."

I had no snappy response to that. A few options went through my head. I considered telling her I wasn't there for Wilkes. Which was kinda true. I wasn't—but the others were. Telling her that wouldn't get us out of the airport before Diwali started.

I nodded. "We're here for Dhanpal. He came to find Wilkes. We have no idea what, if anything, he found."

"If I help you find your friend," she chose her words slowly, "you'll turn over everything you know about the missing admiral then?"

Tania, Miguel, and Cody faced Ms. Chopra with blank faces. A good soldier might think you're giving away state secrets, but they'll never let it show. I could sense their collective disagreement through the tiny electrical pulses their bodies sent out. They considered giving up Wilkes akin to treason. If Ms. Chopra left the room, they'd beat me into something resembling a rug, rectangular and flat.

"Many ifs go with my agreement," I said. "If you can keep up with four highly trained, battle-tested veterans; if you can keep your head when everything goes to hell; if you can trust us with your life—as we will be trusting ours to you; if you can be patient—"

"I read Kipling at University. My part is not in question." She tested us with her toughest glare. Again, nothing like Ms. Sabel. We passed with flying colors. "Will you give up Wilkes?"

I needed the approval of my team. Tania and Miguel knew what I was planning. They'd been against me earlier, but now that I had committed us, they didn't have a choice. Nonetheless, I silently asked their permission. When you've lived through death-defying fights with someone—surviving on nothing more than fear and desperation—you develop a type of telepathy. Without a word, they let me know they were all in. No hesitation. They knew exactly what to do and when. Cody had been through his own battles, but the trust he placed in me was evident. He kept his gaze fixed on a point three miles beyond the wall in front of him. He planned to live out the motto of the 101st Airborne: Rendezvous With Destiny. If he had to break someone's neck in the next thirty seconds, OK. If he had to lay down his life, OK.

"Wilkes means nothing to us. All we want is our friend back safe and sound. We will give you anything and everything he knows about Wilkes."

She looked us over. "Why did that feel too easy?"

"We move fast," I rose and pointed to the door. "We'd like to get moving."

She led us to her rented Tata Safari as dawn broke. Miguel sat up front for the legroom. Tania and I took the middle seats. Cody squeezed in the third row, way back. Chopra drove in the direction of the Dharavi slums. Sticking out of a side panel on her purse, I saw an Air India boarding pass for a red-eye out of New Delhi a few hours earlier.

Along the way, she filled us in on how the Indian government was displeased that an American admiral chose to go rogue in their country. They kept tabs on the local Sabel Security office, the American Embassy and all our consulates, and every other security company operating in the country. The Minister of Home Affairs, a jillion rungs up the ladder from Ms. Chopra, hit the roof when reports of a shoot-out involving Dhanpal and several Americans came in. The largely vegetarian nation did not appreciate American problem-solving methods. Particularly when they evoked images of America's lawless western expansion. When we arrived, she was dispatched to find what we knew about Wilkes.

"You were on duty that early?" I asked.

She stammered before answering. "I work an early shift."

"Oh? You live near the airport?"

"Not that close. I was available."

The neighborhood outside her truck went from airport businesses to poor shops to desperate living conditions. The litter on the streets, the open sewers, the potholes to nowhere, and the shabby state of buildings became increasingly worse. The stench and insects were thick enough to taste.

After making a couple wrong turns and backing out of a dead-end alley, she turned the tables, asking us about our understanding of events. Miguel did the talking for us because he leans laconic. All we knew: Dhanpal went missing. We take care of our own. Doesn't matter who went after him, he's coming home. No shootouts, we're unarmed. And so on.

Mercury sat on the console between the front seats, facing me. *You know she's going to hate you, bro.*

I said, *Can't be helped.*

Mercury said, *Radhika's going to call on Ganesha. He's one tough hombre. Or should I say, dost?* Mercury looked upwards. *Or is it yoddha? I forget. Oh yeah. Yoddha means knight in Hindi. Guess who told Lucas to name his little frog-priest—*

I said, *Who is Ganesha?*

Mercury said, *That elephant-looking god with four arms. Thinks he's all down with wisdom. Ha. I creamed him at Scrabble at the last gods convention. Hindu gods can suck my—*

I said, *I get it.*

I looked out the window and tried to rein in my sanity.

India goes the distance to maintain independence from the US. Their distrust of empire-building nations runs deep. Why they wanted Wilkes bothered me. Was she leverage in some grand diplomatic game? Did Wilkes run off with India's nuclear codes? Did she stiff a cabbie?

We circled the slums driving on streets clogged with scooters and bicycles. Shops barely big enough for the owner to stand in lined every street. We passed a cricket field where a game was in progress. Miguel thumped the footwell. We drove another half mile while Ms. Chopra looked for roads and peppered us with questions.

Packed slabs of concrete formed housing. Salvaged plastic tarps, shreds of corrugated tin, and billboards served as roofs. Wire held most of it together. Piles of garbage filled many lanes making them too small for the Tata. Chopra circled around the cricket field again, still looking for her destination. Miguel thumped the footwell again. Behind me, Cody tapped my neck, signaling he understood the drill. I slipped my phone under Ms. Chopra's seat. Tania did the same. When our driver looked left, Miguel put his in her console. Behind me, Cody dropped his on the floor.

Half a mile later, Chopra stopped in a gridlocked intersection.

All four of us bailed out of her car. Tania opened the back to release Cody. We ran in four different directions, disappearing into the slums and crowds.

Radhika Chopra yelled.

We didn't stop, we didn't look back. I looped through buildings and alleys and passageways. I ran across two pieces of wood forming a bridge over a canal filled with plastic garbage. I ran through the plaza of a twenty-story building, dilapidated and rusting and crammed with human beings.

I kept running until I made the full circle back to the cricket field. Miguel watched the game from a bench. I joined him. Tania joined us a few minutes later. We still hadn't figured out how the game was played by the time Cody got there.

Miguel held a fist up to the new kid. Cody bumped it with a grin.

Tania said, "I don't care what Jacob says, you're all right, Cody."

Cody looked at me for affirmation. I wasn't in the mood. I got up and started walking toward the small crowd watching the game. They followed.

"Wazzup?" Miguel asked.

"Radhika Chopra." I kept walking as Tania came alongside. "She dressed professionally early in the morning. She had a boarding pass for the red-eye from New Delhi. She was looking for us in the passport queue. She had folders with our histories in them. Who told her we were coming?"

CHAPTER 12

PIA TOOK THE FOLDING CHAIR next to Veronica Hunter in the Casey Community Center in Gaithersburg, Maryland. She didn't feel right about misleading the Major regarding her evening schedule. But, she reasoned, why bother the Major with details? Thirty people were scattered in the seats in a meeting space meant to hold two hundred. There were two blocks of chairs with a generous aisle on each side and a big one down the middle. A microphone waited, dead center of the room, for the citizens' question and answer period. At the front was another microphone, no podium, on a stage less than knee high. Aides for the Governor of Maryland scanned the crowd with nervous looks from behind a curtain.

"Thank god, you wore something professional." Hunter looked her over. "Tell me you're finally over the ninja-athletic gear."

"What's the plan?" Pia asked.

"You're late."

"Dhanpal Singh, one of my special agents, is missing. There were more important things to attend to."

"I thought you didn't send anyone to Mumbai."

Pia snapped a quick, icy glance at the vice president. "Who said anything about Mumbai?"

Hunter inhaled and cleared her throat. "We don't have time to go over my plan. Instead, we'll just sit here and listen to the fool prattle on for an hour."

"What is this all about, anyway?" Pia asked. "What do you hope to gain?"

Governor Baylesh poked his head out from behind a small curtain with a disappointed frown. He disappeared quickly.

"You blew the last year trying to take down Roche." Hunter waved at a reporter in the far corner. "You proved he was involved with extorting America's allies. That he knew about an attack on American airliners. That he used his office for personal gain—and what came of it? Nothing. Why?"

"Because I'm nobody, just another conspiracy whacko, or so you constantly tell me."

"When you learn to handle governors and senators, you'll have the first step accomplished. Then you can try the second step, how to handle the press. Lastly, you must learn how to stay in the public mind. After that, you can say anything, even things that aren't true, and people will listen."

Someone stepped to the stage microphone, tapped it, and welcomed everyone. He introduced Governor Baylesh and disappeared.

Baylesh walked out on stage with a purposeful gait. He looked around, recognized Hunter, stared at Pia a moment before glancing at an aide in the front row. Then he started in on why Gaithersburg was his favorite town in Maryland. Even to Pia's inexperienced ear, it sounded like a series of canned phrases used for every event in the state. The aide looked over his shoulder at Pia.

"That guy is trying to figure out who's sitting with the VP." Hunter whispered and nosed at the aide. "He'll hold up a handwritten card after he figures out who you are. Politicians adjust their speeches according to who's in the room."

Pia nodded.

Baylesh rambled on about what great things the Roche Administration had done for Maryland in general and Gaithersburg in particular. A well-known supporter of the president, Baylesh went on and on about Roche's genius.

"Normally,' Hunter leaned to Pia's ear, "he would brag about what great things he's done for the state. But when he saw me, he figured I would report back to Chuck on anything he says."

"Why would he care what Roche thinks of him?"

"Because Chuck could order the Social Security Administration to move their headquarters to Virginia and—just like that—the third largest employer in Maryland would be gone. Baylesh's career ends the day of the announced move—even if it never happens."

Pia leaned back. There were far more moving parts in politics than she'd imagined. She had a strategic plan in her head that had been relatively straightforward. Hunter was right that all her previous attempts to unseat Roche had been tactical and therefore doomed to fail in this complex environment. Was her re-tooled strategy going to work? Could she rely on Hunter to do what Pia wanted? Would playing on her mother's professed interest help Pia bring the guilty to justice?

That required an analysis of how far she could trust Hunter. Working with her on public appearances made sense. It would help Pia improve her public image. But how could she measure Hunter's sincerity? It wasn't like the woman measured up on any motherly-scale. Mothers were all about love and tenderness and caring. They tucked their children in at night and read bedtime stories. They taught their daughters how to bake and microwave. They poured sympathy over every injury. They pick up your soccer bag when you throwdown at the other team's dirty-playing defender. At least, that's how the mothers of Pia's teammates acted. They were the only mothers Pia knew anything about.

Hunter wasn't that kind of mother. Never was, never would be.

So who was Veronica Lodge Hunter? What could Pia expect out of her?

Pia shivered.

Governor Baylesh spoke about tariffs helping Maryland businesses. Pia nearly leapt to her feet.

"He's playing you." Hunter put a hand on Pia's forearm and held her down. "Just listen and learn."

"I see one of our local businesspeople is with us here tonight." Baylesh swept his arm to Pia. "Did you see her get agitated when I mentioned tariffs? You can tell who makes billions shipping Maryland jobs overseas, can't ya?"

A titter of laughter followed him for a split second.

"Stay calm," Hunter whispered. "Don't take the bait."

Baylesh went on about immigrant labor taking jobs from American workers. Pia ground her teeth listening to him.

"President Roche is a powerful man." Baylesh brought his voice from conversational to full oratory. "He is a strong executive and brilliant strategist. Have you seen how he's bringing our competitors to their knees? He is proving the nay-sayers wrong at every step. Everything he has done has been good for your wallet and your family. Don't you think Congress should let him run the country? Tell your elected representatives to stop impeding him. Tell your local news site to stop slandering him. Chuck Roche is the leader we've always longed for. He's the kind of man who makes us rethink term limits. FDR was elected four times, why not Chuck Roche?"

A smattering of applause followed his thunderous conclusion.

He waited until it stopped. "Does anyone have any questions?"

Pia leapt at the microphone as if expecting to fight for it. No one else moved. She heard Hunter tsk.

She looked up at Baylesh. "My titanium supplier for Sabel Satellites is under tariffs. My landed cost for raw titanium went up twenty-five percent because of Roche. Our customers won't pay the higher price. My supplier is now making the parts my employees used to make. He can sell me finished goods because those are not under tariffs. That means I'll have to lay off a hundred specialists in Greenville. Roche's tariff is hurting my company. How can you say—"

"Greenville, South Carolina is not Maryland's problem." His smiling face turned to stone. "Young lady, everybody knows about you. You were born rich, you grew up rich, and your daddy left you rich. It's nice to hear you know where your satellite factory is—but I'll bet $100 you've never been there. Don't act like you have any idea what kind of jobs the hard-working people of Maryland need when you've never held a wrench in your hand. You don't know a tariff from a tadpole. We don't need people like you waltzing into our town halls spouting off jargon you heard on NPR. We need good, high-paying jobs, don't we folks?" He smiled at the applause, mostly coming from his three aides. "We don't need some random rich kid coming in here complaining about how hard life is at her slave labor camp down in the Carolinas."

Pia felt every eye in the room staring at her. She wanted to slither beneath a linoleum tile. It took great strength to keep her mouth clamped shut. Pia took a deep breath, turned, and crept back to her chair. The room was silent.

Pure sympathy covered Hunter's face.

She had the decency not to say a word. Instead, she put a hand on Pia's shoulder and rubbed gently.

"Anyone have any questions about MARYLAND?" Baylesh called out. "Some people fly around in their private jets so often they forget what state they're in. Wouldn't you folks love to have that problem?"

Laughter broke out.

Pia hung her head.

An older man went to the microphone to ask about expanding deer hunting season.

Pia stole a glance at Hunter. The vice president was looking at her with wise, caring eyes. Pia wanted a hug as much as she didn't want it from Hunter. She took a deep breath. "Thanks for not rubbing it in. Yes. I do need to learn. I'm ready."

"You can't be successful if you aren't willing to get punched in the face once in a while."

"My boxing coach used to say that."

Hunter said, "I know."

Pia spotted a unique bracelet hanging from Hunter's purse. Playing for her future high school when she was twelve, Pia helped the team win the state championship. The school gave out custom-made championship bracelets to all in attendance that night. Hunter's was one of those rare bracelets.

Had Hunter been there? Pia wondered if her reluctant mother had watched her grow up from a distance. If so, what did that mean?

They got up and took the exit closest to them. Secret Service agents surrounded them until they got in the armored Ford Excursion. They buckled up and drove away. Hunter didn't speak.

After a mile, Pia said, "OK. I'm ready to listen."

Hunter smiled and met her gaze. "Never feed a wild bear."

"I fed him?" Pia pulled a small notepad and pen out of her purse. "I did, didn't I? Damn."

"When you ask an opponent a question in public, rephrase using his words. For example, 'Govenor Baylesh, why would you tell these good people tariffs are working when I just had to lay off hundreds of people because of them?'"

Pia smiled at her and jotted down the phrase.

"Never state facts, use them. Never tell your story, always attack his." Hunter kept the gems flowing, and Pia kept scribbling all the way back to Sabel Towers.

CHAPTER 13

PRESIDENT ROCHE WANDERED AIMLESSLY INTO the White House living room where his nephew was sprawled on a couch watching *Are You Hot: America's Search for the Sexiest People* on the big screen TV. Roche hadn't slept since that traitorous Wilkes ran off four days earlier. Congress had been breathing down his neck about the *USS Caine* investigation. The admiral's staff had to be sequestered before they started spreading irresponsible stories about Wilkes being abducted.

Roche had been through worse times. He weathered them all because the universe loved him. When he reflected on it, he was the perfect man. Rich, accomplished, loved, and smart. The zenith of all that mankind strives to become. But the damn senators thought they were the anointed ones. Their endless questions about the Redjackets were tiresome. Someone should clean house over there, get rid of the whiners. Then he could get the war going.

Everyone loves a good war. Everyone loves to rally around the flag, make sacrifices for the common good, beat those evil towelheaded terrorists into submission. Why couldn't the senators see the endgame? All that Saudi oil would pay down the national debt instead of funding another terrorist group. The country needed this war. Why was he the only one who could see that?

Part of the problem was the extensive lobbying by the Saudis. Lobbyists crawled all over the capitol, donating money to SuperPACs and bending Senatorial ears against the war. They didn't stop at party lines; they gave generously to both sides. It was becoming an uphill battle.

A text came in from Governor Baylesh with a video attached. Roche leaned against the wall and watched it. Pia Sabel, dressed as if she were a real executive, was being destroyed by Baylesh. The angle suggested it was taken by someone, probably the governor's aide, sitting in the front row. The expression on her face was priceless. Roche burst out laughing, then backed it up and watched it again. Fierce and scowling right up to the point where Baylesh lit into her, she crumpled and turned pale. Pia had no response. She was weak and helpless.

"What's so funny, Uncle Chuck?" his nephew asked.

"Funniest damn video I've seen in years."

"The baby falling off the pickup truck on the highway? Seen it." The nephew shoved his hand in an empty bag of Cheetos and came up with orange fingers.

"No. Here. I'll send it to you." Roche sent it over. "Give me those Cheetos."

"Sorry, Uncle Chuck," the young man crunched the bag into a ball. "All gone."

"Did you get those peace talks scheduled?"

"They both have crazy demands."

Roche raised his voice. "Then the least you could do is get another bag of Cheetos, damn it."

His nephew popped up and ran for the kitchen. Roche called after the kid. "If my sister hadn't begged me to give you a boost up the ladder, you'd still be packing Amazon boxes."

Hartwell Thomas stomped up the stairs and called out. Roche answered him. "In here, the living room."

Thomas stormed in with his arms wind milling and started yelling. "Do you realize what you've done? Three teams added to the one already there? The risks are astronomical. The only white people in that part of Mumbai are missionaries. And they don't stay too long. You have to recall them."

"Who do you think you're talking to?" Roche spat his words. "I'm the president, and you're not."

"With all due respect, sir, you won't be for long if the press gets wind that these here orders came from you."

"And just how would that happen?" Roche nosed into the big Texan's face. "Are you going to sing for the prosecution?"

"Why, no sir. It's not at all like that. It's not me. It's the simple numbers. You added twenty-six people to the operation. That's in addition to the eight currently involved on the ground or in support. You can promise eight people they'll get pardons. You can't pardon over thirty people without destroying your presidency. One of those rednecks will crack under pressure. Someone, if not five, will give you up. You have to recall those people or risk losing everything we've worked for."

"That's one option." Roche let his reply hang in the air between them. He turned away.

Thomas used to be loyal. The man never lost his temper before. Hysterics didn't become him. Sadly, the man didn't understand Roche's plan.

"What options would there be?" Thomas looked scared. His face was pale, his suit wrinkled.

"Options to what?" The nephew handed a new bag of Cheetos to Roche. "Are you talking about Uncle Chuck's death-squads going after Wilkes?"

Thomas's mouth dropped open. He looked at Roche while he pointed at the nephew.

"We can trust him," Roche said. He opened the bag and took a few.

"He's the last man you should trust." Thomas's gaze stayed glued to the Cheetos. "He turned on his dad."

"What's the big deal?" The nephew went back to the couch and took the show off pause. "I got immunity."

Roche considered the risks. Thomas had a point about the number of people involved. If he was right about them flipping, his war might evaporate overnight. Then the Senate would turn their investigations on his administration. They'd dig up his business records and his tax returns and the shooting of the idiot French girl. They'd do everything in their power to make him look bad. But he needed the Redjackets to find Wilkes. They find Wilkes, the war starts. There could be no recall.

Thomas looked at the Cheetos and licked his lips.

Roche turned slightly, moving the bag farther away from Thomas. "That plan of yours wasn't working. I've got senators calling me every ten minutes asking why we were casting aspersions on a US admiral."

"That doesn't matter." Thomas's voice rose. "We are not exactly bosom buddies with India. Why, they'd love to get hold of our Redjackets and put them on display. They'd make fools of us. They'd be laughing at us in the UN. Again. We can't have four armed squads roaming the streets of Mumbai like American coyotes."

"American what?"

"Sorry, sometimes cowboys low on beer money'll bring a few illegals across the border. They call 'em coyotes."

Roche observed Thomas and took another few Cheetos and stuffed them in his mouth. Thomas was still staring at his snacks. Roche held them even farther away, almost at arm's length.

"If there's going to be another shoot-out," Thomas said, "They'll send every officer in uniform after our people. We can't protect them there. We can't grant pardons in India. The boys would flip on you by dinnertime." Thomas tossed up his hands. "I'm not going down for this."

Open rebellion, that's what Roche saw in Thomas's eyes. No loyalty whatsoever. He munched another handful of Cheetos while he thought. Thomas watched the bag like a hawk about to strike a mouse. Roche turned his back on the man.

"Other than recalling them, what options do you have?" Roche asked.

"I don't see any. The risks—"

"You said that already. I get it. Now shut up about it." He considered alternatives. It was an easy decision. There is only one way to go when your options are to run away or double down. "The men are staying. You were going to make Wilkes look guilty. Go do that. Tell them she's in deep with—"

"I don't have the evidence to back up any accusations. I can't go around—"

"Jesus Christ, do I have to do everything myself?" Roche shouted. "Wait here."

Roche looked at his bag, then at Thomas. He marched straight to the kitchen, stashed the Cheetos on a high shelf, then grabbed his cane and made his way to the press briefing room. As he passed the desks where reporters sat around making stuff up all day, he snapped his fingers and promised a good sound bite.

They followed him into the briefing room. He waited until most of them were seated before making his announcement.

"It has just come to my attention that Admiral Wilkes ran from her hotel for a reason. After I turned down a pardon for her murderous daughter, she turned to the Saudis. We presume for money to pay defense attorneys, we don't know. The Saudis dragged her into their evil terrorist plot. I'm sad to say, she fell for it. When the investigators arrived, she knew her treason would come to light, so she fled. I've been told she's desperately trying to get to the Saudi consulate. Every red-blooded American in Mumbai should be on the lookout for her. She's armed and dangerous. I hope no one has to shoot her. Thank you, everyone. That is all."

He marched away from the podium grinning hard enough to hurt. He loved leaving stunned silence in his wake. He was twenty strides down the hall before they started shouting questions. Too late. He headed back to his private quarters.

How Thomas could last that long in the Senate without knowing how to shock the press and walk away was a mystery. Anyone could figure it out. They don't need facts, they need headlines.

Roche took the stairs and went to the living room. Thomas was gone. Which was fine.

His nephew held his phone over his head, laughing with his mouth wide open. "Oh, hey, Uncle Chuck, you were right, this Sabel-chick getting creamed is the funniest video ever. Can I post it on Twitter?"

"Sure."

"Tell me something," the young man started fiddling with his apps, "how come a dumb bitch like her gets a security clearance and I don't?"

CHAPTER 14

MERCURY SAID, *YO, BRUTHA, GOTTA be someone in the cricket crowd who speaks English. Maybe they can help you find Dhanpal?*

I said, *That's what I was going to do.*

Mercury said, *I thought of it first, homie.*

I said, *I think up good ideas too ... oh man, I am totally insane.*

Mercury said, *What makes you say that?*

I said, *Cuz talking to yourself is one thing, arguing with yourself is...*

I crossed the dirt lot of the cricket match, heading for the players and observers. Tania grabbed my arm. She said, "What was that crap about giving up Wilkes?"

"All I could think of to get us out of airport-limbo."

Miguel and Cody wisely kept their mouths shut.

"I got that part." Tania ran in front of me and planted herself. "Now we'll never get the admiral out of this country."

"We can worry about that after we rescue Dhanpal." I stepped around her and kept walking.

She started to say something when Miguel scowled at her. "Leave it."

When he uses his Geronimo-face and Sitting Bull voice, no one argues with him. Tania turned and resumed our march to the crowd. When she got a few paces ahead of us, Miguel leaned close. "We get Dhanpal. After that, you better think up something for the admiral."

"You know what's more important? Think about how Chopra knew we were coming."

Mercury put an arm around me. *Aw homie, only on the ground a couple hours and you've managed to piss off everyone around you. That's a record.*

I kept walking. *Where were you with all the good advice when I needed it?*

Mercury gave me hurt look. *Dude, I was getting down with Muhammad. A lot of his people in these parts. You can learn a lot from the minorities in a city.*

I said, *Are you talking about THE Muhammad, founder of Islam?*

Mercury said, *Oh, you know him too? He's dope, right? Haven't seen him since the big protest at the gods convention. He was out there with David and Ezekiel wanting equal rights for the prophets. But. 'At's just not how it works, know what I'm saying? Going around saying I-got-the-word-of-god-from-angels just doesn't cut it. If you want to be a god—you gotta be created that way. None of this born-mortal crap. Do you think gods slide down a birth canal? Yuu-uuck.*

I said, *I should've taken my meds before we left. I really can't handle stuff like this.*

I thought you liked the behind-the-altars material. It used to make you feel special. Mercury turned left and walked away. *Oh, hey dawg, watch for the nabi, he can help you.*

I said, *The what?*

Plenty of educated Indians speak English, but we weren't in the educated hood. Miguel walked straight up to a bunch of locals who'd never seen anyone that big before. As they stared up at him, he asked if anyone spoke English. They didn't. He asked in French and drew another blank stare. At the other side of the crowd, Tania asked in Spanish.

Miguel and I watched the people trying to communicate with her. I said, "Check the crowd's lassitude. We're not getting through—"

"Lassitude?" Miguel put a hand across my chest. "Did you read the Margaret Atwood book I gave you?"

"I … started it." How do you tell someone, *It was a nice book but I had to look up every fifth word, so I gave up on page twenty*, without feeling like an illiterate?

Miguel tried some more French on the locals.

A young man wearing a white kufi watched him.

Then it hit me, *nabi* means prophet in Arabic.

I shouted in Arabic, "Does anyone speak any language?"

A boy nudged kufi-man. He looked at me. I greeted him in Arabic. "*As-salam alaykom.*" Peace be upon you.

He looked around to see if I was speaking to someone else. I kept my gaze fixed on him. He stepped away from the crowd and eased closer to me.

"I not speaking Arabic." He watched Miguel pantomiming questions about Dhanpal for the others. "My English very, very good. My learning for American banks in customer service. Perhaps helping each other."

His accent was so thick I had to sort the words to get the meaning.

I pulled a fifty euro note and discreetly held it for him to take. I always travel with thousands in euros because Americans are often frowned upon these days, and nothing identifies us more than our currency. While his eyes scanned the crowd, his fingers snaked the bill from my hand like a cobra and shoved it in his pocket.

"Generous being American quality well known. Most thanks." He turned away from the group. "Good to leave quiet in search of what you wish. It is women, yes?"

"No," I said. We crossed the field, heading for an alley. "My friend came here. An American Mumbaikar. There might have been a gunfight."

He looked at me suddenly with some fear. Unlike the US, shootings are rare in India. The shock of them spreads rapidly. So do the exaggerations. He told me five variations he'd heard. One version he heard from his wife. Another from his cousin. And a third from his cousin's brother. I lost track of his family after that.

I snapped my fingers, knowing without looking what would happen behind us. My companions would see me leaving discreetly. They would wind down their attempted conversation, leaving the crowd with the impression all Americans are weird, and then follow at a distance. Intending to keep a low profile, we were instead celebrities because of our rarity. American tourists didn't visit Dharavi.

My new friend's name was Vishal. He'd married a Muslim woman and converted. His family disowned him, his employer fired him. That's how he ended up in the slum. He worked in one of the sweatshops nearby. Every other structure in Dharavi is a sweatshop. The largest slum in Asia is one big manufacturing plant with people living between the machines. When there are machines. Vishal made briefcases by hand.

Stories about the gunfight had grown overnight. The police made a rare appearance in the area to quell rumors that it was a Muslim-Hindu gunfight. The authorities didn't want a repeat of the '92 riots. One story claimed three men fired on a local boy who shot back before succumbing to his injuries. The other end of the gossip spectrum claimed ten gangsters tried to kill a local boy who sprinted away, leaving a trail of dead men behind him.

Vishal insisted he knew a doctor who, for a minimal fee, could tell us where the injured had been taken. I hoped for the best and feared the worst as we wound through lanes too narrow for small cars. Shanties were stacked on top of each other, blotting out the morning sunlight like trees in a rainforest. Everywhere, the stench of human waste hung in the air.

Miguel, Tania, and Cody caught up with us. We stood out in the thin margins between stacked goods, worn out motorcycles, and discarded trash. Years of training kicked in. We spaced ourselves like soldiers on patrol. Close enough to render aid, far enough apart that an attack could only claim one. Cody's eyes ranged over every face with a nearly combative expression. Miguel and Tania were much more subtle, taking in every possible angle of attack through their peripheral vision, minimizing mistrust.

The suspicion was evident. Heads poked out of hovels warily eyeing the Americans. People like us had recently wreaked havoc in their streets. Children were called in, girls hid behind solid objects. Older men kept watch, ready—should the need arise—to protect what little they owned from the potentially violent tourists.

The valleys of the shadow of death I'd patrolled so many times had not been so tightly packed with people. They had been wide open mountain ranges, villages sprawling on the open plains, snipers on distant ridges. Tension overpowered the stink.

We came to the doctor's house, which stood out among the others because of its fresh paint, tiled roof, and single-car garage. We instantly learned how the doctor wound up in the slums. He reeked of alcohol.

With bleary eyes, he discussed my missing friend with Vishal in Marathi, the local language. They began to argue.

Haggling over price involves facial expressions and hand gestures common in any language. I readied another fifty and held it up where the doctor could see it. He smiled. The discussion calmed down a good deal, and Vishal thanked him and turned away.

"In gunfight dies American." He started walking to avoid eye contact. "Morgue need identification persons. You do this, yes."

Mercury appeared with his arm around a four-armed lady in red. *Tough times, bro. But I'm here for you. Let's do this. Just remember, it's not about god's will. Sometimes you stupid mortals do things you shouldn't. That's not on us. That's on you.*

I looked the red-lady over and reached for my meds but found only an empty pocket.

Didn't bring them.

Oh, hey, this is Lakshmi, goddess of wealth and prosperity. Mercury grinned and gave Lakshmi a squeeze. She winked. *We used to date in god college. Then she ran off with Vishnu—her loss. She's not busy until Varalakshmi Vratam—and Vishnu's out of town—so if you don't need any more miracles ...*

That's it, I said. *I've lost it. I'm off the rails.*

"What'd you mean?" Cody's voice had a concerned edge.

"Nuthin." I shoved my fists in my pockets and pushed past Miguel to catch up with Vishal.

The hospital had trees, which made it stand out from the surrounding architecture. My hopes were raised that my friend might have gotten the best care available. The stench of sewage followed us inside, where two policemen had their backs to us. Vishal ushered us quickly down a side hall.

A few minutes later, he spoke at length to a sober doctor who considered us with great suspicion. When I started to reach for more money, Vishal waved me off. I felt terrible assuming everyone was on the take in India.

"Doctor asks of you identity." Vishal gestured to the four of us. "Most thanks. Needing persons of family for identify of body."

"We're his co-workers." I took a deep breath.

After more discussion, the doctor shook his head.

"And he's the brother." I pointed at Miguel who, a foot taller than Dhanpal, had the closest skin tone among us.

The doctor frowned and yelled at Vishal. Then he pointed at me and curled his finger. Everyone else stayed behind while I followed the man down a dark, dank corridor. Dread seeped into my veins. It had been a long time since I'd identified a friend.

"My English rusty—but better than your guide." The doctor pushed open a lightly refrigerated room and switched on the lights. "The wounded persons go to Lilavati in Bandra. This man—" he pulled back a plastic sheet "—not so lucky."

A complete stranger with the gray, waxy skin of the dead stared at the ceiling. He wore a nice suit, a clean shirt, and three-day stubble. One neat 9 mm hole in his heart gave away the cause of death. No autopsy required.

I picked up the lapel of his jacket and found what I expected, a red square of silk. One small star was bleached into the fabric, a captain. Superheated anger flowed into my brain like lava. These bastards knew where to find Dhanpal. Someone must've told them to track him down. Which pissed me off. I changed my mind about going after Americans. These Redjackets, from the leader who'd given the order to the grunt who carried it out, had a destiny with death. I would find them and dish it out.

Then the good news struck me: Dhanpal was still alive. No one else could put a single bullet into the millimeter of space where the left and right ventricles share a wall with the left and right atriums. A shot that rendered the heart irreparable. A merciful death followed in seconds. Which meant Dhanpal was out there somewhere and needed help. *Congress Jacob would never go.*

A massive wave of relief hit me. The tension faded; calmness relaxed my muscles before giving way to another emotion. I became giddy and fought to contain myself. I nearly laughed out loud. Why I ever thought Dhanpal would fall victim to these bastards was a mystery.

I dropped the lapel.

"Sorry, doc." I shrugged. "Never seen this guy before. But he's an American. Call the New York Times' local bureau. Tell them you have a Redjacket who needs to be identified. Guaranteed to get here quicker than anyone from the consulate."

I left him and the dead man in the morgue.

Reunited with my team, I breathed the filthy air with a renewed appreciation for life and filled them in. We sighed collectively and grinned.

I turned to Vishal. "Next stop, Lilavati Hospital in Bandra."

His eyebrows rose the way people's do when I tell them we're taking Ms. Sabel's jet. "Cab needs crossing river."

That took a minute to figure out. "We need a cab because it's across the river? OK." I patted my pocket before remembering we ditched our phones. "Say, would you mind calling one?"

He went to the lobby. We hung back because the two cops were still there, milling about. Vishal used the desk phone.

Outside, a familiar looking Tata pulled up in the sunshine. The cops in the lobby spotted the car and straightened themselves, smoothed their hair and re-tucked their shirts. I put my arm out and motioned my team backwards into the dark labyrinth. Radhika Chopra stepped down from the driver's side, flipped her hair back and headed for the glass doors. Three policemen piled out of her car and followed her in.

CHAPTER 15

AFTER HER PUBLIC HUMILIATION AT the feet of the governor, Pia worked out. A quick 10K followed by punching a heavy bag and lifting weights gave her time to think about her plan. As badly as it was going, she had to keep focused on her core goal. Chuck Roche had paid the hit men who killed her mother and father. She would avenge their deaths. Then she could sleep like ordinary people. Working with Hunter started out painful but might still prove useful. Pia's biggest hesitation came from adopting Hunter's cynical tactics. Was it a reasonable trade off?

After the late evening workout, Pia headed for the shower in her rooms. On her bed lay the little jersey of her childhood. Maria, unsure where to keep it, must have left it out for Pia to decide. She picked it up and buried her nose in it.

The sweet smell of grass was long gone. But the comfortable scent of her second childhood remained. Her first childhood was the dim yellow-tinted memory of a kitchen. A kitchen filled with horror, blood and murder. Her mother's dead body lay on the floor. The killer pleaded for help as he bled out. The big, bloody knife slipped from her little hand. Pia's helpless confusion about what had happened came back to her like a gut-clawing phantom. Why had her world been destroyed in five violent minutes?

The black jersey in her hands was the dividing line between her two childhoods. Before she wore it, all her memories were of the tragedy. After she put it on, life was Alan Sabel. Safety. The cocoon of his caring home, his bodyguards, his steady hand on her shoulder. The unspoken message in his gentle grip: Harm will never visit you again.

A distinct and indelible memory came to her and played out like a movie that was half dream. It was after her second soccer game. She was little, looking up at two grown men facing each other. She stood at their pocket-level. Their sleeves and hands filled her vision. She could see the underside of their jaws, not their eyes. Her coach had just said she was born with talent. Dad disagreed. He looked down at Pia, then back at the coach. "Everyone wants to be a superstar. What separates us from our full potential is our willingness to work for it. What we call talent isn't something you're born with. It's the willingness to do the hard work, practice and practice again, stay focused, give up friends and fun, give up everything. Anyone willing to do the work can become the greatest."

On the way home, she told her dad she wanted to be the greatest. She wanted to do the work. She had no problem giving up friends because Alan, a single father with no parenting experience, didn't know how to arrange playdates. Now that she reflected on it, maybe he feared them for the questions well-intentioned parents might've ask about the highly publicized murders. Whatever the case, she spent most of her time alone with caretakers.

Alan had looked at her that day with fond appreciation and tousled her hair. The next day, she had a new nanny, the recently retired star of the German national team. Pia did the work. She learned to be fast and ferocious, practicing day and night. The harder she worked, the better she outran her demons. Practice became her therapy.

Soccer became Pia's search for meaning. Relevancy. Innocence.

At some point in her youth, she became aware that six people had conspired to turn her world upside down in those five yellow-tinted, violent minutes. She did the work. She gave up friends and fun. She focused on her goal. And since she had learned the names of the conspirators? Four were dead. Two remained among the living. One was in the White House.

Pia tossed the shirt back on the bed. She took a deep breath, let the thoughts go, and showered. She toweled off and put on leggings and a top. Something comfortable for her few hours of sleep.

Bianca sent an email that interrupted her routine. It had a presidential executive order attached. Bianca's email explained how several presidents justified drone strikes. They identified terrorists and their supporters under the War on Terror. They listed those who needed to be killed at any cost. During the Iraq War, soldiers had created a deck of cards showing the priority list for people in Saddam Hussein's regime. Each one was wanted dead or alive. Many of them had rewards. The deck of cards faded into obscurity, but the hit-list remained. Among the many Iraqis on the list were a few foreign supporters. Bianca suggested Pia look for a particular name.

Pia was too tired to read the many pages of bureaucratic jargon, but she found the man's name near the top. It gave her a smile. She combed her hair and made her ponytail. She plumped the pillows and looked at the Margaret Atwood novel Jacob had given her. She glanced at the dictionary next to it. She needed something lighter to induce sleep. Beneath Atwood lay *Death and Secrets*. Perfect.

Then she heard the Major's angry voice coming through her sitting room. "Pia!"

She braced herself as the Major stormed into her bedroom holding a phone in front of her. The Major said, "What the hell is this?"

Pia looked at the screen and instantly recognized herself. She cringed at how awkward she looked. And cringed even more as she realized it was a Twitter post from the president's chief adviser, the first nephew. She couldn't watch her on-screen-self shrinking from the governor's onslaught. She pushed the phone away.

"You didn't tell me about this." The Major leaned forward.

"I didn't tell you because I knew you'd get angry and—"

"Damn straight, I'm angry. I have a right to be. You told me you'd give the company one-hundred percent of your attention. What happened to that promise?"

Pia couldn't face her, the woman who had held everything together while Pia dealt with the tragedy of Alan's death. The woman who had stood by Dad through thick and thin, refusing his marriage proposals, running the company he built like a clone of the man himself. And currently running the company for Pia because she still didn't know the difference between return on assets and return on equity.

The Major's phone rang. She sent it to voice mail.

"I'm sorry." Pia knew the Major deserved better. "I need to do this.

There's more to what I'm doing …"

The Major's phone rang again, this time with her special urgent-ringtone. The woman never took her eyes off Pia.

Pia said, "You should get that."

"Screw it." The Major sent it to voice mail again. "What is wrong with you? You're running off like a child with some serious mommy-issues."

Pia felt that one like a stab in the gut.

The Major stepped back and covered her mouth with the back of her hand. "I'm sorry, Pia. I didn't mean … that was wrong of me to say."

"Maybe a painful truth."

"Sometimes I get the feeling you're using Hunter to find an opportunity to destroy her and other times, the mother-thing. I'm not sure which is scarier."

"Ancestry has twenty million members because everyone wants to know where they came from, who they are. Am I any different? You know your mother. The good parts, the bad parts, everything. I've seen Veronica's bad side plenty of times. Maybe I'm looking for the good."

The Major's phone rang again.

"Take the call." Pia turned and paced the length of the room.

The Major answered. Her conversation was limited to a series of single syllable acknowledgements. Then Pia heard her say, "I understand. We will consult with our attorneys and act according to the advice of counsel."

Pia paced back toward the Major and noticed a concerned frown on her face. The Major bit her knuckle.

Pia asked, "What is it?"

The Major glanced up. "The president revoked your security clearance."

An unexpected move on Roche's part. Pia couldn't grasp the full extent of what it meant. "That's bad?"

"You can't Chair a company with the most sensitive security contracts in the world. But don't worry, we'll get the lawyers involved. We'll have that order stayed. You won't have to give up your position or—"

"The voting shares."

The Major squeezed her eyes shut. "Yes. The board was ready to ask you to step down before this. But they came out of the meeting with more respect for you. You gave them new confidence. We can work with them. They're not big fans of Chuck Roche. They'll consider this an assault on the independence of corporate America. They'll line up—"

"After I step down. They'll crusade on my behalf but only if I take another sabbatical." Pia saw a tremendous upside in this turn of events, more field work.

The Major frowned and nodded. "That's a potential outcome to consider. But I could make the case—"

"You keep asking, *what's best for the company?* Is fighting for the right to run my own company the best thing right now?"

"What alternative is there?"

"Hunter has a plan to ruin Chuck Roche. I can travel with her, gain some publicity that will neutralize his attacks on—"

"No." The Major held up her hands. "That woman is the worst thing that ever happened to you. I know she's your mother, but you must see her for who she is. She's a ferocious fighter for only one person— herself. The only thing she cares about is becoming president-for-life. She'll ruin everyone and anyone around her if it will get her face chiseled into Mount Rushmore. She's singularly focused on getting back into the Oval Office. Veronica Hunter doesn't care about you. All she wants is your checkbook."

"I know."

The Major stepped back to take in Pia's expression and body language. "Once she regains the presidency, she'll dump you like she did when…"

Neither woman spoke for a minute.

"She believes in me." Pia shook her head slowly. "She doesn't have any voting shares, no board of directors to answer to, she simply believes in me. Look how much she's achieved on her own. An unmarried woman who wowed the country well enough to win the popular and electoral votes. Sure, she lost to Chuck Roche. And then she wormed her way into the VP slot. But in contrast, her administration looks golden. She might win next time."

The Major squeezed her eyes shut.

Pia paced again. "I know she has flaws. Everyone has flaws. And I know she was involved in my parent's killing, but she swears she thought they were talking about surveillance, not murder. Before you say anything—I believe her now. She can help me."

Pia's hands floated in the air. "Do you know how many public figures she's mentored from obscurity to the public eye? Do you know how many great things she's done? Passed a lot of legislation that helped people. No one knows the political process like Veronica. Maybe she does it for herself. Maybe she wants to be enshrined on Mount Rushmore. Maybe she belongs there. Whatever the case, she can help me. She can get me inside Roche's administration. She can help me build a platform to expose the corruption I find there."

Pia came back to face the Major and took her hand. "I need Hunter's help."

The Major's head was shaking back and forth slowly. "You're so young. You don't know the evil in that woman's heart."

"Don't talk about her like that. She's my mother."

"You have no idea how much you stand to lose by trusting her."

"Maybe you should trust me." Pia picked up her phone from the night stand and dialed. "Veronica. It's me. I just freed up my calendar. Can I still join you for the forum in Denver?"

Pia watched the Major's eyes close and stay closed.

The Major mouthed, *don't do this Pia.*

"I'll be there tomorrow." Pia paused. "Looking forward to it."

CHAPTER 16

VERONICA HUNTER NODDED AT THE first nephew as she made her way to the secure meeting room in the headquarters of the State Department. Her Secret Service agents waited outside. An aide to Nora Ratched, Secretary of State, offered her coffee, water, or juice.

"It's after midnight," Hunter said. "If you offer me a drink make sure it's at least 90 proof. Right now, your boss is wasting my time."

"Have a seat, ma'am." The aide scurried out of the room and closed the heavy door.

Hunter remained standing. She paced the length of the room speculating why her nemesis had requested her presence for an urgent matter and not held the meeting in the West Wing. The root cause could be any number of things, but the location made Ratched's desperation obvious.

Hartwell Thomas rushed in. "Thank Mother Mary and Joseph you came, Veronica."

He stretched out a hand.

Hunter glanced at his hand then at him. "Madam Vice President to you, Hartwell."

"Sorry." The Texan ducked his head. "Sorry. Sorry. I've been rushed all day. I've been working on this here project for the last couple hours." He straightened up. "Thank you for coming on such short notice, Madam Vice President."

She turned her back on him as the aide returned pushing a cart of crystal decanters. He put the cart against the wall and vanished. She took a glass, dropped three cubes in it, and poured what she guessed was single malt Scotch. Then she propped her butt against the cart, blocking

Thomas, and sipped. "What's this all about?"

"I'd better let Nora do the talking."

"If you think I'm talking to that little tramp—"

"What little tramp?" Nora Ratched entered and slammed the door behind her.

Hunter sniffed the air. "You managed to drag the stench of your trailer park right into the Truman Building."

"Now, ma'am, hear us out." Thomas held his hands up between them. "This is something important."

"It would have to be." Hunter swirled her Scotch. "I take it you're not inviting me to the administration prom."

Ratched reached for a glass on the cart. Hunter slapped her hand away. "I'd rather hear you plead for help without slurring your words."

Ratched turned to Thomas. "This was a mistake."

"Go on, ask her," Thomas said. He looked at Ratched and gestured to Hunter.

Ratched and Thomas stared at each other for too long.

Hunter sipped her drink and cherished their reluctance. More desperate than she'd realized.

Ratched turned to her. "What happens to the President's appointees if he's convicted of a crime?"

Hunter held Ratched's gaze over the rim of her glass while she took a long, slow sip. She finished with a satisfied exhale and smacked her lips. "Depends. If his crime is catching the clap from you, he'll get a sympathy hug from every elected official in the city."

"You're such an asshole." Ratched's eyes flared at Thomas. She wheeled around and stormed out.

Hunter grabbed Thomas's arm as he started to follow her. "Twenty bucks says no more than eight seconds." While holding his gaze, she counted down. "Seven, six, five, four."

Ratched returned and closed the door softly. "If you don't change your tune, I'll release what we've come to call the *Sabel Kill-Video*. You know the one I mean, the one you buried so she won't face murder charges for Popov."

"Could've made twenty bucks, Hartwell." Hunter snorted and sipped and pushed Thomas playfully. "Maybe not. You thought she'd hold out longer, right?"

Thomas hung his head.

"You're negotiating skills suck." Hunter rolled her eyes. "First, Chuck threatened Pia with the release of that video a couple days ago. He won't light that match until Pia's poured gasoline on herself. You're not dumb enough to steal his thunder, because you know he'd fire you so hard you'll never get a job in this town again. Second, you invited me here, which means you need something from me. Therefore, it follows that releasing the video—which will incriminate me—will render me incapable of helping you. Your threat is hollow. Now stop being vapid and tell me about your problem."

Ratched bit her knuckle and paced a few feet. "He's gone too far. I can't stop him now. And this time, we can't cover for him."

Hunter said, "You're not saying what he did—because I don't want to know. Thank you, I appreciate that. I get all the alerts from *Axios* to *Vox* to *Politica,* and nothing's come up out of the ordinary, so it hasn't happened yet. Am I right so far? That head nod's all I need. It's better if you don't open that mouth again. So, this is not the idiotic revocation of Pia Sabel's security clearance. It's not the evidence-free accusations hurled at Admiral Wilkes. Which leaves his beautiful plan to start a Holy War on Islam. Great."

"He's alienating everyone," Thomas said. "Badmouthing Wilkes pisses off everyone in public office who served. Senator Krueger is too pissed off to talk to him right now."

"He was a Navy captain or something, right?" Hunter looked over at Ratched. "And you're an Annapolis girl, aren't you?"

"Have you heard about his new mantra?" Thomas crossed his arms. "He's going to have us all refer to him as Zenith Man. His life is the model for all Americans. It's about how his brilliance in business, his achievements in public service, his attainment of the highest office in the land all qualify him for more than just two terms. He wants the term limits repealed."

"Oh, my god," Hunter nearly choked on her Scotch. "That's what Governor Baylesh said. That was for real? I thought he was improvising."

"Don't pretend you haven't heard this," Ratched said. "You kiss his fingers like the rest of us."

"You kiss something bigger than his fingers." Hunter sipped. "No. I don't kiss his slimy fingers. I know where they've been. That's why he doesn't invite me to his inner circle. You guys don't brief me. You don't—"

"Spare me the lonesome speech." Ratched pushed Hunter aside and grabbed a glass. "I'm not feeling it. Thomas has a problem. Listen to him. If we don't act, it could bring us all down."

Hunter raised her glass at Thomas, giving him permission to speak.

"The Redjackets are an independent group of citizens who act—"

"Just like Hitler's Brownshirts," Hunter interrupted.

"The point is, they're independent. They act on suggestions, vague references, concepts. There is no link between any administration official and the—"

"And you let the fool get the phone numbers to your, what do you call them? Generals?" Hunter sighed and finished her drink. "Since he has no idea how the rule of law works, he's given them specific orders. And he left a voice mail or some form of evidence, right?"

"A couple times he may have made inappropriate calls to the three-star Redjackets. I reduced our exposure and kept the names and phone numbers out of his reach. But then, the other day, he went and found the whole list."

Hunter poured Scotch on Ratched's ice cubes. And finished with a snarky smile. She stepped away from the cart and motioned for Thomas to help himself. She kept the Scotch decanter and poured for him.

"Back to your question, Nora," Hunter said. "No president has gone to jail before. No one knows what happens to appointees that were appointed by a criminal. The judges are appointed for life, so they could stay. If the public outcry rose to the level of tearing down everything Roche built, they might reasonably be expected to step down or face impeachment. The latter would be a stretch. But that's not what you're worried about." She pushed the index finger of her glass-holding hand into Ratched's breast, splashing a drop of Scotch on the Secretary's clean suit. "You're only worried about you. Tradition says cabinet officers should resign to allow the new president to choose his or her own cabinet. And the reason for this meeting," she pointed at both of them, "is to determine your job security when I take office. Or, to put it bluntly, the likelihood that I would pardon you."

Ratched turned to stare down Thomas. Thomas stared at his glass.

"So," Hunter said adding a sigh, "you no longer detest me because you need me. This isn't a peace offering, this is a beg."

"Damn it, Veronica, do you have to be such a fucking bitch?" Ratched slammed her glass on the table. "I'm not begging you for anything. You can take a flying—"

"Hold on now." Thomas grabbed Ratched's arm. "Yes, we are. We're begging. Let her gloat. Get it over with."

Hunter splashed more Scotch in both their glasses. "Before we toast to our new-found friendship, what are you offering me?"

Ratched shrugged and sipped and kept her gaze on the floor. Thomas held his own with Hunter for a moment. Then he looked away.

"What could we possibly offer a woman of your high caliber?" he asked.

"We can rule out loyalty." Hunter refilled her own glass. "But I have some ideas."

"What are they?" Ratched looked up quickly like a victim who hears a round chambered.

"We'll dive into specifics as needed." Hunter raised her glass to them. "First, let's toast to your capitulation. From now on, you're my dogs. You come when you're called. You sit when you're told. You heel when I snap my fingers." She raised her glass a little higher to encourage their acceptance. "*Santé!*"

The other two mumbled the French toast in reply and clinked glasses. They drank with suspicious eyes darting from one to another.

"How do we know you'll keep your end of the bargain?" Ratched asked.

"Well," Hunter laughed, "a pardon written on vice-presidential stationary won't do you much good. You'll have to trust me."

"What are you going to do with that Sabel girl?" Thomas asked.

"Chuck's been asking me where she is on the Kubler-Ross scale."

"The good governor moved her from bargaining to depression. Try not to focus on that. She's our insurance policy. If Roche doesn't go down in flames, we bring her into the administration and fund the next campaign out of her checkbook. If he manages to stay in office…"

"We go and fund the next campaign out of her checkbook." Thomas offered another toast with a grin.

"How do you know she's not playing you?" Ratched asked. "She's dangerous."

"That child?" Hunter clinked with Thomas and sipped.

"I want something in writing," Ratched said. "I want a guarantee."

"The only certainties in life are death, taxes, and your stupidity." Hunter glared at the Secretary of State. "If you want a pardon, I need to be president. Until then, you get nothing from me. You need him to resign of his own accord. Anything else sinks all our ships. He must resign before whatever it is that forced you into my arms becomes public. And, given your trembling hands, I'm guessing we have a week or less."

They nodded in silence. They drained their drinks, then set down their glasses, and filed out.

As they walked silently down the hall, Hunter smiled to herself. There was no way she could trust these two to hold up their end if Roche exposed their little conspiracy. But something Ratched had said made her swell with pride. Pia had managed to make the Secretary of State afraid of her. Ratched had called Pia "dangerous." Her daughter had already made waves in the biggest pond.

When she was alone in the elevator with Thomas, she said, "I expect the Redjackets to do a little favor for me in the next few days. I'll let you know when. Are they still mad at Pia Sabel for landing their fearless leader in jail?"

CHAPTER 17

To avoid Chopra, we slipped out the hospital's side door. It led to the only walkway. Which took us back to the front. Not good. At the edge of the wall, I stopped and checked the situation. A couple people milled around in front. Chopra's Tata was the only vehicle in the dirt lot at the end of the dead-end street. Everywhere else we looked were the back walls of shanties stacked four and five high. The only way out was past Chopra.

Mercury and Lakshmi, his goddess in red, walked around the corner. She winked at me. He said, *Hey homie, what're you waiting for? Chopra left her keys in the car along with her purse, her phone, everything. It's like she wants you to steal it.*

I said, *That's how Roman morality works? Just steal stuff? What would Seneca say?*

Mercury glanced at Lakshmi who was laughing at him. He leaned in and whispered, *Don't be making me look bad in front of the ladies, bro. What kind a disciple does that shit? C'mon now.* He straightened up and said, *Seneca said, 'We suffer more from imagination than from reality.' You want out of here, take the car the gods are offering you.*

My imagination conjured up the image of Chopra and five cops with guns drawn surrounding us in two seconds.

Mercury waved his arms to push me. *I'll smooth things over with your girlfriend. I gotcha six, dawg.*

I said, *Chopra's not my girlfriend.*

The eyes of my three coconspirators fell on me like cattle-prods.

Miguel said, "Chopra? She's sweet on you, but we never said—"

"I'm driving." I started out. "Each of you pick a door and climb in."

We trotted across the dirt. Each of us yanked open a door and jumped in and buckled up. The keys were in the console. It started up without a moment of hesitation. I dropped it in gear and stomped on the pedal.

In the rearview mirror, Chopra stood in the hospital doorway. I've not seen a woman that mad since I told my last girlfriend I'd called Interpol.

Behind Chopra, Vishal emerged and spoke to her.

With the aid of a translation app, Miguel programmed the dashboard mapping system to find Lilavati Hospital in the Bandra West neighborhood.

The route took us across a bridge and into a different world. Dharavi was a cesspool. Bandra was upscale. For Mumbai. The streets were still littered, and the paint on the infrastructure needed several new coats, but the smell was gone. Potholes were more like American potholes, not entrances to the underworld. Traffic became dense with every kind of vehicle imaginable. We shared the road with motorcycle rickshaws, scooters, sedans, trucks, busses, and the occasional limousine. At any given point in time, regardless of the speed, an inch separated us from any vehicle.

The buildings were infinitely more prosperous. Especially Lilavati, the exclusive, private hospital. Their motto, written in English hung over the entrance. It said, *More than Healthcare, Human Care.* Apparently, there wasn't room for the rest of it: *For those who can afford it.* A hundred people stood around the entrance. Some were uniformed valet parking attendants. Their work looked like an interpretive dance of eternal gridlock. I backed us out quickly and drove around the block.

We abandoned Chopra's Tata behind the ten-story Mumbai Educational Trust building. From their empty lobby, we could see the entrance to the hospital.

The pilots were supposed to meet me at a specific place and time, which was about now and about several miles away. My beautiful arsenal would not be available for our impending confrontation. Which was annoying.

Cody tapped my shoulder and handed me a phone. "Found it where a cop might've dropped it. Our phones are gone too."

"Perfect." I gave him an appreciative nod. "This might come in handy until they track it."

I dialed Bianca Dominguez's direct number at Sabel Technologies. She answered on the first ring. "We figured you dumped your phones. Don't speak. The NSA is scouring all calls out of India. Plan C."

She hung up.

For Plan C, I'd need a phone with internet access. The ancient piece of tech I held in my hand looked close to twenty years old. I folded it up and tossed it in a trash can.

Tania pointed out the window at the hospital entrance. "Two Americans in suits in that crowd."

"Redjackets," Miguel said. "Scanning the arrivals."

"They missed us?"

"I don't think so." He thumbed at an old-fashioned newspaper in a rack a couple steps away.

I checked it out. The *Indian Express* in English. A headline story referenced the search for five Americans who attacked an American admiral in the Hilton a few days earlier. Not the same story being told in the American press. The paper claimed they were the same men involved in the attack on a local man in Dharavi. One dead, two wounded.

I looked at Miguel. "You're figuring Dhanpal is one of the two wounded they brought here. Making two Redjackets out front and a third trying to circle around behind us?"

Miguel didn't answer. He looked over my shoulder with a cold stare.

I turned around and stepped to the left while Miguel stepped right. We were facing an American in a suit with a pistol leveled at us.

Tania said, "Two guys holding across the street. You two handle this asshole."

"Stay together where I can keep an eye on you," the gunman said.

"Screw that." Miguel kept separating from me.

"I'll shoot your girlfriend."

"Go ahead." I continued flanking the guy. He began to realize the emptiness of his threat. Despite what you see on TV, pistols are horrifically inaccurate weapons even at close range. If he escalated the situation by shooting one of us, the other two would pounce on him before he could get off a second shot.

Mercury stood behind the man. *Chill, my brutha. Your man Cody has this handled.*

My gaze darted around the room. The new guy was nowhere in sight.

Mercury said, *I told you he can see me. The young blood heard me! Ain't that sweet?*

God only knew—literally—what Mercury told him, but sometimes, against my better judgement, I trust my forgotten deity.

I nodded at the Redjacket. "I saw your boss's corpse. Not pretty."

Miguel was now three yards to the man's left. One big leap and he could neutralize the guy. I moved a little more to my left, putting the two of us on opposite sides of the guy. His barrel remained trained on Tania.

"Check it, Vishal just showed up." Tania never took her eyes off the hospital entrance. "Redjackets are still there. Chopra and the cops can't be far behind."

Confusion crossed the Redjacket's face. The new names weren't on his list.

I said, "The guy who killed your boss is one helluva shot. He was a Navy SEAL, y'know. You guys don't have a chance."

"Yeah?" He sneered. "How come Bobby winged him then? Too bad his friends got him out of there, or we'd have finished him off."

Cody appeared out of thin air with a chair in his hands. The leg crashed into the gunman's head with extreme force. He crumpled into Miguel's arms.

Miguel disarmed the guy and put his shoulder under the armpit of our would-be killer to keep him standing. The man's knees buckled and his body weaved like a reed in a breeze and his head wobbled around a few times. Blood started running down the back of his neck and into his shirt.

Cody put the chair down. Miguel fished a phone out of the man's pocket before dropping him into the chair.

"Call your friends." Miguel handed the guy the phone. "Tell them to come on over."

The guy was just woozy enough to do it. He dialed.

"SHIT!" Tania turned from the window. "Chopra's over there. She's going in with five uniformed cops."

Mercury rested his elbow on the Redjacket's head. *See what I'm talking about, mortal? You taught Intelligence Bureau Special Agent Chopra a valuable lesson today: never leave your keys in your car. She'll be grateful—*

I said, *Yeah, after I spend thirty years in Kaala Paani.*

Mercury said, *You've been researching the worst prisons in India, homie?*

I said, *That's where they were going to send Tania last time she was here.*

People crossed the lobby in rapidly growing numbers. Classes had let out. They walked past the Redjacket with suspicious glances followed by disapproving looks at us.

I said, "We don't need a fight right now."

"Or selfies with our victim," Tania said.

I pointed at the guy and looked at Miguel. Cody tried to decipher our telepathic communication with a glance back and forth.

Miguel hoisted the guy to his shoulder and followed me out the door. We shoved him in Chopra's passenger seat. We tossed in the guy's phone. A voice on the other end was asking, "Mike? Mike? Are you there?"

Tania lashed his shoelaces to the seat's anchor bolts. We slammed the doors. I locked it up and slapped the keys on the hood. We walked down the street and took the first alley.

A voice called out louder than I would have liked. "Jacob! Jacob, for me now waiting up."

Vishal let half of Bandra know where we were. I bit the inside of my cheek to keep from calling him names in a voice loud enough to alert the other half of Bandra. I shushed him with a finger to my lips and wondered if it meant the same thing in India. Sometimes gestures convey entirely different meanings in other countries. For example, I learned the hard way that the thumbs-up gesture is akin to the middle finger in much of the Middle East.

Our guide for the day was woke to Western gestures and lowered his voice. He trotted up to us.

"Cabbie for us waits one street." He pointed around the corner. "Much telling news. Hurry."

We followed him to a black and yellow Suzuki cab built to hold three Indians or one and a half Americans. Or Miguel. The cabbie looked at us and pointed to the roof. I shook my head. Another cab came around the corner. I flagged him down with a hundred euro note. He tossed his passengers out and took Miguel and Tania. Vishal, Cody, and I got into the first one. We took off.

"Friend of yours leaving last night." He gestured wildly. "I did told Police you go to AHI in Bandra East. But. Lie no good. No believing Vishal. Oh. Also. Lost job."

He hung his head.

I sighed and pulled the last few hundred euros from my pocket. I cut the pile in half and gave Vishal the equivalent of two months wages.

He smiled. "Dhanpal Singh is having many grandparents in Promenade."

I looked out the window and wondered how the American banks could possibly succeed without this guy leading their customer service. His English was a jigsaw puzzle, but the results were indispensable.

Our cab-caravan turned the corner and stopped. A wall of police standing shoulder to shoulder cordoned off the road. The center cops parted and out stepped Radhika Chopra.

CHAPTER 18

The skeptical usher checked his invitation list for Pia's name. He called his supervisor who discussed it with someone else. They exchanged bureaucratic speak in hushed tones. She looked around the lobby of the historic Brown Palace Hotel in Denver, Colorado.

She tugged the usher's sleeve. "Forget it. I'll go back to Washington. Please give my regrets to Vice President Hunter. I'm supposed to be at her table right now."

As Pia turned to leave, she heard his rushed explanation to the boss. Crossing the lobby slowly allowed him time to catch up. His panicked footsteps followed a few seconds behind her.

"Ms. Sabel, please forgive us." He called as he trotted up. "This is an exclusive affair. We are concerned that the radical-mainstream press might impersonate invitees to infiltrate this event. If you will be kind enough to follow me. I will escort you to Vice President Hunter's table."

Pia looked the man over before taking his offer with a nod. As soon as his back turned, she glanced again at her notes. The list of attendees with their hobbies and children's names peeked out of her purse. Half of the people she had met through her father. Many of those she could pick out of a crowd. She only needed to greet three before news of her arrival would be whispered throughout the room. Her purse snapped closed while she silently thanked the Major for the tip on preparation.

A cringe tightened her face as she thought of their last conversation. The rudeness was regrettable. One day, she would make it up to the Major. When the smoke cleared and Roche was gone, the Major would forgive her. Maybe.

The usher led her to the Brown Palace Club, a classic of the Old

West. Its wood paneled walls framed stained-glass windows as they rose to the coffered ceiling. At the narrow end of the darkened room, Senator Krueger addressed the small crowd of billionaires. The last dinner plates were being hauled away by the serving staff. The usher walked straight to Hunter to verify Pia's invitation.

Pia stopped at the table nearest the door and whispered greetings to a couple she'd met at one of her father's famous dinner parties at Sabel Gardens. They greeted her with feigned smiles and suspicious glances. When she moved to the next couple on her list, she heard a trophy wife ask her husband, "I thought she hated the administration."

She repeated her greetings at two more tables, the notes working flawlessly to endear her to the guests. They were astounded that she remembered them. Soon the whispers circled the room ahead of her. People began calling her over. Some tested her memory and sounded a little surprised that any daughter of Alan Sabel would speak to them. These were the billionaires who had stiffed or sued or scammed Sabel Industries in some manner. Her father's policy, make no enemies, had saved the perpetrators from prosecution. All is forgiven. Never forgotten.

Eventually, she made her way to Hunter's table. Before she could say anything, Hunter said, "You're late."

Pia shrugged. "Lots of Dad's former friends in here."

"We were supposed to meet earlier this afternoon to go over my plan."

"You emailed it. I've got it down." Pia smiled. "Probably."

Hunter squeezed Pia's forearm hard under the table. "We do things my way. I said we meet at my suite before dinner."

Pia nearly snapped at her mother before catching herself. She saw something in the woman's eyes: hurt.

A wave of guilt seared Pia's heart. Her tardiness had been intentional. She wanted to make her own entrance, conveying that she was an independent woman.

In Hunter's face was a different story. Veronica had imagined tutoring Pia, then taking her by the hand, and introducing her to this evening's guests as they arrived. It would've been a huge coup in political circles. *Look who I brought.* For Hunter, it would've been a proud moment in her suddenly invigorated motherhood. Like a proud mother at her daughter's debutante ball, she'd dreamed of introducing her secret-daughter to political society. She'd hoped to make it an emotionally bonding evening they could share.

Pia had crushed the woman's dream. Despite it being a self-interested manipulative dream, Pia could tell her mother had imagined being proud of Pia. A rare emotion for Veronica Lodge Hunter.

"I'm sorry." Pia gently squeezed Hunter's hand. "I won't do it again."

Hunter's eyes searched Pia's, bouncing from one to the other, looking for a hint of insincerity.

There wasn't any.

Hunter accepted her apology and ran through the bullet points from her email. It felt like a test which Pia answered in detail and passed. Satisfied that her student was ready for her first intentional public appearance, Hunter relaxed and leaned back in her seat.

Senator Krueger prattled on about taxes.

"Now," Hunter leaned to her ear, "tell me why your people are causing trouble in Mumbai."

Pia tried not to face her with a glare. She failed.

Hunter met her gaze and cut her off before she spoke. "I get intelligence briefings every day. Our people gather information all over the world. There is an Indian agent named Chopra who's hopping mad about Americans searching for Dhanpal Singh. Why don't your people go through channels and work with the government?"

"What makes you think the Americans are my people?"

"Who else would they be?"

"Redjackets."

Hunter recoiled as if it were an impossibility. Pia sensed a concern in Hunter's eyes as well.

Pia's moral compass roiled. If Hunter were involved in the Redjackets, Pia couldn't keep company with her. It would be like sitting next to a bomb. Yet Pia wasn't close enough to Roche to destroy him. Only Hunter could get her that close. And she was learning a good deal from the savvy politician.

Still, she had to know, even if Hunter would deny it. "Are you involved in the Redjackets?"

"Of course not." Hunter frowned with practiced indignation. "Those are completely independent operators working on their own. Though, I do wish Chuck would denounce them."

Pia turned the words over in her mind. Carefully devoid of any personal connection, Veronica also passed on the opportunity to denounce them herself. Not a conclusive statement.

Hunter returned her attention to Senator Krueger. The senator said, "Government cannot create prosperity, though government can limit or destroy it."

Hunter and the others applauded. Pia missed whatever Krueger said leading up to that and felt confused by the applause. Hunter elbowed her and gave a nod. Pia dutifully clapped.

"And that's what those radicals in congress are trying to do," Krueger raised his voice. "With your support, we can elect more representatives and senators at the state and federal levels who will reduce your taxes instead of raising them. Why should you pay for the problems of deadbeats and losers?"

While the crowd roared their approval, Pia wondered about her whole plan. Maybe it was time to take the Major's advice and leave politics to the politicians. But she'd often heard her coaches say, *play your game, not the other team's.* She considered Hunter's ideas. She knew what she was supposed to do.

"Any questions?" Krueger asked.

Pia was ready. Hunter had given her pointers in that email and Pia had extrapolated from there. She could ace this test. She rose and strode to the middle of the room where an aide held a microphone.

The clean-cut young man saw Pia coming and quickly looked to the podium for instructions. Krueger gave a predatory smile and nod. The aide handed Pia the microphone and stepped aside. A spotlight hit her in the face.

"Welcome, Pia Sabel," Krueger said, "We're all surprised to see you—sitting—among us after the spanking Governor Baylesh gave you."

Pia waited for the raucous laughter to die down. Taking pride in the fact that she hadn't blushed, she lifted her chin and smiled at the crowd before turning back to Krueger.

"I'll leave the petty wisecracks to you." Pia felt her voice grow strong and loud. "Your childish remarks don't reduce the regulations restricting our companies' growth." She wafted a hand at the billionaires around her and caught a few approving nods. "They don't help our companies create new jobs. If you want my money for your campaign, you'll listen to me. You're wrong about tax breaks for us, the richest people in America. Here's why. Middle class moms don't begrudge me flying here tonight on one of my Gulfstreams. They envy but don't mind my exotic car collection. What they do care about is why their kids' schools have fallen behind Vietnam. When did that happen, Senator Krueger? When did the USA drop below Latvia in global education rankings? From where will we fill our top executive positions in ten years, Singapore? Russia? Ireland?"

She stared down Senator Krueger. He stammered through an answer that redirected the education problem to lousy parenting. She felt the support of the people around her. They'd all used H-1B visas to import cheap executive talent to their company. A solution that had become difficult with the growing hatred of immigrants. The best and brightest were shying away from the program fearing for their families in the new environment.

Pia handed the microphone to another dinner guest waiting his turn and wound her way back to Hunter's table. She was proud of herself. She'd played her game, not Krueger's.

As she passed by, the guests smiled and congratulated her in polite, but not supportive terms. Pia took her seat next to her blank-faced mother.

"Was that our plan?" Hunter asked.

"Not exactly." Pia felt stung by the harsh question. "But it went well. Didn't you like how I handled him?"

Hunter rose and signaled to her Secret Service agents. "We'll talk at breakfast."

"But didn't I do well?" Pia watched her walk away. She searched for the right way to address her. She wasn't ready for mom. "Veronica?"

CHAPTER 19

HUNTER WENT TO HER SUITE cursing the ungrateful, spiteful, disrespectful child. She had to find a way to get that willful girl under control. She stopped in her tracks and realized something. When Veronica's father was mad at young Veronica, he called her "willful". Maybe it was hereditary. For a moment, she felt proud of Pia for swatting Krueger. But still, she needed to get that willful girl under control. Her aide stood in the suite's sitting room with a laptop open, facing her.

On the screen, Chuck Roche's face stared blankly back at her.

"The President would like a word," the aide said. "Don't worry, ma'am. I've muted both audio and video."

"Let's get this over with." She took the laptop, set it on the desk, checked that the secure scrambling system was engaged, then turned on the video stream.

"Who released this damn video?" Roche asked.

Hunter shook her head, worried that Nora Ratched had screwed her over by releasing the Sabel Kill-Video. "Which video?"

"Pia Sabel making a fool out of Krueger." Roche looked about as mad as she'd ever seen him. "Most people accept their fate by now. Who's been coaching her? You?"

"I'm working her into your campaign." Hunter clenched her teeth. "It will take time."

"Have you seen this? She stepped all over Krueger's pitch for Zenith Man. Why didn't you stop her?"

"Where is it? Twitter?" Hunter pulled it up on her phone. There was Pia Sabel, front and center, looking like a tiger pouncing on the aging

Krueger. "This was taken from the front left. That's where security and wait staff stand."

"Did you rehire those murderous Secret Service agents, Dan and Catherine?"

Hunter looked over the top of her screen at gray-bearded Agent Dan and eye-rolling Agent Catherine. She muted the feed and waved them out of the room. She clicked back online and said, "Of course not."

"I'm going to purge this administration of the disloyal, Veronica. If I find you've—"

"Just a reminder," Hunter said, "you need half of congress to vote me out. I have dirt on more than enough of those fools to keep my job."

"Fine." Roche blew out his frustration. "But I'm serious about everyone in the administration backing the Zenith Man concept. Our marketing people have tested it and found great results. Everyone— including you—needs to be onboard. I'm getting rid of anyone who doesn't like it."

"You never sent me the memo," Hunter said. "What is Zenith Man?"

"Me." He scowled, surprised at her ignorance. "My rise from nothing to billionaire. My tenacity in overcoming adversity when the American banks foreclosed on me. I came back from the financial graveyard four times. Did you hear me? FOUR TIMES. And now, I've won the approval of a vast majority of Americans. I am President of the United States of America because I'm the pinnacle—the zenith—of man's achievement. I've overcome more adversity, accomplished more business triumphs, won more lawsuits, screwed more beautiful women, and gotten more votes than any man in history. I am the prime example of what every man wants to be. I am Zenith Man. You need to put that in all your interviews." He paused long enough to take a breath. "That is if anyone cares to interview you."

Hunter clamped her tongue between her molars to keep from correcting him on nearly all counts. A certain amount of pride lay in her patience. She nodded. "I'm sure I can refer to your record from time to time. Subtle mentions. You don't want to overdo it."

"Back to that girl." Roche nearly spat. "Congress is fighting me on the war. Saudi lobbyists crawl across the Capitol like cockroaches. You have to do something to get this impulsive little bitch in the program. Get her to recall her agents from Mumbai. We need the Wilkes problem solved today. Tell her, if she doesn't, I'm going to release the Kill-Video."

"How many checks will she send your campaign from death row?"

"Did you read the intelligence briefings? Her people are looking for Wilkes."

"The Kill-Video is your ace." Hunter's patience thinned every second. "Don't ejaculate that ace prematurely. Wait until she's done something impulsive. Wait until she pours gasoline on herself before you light that match."

"If we don't get this war going, these cretins are going to tear down my administration. They're investigating my business operations now."

"You're bogged down in the weeds on this, Chuck." Hunter used her soothing voice. "You need to keep your head up. Be the commander in chief with capital Cs. You'll never achieve your goals if you spend all day worrying about some runaway admiral in India."

"Everyone keeps getting in my way," Roche snarled. "I never should have asked for a declaration. I should've done what the rest of them did, just start bombing the hell out of Riyadh and Mecca. Now, I have to announce a shoot-to-kill order on Wilkes and anyone aiding and abetting her."

Hunter almost choked. "How would the Indian government react to that?"

"Don't know, don't care."

Hunter visualized the country's future. India has always been popular among the non-aligned countries. They successfully stood up to the British. They rejected American overtures because of Nixon's affinity for Pakistan. They played Russia and China against each other. For the wannabe countries, India was a model of independence. India could align a powerful reaction if Roche pissed them off. Nothing would piss them off like issuing a shoot-to-kill order on their sovereign soil.

Never mind the fact that Roche couldn't legally do such a thing. The law didn't matter in Roche-Reality. Worst of all, the rule of law took too long to catch up with him. His Redjackets would kill Wilkes. The proclamation would create a get-out-of-jail card for them. She could hear their defense attorney, "They assumed they were working on the directive of the President of the United States of America, like a soldier in a war zone." It wouldn't hold up long, but it would make Roche look like a caped crusader to his base. Even so, the Senate might censure him. The House would vote to impeach. All of which could put her back in the White House. But with a cloud ten times worse than Gerald Ford's. That would not do.

"You want that war with the Saudis?" Hunter asked. "Don't go around chasing some lowly admiral. Meet with your generals. Get lots of pictures of you poring over maps next to men wearing medals. Be what you were elected to be, the commander in chief. Do you know what your actual title is in Article II, Section 2 of the Constitution?"

Roche squinted and shook his head.

"Commander in Chief of the Army and Navy of the United States, and of the Militia of the several States, when called into the actual Service of the United States." She beamed confidence to him. "That's a title worthy of Zenith Man. Be that person. Surround yourself with the highest-ranking officials. Call in the Joint Chiefs. Call in the CIA and the DIA. Make it known that you're planning to neutralize the threat while Congress twiddles its collective thumbs."

"Say." Roche twisted his face while he thought. "I could bring in the Joint Chiefs and hold meetings. But what if Wilkes pops up?"

"I'll handle that." Hunter softened her face to plead. "I need something important to do. These fund raisers are boring and useless."

"Yeah," he said while nodding. "I'll bet you could make her disappear. You have considerable experience in that department. OK, but you better not fuck this up, Veronica. If you do, the Redjackets will come for you."

"I'm on it, Chuck."

"First thing you'd better do, neutralize that Sabel girl. Do something that will get her video off the front page of every website. And don't let her make a fool out of Krueger again. Now get going." He clicked off.

Hunter let out a breath. Crisis averted. But how long would that last?

First on her list of things to do, take Pia down a notch. She found the tweet with Pia's video and retweeted it, adding, "Isn't that cute? It's as if she grew up a little since Governor Baylesh slapped her."

CHAPTER 20

ZXZXZX IF YOU EVER HAVE the opportunity to be a guest of the Municipal Corporation of Greater Mumbai at their Arthur Road jail—skip it. Tania had had the foresight to bail from her cab at the first sign of trouble. She immediately evaporated into the densely populated city before the police had time to swarm our cars. Miguel struggled just enough to cover her escape. She had a lot to lose should the local authorities realize her current passport didn't match the identity she'd used on her last visit to India.

We weren't so lucky. We were dragged in without anyone reading us our rights, giving us a call or any of the comforts of the legal system back home. We spent the first few hours in the general population which is packed in like sardines. Little oil and no condoms. Somewhere around midnight, we were moved to Barrack 12 where they keep the high-profile criminals.

We were given a cell of our own. Miguel and I, accustomed to falling afoul of authorities from time to time, slept soundly on the cement floor. Cody paced all night, unable to believe he'd fallen in with the kind of people who steal cars, much less steal them from India's equivalent of a CIA clandestine operative.

Mercury materialized in the small space between the solid steel outer door and the classic jail bars that formed the inner door. *Homie, good news. Jupiter talked to Mahā-Ambā and we're springing your ass. Sweet, right?*

I said, *Who spoke to who?*

Mahā-Ambā, or Mumba. Mercury's disappointment drooped his face. *Holy Minerva, boy, when you visit a place, the least you could do is learn the patron goddess. Just common courtesy. Y'know, when I get coffee with the other gods, they always ask why I bother with a loser like you. I'm beginning to wonder myself.*

If you have better believers, don't let me keep you, I said. *If you're springing us, why are the doors still locked? Oh, no. Don't tell me. Is there digging involved?*

Mercury shook his head sadly. *After all I do for you, this is how you treat me? Dude, even Jesus is ashamed of you. And he hangs with whores and tax collectors.*

The outer door opened. Radhika Chopra, flanked by three prison guards, stood silhouetted in front of high windows. One guard came forward, opened the jail doors and barked something in Marathi, the official language.

Miguel rose from a sound sleep and marched out without a second thought. Concern held Cody in place. I motioned him forward. If we were getting the death penalty, at least we'd be in the daylight and out of the dark cell. I followed. In the hall, they cuffed and shackled us. We shuffled along with Chopra and a guard in front, the other two behind us.

They led us down hallways. Complex door systems clanked open and closed, controlled by unseen operators. Eventually, we emerged into the outer lobby. Fifteen men and two women in expensive suits waited for us. The cuffs and shackles came off. The questions flew from the suits' mouths. Were we mistreated? Were we assaulted in any way? Do we harbor any ill will toward the representatives of the city or the government of India? Do we have any grievances against Radhika Chopra? And so on.

Cody couldn't believe they weren't fitting us with blindfolds. Miguel and I answered the questions. We were fine. No harm. No foul. When they were satisfied, they gave Chopra a nod. She offered us paperwork written in the Devanagari script which meant nothing to us. An attorney gave us a smile. We signed. Our personal effects were given to us. We signed more forms.

The attorneys offered us rides to anywhere in the country. We declined. They left. Which put us outside on the street with Chopra. She was not happy.

"As it turns out," she said in her crisp British-accented English, "every advocate in Mumbai uses Sabel Security for personal protection. So does every banker and hedge fund manager on Dalal Street."

Mercury grinned over her shoulder. *Dalal Street rhymes with Wall Street. The financial center of Mumbai. That's where the Caesars live, dawg. You're inches away from having important people you can tell about me and how my grace saved a wretch like you.*

I said, *What happened to your girlfriend, Lakshmi?*

He looked away. *Sometimes old flames are looking for revenge, ya feel me?*

I held Chopra's gaze without responding. Miguel sniffed the wind. Cody wondered, as he had since he first met me, what the hell was going on.

"The Minister of Home Affairs sent a police squad to wake me at my hotel before dawn." Her scowl detracted from her otherwise pleasant face. "I would love to be on the minister's radar, yeah?—but not for arresting well-connected car thieves. You caused a career fail for me."

I shrugged.

"Don't you have anything to say for yourself?" She stuck her nose in my space.

"Not yet."

"Why do people think it is fine for you to nick my car, blow up our deal, scarper, and … and … wreck India—not to mention my career?" She watched me shrug again. This time she leaned in nose-to-nose. "Why is it OK for armed Americans to shoot each other in the slums of Mumbai like cowboys in some stupid American movie?"

I waited.

"Bloody hell." She took a deep breath and glanced around the street. "You are free to go. Leg it before I change my mind, and have you arrested for loitering."

Dhanpal was out there somewhere, wounded and needing our help. I should be in a rush to get moving. But Cody wasn't the only one with questions. Since when did Sabel send seventeen well-dressed lawyers for a little grand theft auto? I barely got the lone fat guy when I was arrested for murder. I said, "No."

"What?" She snapped an angry glance at me. "Get out of here. Get out of my life."

"Coffee?" I asked.

Her eyebrows went up. So did Cody's. Miguel pointed to a café down the street. As he did so, his gaze bounced off three cars. I gave him a discreet nod to confirm receipt of his message. His recon had been productive in several ways.

I said, "There's a little American-style coffee shop down the block."

"This better be good." She fell in behind Miguel. "What do you want then?"

"To know what you want."

"I told you, we want Wilkes."

"Why?" I asked.

"What is the American expression? That is above my paygrade."

"Who told you we were coming?"

"My boss."

"He woke you out of your warm bed in New Delhi and sent you to Mumbai in the middle of the night. You care about your career. You weren't about to sign up for a fool's errand. So, you asked him. And, like you, I want to know: who provided the intel on our arrival?"

She huffed and thought and walked and huffed again. "One of your pilots was in touch with him when you stopped in Stockholm."

Miguel shot me a glance when he held the coffee shop door open for us. I answered his unspoken question with a minimal shrug. Someone's giving away our position, but I'm not taking her word for it. Cousin Elmer picked pilots on a rotation basis. They had no idea who or where they were flying very far in advance. The likelihood of pilots calling someone about us was minimal.

I asked her, "Why are you being honest with me?"

She said, "I don't know. I reckon…"

She ordered a drink while she thought up a good one. She turned back to me. "I reckon I like you. Even if you're a bit daft. You seem genuine enough. You believe in your mission. You want to save Wilkes."

"You're lying." I pointed at something on the menu, the girl behind the counter nodded and disappeared. I faced Chopra. "You know I'm a dishonest car thief. You don't like me and the yellow dot on your forehead might be fashion to match your blouse, or it might be an indicator that you'd never date outside your caste. Drop the flirty stuff. I'm not in the mood."

She started to protest when she caught a glimpse of the look on Miguel's face.

"Quite the fantasy life you lead, innit." She took her drink, which had whipped cream piled on top.

The server looked at me and said something that must have been the amount due. I reached in Chopra's purse and pulled out her wallet. The money looked like play money, so I handed over a credit card. While Chopra stared with an open mouth at my brazen moves, I palmed her phone. The cashier coughed. Chopra sputtered and huffed and signed the bill.

We took a small table in the corner. Cody remained standing with his back to the wall, his eyes scanning the room and the street, and everyone who passed by. He was good. Vigilant but with a little too much darting in his eyes. The darting indicated growing stress. He was used to planned missions, with intel and communications and comprehensible command structures. He wasn't used to stealing cars and sleeping in a concrete cell. All of which he'd learn to love someday. But right then, something about our situation was dredging up unpleasant memories from his combat tours. I checked Miguel. He'd noticed the signs of PTSD in Cody too. He took the kid outside where they leaned against a wall and talked.

"Why do you want Wilkes?" I asked Chopra.

She stared at her cup, turning it slowly as she thought.

"In case you think we're stupid," I said, "Miguel spotted three of your co-workers sitting in cars outside Barrack 12. Your little dog and pony show of setting us free didn't fool us for a moment. Three cars is a complex tail. One that means you have some serious juice at IB. And that means there's a whole lot about this you've been lying about. I'm turning the tables on you. We're having coffee until you call them off. Then you're coming with us."

She looked up quickly. "Your friend never said a word."

"We communicate."

"How?"

"Why do you want Wilkes?" I asked again in an impatient voice.

"Career move." She sighed. "It would be what you call 'high profile' to rendition her."

"Bullshit." I tapped the table. "But I do like how you integrated the word rendition into your vocabulary. Nice touch. I have a warm spot in my heart for how Dick Cheney rephrased 'kidnapping off the street.'"

"Why do you want Wilkes?" she asked.

"I don't care about Wilkes. My friend has a bullet in his shoulder. He's lying low somewhere in this city. When I find him, I'm taking him home where he can get proper medical care—and the Redjackets can't touch him. If he can give you Wilkes, fine. If not, too bad."

"OK. Why take me with you?" She waited until she realized I wasn't going to answer. "You want to keep your enemies close. So, I don't have a choice, do I? If I refuse, you'll continue to wreck my career."

"Ready to go?"

"Yes." She hung her head.

"One more thing." I held the door open for her. "I need Vishal. He's over there in the backseat of your man's car."

CHAPTER 21

THE LIFE OF AN INSOMNIAC involves a good deal of wandering. For Pia, early mornings became her daily run many years ago. Long before dawn, she ran east through downtown Denver to the City Park, circling it once before heading west to the banks of the South Platte River. She ran from the northern end of Confluence Park down to Mile High Stadium before turning back for the Brown Palace Hotel. Near the end of her twelve-mile loop, she sensed someone running a parallel route. Not exactly parallel. The shadow took advantage of the triangular streets in the central business district to run an intercept course.

Pia ran alone at four in the morning. The only serious runners among her staff were in India. The early hour and her world-class speed usually kept her safe from criminals. Now that she'd raised her public profile, threats were pouring in every day. She checked her fanny-pack for her pistol. It was there and ready.

She kicked up her speed, turned a corner and circled the block. Her route brought her behind her pursuer. She closed on the dark figure at sixteen miles an hour. The other runner had a woman's figure and a respectable but not fast pace, lowering Pia's concern. When Pia blew past the surprised runner, she stopped.

The figure also stopped and gasped, "Pia, it's me, Gina Wind."

Pia walked back to her under the streetlights. "Gina, it's been years. How are things at ESPN?"

"Not ESPN." Gina held up a hand while she fought for breath. "Anymore. *Politica* now. Big leagues."

"Congratulations then?" Pia wasn't sure why a decent sports journalist would stoop to political coverage.

"Thanks." Gina gulped air several more times. "Mind if I ask you a couple questions? Like the old days?"

Pia looked around them in the dark. Gina had written several favorable posts and did a couple flattering video interviews during her soccer career. The journalist was a couple years older and a fair athlete in her own right. There were no other people on the street. It appeared safe.

"You followed my route for an interview?" Pia asked.

Still breathing hard, Gina nodded and reached for her water bottle and drained it.

"Admirable. You always were a go-getter." Pia smiled and waved in the direction of the hotel.

"OK, if we walk?" Gina gasped. "I had a baby a few months ago. I'm not back to my old speed, let alone yours."

"Congratulations. Boy or girl?" Pia smiled.

"Girl. One of your posters hangs over her crib."

"Trying to scare the hell out of her?"

They laughed and walked up the block.

"Why are you working with Veronica Hunter?" Gina asked.

Pia felt ice run down her back. "Where did that come from?"

"You're in Denver. She's in Denver. You went to the super-secret fund raiser last night. She was there. What's the connection?"

Pia considered spilling her story. All of it. From birth to adoption to orphaned to adopted again to discovering why the former president, now vice president, paid her so much attention. It would feel good to bear her soul. It would feel good to tell someone about the sickening, out-of-control rollercoaster of her life. Gina was the kind of reporter who would understand. Why not tell her all about it? Put it out there for the world to see.

She took a deep breath.

"How many children do you plan to have?" Pia asked. She wasn't ready to spill.

"We're going for two." Gina glanced up at Pia. "One girl, one boy ideally, but we'll stop there no matter what. My sister has four boys."

"I'll bet she loves your little girl."

"Hunter's your enemy." Gina stopped and touched Pia's arm.

"Everything you've ever said and done would lead a reasonable person to think you hated Chuck Roche and Veronica Hunter with a murderous passion. Like the rest of us."

The journalist had the murderous part right. Pia considered the woman. What had Hunter said about reporters? They feed on three things: pictures, mistakes and attacks. Pia handled the sports press well in her day, but they were minor league compared to political reporters. Talking to Gina without preparation could be a big mistake.

Hunter would be as happy about this sidewalk interview as she was about Pia's attack on Kreuger. Some mothers are hard to please. Pia considered making an attack. That would get Gina off her and onto someone else. But on what or who?

Hunter was right about one thing; Pia wasn't ready for the national press.

Yet she was smart enough to handle anything she put her mind to. And, Gina was a decent woman. By getting up long before the world around them, Gina had showed the assertiveness Pia admired most.

She resumed walking. Gina kept up.

"My father taught me an important lesson growing up," Pia said. "Make no enemies."

Gina tipped up her empty water bottle, then slid it back in her fanny pack.

Pia handed over her bottle. "I keep it for emergency-use. Untouched."

Gina hesitated before taking it. "Thank you."

They resumed their walk.

Gina said, "The Roche administration has passed laws and regulations that I know run directly against your personal beliefs. That is, the Pia Sabel I used to know."

Again, Gina hit it right on the head. Pia's thoughts ran through all Roche's crimes and Hunter's involvement in them. Did she really believe Veronica's excuse that she didn't know Roche and company were going to kill her parents? Did being an egg-donor to Pia's life give the woman a pass for her sins? What the hell was Pia doing in Denver, pursuing a mother-daughter relationship with a cobra?

Gina kept an inquisitive gaze on her. The journalist deserved an answer.

"No enemies," Pia said, "means respecting the dignity of every human being. Even if that human being is in the Roche administration."

"Are you telling me you respect Veronica Lodge Hunter?"

A small laugh bubbled out of Pia before she could gather her thoughts.

"Roche wants to start a questionable war with Saudi Arabia. Are you OK with that?" Gina took a couple long strides, turned and walked backwards so she could face Pia while asking the next question. "You accused President Roche of complicity in the Russian conspiracy to kill 365 Americans in the airline disaster last year. Have you forgiven him?"

Pia felt tension run up her back like a jolt of electricity. There was no forgiving Roche. "Ask Senator Krueger what he did with the evidence I gave him."

"I'm asking you, Pia." Gina stopped in her path. "What the hell are you doing?"

That was a very good question. One Pia didn't want to answer. She walked around her former friend, continuing on to the hotel.

"Rumor has it, you're angling for a position in the administration. Is that true?"

The question felt cold in Pia's ears. She heard herself retort quickly, "Once upon a time, rumor had it you were sleeping with the Brazilian coach. Was that true?"

"Yes."

Pia turned back and faced Gina at the extraordinary admission. Gina had scooped the rest of the press on World Cup strategy and vehemently denied accusations of using sex for access later. Several years and a career change muted the past. Whole floods had passed under that bridge. Could the same passage of time purify Roche and Hunter?

"Tell me what's going on, Pia." Gina approached her. "I'm not buying your bullshit. Two viral videos in two days. Veronica Lodge Hunter in the background of each. You're smart. You used to pick a path through a defense a week before the game. You always played it the way you planned it. You're a strategist, Pia. Always were, always will be. What's the long game here? What are you doing?"

The sharp accusation coming from a former friend struck Pia hard. Definitely out of her league. Political reporting had toughened Gina. If Pia were smart, she'd blow off this interview by outrunning the young mother and seeking Veronica's advice. But she had to respect Gina's tenacity. Afterall, Gina got up three hours before her peers and tracked Pia down. That had to count for something.

Pia carefully considered her response.

"I'm a businesswoman," Pia said. "It benefits the employees and customers of my business if I am close to any administration rather than in conflict with it. That's what I'm doing."

"Some people say there is a video of you shooting Viktor Popov nine times in cold blood." Gina's eyes narrowed. "Are you working toward asking Roche for a pardon?"

Pia's breath left her. Where had that come from? Roche had threatened to release the video. Was he building anticipation for it by teasing the story? Fear chilled her body and emptied her resolve. Hours of executive training for press relations vanished at Gina's question. None of Hunter's training had prepared her to deal with her biggest crime. A crime she'd hoped would remain forever hidden.

Pia reverted to her instinctive reaction to adversity. She turned and ran at a pace fewer than ten women in the world could keep. Gina didn't even try.

Back at the hotel, Pia lifted weights, she showered, she tried to read a book, she flicked on the TV, she paced her suite, she strolled the lobby. Dawn broke, people filled the street below her window. She still couldn't call Hunter. She would have to wait for their scheduled breakfast meeting. The way they'd left things the night before, she couldn't come crawling for help now. It would weaken her already dismal standing with the woman. Usually, Pia wouldn't give a damn. Hunter was being difficult to please as a power play.

What made it worse was that her mother was right. She just wasn't ready for the national press. They went after blood.

The call came, breakfast waited at the nearby Hyatt. Secret Service agents Dan and Catherine came to escort her for the short walk. A few months earlier, they had been reassigned to a broom-closet job after doing Pia a favor. Once they'd regained their previous seniority, they'd been fired for insubordination by Chuck Roche over a fight Pia had started. They were later reinstated after a groundswell of support from the entire Secret Service.

They rode the elevator to the ground floor in silence. Pia broke the tension. "I see you're back in the civil service. Everything turned out well then?"

Catherine gave her a cold, over-the-shoulder glare. "We get to work overtime—without pay during the shutdowns—the president is a prick, the vice president is a bitch. Yeah, turned out great."

Dan said, "Whatever you're up to this time, please leave us out of it."

It was the last thing either of them said during the long, silent walk to the Hyatt and up the elevator to Hunter's suite. Catherine pointed to a chair at the vice president's table. Pia took it.

Without a greeting, Hunter held up her phone to *Politica's* website. The headline and subhead read, *Pia Sabel Chooses Oldest Profession: Better to have Economic Ties with the Administration than Stand on Moral Principles.*

"You gave an interview." Hunter sat behind a coffee cup and a croissant.

No other food adorned the room service table. Pia had burned two thousand calories before Hunter pulled off her eye mask. Her stomach growled. Hunter looked disgusted.

Pia looked for a waiter or butler.

"You didn't say anything about me." Hunter pulled her phone back. "It's all about you and your company. You're not even running it."

"I did what you told me." Pia got up and retrieved a room service menu from a nearby table. "Tease the news, don't blurt it out."

Pia recalled the elaborate Secret Service rituals. She had to give them her order so that no unvetted people came and went from the suite. She got the attention of the young man at the door. "Yogurt, ham and cheese omelet, toasted bagel, cream cheese, lox and onions, and a big bowl of steel cut oats."

Hunter's brow rose as Pia took her seat. "Hungry?"

Pia shrugged.

When they were alone, Hunter said, "You seem to think this is a game. We're not playing for gold medals here. We're playing for people's lives. Chuck Roche came this close to issuing a shoot-to-kill order for Wilkes and 'and anyone aiding and abetting her.' That means your people in Mumbai. I talked him out of it. The Secretary of State and his chief of staff think he's done something criminal—again. It's so bad, they won't even tell me what it is."

Hunter rose and went to the window. She waved Pia over to join her. Together, they looked at the people on the street far below.

"Pia, I am all that stands between these citizens and Chuck's war with Saudi Arabia. You know how that war will go, every breathing Muslim in the world will descend on us. World War III. And some of those countries have nuclear weapons. We are inches from the end of civilization." Hunter took a deep, solemn breath. "I am all that stands between their lives and that lunatic. If you don't do as I say, tomorrow's breakfast could be served in hell."

CHAPTER 22

VERONICA HUNTER STORMED THROUGH THE West Wing to an empty Oval Office. Roche's secretary pointed her to the Cabinet Room. She glanced in the open door.

Chuck Roche leaned over a massive map stretched across the expansive meeting table. He wore a suit with epaulets that looked vaguely military, like a Brioni uniform. On either side of him stood generals and admirals in real uniforms with all their medals shining. They held long pointers. The pointers moved toy ships, airplanes, and tanks around on the map. Roche used his silver handled cane to move some aircraft carriers. Opposite the performers, a wall of media photographers snapped and flashed away at the scene.

A finger tapped her shoulder. When she turned, Hartwell Thomas gave her a nod toward the hallway. She followed him and nodded good morning to the first nephew as he passed by.

After a few silent steps, Hunter grabbed Thomas's arm and made him face her. She pointed back to the Cabinet Room. "What the hell was so important about this that he had to summon me straight off the plane from Denver?"

"He didn't summon you, madam Vice President." Thomas hung his head. "I did. Sorry for the subterfuge. Something…" He looked up and down the hall. "We need to speak privately."

He led her down the hall to a small office. Waiting inside the cramped space were Nora Ratched and the Secretary of Defense, Robert O'Brien. Hunter smelled fear and sweat.

"Well, Nora," Hunter said, "your gang's grown by fifty percent. How many more will come crawling out of the woodwork?"

"How's the Sabel girl coming along?" Ratched asked without looking up.

"Fine." Hunter examined O'Brien, who also hung his head.

"You're supposed to be getting intel out of her about Mumbai." Ratched still didn't look up. "What have you learned?"

"That you're not as smart as she is." Hunter waited for the sharp look from Ratched before continuing. "What happened that you needed to see me?"

A disaster had brought these people together, and it hadn't gotten better in the last twenty-four hours. She had a hunch what their problem was but would have to play her hand carefully. There is opportunity in disaster. Hunter always believed that.

"Pia gave me some interesting news." Hunter waited until their heads came up. "She believes her people will apprehend the Redjackets who kidnapped Wilkes within hours."

"Holy shit," O'Brien rubbed his face.

Ratched looked sick. Thomas shook his head.

"That's not good?" Hunter asked. Her lie worked. Pia had said no such thing, but, as she suspected, these people feared that outcome. "We don't want an American admiral rescued?"

"We don't want the Redjackets caught with—" Ratched stopped herself from saying more. "They tie back to…" She pointed toward the Cabinet Room.

"How many Redjackets does she think there are?" O'Brien asked.

"Pia's not on board yet." Hunter shrugged. "It's a delicate conversation. And I don't know what to ask because—thankfully— you've kept me in the dark."

The three of them didn't offer any details. They stared at the floor.

"Time to fess up, kids." Hunter snapped her fingers, drawing every eye to hers. "You're standing in a tiny office, looking for the solution to a problem so bad you can't even say it out loud. Don't sugar coat it, tell me what it is."

"We can't win the war." O'Brien straightened up. "We can take down the Saudis in an afternoon but…"

He turned away.

Ratched looked at him with disgust. She said, "Every NATO country says if we don't produce the Weapons of Mass Destruction, they won't send so much as a tow truck to help with—"

"The Saudis sank a ship, there aren't—" Hunter stopped herself. "Right. They looked like idiots when they went with us into Iraq only to discover we never had any WMD intel to begin with. They're not going down that road again."

"Worse," Ratched said, "Pakistan and Turkey have stated through channels they'll defend the Saudis. Russia, China, and India have told us they will not sit idly by while we invade a sovereign nation, again. Draw a line from Dakar to Shanghai and every country along the way will stand against us."

"The lot of you were fine with the Saudi war until it became clear we couldn't win it." Hunter hurled her words at them.

"We expected a few allies." Thomas shook his head. "We thought some country or other would have the decency to back us in our hour of need."

"After we told all of them to pound sand?" Hunter asked. "So, where are we with the naval investigation?"

"Shortly before five Redjackets tried to fake Wilkes's suicide," O'Brien shot a nasty look at Thomas, "Wilkes told her chief of staff she had evidence the sinking was an inside job. So far, we've kept a lid on that."

"Suicide? Nice touch." Hunter waited until their surprised gazes met hers. "OK. We recall the Redjackets, let Sabel win that battle. She brings Wilkes back alive, we get evidence that buries President Roche, he resigns in shame."

All three of them turned their heads away in different directions.

"Jesus," Hunter said. "You're all involved? Fucking brilliant. All right. Let's not worry about that right now. Wilkes testifies in Congress, we apologize to the Saudis, Roche resigns, I pardon you—just like GHW Bush did with the Iran-Contra conspirators. Won't that work?"

"He's gone and taken direct control of the Redjackets," Thomas said. "A pardon won't do us much good if we're dead."

"He threatened us," O'Brien said. "He sent three squads after Wilkes.

Told them it was a competition. Whoever comes back with the head of Annie Wilkes wins. When I found out, I objected. It's crazy. He listened, then he acted nice. At two in the morning, someone called me and told me to look out my window. Fifty Redjackets holding shiny gasoline cans stood in a circle around my house. They didn't do anything, they just stood there." O'Brien faced Hunter. "My bodyguards were with them, Veronica. My goddamn security detail."

He glared at Hartwell Thomas.

"You should've let me handle it," Ratched said. "We agreed—"

"I never signed up for murdering an admiral." O'Brien leaned into Ratched's face with his fists clenched. He huffed and faced Thomas. "I had no idea what your people were capable of."

"You joined the Roche administration," Hunter said. "When it all comes out, that alone will be enough for a public hanging." She let her words float in the air for a moment. "Unless you fall in line and do as I tell you, we're all going down. But don't worry. I've gotten out of worse jams than this."

"That doesn't surprise me," O'Brien sneered.

"Don't play high and mighty with me, mister Ivy League." Hunter glared at the man. "You joined up to feed contracts back to your former employer. A simple game of graft. One that will make your stock options explode in value. You want us to believe rigging public bids is where you draw the line in criminal activities? You're here. You're in. Now get your head in the game and quit whining."

All four huffed out anger like sparring prize fighters.

"Let me recap what I heard you say." Hunter stared each of them down. "No matter what facts you put in front of him, the president refuses to see the escalation problem, right? OK. And we know his morality begins and ends with what's best for him. He has no concept of collateral damage. He'll be fine with escalating the war as long as people rally round the flag and him. Roche will survive, of that, he's dead certain. He doesn't care about the rest of us. And you guys fear all that recklessness will cause a backlash that will expose your involvement. Is that a fair summary?"

The group muttered their agreement.

"Your boys are out of control," Hunter said to Thomas. "What happened?"

"Chuck found all their contact information. He has them reporting directly to him now. They're never going to answer any of my calls or texts."

Hunter thought for a moment. They needed Wilkes to die quietly. With Roche ordering a competition, gunfights in the streets of Mumbai were eventualities. Up until now, all they were asking was to guarantee pardons. Getting involved in solving the problem could implicate the VP herself to an irredeemable point. The risk was astronomical. It was a potential suicide mission, nearly impossible to pull off, but they needed her.

Hunter loved to be needed.

"What you're telling me is," she said, "we're screwed if we save Wilkes, and we're screwed if we don't. We need control of the Redjackets."

"You think we haven't tried that?" Ratched asked. "There are more Redjackets than active military. You think Chuck's going to give them up because you ask nicely?"

"He needs an incentive," Hunter said. "Since you're already giving him blowjobs for free, you'll need to try something else."

"You bitch!" Ratched clawed at Hunter.

Thomas and O'Brien caught her arms before she drew blood. Thomas said, "Stop it, you two. We need this problem solved."

"What incentive do you have in mind?" O'Brien asked Hunter.

"I'll ask him." Hunter shrugged. "Worth a shot."

Ratched grabbed her arm. "Do you think you can pull it off?"

"You better hope I do." Hunter looked at the conspirators one at a time. "I'm all you've got."

She peeked out the door and waited until no one was walking by. Then she headed for the Cabinet Room and waited outside until the media began filing out.

She swam upstream through the crowd to where Chuck Roche gabbed with real generals. They looked decidedly unamused at his jokes. As a matter of fact, they had no interest in his photo op. They politely brushed aside his suggestions telling him they would, "study the idea." Then they left. Hunter closed the door behind the last man.

"Oh, Chuck," she crooned and stood across the table from him, "you look so regal. The emperors of Rome never looked so," she paused for emphasis, "commanding. The interns must be lining up to kneel at your waist."

"It went rather well." He tapped his cane on the table. "Look, we have a map of the Middle East with ships of the Fifth Fleet and everything."

He pushed one of the ships back and forth with his cane.

Hunter looked at the tableau. One of the models looked like an obsolete battleship. She reached across the table, picked it up and examined it. Written in tiny lettering along the side: *USS Arizona.* She picked up another ship that read, *USS Indianapolis.* One of the carriers bore the designation, *USS Hornet.* All three of which were lost in World War II.

"They told you this was the Fifth Fleet?" She caught herself. "It's a perfect representation. There's so much intricate detail."

Roche tapped his cane on the floor to get her attention. "I'm thinking of having a military uniform made out of this. Add some medals, some gold braid. What do you think?"

She inhaled long and deep. A president who never served wearing a military uniform was so banana republic she wanted to laugh in his face. "You would outshine the generals and admirals. It would be perfect if Congress finally declares war."

"What's wrong with those bastards?" Roche marched the length of the room and back. "Everyone wants this war. The sooner we get started, the sooner they'll enshrine me the way they did Abraham Lincoln. But Congress sits on their hands. They're waiting for Wilkes to surface. Well. News flash. She's never going to surface. I've seen to that."

"Good for you, Chuck," she purred. "Wait. What do you mean, you've seen to it? You can't be involved in any ground operations to… What have you done?"

"Don't worry." He smiled and tapped his cane. "Channels and CIA and special ops take too long. And they insist on having written orders. Fuck that. I used the Redjackets."

"No." Hunter covered her mouth. "Chuck, you didn't talk to them directly, did you? Tell me you didn't."

"They're loyal to me," he pounded his chest. "I'm Zenith Man. They know it. Finally, there are people who get me. I tell them to jump, and they jump. They don't have to do an environmental impact study. They don't need to check their protocols. They don't say, let me consult the uniform … military code of … whatever."

"Uniform Code of Military Justice," Hunter said. "But they do. Unless they want to be tried for murder."

"They won't get caught. I sent three squads and told them it was a competition. They love to win."

Hunter gasped dramatically and stepped back and held her hand to her chest. "Chuck, the winner isn't the problem. What about the two losing squads? Did they record your call? Did they save your texts? Will they offer evidence to Congress in exchange for immunity? Will India offer them a plea deal? Have you ever seen the inside of an Indian jail cell? They won't last a day. Why do you trust them?"

Roche looked confused. Then angry. He swept his cane across the map, flinging the ships to the floor. "Unlike you, they're loyal to me. They'll die for me. And they know I'll pardon them."

"Chuck, India is not an ally of ours. If they catch the Redjackets, they'll parade them before the international media. You can't pardon them over there."

Roche pinched his eyes and thought for a long time. "You're right. I should have someone else handle the Redjackets for me. That way I can deny I knew anything about it. But I can't trust Thomas. He built that organization; he'll use them against me. Who can I trust to handle them for me? It would have to be someone no one would suspect. Someone who would never draw suspicion. Any ideas?"

The hairs on Hunter's neck rose as if she'd grabbed a live electric wire. This was the opportunity she wanted, but the feel was all wrong. Eager people are always suspicious, but he seemed more suspicious than usual.

"Nora Ratched fits that bill." Hunter bit her thumbnail as she thought. "Maybe your Defense Secretary, is he loyal?"

"What about you, Veronica?" Roche put his hands on the table and leaned as far across it as he could. "Wouldn't you be the best person to run the Redjackets?"

"Whoa!" Hunter growled at him. "Don't you dare try to saddle me with your subversive conspiracies. I'm not going to take the fall. The last time I arranged killers for you, they were supposed to surveil Pia's parents, not strangle them to death. You think I'm going down for you? No way."

Hunter turned and strode straight for the door. She moved with purpose and determination.

"Wait!" Roche called out and trotted to intercept her. "Here, take this phone. It's the command phone. It has all the phone numbers in it. I'll send a group chat telling them I don't have time. They're to take instructions from you and only you."

She stopped with one hand on the door. He approached, holding out a phone in one hand. It might as well have been a rattlesnake.

"That's not a phone, it's a ticket to a lethal-injection at Terre Haute Penitentiary." She turned up her nose, spun around and slammed the door behind her.

CHAPTER 23

I DROVE CHOPRA'S TATA WHILE she protested from the backseat. We knew the Singh family lived in the section of Bandra West called the Promenade. But the neighborhood counted a million people. It's a boulevard of ocean-facing high-rise condos. We didn't have an exact address. I figured Chopra did, but she wasn't sharing. Since I had no idea how to read the alphabet on the SUV's map or understand half the street signs, I drove until we were thoroughly lost. Eventually, we came to rest staring at the rusted hulks of ships in the Coal Bunder district. I parked. We got out.

Mercury strolled around the back of the truck, inhaled deeply and patted his chest. *I love the places you find, homie! Look at all this soot and grime. If you were a location scout, this is where you'd shoot a post-apocalyptic movie.*

I said, *If you have anything to tell me about where to find Dhanpal's grandparents, this would be a good time.*

Mercury laughed and strolled across a slag heap.

Chopra crossed her arms and scowled. "Are you worried about your friend, the girl with the wild hair?"

"Tania will show up." I smiled. "Can't get rid of her if I tried."

We took Chopra with us and left her Tata behind. I suspected her people were monitoring its location. We snagged two motorized rickshaws because of their anonymity and lack of GPS. They dropped us on the far side of Mumbai. By mid-afternoon, we were on a rail system back to downtown. All the stations were crowded with entrepreneurs hawking cologne in the bathrooms or pay-per-use cellphones in the open areas. We caught another pair of rickshaws. And so went most of the day. If any of her people were following us, we'd lost them. We were what the spies called *clean*.

Finally, Chopra broke down.

"I might know where they live then." She huffed and clutched her purse. "But I need my phone back."

"Sorry, I tossed it on a coal tender heading for Shanghai." Which was the truth. One must assume the IB can track a cellphone the same way everyone can, like Apple, Google, Amazon and small-town cops.

She rolled her eyes. But it worked. By rush hour, we stood outside an uninteresting building of well-heeled Mumbaikars. She waited in the condo's marble lobby with Miguel while Cody kept watch on the street.

Vishal and I went to the fifth-floor apartment and knocked.

No one answered. We knocked several more times until the neighbor came out. She was old and wrinkled and gray and angry. She argued with Vishal for a long time then slammed the door.

My translator and tour guide turned to me. His hands flopped at his sides. "No liking Singhs the lady. Bad boy Dhanpal maybe. Many Americans once came. Five of them grouped. Singhs go away much with violence. Called police she believed. None were coming still."

It took me a minute to unscramble his words, then I said, "Did the Americans who kidnapped the Singhs have red patches inside their jackets?"

Vishal knocked on the old lady's door. They discussed it. She gave me another disdainful glare and slammed the door again.

"Inside jackets," he pointed to an imaginary jacket, "yes the squares red."

We went back to the lobby where I filled the others in on the story. Our gazes bounced off each other while we drew blanks on what to do next. Dhanpal's grandparents were our only idea. Now we had three people to rescue.

A resident couple came in off the street. They looked at us with suspicion. Chopra cornered them. They spoke at length. They were disgusted at the mention of the Singh family and darted away.

"They don't think much of Dhanpal's associates," Chopra said. "They seem to think he associates with prostitutes."

Vishal turned to me. "Women you said no."

Mercury elbowed Chopra out of the way. *You get it yet, dawg? Congress Jacob would never go. Aw, c'mon, tell me my favorite disciple isn't as dumb as he looks. Think, young blood, think. What kind of congress are we talking about here?*

I said, *I don't do politics.*

Bro, you also don't do... what? Mercury ran out of patience. *You hired Vishal, why not listen to him?*

I said, *The guy is barely literate, why would I ... wait a second. The first definition in the dictionary isn't about legislative bodies.*

I turned to the others. "I know what it means! *Congress Jacob would never go.*"

At that moment, a janitor's closet door opened. Tania crashed out along with a mop and bucket. "What's the answer?"

I turned to Chopra and thumbed at my sprawled associate. "Told you she'd show up."

Tania picked herself off the floor and dusted herself off and noticed Chopra. "What the hell is she doing here?"

Chopra's inclusion in our expedition meant I couldn't explain my theory. At times like these, a nice diversion comes in handy.

"Why did you volunteer for this trip, anyway?" I tilted my head at Tania. "Does this mean the dinner with Jaz didn't go well?"

"What the fuck is wrong with men?" Her eyes lit up with anger. "Not a single one of you can commit to a cupcake much less a relationship."

"I can." Cody decided it was a good time to come out of wall-flower mode. Boy, was he wrong.

Chopra and Tania silenced the young man with steel gazes.

"Spot on," Chopra said. "What happened?"

Mercury said, *You waited this whole trip for the right moment to shut her up by asking about Jaz Jenkins? You be the divinely inspired mortal of the hour, my brutha. Did you think that up on your own or has Minerva been whispering in your ear?*

I said, *How am I going to get rid of Chopra now that I know where Dhanpal is?*

Mercury said, *Rid? What's wrong with you, homes? She's your hostage. Your get-out-of-India card.*

Making a hostage out of an IB agent sounded risky. So did leaving her behind.

The women commiserated over elusive bachelors while I filled Miguel and Cody in on Dhanpal's whereabouts. When the ladies realized they were missing out, they insisted on getting the intel. They pushed into our midst.

Decision time. I'd already ditched Chopra twice, stolen her car, and forced her to come with us. We could tie her up in the Singh's apartment while we rescued Dhanpal. We could take her with us and risk having a brigade of Indian Para Commandos crash our party. Or, we could take her along and hope for the best. But, there is always a better option.

"If Tania got here before us, what are the chances your people are watching us right now?" I asked Chopra. "Too big a risk. We're going for another loop around the city."

During our public transportation ride, Radhika Chopra explained where she'd learned all the foul language she'd thrown at me back at the high-rise. She had been raised in London and attended Cambridge before coming home to join India's Ministry of Home Affairs. She had broken up with her boyfriend of five years because he gave her a ring for her birthday that was not an engagement ring. Tania commiserated with her.

We switched to rickshaws, then busses, then cabs, and more rickshaws. Somewhere after three in the morning, Chopra was tired, yawning and asking for coffee. The rest of us had discreetly downed Provigils, the soldier's go-to stay-awake pills. The streets emptied before I was confident we were no longer followed by Chopra's team.

We turned into Kamathipura, the district where legal prostitution still exists. The streets were filthy and stank almost as bad as Dharavi. Pimps and hookers wandered the wide sidewalks offering end-of-evening deals. Propositions that lacked even a hint of excitement or enthusiasm. Even Tania and Radhika were offered some fascinating opportunities. Which they turned down. The brothels lining the road were shops the size of two shipping containers stacked on top of each other. The bottom floors housed primitive bars and lounges. The main attraction was upstairs where customers were allowed to go only after pimp-scrutiny that ranged from a gangster-stare to a pat-down to the straight-up robbery of drunks.

I didn't know that from checking it out. I'd heard stories from soldiers coming back from leave. Dhanpal and I once listened to a lengthy and detailed story about such an expedition from a new recruit to Sabel Security. He'd tried every brothel in Mumbai and concluded that a place called Congress House had the finest women in the world. Dhanpal and I had looked at each other and said in unison, "I would never go there."

We approached Congress House from an angled alley. Bigger than any other brothel by a factor of ten, it was rocking. The lights were on, people partied in the bar, music, and smoke poured out the front door. Two tired Americans in suits leaned against the wall near the front door.

A breeze blew, and a jacket flapped, revealing a red square of silk.

CHAPTER 24

PIA CONSIDERED BLOWING THE WHOLE thing off. It was a beautiful day in early May, she had the McLaren's top down, and Skyline Drive in Shenandoah National Park was only an hour from town. She pulled in to the Mayflower Hotel and stopped and thought and took a deep breath. Freedom of the open road beckoned.

In the hotel was another siren call: vengeance.

She tossed her keys to the wide-eyed valet and resigned herself to another meeting with the mother. One she was determined to conclude with some form of approval. There would be considerable effort involved, but she could win over the tough campaigner who held Congress at bay for four years. It wasn't impossible.

She walked past the elevator to the stairwell and began the five-floor climb to the Reelect Roche Campaign headquarters.

Hunter's interest in Jacob and his team gave her pause. As did Gina Wind's knowledge of who killed Viktor Popov. That leak could've come from Hunter, but more likely came from Roche. Then again, for all Pia knew it could have come from the Russians.

Dan and Catherine, the reluctant Secret Service agents, met her at the stairwell. They were not in a chatty mood when they walked her to a large suite. It had been converted into a cramped office filled with staffers. Hunter stood at the far end giving orders to someone. She saw Pia and waved her over.

The worker glanced over his shoulder, saw Pia and disappeared. Hunter opened a door and led them into a small but quiet office space. "Given your early rising routine, I presume you had breakfast. Coffee?"

"Why did you backhand my Krueger-takedown video?" Pia asked.

"Here's a lesson in real life," Hunter waved away her question. "When a powerful person gives you time and attention, the first public thing you do is honor her. You chose to make your two appearances about the great and powerful Pia Sabel. My tweet was a simple reminder of who got you into those forums."

Pia fought her rising anger. Blowing up would make things worse and distance her from her goals. Then she caught another glimpse of the bracelet hanging from Hunter's purse. Had Hunter been at that game? Pia said, "You're right, as usual. What should I have done?"

"Mention what an honor it is to be here and thank the woman who brought you. Then attack whoever."

"I could've done that." Pia tried to look pensive while she fought the urge to snap at Hunter's reluctant motherhood.

"At least you followed your boxing coach's advice." Hunter poured herself a cup of coffee and waved the stainless-steel carafe at Pia. "What was it he used to say, 'Hit first; hit fast; hit hard; hit last?'"

"How do you know so much about my teenage years?" Pia nodded at the coffee offer. "Were you stalking me?"

"We have a problem with Roche." Hunter held out a mug. "How close are your people to finding Admiral Wilkes?"

Pia considered denying she had people in India again, but they both knew better. Jacob had arrived by Sabel jet before dropping off the grid. That was easy to track for any intelligence agency.

"I don't know." Pia held the mug while Hunter poured. "I'm not saying that because I don't trust you—and make no mistake, I don't trust you—I'm telling you because they went offline."

"The vaunted Sabel Technology system that no one can hack is not reliable?"

"We had this discussion."

"Oh right," Hunter added cream and sugar to her coffee and started to offer the same to Pia before remembering Pia drank it black. "Chuck told you he has Redjacket moles in your company."

"Are we on track to destroy him?" Pia blew across her mug. "You promised that's where this would lead."

"You know what Helmut von Moltke said, 'No battle plan survives contact with the enemy.' We have to adjust. The plan has gotten bigger than the two of us. There are others who have tired of his—"

"You promised it would take a month at most."

"As I was saying," Hunter sipped, "there are adjustments to be made. Your people landed in jail. Someone had to spring them. That cost me favors. Politics works just like business, you need a favor, you do a favor. We all help each other."

"You got them out of jail?" Pia squinted.

"There were a few people involved," Hunter said. "Now I owe them favors. And we're not done yet. Chuck is threatening to release the Kill-Video."

"Someone's already leaked its existence to the press."

Hunter's expression of shock looked genuine to Pia. Although Hunter was hard to read.

"Who?" Hunter asked.

"Gina Wind asked me about it yesterday."

"We need to work together more than ever, Pia." Hunter took her arm and gave a gentle squeeze. "You don't trust me, but you must. Several high-level people are looking to take Chuck out of office. We have to include them in the process. They want to know what's going on with Wilkes. What can you tell me?"

"Just what I told you, I don't know anything."

"What can you find out?"

Pia looked her over with a suspicious gaze.

"Need I remind you that Hartwell Thomas is itching to take my spot as VP? If he gets more power, no one will ever get the truth out of this administration. They're working on getting rid of term limits. They're going to call him Zenith Man, the most perfect person. And this perfect person wants a war that will consume every Christian and Muslim in the world. Thousands of lives are at stake, Pia. Thomas's Redjackets will intimidate anyone who stands against them. They'll make the Nazi Brownshirts look like children. We must work together."

Pia's head swirled with conflicting concepts. How could she trust Veronica Lodge Hunter? A list of the woman's crimes against the nation could earn her the death penalty. But the alternative future she painted was more than bleak. Was Hunter telling the truth about liberating Jacob and his team? Was she telling the truth about others in the administration? Was Hartwell Thomas the source of Roche's evil power?

"I'll find out what I can." Pia took Hunter's arm. "First, you have to tell me something I don't know. Prove to me I can trust you."

Hunter held Pia's gaze. Pia could almost see the wheels turning in her head, deciding what to share and what to keep to herself.

"I'm not sure of this," Hunter said, "But I overheard a rumor. Three squads of Redjackets are hunting for Wilkes and anyone helping her. Roche made it a competition. The first one to find Wilkes is the winner."

Pia felt dizzy, Jacob and his team were being hunted like animals. The need to get word to him squeezed out all other thoughts.

"You need to report this." Pia leaned over the shorter woman. "You need to go public. Call Emily Dominguez at the *Post*."

"And have Roche release incriminating details from my administration? He'll push me out, and Thomas will be in. I'm telling you this so you can save your team. You can't tell anyone—anyone at all—or I'm dead meat."

"That is a good exchange of information," Pia said. "I'll contact them and find out what I can. But just asking my people to make contact could go straight back to Roche. I need to know, who is the mole in my company?"

CHAPTER 25

HUNTER LEFT THE CAMPAIGN HEADQUARTERS and made her way to the White House five minutes before the scheduled meeting with the president. When she poked her head in Thomas's office door, he shooed away the three people. She stepped in and stared out the window with her arms crossed.

Hunter said, "Sabel's people are off the grid. She can't get hold of them."

"Doesn't matter none," Thomas said. "Roche said they've walked into a trap. That problem should be all over soon."

She kept her gasp to a minimum. If Thomas were right, Pia would think the worst of Hunter. Right when she'd begun to see the good side of her daughter. She had come to admire—and loathe—the spirit in that girl. Part of her wanted to drop out of the Roche administration and be a mother to Pia. And part of her knew Pia would never accept her no matter what she did.

She held a steady gaze on Thomas. "Which means the next problem will be starting."

They shared a dejected moment of silence. The Indian government would not tolerate Americans killing each other in the streets of Mumbai. An investigation beyond the administration's control would begin, and it would lead right to a desk in the White House. Roche was in deep. Thomas was in deeper. Ratched and O'Brien must have gotten into the mix somewhere as well.

"Chuck said you went and refused to take over the Redjackets." Thomas had a superior tone in his voice and a disdainful look in his eye.

"He didn't offer me control. He tested me. If I'd agreed, he would've yanked it back."

"You had a shot. You turned it down. You lied to us."

"It wasn't legit." Hunter tried to keep her voice down. "It was just a setback. I tried to con him into giving me control, but he figured it out. There was nothing I could do."

Both their phones buzzed with an alert to a presidential tweet. They simultaneously read the latest blast.

"Who the hell told him he could issue a shoot-to-kill order?" Hunter shouted at Thomas.

"I brought in the attorneys. They told him in no uncertain—"

"He named Jacob Stearne along with Wilkes." Hunter felt sick.

"He's gone and done it." Thomas moaned. "He tweeted an order to commit murder. How in God's name are we going to spin this one?"

Thomas's secretary opened the door to remind him they were wanted in the Cabinet Room.

Hunter led the way. Nora Ratched joined them in the hall. Robert O'Brien and a new guy, the Secretary of Homeland Security, Ed Rochester waited by the door.

When she saw them, she whispered over her shoulder to Ratched, "Rochester, is he in this too?"

"He came looking to save his career."

They greeted each other in somber tones. No one made a move to enter the meeting. When Hunter peeked around the corner, she saw why. Chuck Roche stood at the center of the table in full military uniform, pointing his cane at the map of the Middle East, while an artist painted his portrait.

It was Hunter's fault and she knew it. He'd mentioned the uniform plan. She could've shot it down then. Instead, she blew smoke up his skirt. Now, someone had to tell Zenith Man his uniform would piss off everyone who'd served. She patted her face with her hand and took a deep breath.

Hunter coughed. The artist looked up with a pained expression, begging to be dismissed. She obliged. "We have a meeting scheduled, Mr. President."

"I can work from the photos, sir." The artist grabbed his paints and easel. "There's no need to take up your valuable time."

"You sure?" Roche looked up. "I want the finest work you've ever done or I'll arbitrate your fee."

"The subject matter alone dictates the resulting quality, sir." The little man scurried through Hunter and her associates like a rat sprinting through the rubble of an earthquake in progress.

Thomas and the others approached Roche to kiss his fingers. He held up a hand and pointed at the chairs facing him. "No time for your rituals today. I have this all set up exactly the way it needs to be for the portrait. I don't want you screwing it up."

They dutifully stepped back and stood at attention in the space vacated by the artist.

Roche sat down in his chair. "Why the sour expressions, people?"

He swept his hand toward the chairs, granting them permission to sit.

"Your tweet ... it was," Ratched couldn't find more words.

"Surprising," O'Brien chimed in. "That was a bold step."

"The treachery and treason of Annie Wilkes cannot go unanswered." Roche slammed his cane on the table, upsetting all the World War II models. "We will send a message to anyone plotting with the Saudis. We will be resolute and unwavering. No one can get away with aiding an enemy of the United States. I am taking care of our enemies one person at a time. If Congress doesn't approve my declaration, I'll destroy the whole Saudi kingdom myself. Why? Because I'm the only one who seems to care about this country. I'm all that stands between us and a bunch of towelheaded terrorists who want to rape your sisters."

All five of them inhaled at once.

"What's that noise mean?" Roche peered at them. "You're not up to the job? Don't you care about defending our country?"

"We were expecting to use more legal ... uhm, conventional channels," O'Brien said.

"You committed a crime, Chuck." Hunter rapped her knuckles on the table to get his attention. "You tied yourself directly to a premeditated murder, and you did it on a public forum. You already sent the killers, and you just sent the orders. You're fucked. And—thank you very much—you fucked the rest of us along with you."

Her four associates faced her as if she'd committed the crime.

"Why?" Roche asked. "Presidents order assassinations all the time."

"Executive Order 12333 specifically bans political assassinations."

"What about all the drone strikes?"

"Those are part of the War on Terror," Hunter said, "authorized by Congress and justified by Obama for use in 'areas of active hostilities.' There's a Top-Secret list attached to Executive Order 15388, Enemy Belligerents in the War on Terror. But Mumbai does not qualify as an area of active hostility. Nor does Saudi Arabia for that matter. Not until Congress approves your war."

A thoughtful silence descended on the room. Roche examined his fingernails. The others stared at the table.

"I've made some adjustments to that order." Roche rubbed his chin while he thought. "So what ties me to the Redjackets?"

"The fact that you sent them there."

Roche pulled a phone out of his pocket. It had a red back and a picture of President Roche in his new uniform on the front. He spun it across the map, sending several model ships flying in different directions. "I didn't have anything to do with them. You did. Remember when you said you would take care of Wilkes? I did some research and figured out how you were doing it. That's your phone. That's how you communicate with them. Do you see her phone right there in front of her, Nora? You see it, Hartwell?"

The phone slid to a stop an inch from the edge, directly in front of Hunter.

Every eye in the room turned to the phone. And from there, rose to Hunter. She felt them more than saw them. Her gaze was fixed on the phone. It may as well have been a nuclear bomb.

"Yes, Mr. President," Thomas said. "That there would be Madam Vice President's phone. I've seen her carrying it everywhere she goes."

"That's a special CIA phone," Ratched said. "The encryption is the highest level. No one can eavesdrop on that type of phone. They're all accounted for under tight security. I'm sure we'll find out that one was assigned to the VP, sir."

Hunter gave her coconspirators a slow, icy stare. Thomas gawked at the table. Ratched returned Hunter's glare with equal intensity.

The Vice President looked back at the phone. Last night she laid out a plan based on reverse-psychology. Had things gone according to that plan, Roche would do what he just did. But that was before he publicly ordered a murder. Now, her own plan had come back to bite her. And hard.

If she touched it, she would own it. Everyone in the room had asked her to help. She'd lorded it over them. Now they would have leverage of their own. She could feel them breathing a sigh of relief. They weren't in the clear, but they were no longer her dogs. That could be a problem. From here on in, the palace coup was on unsteady ground. They could stand with her and dispose of Chuck Roche. Or they could band together without her and depose both the president and vice president in one fell swoop.

They weren't as menacing a coalition as they imagined themselves. Hunter had experience living with packs of dogs that resorted to cannibalism. She could take that risk and win.

There was something else to be considered. The power packed inside that phone was astonishing.

It was a conduit to the most extraordinary weapon the nation had yet seen. Thomas might be whimpering today because he stood on a precipice from which one false step could land him in jail for life. But a week ago, he was a strutting Senator from Texas. He had built a network LinkedIn only dreamed of. Whispered from cubicle to board room, insiders were given promotions. Loyalties were pledged. Promises were made. Connections combined a spectrum of talents into a fantastic labor pool. From blue collar laborers to Fortune 50 executives, they all vowed to act when called upon because their individual cause had been singled out and a solution assured. And this vast pool of energy waited for the unifying leader who would champion their personally energizing issue.

Thomas had been brilliant. Until he made that one fateful mistake. He had actually believed in Chuck Roche.

From that phone, threaded connections could bring fifty men with gas cans to flash-mob the home of the Defense Secretary. With only vague, deniable instructions, the Redjackets had changed the editorial direction of the *Tribune* and the *Herald* and the *National News Network.* The resistance groups in various cities had disbanded in terror. In the right hands, Thomas's formidable little organization could be a force for good.

But time was short. Any seasoned politician would know the downside to promising everyone balm for their outrage. The solution to one problem almost always exacerbated another. As Pia had pointed out, stopping immigration pleased bigots but angered executives looking for cheap engineers. Tax breaks for one group inevitably led to higher taxes for someone else. Or the end of services for both. Before long, half the Redjackets would realize they weren't going to get whatever they were promised. The entire group would fall apart.

Until then, there was only one way to get rid of Roche and preserve her position on top of the rebellious Cabinet members.

Veronica Lodge Hunter picked up the phone. "You want me to take the fall, Chuck? No problem. You know I'd take a bullet for you. There's just one thing you have to do first."

Her four coconspirators gave a quiet sigh of relief. They'd held their breath in fear of being the next to be assigned the poisonous phone should Hunter refuse.

She gave the phone a shove back to Roche. "You need to record a video transferring operations from you to me. Send it to the leadership and leave a copy on the phone in case I run into rogue operators."

Hunter felt an elation lightening her head that was neutralized by a sickening twist in her stomach.

CHAPTER 26

MERCURY LEANED OUT OF THE alley to have a look at Congress House. *Hey homes, you thinking what I'm thinking?*

I said, *I'm thinking that a loving god would've told me where to find Dhanpal yesterday.*

Loving god? Mercury sneered. *Where do you get that crap? Christians and Jews and ... I don't even know how many other wimpy religions are out there peddling that baloney. What loving god blows a volcano on a city? What loving god spins up a petri dish full of Ebola? What loving god lets you fools drop an atom bomb on Hiroshima?* He huffed his disdain. *Besides, brutha, you know I can't be talking shit about your future. Where's the fun in that?*

I said, *OK, what are you thinking then?*

Mercury said, *You've run into smart Redjackets and dumb Redjackets. So why are those two standing in that particular spot?*

It was a good question. We'd circled the city for hours to tire them out, wait for their weakest moment. This was it. But two guys were standing under a light by the entrance. As if this was just another day at the whorehouse. That was not good. My crew knew it too. We exchanged glances that spoke volumes.

Even though I'd kept a short leash on her, Chopra was the only one who could have alerted the Redjackets. Tania pulled the Indian back into the dark corner of the alley. Miguel and Cody and I completed the circle around her.

I asked, "How did they find their way here?"

Radhika Chopra lifted her chin in defiance.

We had checked her out, taken her phone, rifled her purse, even flexed her shoes, everything short of a cavity search, and found nothing. We knew she had no communication devices, no way of her co-workers tracking her after we abandoned her car in the Coal Bunder district.

Dhanpal and I worked on many missions together. His family was as tight as any family I'd ever met. His grandparents would've withstood torture and death rather than give up his hiding place. He wouldn't have told them where he was because that would jeopardize their safety. The Redjackets didn't hear it from the grandparents.

So how did the Redjackets decipher a clue even I had trouble unwinding?

"Two questions," I pushed into Chopra's space. "How did you get word to them? And: you seem like a nice, educated young woman, why in god's name would you betray us to the Redjackets?"

"How would I know how they got here?" She snarled back at me. "There's only two of them. There are four of you. Take them down. Or are you a bunch of bloody cowards?"

Two men under a light is an invitation only a rookie would fall for. The math was simple. Five came for Wilkes. One was dead. Another was wounded. We disarmed and gave a third to the cops. That leaves two from the original crew. Yet, five had kidnapped the Singhs. Which could only mean, reinforcements had arrived. More Redjackets were flanking us while we deliberated.

Tania lost her patience. She grabbed Chopra by the throat. "Why?"

An expression of regret crossed Chopra's face when she saw Tania's anger. They'd shared a moment in their shared struggle against the patriarchy, and now she was regretting it. But only for a second. Then she reclaimed her defiant look.

Vishal dropped to his knees in front of us. "Family is many in India. Threatens did she jail, also death. On behalf of her Vishal calls at depot train. Sorry. Sorry. Sorry. Beating is deserving of me."

Chopra had been speaking Marathi to Vishal every now and then. It had sounded like small talk in pleasant voices. She snuck it right past my ear.

"I'm not going to beat you, Vishal." I pulled him to his feet and gave Chopra my soldier-stare. It's the one seasoned veterans use when they must decide between slitting your throat and watching baseball. Which is the more boring endeavor? All the muscles in your face relax, all hope for excitement vanishes, you resolve yourself to finishing a job as fun as analyzing actuarial tables. In a tense situation, such ennui is disconcerting.

Chopra flinched.

Mercury leaned over her shoulder. *Ennui? You're thinking in three-dollar words. Dude, you been reading books again? I'm almost proud of you.*

I said, *Not now. I'm trying to intimidate her.*

Mercury said, *Good luck.*

Chopra said, "I have orders."

"I'm trying to rescue a friend of mine. We had a deal."

She shrugged. "You nicked my car."

I pushed Vishal away from the others and reached into his pocket and extracted the wad of bills I'd given him. "You can walk right past those guys. They're not looking for locals. You find my man, Dhanpal Singh. You come back with recon, including an exit, and I'll give you all the cash back."

He nodded and walked away into the dark.

Maybe it would work. Maybe not. Next item on my agenda: find the rest of the welcome committee.

Tania held Chopra in a chokehold and stayed in backup mode. Miguel had the pistol he took off the Redjacket back at the hospital. He gave it to Cody who tucked it in his belt as a reserve. We were equalized. Miguel had his size advantage. I had my used-god advantage. Cody had a gun.

Mercury leaned against a boarded-up shop and thumbed over his shoulder into the third darkened alley. *Three on the ground, two on the balcony, three doors down.*

I led the way in with Cody on one side of me and Miguel on the other. Three Redjackets held pistols on us from a position directly below a second-floor railing. Their plan was simple, they were going to shoot us. At least, that's what they wanted us to think. The noise of handguns would draw unwanted attention.

I sprinted forward to rush them. Miguel and Cody followed suit, a half step behind me.

Our suicide mission confused them. They backed up, repositioned themselves and raised their weapons.

As we reached the ambush point, I tugged my comrades' arms and stopped. The men had already timed their jump to land on us. Instead, they landed on the concrete. No matter how easy stunt men make it look on TV, jumping from fifteen feet up stings your feet and ankles. In their moment of agony, we lit into them. Their pistol-packing friends were neutralized by the potential for friendly-fire accidents.

Miguel picked up his man in a bear hug and rammed the guy's head into the nearest wall. That pretty much concluded that Redjacket's participation for the evening. Miguel used the man's body as a shield and began walking toward the shooters.

The other man pulled himself together and swung a cricket bat at us. After ducking it, Cody landed a couple blows on the guy. I slammed an elbow into his lower back as his follow-through turned him away from me. He howled in pain, which opened him to a series of rabbit punches from Cody.

Recalling a trick I'd learned from Ms. Sabel, I pounded my foot into the side of the guy's knee, then powered my other knee into his butt. At that point, the guy had no working legs. An effect that only lasted a couple of seconds. But that was enough time for Cody to land a quick combo to his core followed by another combo to his chin. The man was out.

Cody copied Miguel's method and bear-hugged the guy and started walking forward.

Which left me without a human shield. I grabbed the cricket bat and fell in behind Miguel. He's bigger.

We pushed the three gunmen to the far wall. We knew they weren't going to shoot us because that would bring out the pimps in large numbers. Pimps don't like shootings. It's bad for business. From the looks in the Redjackets' eyes, they knew we knew. Miguel slammed his passed-out hostage into the first man and disarmed him.

The other two brought out blackjacks and got in some nasty licks.

Someone tapped me on the shoulder. I swung the cricket bat as I turned, barely nicking the top of Vishal's head.

He felt the growing lump as he rose up. "Madam Aditi acquaintance I insist. Alone you are."

Not sure what that meant, but he waved me out of the alley toward Congress House. This Madam Aditi might have answers for me in there. She might have Dhanpal. But she might have a gauntlet of death waiting for me too. If the Redjackets were waiting for us outside the place, how many were inside? Somewhere between zero and hundreds. It could be a bloodbath. My imagination dialed up images of armed men raining lead from the balconies. If our enemies weren't inside, how many more were about to jump us in this alley? I looked around and saw nothing.

Vishal waved with growing impatience. He'd betrayed me once. Would he do it again? What about Madam Aditi? I knew nothing about her except her involvement in an ancient and not-exactly-honorable profession.

Cody and Miguel were engaged in a terrible fight against overwhelming odds as one of the concussed Redjackets came back to life. Running out on them was out of the question. My gaze rolled back to the whorehouse. Dhanpal was in there. And he'd been winged by a Redjacket two days ago. He needed help.

"You hurrying are now alone." Vishal gestured with more urgency.

Mercury grinned. *They got this fight handled, my brutha. Monster Slayer never loses. I'm not so sure about Cody. He's kinda small. But don't worry about them. Go have fun with Miss Aditi. She's got Dhanpal. She may as well have you too.*

When I get instructions from god, I follow them. Sometimes. In this case, I caught Miguel's eye. He understood, then body slammed his opponent to the ground, face first. Hope that guy had insurance, he'd be needing new teeth. Mercury was right, as long as the odds were a few to two, Monster Slayer had it under control.

I followed Vishal across the street. The two Redjackets who had stood outside were now held in the arms of four powerful local boys. They looked to me for mercy as I passed them and went inside.

A raucous party was going on. It was dark and smoky. Music so loud the walls and tables and chairs shook. Women danced in revealing but tasteful outfits. They were several classes above the street hustlers we'd seen earlier. The clientele looked a little nicer too, which wasn't saying much. Vishal waved me onward, deeper into the cavernous building. Tough young pimps swarmed in behind me, closing off my retreat.

At the far end of the building, with fifty pimps behind me, Vishal started up a dark stairway. I hesitated at the bottom step. He waved me onward. I looked over my shoulder at the pimps. They seemed as friendly and yielding as a brick wall. I climbed into the dark.

CHAPTER 27

PIA STOOD AT THE GUARD station in front of the White House when she dialed Hunter's cell phone. As soon as Hunter picked up, she started talking. "Get me in, I want to hear him explain his first-degree murder conspiracy to my face."

"Calm down, Pia," Hunter said. "He retracted it."

"'Just kidding' doesn't cut it. You want to work together. This is it. I demand to see him right now."

"Everyone wants to yell at him in person. You don't get special privileges."

"He told people to kill my employee. What more do you need for some kind of outrage to take hold?

"What do you hope to accomplish coming here?"

"To find someone with a hint of backbone who will force him to resign."

"Any resignation will have to be voluntary," Hunter's voice sounded as if her calls were recorded and sent to Roche. "He would never think of it even if there was an overwhelming public outcry."

"From where I'm standing, I can see six reporters doing their headshots in the circle. I can create a one-woman outcry right now. I'm sure they'd like an angry sound bite from Jacob Stearne's—"

"OK, you win," Hunter growled. "I'll get you cleared through. You'll have to drive in from the EEOB entrance—"

"My limo dropped me. I'm at the White House entrance."

"Damn. OK. Stay away from the reporters and go directly to the West Wing entrance."

They clicked off. Pia waited until word reached the guards. From where she stood, the famous portico of the White House waited on her left. The lesser known, but more often used, entrance to the West Wing stood on her right. A pair of sidewalks split off to each entry just beyond the guard house.

A guard ushered her through to the foot path. She began walking toward the West Wing. Part of her wanted to call out to the reporters. The other part knew she didn't need to. They had better vision than eagles. She strolled down the path. Still wearing what Hunter referred to as ninja-athletic gear, she would look like a fish out of water on the buttoned-down grounds.

It didn't take long. Halfway down the walkway, Pia heard the first voice calling her name. With a quick glance over her shoulder, she stopped and waved at Philip Haberman. He crossed the lawn as best an out of shape man his age could manage. She turned and resumed her stroll. He continued yelling for her to stop. She played him for another few strides until the West Wing entrance with its guards and attendants would serve as her backdrop. Then she faced him.

This time, she was ready for the national press. Outrage is an excellent method for preparation.

Twenty yards behind Haberman came every other TV reporter assigned to the White House and their camera crews.

When Haberman reached her, he was out of breath. "Ms. Sabel, uh, whew. Could you—"

Pia said, "I'm honored to be an invited guest of our experienced Vice President, Veronica Lodge Hunter. I am deeply grateful and thankful for her help. While our mobster-moron president may be unwilling to show his cowardly face, at least Madam Vice President has shown some backbone."

Haberman stared at her with his mouth open for a moment before composing himself. "What do you think of President Roche's declaration that his tweet was meant in jest?"

"Kind of hard to call a bullet a joke after you pull the trigger, isn't it?"

"Will you demand charges be brought against him?"

"I would, but you know the problem with that idea."

"Charges would have to be filed by the Justice Department—and they work for him." Haberman squinted. "Will you ask Congress to impeach him?"

The horde of other reporters and photographers arrived and set up. Mics and lenses were shoved into her face.

She said, "Not even the fictional Godfather acted in such an irresponsible and criminal manner. Impeachment would be too good for him. He should resign immediately due to his utter incompetence. The charade of having an armchair quarterback running the nation needs to end now. Calling for the murder of a decorated veteran—a man who found the courage to face death on daily basis for eight tours of duty—is too much for his party or this nation to suffer any longer. Surely Congress will lead the charge to force his resignation."

"If he resigns, then will you press charges?" Haberman asked.

Pia turned and began to walk away.

"Ms. Sabel," Haberman called, "is it true there is a video of you shooting Viktor Popov?"

Pia faced him. "Phil, you're not the kind of journalist who would work on rumors. A man of your caliber works only from firsthand, verified information. Does your question imply that you've seen such a video?"

Haberman's face drooped as he realized his source had used him. "I've not seen any such video."

Pia picked up her stride and marched through the doors and into the recesses of the West Wing. Agent Catherine escorted her from the lobby to Hunter's office.

Pia said, "The VP still a bitch?"

Catherine gave her a quick, cold glance. Apparently, their relationship had not thawed.

Wordlessly, they entered the office. Hunter's face was red. Her finger pointed to a live broadcast on TV. Her mouth opened and closed, but no words came out. Then she turned to Catherine and said, "Privacy for god's sake."

Catherine rolled her eyes and left.

When the office door closed, Hunter—her finger still trembling at the

TV—said, "What the hell was that?"

"Why, mother dearest, you did tell me—and I quote—'*Mention what an honor it is to be here and thank the woman who brought you. Then attack whoever.*' And that is exactly what I did. Are you not pleased?"

Again, Hunter's mouth opened and closed without the accompaniment of sound.

Pia parked a hip on the edge of Hunter's desk. "How the hell did you and your goons let him issue a shoot-to-kill order for Jacob Stearne? Who—I will remind you—served his country with distinction. Unlike the president."

Hunter waved her hands in the air. "Chuck's out of control. He's worried about Wilkes. I don't know how or why, but it's driven him mad. She must have something terrible on him."

"Not that it'll do her any good. I had him cold, turned all the evidence over to the Senate where Krueger managed to bury it. Thanks for all your help in that pursuit."

"Don't get clever with—"

Hunter's phone rang. She picked it up and said, "I'll be right there."

She hung up and stared at Pia. "You caused a panic in the Oval Nursery. They need adults in the room. I'll be right back. Stay here."

Hunter ran out, leaving the door open.

Pia glanced at the desk. On top of everything, within easy reach, lay the fabled President's Daily Brief. With her security clearance revoked, she shouldn't have been left in the room. Which Pia took as a sign that Hunter must have wanted her to read it. She listened intently for footsteps or voices, any sign of someone approaching. Nothing.

She picked it up and skimmed through, looking for reference to the Mumbai operation. There wasn't one. Movement outside the office caught her eye. She looked up and exchanged a nod as the first nephew passed the open door. She placed the PDB back exactly where she saw it. On the far side of the desk lay a phone with an unusual red backing. She reached for it and brought the screen to life.

The lock screen was a picture of Chuck Roche in a ridiculous uniform covered in medals. The facial recognition system failed and asked her for the PIN. Pia looked around the room. As in all government offices, a portrait of the president hung on the wall. Pia swiped the phone to repeat the facial recognition attempt and held it to the photo. Unlocked.

Pia froze. This was a line she should not cross. Searching the contents of the phone had to be illegal. Nothing good could come from handling it. She had come to the White House to demand Roche's resignation. What if something inside that phone could force the issue? Would prison be worth the incursion? Absolutely. Since Roche's irresponsible shoot-to-kill order, her goal was more than revenge. It was now about saving the country. If she didn't act fast, Roche might dump Hunter, cutting off Pia's access and putting Hartwell Thomas, founder of the Redjackets, into the heartbeat-away role. She decided to go ahead.

What if it were an old phone from before the election and held nothing? Could it have been planted to test her loyalties?

On the one hand, it was thicker than the average consumer phone. Sabel Security phones were equally thick, the extra encryption board forcing a couple millimeters and a little weight. This one was slightly thicker than the Sabel phones. Indicating it was the CIA's alternative phone used for when they suspected the government's biggest contractor, Sabel Technologies, of eavesdropping. Which suggested the phone was a real operational phone used by Roche.

What was it doing on Hunter's desk?

None of that mattered, she decided. What she had was an opportunity to snoop illegally. It was a matter of act now or lose the chance. She dialed the special Sabel Technologies phone number that would trigger an automatic upload of the phone's internal system to a secret server. From there, Bianca could later decode it and discover its secrets.

The lengthy upload began.

"What the hell do you think you're doing?" Hunter stood in the doorway.

Pia held the phone up. "Why do you have Chuck's phone on your desk?"

Hunter's eyes flashed, and her face flushed red. She charged at Pia, grabbed the phone from her hand and slapped it down. "You call whatshername right now and get whatever you just did erased from Sabel's servers. You're playing against the most powerful man in the world. You cannot afford to play into his hands, Pia. Make that call."

Pia assessed the vice president's intensity and reassessed her association with the woman. Everything Pia had done to bring down Roche had failed. But nothing Hunter was doing brought her any closer. Was it worth it?

"Make that call right now, Pia. If you don't, I'll have to call security—to have you arrested. I swear to god, I'll do it."

That tipped the scales against uploading the data. Pia would never force Roche out of office from inside a penitentiary. Worse. She still needed Hunter.

Pia said, "OK, Veronica. I'll make the call. But you need to tell me what's on that phone and why you have it."

"I'll tell you nothing. A couple hours ago, you asked me to uncover the mole in your company. That requires mutual trust. Just now, you lost all of mine."

CHAPTER 28

PRESIDENT ROCHE WALKED INTO THE White House living room where his nephew was sprawled on a couch watching midget wrestling on the big screen TV. Roche picked up the remote and changed the channel to Fuchs News. "Did you finish off another bag of Cheetos? Damn it, boy. Go get a new one, pronto."

The first nephew scrunched the empty bag into a ball, hopped up and ran to the kitchen. He returned seconds later and handed over a bag of his favorite snacks. "Sorry about that, Uncle Chuck."

"Where are we on the Peace process?"

"They really aren't interested in working things out. Every time I set up meetings, they cancel them. Now all the countries involved banned me."

"Won't matter if Congress gets off their lazy asses and votes for war." Roche tugged at the unopened bag without result. "What about the other task I gave you?"

"What task, Uncle Chuck?"

Roche stared at the first nephew as he struggled with the Cheetos bag.

The younger man began to quiver with fear. He eyed the bag problem as he thought.

"Oh yeah," he relaxed a little, "I remember. You were right. Thomas and Ratched are plotting something with Hunter. I think O'Brien's in on it, too. Maybe Rochester, but I'm not sure about him. I couldn't hear what they're doing, but they don't think we can win the Saudi war. They want to stop it."

"GODDAMN IT!" Roche handed the Cheetos to the boy. "Open this stupid bag."

His nephew pulled it open in one tug and handed it back.

Roche pulled out three Cheetos and ate them. With his mouthful, he said, "Why would they back out of the war?"

"Maybe that," his nephew pointed to the TV.

The scroll below the reporter read, "United Nations resolution to condemn the US for blaming Saudi Arabia passes."

"Where is my UN Ambassador?" Roche asked. "Why didn't he veto that?"

"You haven't appointed one since the last guy quit."

Roche ate more Cheetos while giving his nephew a scowl. As he recalled, the top five positions had resigned en masse to protest something. Roche set the bag on a far shelf and pulled his phone. He texted all the people his nephew implicated—except Hunter—and ordered them to the White House living quarters. Then Roche handed his phone to his nephew to get the orange bits off the screen before slipping it back in his pocket. He continued watching Fuchs News and eating Cheetos.

"Say," Roche said, "you'd better slip out the servant's stairs. I don't want them figuring out who fingered them. They get nasty about that kind of thing."

The first nephew vanished an instant later.

Thomas arrived first. He knelt and kissed Roche's Cheeto-encrusted fingers. "Why, you looked damn smart in that uniform, sir. You should've kept it on. You are the commander—"

"That's why you're a loser, Hartwell." Roche motioned for Thomas to rise. "I'm keeping the uniform and the portrait under wraps until Congress approves my declaration. I'll wear it to the signing."

Thomas paled and swallowed. Roche watched him and wondered if his fear arose from calling him a loser or wearing the uniform in public. Neither of which mattered to the president. He said, "It's come to my attention that you're not happy with my declaration, Hartwell. Is that true?"

"Oh, no, sir. That's not—"

"I hear rumors that you and Ratched and O'Brien don't think we can win the war."

Thomas lost all his color. The first nephew had been spot-on with his eavesdropping. Finally, he'd found something the boy could get right.

Thomas spluttered. "That's not … we're concerned about … Did you see the UN resolution?"

Roche stayed quiet. He preferred letting people talk themselves into a conviction. Thomas had once been a boisterous cowboy, swaggering from bar to bar. Now his knees were shaking.

"The number of countries pledging troops to defend the Saudis … there could be a big downside risk to … It was Nora's idea. She thought Sabel's people were going to find Wilkes and she done went loco."

"I went loco about what?" Ratched screeched from the doorway.

Roche faced her and tapped his cane on the floor. When she dropped to one knee and began kissing his fingers, he ran the fingers of his free hand through her hair. She looked up at him.

"You do that so well." He grabbed her hair roughly. "But tell me, why are you plotting to destroy my war plan? Don't you realize what will happen if we don't rally the American people? Congress will start investigating things. Things like, what kind of explosives were involved in the sinking of the *USS Caine*? Where could those have come from? Who used to be top dog at the CIA and had access to those specialized, high-density PETN explosives?"

He held her in place and watched the color drain from her face. Just as weak as Thomas.

He said, "Tell me who's in your little conspiracy to turn me out of the office I was elected to hold, Nora?"

"Hunter." Nora looked up with pleading eyes. "Veronica told us the Sabel people were going to bring Wilkes in and she had—"

Roche yanked her head to make her stop talking. "Did I not promise to solve the Wilkes problem?"

Ratched nodded in small bobs, her hair still held tightly in his fist.

"And you believed Sabel could beat my people?" he asked.

"Hunter's been working with Pia day and night. You saw the videos. You know they have something going on. Veronica's convinced the Sabel people…" Tears formed in Ratched's eyes. "I failed you, sir. She led me astray. Forgive me. She made me think terrible things. But I have a plan. I can make it look like she did it. The whole thing."

"We'll talk about that later, when you're not blubbering."

She broke down in whimpers. Which Roche hated with a passion.

He shoved her away and crossed the room. His people were cowards and liars and traitors. How could he protect the nation from evil Wahhabis who blow up American ships with these feeble creatures? He considered beating some sense into them. But that wouldn't help get his war back on track.

A tentative knock on the jamb drew Roche's attention. O'Brien stood at the doorway, surveying the scene as if he'd never seen a woman crying on her knees before.

"C'mon in," Roche tapped his cane on the floor. "Confess your sins against your president and all will be punished and possibly forgiven."

O'Brien came forward, his face following the new snow-white fashion. He took a knee and kissed the fingers. He withdrew without lavishing praise on the administration.

Roche said, "You're fired."

O'Brien's eyes blew wide open. "But, why? I've not—"

"You weren't part of this conspiracy to force me out of office?" Roche leaned toward the taller man, jutting out his chin. "If there's one thing I hate, it's a liar."

"Wait," O'Brien said, "I need this job. I'm not rich like the rest of these—"

"If you want your job back, tell me the truth. What have you and your little friends been up to?"

O'Brien looked at Ratched, then Thomas. Roche could see the gears working in the man's head. He was piecing together the story they'd told from what little he'd heard.

"Hunter has a plan to get rid—"

"I've heard all that. Tell me something I don't know."

O'Brien thought hard. All his high-priced education should count for something good. Roche couldn't wait to hear it. But O'Brien was saved by the appearance of Rochester.

They repeated the ritual. Rochester confessed as quickly as the other three. But none of their confessions solved his problem.

"I need my declaration approved by Congress," Roche said. "I don't need my people plotting against me."

The four of them began chattering about how they could be trusted from now on. Roche turned his back on them and thought. Obviously, he needed to get rid of Hunter. If the Redjackets wound up in an Indian prison, he would turn her over to the Justice Department. If she didn't resign, Congress would take care of it. Easy enough. But, if the Redjackets found Wilkes and eliminated her, he'd have to find another way to get rid of Hunter. He could start by undermining her on Sabel's Kill-Video. He could think of no reason to delay that avenue.

He sent a tweet, "Did Veronica Hunter cover up a murder by a donor when she was president? #whathappenedtoPopov."

Roche turned back to his personal Gang of Four. "How am I going to trust you?"

They all started chattering again. Roche hated people when they begged for their professional careers. He wondered if the Roman Emperors experienced the same weariness when gladiators begged for their lives.

He held up a hand to silence them.

"I want that war." He stared them down. "You're going to make it happen for me. I don't care what the Russians say. I don't care about the Chinese or the Pakistanis or the Egyptians. You're going to find conclusive proof that the Saudis sank the *USS Caine*. I don't care what prison you have to dredge to find Saudis but find them you will. I don't care what promises you have to make them but promise them you will. I don't care what lies you need to feed them but feed them you will. I want witnesses who will come before Congress and testify that they helped build the bomb. I want witnesses who will testify that they helped plant the bomb during resupply stops." He paused for effect. "Am I making myself clear?"

The four of them looked at each other. They elected Ratched to speak for them. She said, "What about Hunter?"

"Did I tell you to worry about Hunter?" He waited until they all shrank back. "I have Hunter handled one way or another."

"Sir, what I meant … who gets her job?"

"Naturally, the first one to put a witness in front of Congress." He waived his cane toward the door. "Dismissed."

CHAPTER 29

VISHAL WAVED FOR ME TO follow him up the stairs. With a wall of dangerous looking pimps behind me, I jogged up. He led me down a hallway lined with fashionably dressed women and drunk men. After passing through what once were walls between separate buildings, now just passageways between a consolidated enterprise, we emerged into a large, dark office.

Mercury whispered in my ear. *You're in the bigtime now, homie. This place is as big as the best houses in Rome—back in the day. Madam Aditi likes money and attitude. She's got a hate for the weak. The guy who's going to pat you down will step up behind you. Taking him down will impress her.*

Sometimes Mercury gives me advice that would go down great in ancient Rome but not so great in modern industrialized countries. This advice was questionable at best.

I checked the attractive, middle aged woman in a big chair behind a big desk. A green light behind her bathed the room in an emerald hue. She wore a silk sari with a fancy pattern on it. A jeweled bangle dangled over her forehead. In front of the desk was a stuffed elephant head. Tusks and all. Smart interior decorating. No one could charge her.

On either side stood guys with hard faces. They'd handled their share of drunks and angry customers. They thought they'd seen some tough fights. Not like mine, though. They'd never stood up to a crazed fundamentalist convinced that my death would ensure his place in heaven. I gave the one on the left my soldier stare. He almost flinched. Madam Aditi noticed.

Maybe Mercury was right about her disappointment in weakness. I can never tell if he's right about a situation until it's too late. But this place did resemble ancient Rome more than Washington, DC.

I sensed a third man stepping out of a hidden space in the wall behind me. I stood still until I felt the nearly imperceptible electric charge given off by his arm. He planned to put me in a surprise headlock to allow his friends to search me for weapons before robbing me. I twisted to the right, slamming my rising elbow into the bottom of his jaw. His body began to fall away from the vicious blow. My left foot landed on his, pinning him in place while I delivered another elbow to the top of his head. He lost consciousness. His knees buckled. He pitched forward.

I caught him in a headlock and pulled a pistol from a sash he wore for a belt. I took his wallet and dropped him on the floor.

All this happened before Madam Aditi's bodyguards could react. In fairness to them, it was the first time their jack-in-the-box act failed. They lost valuable seconds processing what had just happened.

"It's an honor to meet you, Madam Aditi." I smiled and tucked the pistol in my belt.

Her two goons leapt forward. One with a *bagh naka*, tiger claws; the other with a *maduvu*, a nasty looking serrated stick with points on both ends. I tossed the stolen wallet to tiger-claws and aimed the pistol at the other. They both stopped. The guy catching the wallet looked embarrassed. I moved the barrel to their boss.

Madam Aditi never blinked. She gave a sharp laugh and snapped her fingers. The goons picked up their friend and carried him out. They closed the door behind them.

Vishal bowed and left. I started to tell him I still needed his services, not to mention his company. Madam Aditi hushed me.

With very little accent, she said, "You pick the only Mumbaikar who speaks English badly. Why?"

"He was available."

"Interesting." Her t's came out more like d's, and her pronunciation was crisp, melodic and very fast.

Mercury stood behind her. *Don't be getting cute with an educated woman, my brutha. Madam Aditi's intellect is a tremendous advantage in this rough business. Be straight up with her, she'll do the same for you.*

I said, "I'm looking for my—"

"Dhanpal." She smiled. "We need to talk about him."

It took me a minute to understand what a handsome, traditional Indian in this no-holds-barred sex shop wanted to talk about. I had imagined I would walk in, get Dhanpal, kill a couple Redjackets and go home. It dawned on me that I was in a whorehouse. Thousands of years ago, transactional deal-making originated in the very first such establishment.

"Sorry, where are my manners?" I smiled. "My friend is blessed to enjoy your protection in his hour of need. We are forever in your debt for your gracious hospitality."

Her gaze flowed over me like an enveloping fog. It absorbed every clue on my person for status, wealth, and intent. Which made me regret my t-shirt choice. It read, "Army Ranger: a constitution enforcing, death-dealing, sex tornado." Beneath that, "Sua Sponte, motherfucker."

I tried to cross my arms over the sex-tornado bit which seemed way awkward in the environment.

"Uh. How much do I owe you for taking care of my man?"

"Ten lakh."

One lakh is a hundred thousand rupees. Ten works out to roughly fourteen thousand American dollars. That's if Madam Aditi offered the going exchange rate. It was a good deal more than I had on me even if I gave her the money I'd promised Vishal. "That's the regular price, what about for Dhanpal, the grandson of prominent locals?"

"You are not negotiating here. President Roche put out a shoot-to-kill order for you. Everyone is looking for you, Jacob Stearne. Ten lakh."

"You don't expect me to carry that much money on me, do you?"

"Dhanpal came to me in need of medical attention." Madam Aditi rose. "I have spent lavishly on him. He said his friend Jacob would come and settle the bill. He said Jacob is a trustworthy and resourceful man who can pay any bill. Did he lie?"

She stepped out from behind the desk with a shiny dagger in her hand.

"He is a ..." I paused while I searched for words other than bald-faced-liar. "Worthy of your generosity. Uhm. I just need to make a phone call to arrange that kind of transaction."

Mercury laughed, holding his belly. *Oh homie, I can't wait to hear what excuses you give Sabel Security's accounting department. They're still talking about sending you up the river for your gambling debts in Monaco.*

I said, *I won that money back.*

Mercury said, *Oh, you won that money? You? All by yourself? Who told you 'fifteen' on that last spin of the wheel? Do you have any idea how long the Dii Consentes interrogated me about breaking my vow to never help mortals win money?*

I said, *OK, so you stuck your neck out for me once. Big deal. How am I going to come up with that much money?*

Mercury said, *Dude, just give her your credit card. This is a modern establishment.*

"Do you take credit cards?" I half-joked the question.

She squinted at me and emphasized the last word. "Do you have that kind of credit line—soldier?"

Now things were in my favor. The real reason Dhanpal invited me on this trip, and the reason my teammates always asked me to join their missions, was because Ms. Sabel—in all her infinite and misplaced wisdom—had authorized me for an American Excess Centurion card. It was part of her decision that, because of Mercury, she and I shared a type of PTSD-induced madness. She thinks of me as the sibling she never had. Plus, I've saved her life a couple times. I get a lot of special treatment. Which doesn't suck. The result is that the team never invites me because of my brilliant tactical leadership or my winning personality. Including me brings my little black card that American Excess only issues to an exclusive group of its biggest spenders. It's so private you can't apply for it. It comes with no spending limits. At all. A mission without me is usually capped at flying coach with budget-minded per diem expenses for food and hotels. With me, the same mission becomes an unlimited and rarely questioned (except when world-famous gambling institutions are involved) mission using one of Ms. Sabel's private jets, first-class hotels and Michelin starred restaurants.

Any businessperson who deals with people Forbes writes articles about knows this card at a glance.

I pulled the titanium credit card from the secret compartment in my belt and held it up for Madam Aditi. She smiled and snaked it from my fingers.

"For an extra five lakh, I deliver intelligence on your enemies. And, for an additional five lakh—" she lowered her voice for effect "—escape transportation for five people."

I wondered how much the escape route and intel would've cost if not for the Amex. I took the whole package. She ran the card through her handheld card reader.

As the electrons flew across the internet to North America and back, she said, "There are twelve Americans with those little red squares in their jackets who paid two lakh for the rights to ambush you at Dhanpal's room. We will need a few minutes to relocate them."

Mercury said, *Are you paying attention right now, homes? This is how you succeed in business. You charge people for an ambush, then send them packing when a higher bidder comes along. No refunds. Madam Aditi would make a pretty good Caesar. Tell her about me. Tell her the god of commerce is taking an interest in her.*

I said, *Let's get Dhanpal out of this first.*

As soon as the approval code came through, her team sprang into action. I sent Vishal to bring my team inside. The two hard-nosed guards became instant friends and led me through a maze of corridors.

Dhanpal sat up in a shabby bed with stained sheets. Shirtless, a fresh bandage covered most of his right shoulder. Naturally dark, he looked as pale as his bandage. His woozy eyes caught sight of me. A weak hand raised to half a wave.

I ran to his bedside. "Dude, I am so sorry for turning you down. I should've been there."

"Good you didn't come." His voice was weak. "It was tough for a SEAL; a Ranger would've peed his pants."

Normally, I'd have decked him for that one. He was already decked.

"Wilkes is safe," he said.

"I don't care about her. We're getting you out of here."

"My grandparents smuggled her out."

I paused and looked him over. This was not a good time to tell him the latest news about his grandparents.

Mercury said, *Dude, something's not right there. If the Redjackets took his grandparents, why are they still looking for you guys? Either they don't have the old folks or—*

Or they're asking the wrong questions. I considered the odds of either scenario. *Not my circus, not my monkey.*

I checked Dhanpal's bandage. I could smell it before I peeled it back. Gangrene. He needed evacuation. He needed a week with intravenous antibiotics in a decent hospital. There were several healthcare options in Mumbai. None out of reach of the Redjackets.

Miguel, Tania and Cody filed in behind me. Vishal hung back in the hallway. One of them mentioned having left Chopra tied to a fence. Miguel sidled in next to me, took one sniff, then looked at me with grave concern.

Elsewhere in the building, a fight broke out. Shouts and screams reached us. Chairs were breaking. American voices rose over the din.

Madam Aditi pushed in. "The other Americans are forcing their way back in. Appalling manners. You will go now. Five of you can get out." She nodded over her shoulder at Vishal. "They saw him. He has no chance now."

She ran down the hall and waved for us to follow. Miguel picked up Dhanpal and carried him. Tania and Cody were right behind him. The team rushed for the exit Madam Aditi had promised. Five people.

Vishal stood in the hallway like a man facing a death sentence.

Mercury said, *Aw, don't be looking at him like a lost puppy now, brutha. Follow the others. Get moving.*

I said, *It's more than that.*

Mercury said, *You're my favorite disciple, homie. The Dii Concentes needs you alive to proselytize for us. Which, by the way, you've been slacking on. And I mean slacking with a capital—*

I said, *Aditi could easily let the Redjackets catch us. I don't trust her.*

Whoa, dude. Mercury checked my eyes for drug use. *You thinking clearly? You been saying you only care about rescuing Dhanpal. You did that. Right now, you can save yourself and leave the expendable guy to take the fall. So, take my advice, RUN!*

I dug Vishal's half of the money out of my pocket and pressed it into his hand. "You did well. Now I need you to catch up with my team. Take my place. Tell them, Leonidas sends his regards. Make sure they get to the jet. Tell them to file a flight plan for Dubai but go to Singapore. Now go."

His face scrunched up as if he were about to say he would do the noble thing and stay behind. Then a gunshot echoed a hallway or two away. I gave him a push-start. He took off running.

I pulled the pistol I'd taken from Madam Aditi's guard and slid into an unoccupied room.

Madam Aditi's people backed through the hall past my open door. They slashed the air with their weapons, fending off pursuers. I waited. Footsteps tromped closer to my hiding place. The guards receded into the blackness of the hallway.

I made out three distinct pairs of feet. Three of them meant the others were clearing other hallways in the labyrinth. That meant taking this squad silently would keep my location and strength secret. My calculations figured they had one guy on point, one covering him and the third covering their rear. They were too close to each other to be veterans. That meant they were nervous and figuring they should stay in physical contact with each other. Which meant I could grab the first guy as a hostage and threaten the second before he could react. The third would be useless because he would have two bodies in front of him.

As the man on point reached my doorway, I reached out, grabbed his collar and shoved my gun into his ear. "Drop it."

He complied.

They were definitely not veterans. Which was a problem. They were scared and tense and jumpy. When I surprised them, the second guy in line emptied his magazine. At least five of the nine bullets went through his friend's body. My hostage fell to the floor dead.

CHAPTER 30

PIA DROVE TO THE WHARTON School in part because the two hours of travel would give her time to think about her mother. And what better place to do some thinking than on the highway in her Aston Martin convertible?

She buzzed Cousin Elmer to let him know she was keeping the car out awhile longer. Then she started thinking.

The acrimony had been thick when Hunter departed for her speech at the business school's banking seminar. Had it been any other president's picture on the face of the phone, Pia wouldn't have touched it. She didn't feel bad about attempting to hack the contents. But Pia hadn't liked getting caught. Should she apologize and piece their relationship back together? Or just dump the mother-drama and go after Roche on her own? She certainly had the ammunition to call for impeachment. But it would only work if someone killed Jacob Stearne. That was a price not worth paying.

Her thoughts turned to her team in Mumbai. Bianca convinced her not to attempt contacting them for fear it would expose their position. They had survived warzones for years; this scenario was nothing new. Bianca had a backchannel for communicating with them that was sporadic at best. Last word: they knew where to find Dhanpal. Nothing about Wilkes. Which led her to speculate on what the admiral could know that made her so valuable. In the end, she decided if the Redjackets wanted Wilkes, why didn't matter. Pia needed to find her first.

By the time she flew past the Philadelphia Airport, she had concluded her plan. No matter how she went about it, she needed Hunter's blessing. Which meant she had to keep on Hunter's good side. Which meant apologizing to a mother who'd abandoned her. Which sucked.

Was the Major right when she accused Pia of *running off like a child with some serious mommy-issues*? Who could blame her?

With lots of time before arriving at her destination, she decided to call her attorney. After exchanging pleasantries, she asked, "Hypothetically, if I plead guilty to murder, can I use the Texas Defense?"

"You mean, will the jury let you off if you can prove he needed killing? Most, but not all, juries go for it. It's a big gamble."

"What if the dead man was on a list of enemy combatants targeted for death during the War on Terror?"

"That would help the hypothetical Texas Defense, but the Feds would go a long way to blocking any such list. For political reasons, they'd claim a matter of national security and squash you like a bug."

Not the answer she was hoping for, but realistic enough. She thanked her attorney and clicked off and turned off the highway into downtown Philly.

Wharton's downtown campus bustled with activity. She had rounded the block before she found a parking space on the street near the lecture hall's back door. She did a doubletake when she realized why it was open. Secret Service agents protected the VP's official limo, making the space look unavailable. Pia parked in it and walked around to the front entrance.

She'd left her bodyguard back at Sabel Gardens. Not intentionally, the trip had been one of her many instant inspirations. She went when she realized there was just enough time to get to Hunter's lecture on international commerce.

She strode into the lecture hall without a clear idea of what she would say or do. Maybe catch Hunter on the way out, after the autograph hounds were exhausted. Too weak. Or wave to her from the hall like a fan. Too pathetic. If Dan and Catherine were on duty, she could wait in the limo. Too risky—for them. She couldn't get them in trouble again. No matter how she went about it, she would end up looking desperate. Which sucked.

She would have to think of something to get Veronica's attention.

She found a seat near the center of the auditorium minutes before the school's dean made Hunter's introduction. The lecture was pure politics. Precisely the kind of speech one might expect from a former president currying the favor of Wharton's illustrious alumni. Hunter spoke about how the government ensured secure business environments for Americans doing business in foreign countries.

Pia checked out the attendees. Among the students and faculty were many notable business leaders. It was a reserved, quiet, and respectful group. A small knot of business reporters shared space with a handful of political stringers in a corner of the room. One of them stood out, Gina Wind. As if sensing Pia's gaze, Gina looked up.

Pia straightened her posture and refocused on the speaker. Hunter bragged about her accomplishments during her term as president. She promised to bring the current administration into line with the needs of international banks and businesses. Then she concluded her remarks saying, "The Roche administration does everything possible to make the world safe for commerce."

"Why do you lie to these people?" Pia was on her feet shouting loud enough to hear her own echo—and instantly regretted her uncontrolled outburst. Of all the ways to get her mother's attention, this was not ideal. Every eye in the room turned to her as she spoke. Even though everyone knew the source of her outrage, it would've been wise to carefully plan her reaction. But, she figured, once you've started, why hold back? "How can you say you're making the world safe for commerce when your boss put out a hit on Jacob Stearne, one of my top employees?"

"Everyone heard the President's explanation. It was simply a joke that didn't work."

"When you repeat his lies you denigrate yourself, Madam Vice President. Why won't you denounce his shoot-to-kill order? Why won't you—"

"We understand you're upset, but this is neither the time nor place to address this issue." The microphone's amplified volume overwhelmed Pia's voice. "Don't make a fool of yourself in public, Ms. Sabel. Now then, does anyone have a grownup question?"

A silence fell over the room. Security guards made their way through the rows. One of them was Agent Dan. He curled a finger. Pia obeyed.

Better to leave standing up than dragged out with Gina Wind watching. Dan led her down the aisle toward the backstage exit.

With everyone staring, Pia began to think about working with Veronica. Nothing to date brought Pia any closer to Roche. Was Veronica deflecting her? Why had she been so sensitive about the red phone? Thinking about the phone's cover with Roche in the ridiculous uniform made her ill. Roche wanted that war. And the red phone had something to do with it. She should've let the upload finish. It was time to go around Hunter. Pia held her head high and marched down the side aisle.

As she passed the reporter area, Gina stepped into her path with her phone in record mode.

Gina said, "What did President Roche mean when he tweeted, 'Did Veronica Hunter cover up a murder by a donor when she was president? #whathappenedtoPopov?'"

Pia studied the woman for a second and realized why she asked hardnosed questions. Gina was climbing the journalist's ladder from sports reporting to the White House. So far, she'd only made it to the level of vice president's coverage. A bleak and featureless plane on which careers stagnated and foundered.

"No one knows what Roche means when he tweets," Pia said, "not even Roche."

"Is it true—"

"Walk with me." Pia continued making her way out. "I hate getting kicked out alone."

Gina let a laugh escape before she followed. "Serious allegations are stacking up against—"

"Gina, why don't you meet me at Sabel Gardens for a proper interview? Anyone who gets up hours before dawn deserves more than a hallway sound bite."

Gina snapped back in shock. "Are you talking on the record?"

"Depends on your questions," Pia put her head close to Gina's and whispered. "Nothing about sex or relationships, right?"

Gina laughed again. "I'm serious about the allegations though."

Dan opened the exit and waved to another agent before gesturing Pia through. Gina followed. Dan slammed the door closed behind them.

"Damn," Gina said, "I need to be in there."

"Why? I can tell you everything she's going to deny."

An amused reporter is much nicer to you than an ignored reporter, Dad had often told her. It looked like good advice. They stood near the exit door and chatted about travel and sports and kids and Gina's new career trajectory.

Applause inside indicating the end of the lecture wafted to them in the late afternoon's warmth.

"If you stand right here," Pia said, "you can follow up on my question to Hunter. She'll come out that door, walk past my car, and get in one of those limos."

Gina looked at the angles, calculated the number of Secret Service agents and realized Pia was right. They wished each other well and parted. Gina took up her intercept position. Pia crossed the small plaza to her car.

Three men leaned against the Aston Martin. She clicked a sequence on the key. The car blasted its horn three times, making the men jump.

One held a baseball bat. The other two gave Pia hard glares.

"You better stop attacking Zenith Man." The guy with the bat tapped the end in his palm. "We're sick of little shits like you pissing on Chuck Roche's legacy."

"You're right," Pia said, "he's doing a fine job of pissing himself."

"Hey, a little respect." The bat came down on her windshield with a crash. A spider web of cracks crossed the length and width. "We don't like what you said in there."

"Too many syllables?" Pia moved closer to the man. "I can dumb it down for you."

"Don't get smart with me." He smacked the hood of her car, leaving a significant dent.

"My bad." Pia came closer still.

The leader slapped the bat into his free hand for noise. He made a strong stance, feet wide apart, the bat as menacing as he could make it.

Pia came within an arm's length, negating the bat's swing. She said, "If you touch my car one more time, you'll end up knocking his teeth out."

She pointed at the second man who stood a foot behind the leader's right hip.

He squinted. "How d'you figure—"

Pia slammed her knee into his groin and rolled around his right hip, tugging his shoulder. The leader spun quickly, inadvertently crashing the bat into his friend's mouth. Pia smacked her knee into the leader's butt, disabling one leg.

Gina shrieked from thirty yards away.

The leader fell backward. She bent at the waist, throwing his weight over her shoulder to the concrete sidewalk. He landed with a thud. His friend held a hand over his mouth while blood and teeth gushed out.

Gina shouted. "Hey! Secret Service agents! DO SOMETHING!"

The third man was slow to react but quick to land a fist in Pia's ribs. As she rose to face him, he slammed a second and third punch in her stomach. They were expert blows. His fist twisted and rose with each contact. The effect pushed her guts upward, compressing her diaphragm into her lungs, forcing out all her air. She couldn't breathe.

"I'm calling the cops!" Gina yelled.

He pulled back for a knockout punch to the face.

Pia twisted her shoulders enough to send his fist glancing off her back. She came at him, powering off her back foot to land an elbow on his chin. A knockout blow for the average street fighter.

Her assailant staggered two steps back.

The fighter hunched down and rushed her, his eyes alert for any opening. He jabbed and feinted and bobbed and landed a power blow to her ribs. She managed to glance a couple jabs off his chin. He was too seasoned to let her land anything substantial. While her fists were up, aiming for his head, he landed a hammering punch to her temple followed by a combination to her core.

He was a big man. His blows were powerful. The pain shocked her. Her responses slowed. He landed another combination to her core. Her defenses weakened. Hands drooping to her sides, her vision became an unsteady double image.

Somewhere behind her, Gina screamed for help.

"You don't come round here talking shit about Zenith Man." The man landed a hard left on her chin. "Redjackets RULE!"

He punctuated his outburst with a right cross to her chin.

Black and silver stars formed an edge around an outer ring of darkness in her vision. Pia's consciousness waned. Another fist landed in her core and pushed up into her lungs.

She fell to the sidewalk. Her world went sideways.

In the distance, she saw Hunter watching her from the open door of the limo. Cold, dispassionate eyes; as if she were watching a pigeon in the park. Hunter shook her head before she got in the limo. The door closed.

Pia's world went dark.

CHAPTER 31

CHUCK ROCHE LOOKED AT THE caller ID. Hunter calling. What on Earth had possessed him to make her VP after his first one resigned? Ratched's plan to dump her couldn't work fast enough. He clicked on. "What is it, Veronica?"

"Your Redjackets just beat the crap out of Pia Sabel."

"Are you calling to complain—or brag—about your operatives?"

"This is no joke, Chuck. You need to disband that group. They're acting—"

"Are you recording this call?" He snarled. "Do you think you can get me to say something incriminating over the phone? OK, here's the truth. If the Redjackets do anything, it's at your instruction. You asked for it— and Thomas gave you full control. They only do what you tell them, Veronica. Don't try to pawn off your failed operation on me."

He could barely contain himself. He wanted to laugh at her predicament.

"What are you talking about?" Hunter screeched. "You know I would never—"

"Your little coup d'état failed, Veronica." He relished the silence she left. "Your coconspirators ratted you out. Thomas, Ratched, O'Brien, Rochester—all of them—begged for my mercy. They blame you for leading them astray. We'll have a meeting when you get back from the Italian Prime Minister's funeral."

He clicked off. She called back. He blocked her calls. He said to his empty office, "Shoulda done that a long time ago."

He rose and crossed the West Wing to his next meeting. The Secretary of Defense and the Chairman of the Joint Chiefs plus various military types were seated at a table with a big screen PowerPoint presentation. The brass all remained seated. Pin a star on a man's shoulder pads, and he'll find a way to avoid kissing the presidential fingers. Somebody conjured up an order from the Pentagon's medical team and got all physical contact involving lips barred as a general practice. Unsanitary procedures reduce military readiness, they claimed.

"Is this the battle plan?" Roche pointed to the screen.

"We want you to have the latest facts," the JCS Chairman said. "There are alternatives to war that might be advantageous—"

"Are you the commander in chief?" Roche felt like caning the man. He settled for striking the desk. "I asked for a battle plan. Not alternatives. Are you deaf? Do you not understand how orders work? I give them. You carry them out."

"If you would hear us out," O'Brien said. "We have a few paths we could take. We need your guidance on which would be the best route."

Roche caught a glimpse of himself reflected in the window. He looked different. His face was harder, more muscular. His shoulders wider, brawnier. He was physically transforming from a mere president into Zenith Man. They needed his guidance. Roche nodded and rolled his hand for them to proceed.

The Chairman began reading from the slides. "The Saudis have placed sell orders for nearly a trillion dollars of stock in American companies. We've asked them to put that order on hold. So far, they've complied. But then they announced an auction of two hundred billion of US Treasuries."

"Blackmail." Roche imagined the panic such an auction would cause on Wall Street. "How bad would it get?"

"The Fed chairman says in a best-case scenario it would cause a slide, but other investors would pick up the slack. Ben at Treasury thinks the devaluation of Treasuries might cause a buying-frenzy. He thinks he can tip the balance in our favor."

"And worst-case?" Roche asked.

"An auction of more than one percent of our national debt could trigger a sell-off. We could be in an instant depression."

An admiral, whom Roche had never seen before, said, "China has threatened to join the Saudi auction, sir. They hold $1.1 trillion of our securities. A sell off would hurt them. But selling would hurt less than holding them through a sell-off. In other words, if they don't join the Saudis and there is a run on US Treasuries, the value of the Chinese investment could be cut by 40% or more. They believe it would be smarter to sell as much as possible in the first wave."

"Which would ensure a sell-off." Roche felt sick. "Japan, Brazil, Ireland are next in line for holding our debts. What is their position?"

"Pretty much the same, sir," the admiral said. "They'd have to sell to protect their reserves. If those top four join the Saudis, that's over $3 trillion in one auction."

"Worse," O'Brien said, "our allies have told us they will not buy US Treasuries if we declare war. Which means—"

"I'm not stupid." Roche slapped his cane on the table. "I get it. We can't finance the war effort."

He sat in silence. They stared at him. He hated it when they stared at him. They all thought they were superior. They all thought they were better and smarter. Why didn't it occur to them the people of the United States of America had elected him to be their boss? He was the ultimate American, elected to the highest office, not them. He was Zenith Man, and they were just grunts taking orders.

He got up and paced before coming back to rest his elbows on the back of his executive chair. He said, "You need to come up with a plan to counteract this problem."

"Well," O'Brien said, "we have a kind of a plan. And that's where we need your advice. We think it would prevent a Great Depression from happening on your watch, sir. When I heard it, I liked it. I think you will too. Mr. Chairman, will you explain it please?"

The Chairman coughed and switched to another slide. "We can replace the current investigating team with some special investigators. The team I'm talking about are top guys. They follow their orders and never leak a word of their operations. If their commanding officer gives them the order to discover a breach in safety protocols, we can rest assured, they will find a safety breach. We could wrap up the investigation and declare it an unavoidable accident. We would hold

Admiral Wilkes responsible. We could then diffuse—"

"Bury the whole thing?" Roche's question shook the room. He looked each of the men in the eye. What a collective disappointment.

Without the war to draw the people of the country together, the forces of evil would broaden the chasm between ideological groups in America. Investigators would continue to tear apart his brilliant record. People would whine about equality and fairness instead of relying on hard work to get ahead. Endless lines of people would stick out their palms expecting the government to fill them with gold. People from all over the world would stream into this country bringing their disgusting foods and filthy habits with them.

It was up to him, Chuck Roche, to save the country. No one else could make it happen. Tremendous undertakings always fell upon Zenith Man. It was his duty. One he was born to. It was time to fulfill that destiny. Time to become a great orator who could hold the country together in its hour of need. It was time to complete his transformation.

Roche turned to the window and stared into the dusky shadows. He started speaking quietly. "Those sailors who lost their lives on the *USS Caine* were the finest men ever to sail under our flag. What would I say to the red stain of American blood floating in the Persian Gulf if I were to give into your cowardly 'alternatives?'"

He turned to face the meeting room and scanned their faces again. Weak men.

"I don't make apologies." Roche crashed his cane on the table. "I don't bury reports. I take it to the terrorists who drew American blood. I swear to you, my fine gutless generals, I will rain down terror on our enemies. Fury will drop from our bombers—onto their heads. Death and destruction will become so common they'll think nothing of finding their dismembered babies in the rubble of their shopping malls."

The decorated generals went pale and pushed back in their seats.

"Our allies will fall in line when the missiles fly." Roche felt his voice reaching its optimum timbre. "Our enemies will tremble at the sound of our jets screaming over their cities. The modern shrieks of revenge. American vengeance for the cowardly way the Arabs have treated the United States for the last fifty years. NO MORE! Do you hear me? NO MORE!

"I will have this war. I will cut out every tongue who dares to speak against me. Whether it's ours or theirs. Only one voice will be heard in this country, and that is the united voice of all Americans standing together and demanding action. Blood for the deaths of our sailors! Blood for attacks on America!"

Using his cane, he pointed to the door. After a moment of hesitation, the officers grabbed their things and fled the room. O'Brien stopped at the door. He turned, papers falling from his clutches. His mouth opened. He changed his mind, turned and left.

Roche pulled his phone and brought up Twitter. He sent, "Call your representatives. Demand blood for the deaths of the brave sailors of the *USS Caine.* We are ready for this battle. We are guided by the spirits of the 9-11 victims. The murdered and beheaded missionaries, the strangled women and children cry out for vengeance."

He had one more thought that wouldn't fit in Twitter's 280-character limit. He started a second tweet. "This war will break the enemy and bring revenge for our people. We have been the victims of terrorism for too long. NO MORE! Shout it from the roof tops, send it in emails, call your congressman, tell the world, NO MORE!"

CHAPTER 32

MERCURY GRABBED MY COLLAR. *DUDE, did I say run? Did you? Think about this. Redjackets are not dumb. Why are their untrained wannabes clearing the exact place they expected to find you?*

I cringed. There are times when the holy messenger is right. *Where are the rest of them?*

Coming atcha from all sides now. Mercury folded his arms with an I-told-you-so expression on his face.

What's my best escape route? I asked.

Fold your hands on top of your head, get on your knees, hope they don't kill you right off.

I said, *Or I could fight long enough to make sure my friends get away.*

Leading with my pistol, I poked my head around the corner. One dead, one on the floor wounded, and the third aiming for my head. He squeezed off four bullets.

"Yo," I said. "Haven't you guys done enough damage to each other? Don't go shooting over your partner's head."

There was silence. I estimated the shooter's position and fired a round at thigh-level through the thin wall. Plaster dust kicked up along with the Redjacket's howl.

I said, "Toss your pistol my way, and I won't kill you."

"Do it, Ben," the wounded man said. "Before you shoot me again."

"Well, you shot Mike."

Ben didn't sound like he was going to win any lightning rounds in the IQ test.

The clatter of two guns hitting the tiled floor came next. I ducked out and back in to get a sense of the layout and to see if they had any other weapons. Nothing happened. No shots fired.

I picked up all three guns and ran down the hallway, tossing magazines one way and weapons in the other.

The hallway turned a corner at what had to be the back of the building. A quick peek into the darkness beyond showed me three Redjackets coming my way. I looked for another way out.

Mercury leaned against the wall. *Hands on top of your head in three… two…*

I said, *Did they get Dhanpal out of the building?*

Mercury said, *Yes, but your time is up.*

"Hands on your head." Chopra's voice.

I complied and made a slow turn. She held a rifle. Three Redjackets covered her in perfect formation. They were the veterans I should've known were using Ben, Mike, and the wounded guy as bait. They had me cold.

"On your knees." Chopra's command voice was a lot different from her casual voice.

I fell to my knees. They pulled my hands behind my back and cuffed them. Chopra slammed her rifle butt into my face.

I ALWAYS WANTED TO BE one of those movie heroes who gets hit with a skull-crushing sledgehammer and gets right back up. Never happens like that in my life.

My consciousness came back slowly. Like other real people, I was confused about what had happened, what day it was, what city I was in. I was being carried to a filthy room in a filthy building. Not the whorehouse. Cold water splashed on my face several times over a period of what felt like months but was probably a few minutes.

"Where did they go?" Chopra's voice again. It sounded familiar as if she'd been repeating that phrase for a while.

"What?" The question came out involuntarily.

"Surprised to hear my voice?" She put a gloat in her words.

"Not at all." I tried to sound cool and collected. "You're a terrible actress. You were far too easy at the airport. Would the IB share intel with foreigners? Please. You left your keys in the car in the bad part of town. That was a big clue."

She huffed. "Where did your friends go then?"

"Dushanbe or Samarkind," I said. "Whichever has the best WiFi."

She slapped me hard. Three men chuckled behind her.

"Does this mean you're not interested in dating anymore?" I asked. "Or is this some kind of BDSM courting ritual?"

Her audience chuckled again but cut it off fast. She must've given them a silencing glance. Which made me realize my vision wasn't what it used to be. It was all dark. The sensations of a blindfold came to me. Along with the pain of a broken nose. I was lying on a table or something with minimal cushion.

"Where did they go?" she repeated.

"If I knew, I would've gone with them."

"Where is Admiral Wilkes?"

"She's not with them?"

My smart-alec response earned me another slap. This time, one of Chopra's friends dropped an anvil on my chest. Felt like an anvil anyway.

"You promised me Wilkes," Chopra said.

"India doesn't care about Wilkes. Why do——" Another anvil landed on me.

"You're not going anywhere until I get Wilkes."

"Why go rogue? You have a career ahead of you. Had."

"Wilkes is critical to my country. We will be quite generous and grateful if you tell me where to find her."

"You think these Redjackets are going to help you in some way? You must've missed the intelligence on them. Backstabbing, disloyal, traitorous—" Another anvil. "—oof."

Mercury said, *Are you keeping this up until I tell you the team is safe? Aw, homes, that's like something honorable. I thought you quit risking your life to save others when you left the army. Are you back to being honorable? You da man.*

I said, *Let me know when they're in the air. Then these clowns can kill me.*

Mercury pulled up my blindfold. *Kill you? No way I let these mortals kill one of my disciples. Huh-uh, brutha. I get to do that. No god smites like I smite.*

I said, *OK.*

Chopra dropped the blindfold back in place. "OK, what?"

"I get it." I took a deep breath. "Someone promised you a visa or something."

"I'm going to step up the interrogation." She shuffled around a bit. "You could die, yeah? But that's a risk I'm willing to take."

An electric shock ripped through my body like a bolt of lightning. The pain seared through every cell from head to toe. My muscles violently convulsed as if they were tearing themselves from my bones. Then it stopped. I felt an overwhelming thirst. Then came another shock.

"As I said," Chopra continued, "this could bloody well kill you."

Zap. My muscles convulsed hard enough to break bones. My head hit the table, my feet spasmed. The thirst returned. All I could think about was water.

Mercury's voice slid in my ear. *Holding up fine, my brutha. But a dead disciple is not a very good disciple. Tell her what you know. Tell her about the grandparents.*

I said, *Never. Fuck the Redjackets.*

"Fuck who?" Chopra gave me another jolt electricity.

Mercury said, *Honorable, bro, but what about saving Dhanpal makes you hold out against letting them find Wilkes?*

I wasn't entirely sure. I said, *Dhanpal thought she was important enough to go through hell with these guys. Maybe she knows something the world ought to know. Beats me. I'm doing this for Dhanpal.*

"Live up to your commitments, Jacob." Chopra's face was close enough to feel the heat of her skin. "You committed to giving me Wilkes."

I gathered all my strength just to speak. "I committed to support and defend the Constitution of the United States, which is more than your scumbag friends ever did."

"I served, asshole." Someone in the back of the room had shouted that shortly before being slammed by his friends.

"What unit?" I asked.

"75th Rangers."

A Ranger like me. That was depressing. But then, all kinds of good people have been fooled by the Con Man in Chief.

Thirsty. Like never before.

I heard feet scuffling out of the room. A door closed.

The shock treatment came back in force. My back rose off the table and slammed down with incredible force. Water. Cool, clear water.

Chopra said, "I need to know what your friend did with Wilkes. Dhanpal isn't getting out of the country. I have every airport checkpoint looking for your friends. They're going nowhere. So you may as well tell me."

"Did Roche promise you citizenship?"

"Wilkes. I want Wilkes."

More electric shocks. More thirst.

"Oh, I get it," I said after the pain subsided a little. "Look, I'm sorry I turned you down for a date. I know that had to sting after you summoned all your courage to ask me out. But. Hey, I could put up with you for one round of drinks—as long as I don't have to put out afterward."

Surprise. A much longer shock followed that one.

Noises of people coming in and going out were followed by silence. We were alone. Maybe. I was still thirsty. Like dying-in-the-desert thirsty.

Mercury said, *Smartass much, homie? Get ready. She just stepped out of the room for a few seconds. There's a loose screw on the edge of the table near your left hip. Rip the plasticuffs with it and get out of here.*

I said, *Thanks. You're the best god I ever believed in.*

Mercury said, *Aw, dude. You're finally coming around. But then, you never believed in any of us, so you're not fooling anybody.*

I started squirming for the edge of the table. I felt the screw, right where he said it would be. Praise be to Mercury.

My wrists barely made it to the edge. I nearly fell off before I could get the right angle.

Wait a second. Mercury sounded panicked. *Never mind. They decided to kill you. They're coming back. Well. It was nice knowing you. Ima check out Cody. I think he can see me.*

I lay back down. The plasticuffs felt frayed but not broken. I struggled against them.

Chopra ripped my blindfold off. My eyes squeezed shut from the pain of sudden light. Then I made out Radhika Chopra's angry face. She was a lot prettier without the scowl.

"Citizenship, right?" I asked.

She held an old but shiny revolver to my forehead. The safety was off. She noticed me looking at the gun. "Like it? It was my grandfather's."

"He must be so proud."

"Last time, Stearne." She pressed the barrel hard against my skin.

There is something about spending years in battle that gives a soldier some insight into the soul of the enemy. To take the life of another human being you must be a total psychopath like me, or so angry your face shows it in excruciating detail. I'd looked into the eyes of enough people at close range to know the difference. Chopra belonged to the angry group. She was angry enough to pull the trigger, but she wasn't enough of a psychopath to go through with it. Her fingers tensed on the grip.

"You got me." I sighed. "New Delhi. Holiday Inn, downtown. Say, could I get some water?"

"This is no joke." She raised the pistol to emphasize her point. "You are going to die if you don't answer the question."

"When you join the army, you figure you're already dead. Every day after that is like a gift. All you're telling me is that I've run out of gifts."

"I'm bloody serious." Her voice was cold. Her gaze went slack like a soldier's stare. She mentally moved from angry to psychopath. Welcome to the club.

Mercury said, *Tell her about the grandparents.*

I said, *Why?*

Mercury said, *Dawg, are you in a coma? Dhanpal's grandparents are the only ones who know where Wilkes is. The old man is the one who squirreled away the admiral. Chopra has the Singh's stashed somewhere. Turn them over and you could go home. You claimed you never cared about Wilkes.*

He was testing me. I hate when the gods do that. If I fell for it, he'd unleash some ancient Roman torture on me.

I'm not giving her spit, I said. *Did Miguel get the team to safety yet?*

Mercury said, *They're on the apron, waiting for clearance to take off. It's morning, there's a rush hour for runways.*

I said, *Then this is it. Chopra gets nothing. Dhanpal gets medical care. I go to the big pantheon in the sky.*

Mercury said, *That's dope, dawg. You're actually going the honorable route. Cannot believe it. But dying isn't going to accomplish anything.*

I said, *She's not going to kill me. She doesn't have the stomach for it. Besides, women find me irresistible.*

I struggled against my plasticuffs. The last bit of plastic stretched but didn't break. I couldn't take the gun from her. I caught Chopra's gaze. I gave her my puppy dog look. It didn't work. Our eyes locked in mortal combat. She hated me with a deep and irreversible passion—and she'd reached her inner psychopath.

I reassessed my estimation of her.

Apparently, she did have the stomach for it.

I turned to Mercury, *What about the woman I want to spend the rest of my life with—don't I get a chance to find her? I want kids. Don't I get kids? How about a chance to say goodbye to Mom?*

Mercury shrugged.

Chopra's finger wrapped tighter around the trigger. She squeezed it. The cylinder turned. The round copper heads of bullets rested in every chamber. No chance for Russian Roulette. The hammer reared back. The trigger reached its release point. The hammer slammed down.

CHAPTER 33

PIA'S DOCTOR RODE WITH HER in the helicopter. Ice packs were like an old friend from her soccer days. The one she held to her eye wasn't big enough to cover her chin at the same time. She lowered it a little and glanced out the window. They were flying over the Sabel Technology campus. Halfway home.

She wondered if the cops would get anything out of the Redjackets. Then a horrible thought occurred to her. When she'd regained consciousness, cameras were flashing all around her. She'd been too dazed to shield her face. Had Gina Wind helped? Or had she snapped her own photos? Pia couldn't recall. Nothing she could do about it now. Besides, the public had seen it before.

The flight took her to Shady Grove hospital at the doctor's insistence. She didn't need an x-ray, she knew her nose was broken. She'd broken it enough in games to know the severity by the throb. Her cosmetic surgeon used to joke about keeping him on retainer.

The Major waited for her on the helipad. She didn't speak, she just took Pia's hand and walked with her to the radiology department. They waited for the radiologist in the emergency room.

"Thank you for not saying I told you so," Pia said.

"Hunter didn't respond because protocol wouldn't let her." The Major crossed her arms. "At the first sign of violence, the Secret Service secures and evacuates their principal."

Logically, Pia knew that to be true. Yet the image of Hunter's cold dispassionate eyes had burned itself into Pia's memory.

"How did they know I was there?" Pia adjusted the new ice packs the nurses had given her.

"Not even I knew where you were until I got the call," the Major said. She sat in the plastic chair next to the exam table. "Roche told you he had a mole. We need to find—"

"No one knew." Paper crinkled beneath her when she hopped off the bed. "I wasn't sure that's where I was going until I left Baltimore. They must have spotters."

"Everyone knows you've been hanging around Hunter lately." The Major's bitterness was understandable. "They could follow her schedule to find you."

Pia let it go. Maybe the Major would understand one day. Maybe not. But the incident pointed out one obvious thing to Pia. The operation with Hunter wasn't working. She was playing Hunter's game. Her coaches' mantra replayed in her head: play your game not the other team's. The Major had been telling her the same thing in a different way.

"You don't have to worry about Hunter anymore." Pia got back on the examining table, lay down and tried to comfortably balance the ice packs on her face.

The doctor came in with a big smile. He said, "I love the question you threw at the VP! 'Why do you lie to these people?' Someone needed to call out the administration on this stuff. Have you thought about running for office?"

He explained the nursing staff had been watching her clip on a news site. Then he showed her x-rays. Her nose was indeed broken again. And her orbital socket had a hairline fracture of the rim that ran through a few older, healed fractures. She'd lost a tooth, but the jaw remained intact. There was nothing they could do for the orbital rim. They would schedule follow-ups for a new tooth and nose job. Then they released her.

The Major led her to a waiting limo. They drove off in silence.

"It had to be Hunter." Pia's statement hung between them after they'd ridden for miles. "But she was on stage when I arrived. She didn't text anyone. Would she have arranged for Redjackets to follow her? Stake out her appearances, knowing the Secret Service would keep her out of it? Complete deniability."

"Why do you trust her?" the Major asked.

"It's not trust. It's access. Hunter gave me hope. She promised to get me close enough to Roche to avenge the murders of Lloyd and Sandra." Pia used the first names of her first adoptive parents.

"Avenge? Pia!" The Major faced her and grabbed her arm. "You can't kill the President of the United States."

"Killing's too good for him. What's worse than death to a narcissist? Public humiliation. Shame."

The Major took a call while Pia immersed herself in thought. The Major dropped her at Sabel Gardens and returned to the office. She took a bag of peas from the freezer—better than anything medical supply companies produced—and headed to her wing.

She felt alone now more than ever. She'd always been alone. Even though her economic situation was the opposite of slaves, she felt the words of their old spiritual. *Sometimes I feel like a motherless child. A long way from home. Sometimes I feel like I'm almost gone. Way up in the heavenly land.* She felt the words in her marrow.

Thoughts flooded her mind, fast and disorganized. Again, the image of Hunter's emotionless face watching Pia collapse in pain and agony surfaced. Hunter had promised the end of the Roche Regime. She'd promised to let Pia unleash her rage. What happened? Hunter had reacted harshly when Pia tried to upload the contents to her server. Was that the catalyst for this attack?

Pia knew from the beginning Hunter was duplicitous. The VP had convinced Roche that Pia would bring youth, money and vitality to his campaign if he brought her in. At the same time, Hunter promised Pia she could better find dirt on Roche from within the administration. A typical fulcrum for a politician, playing both sides to see which one had more leverage. Pia felt no compulsion to play that game anymore.

Pia noticed something new in her sitting room. A painting had been removed and her little black jersey, pinned and mounted in a frame, hung in its place. The dividing line in her childhood. The tragic horror followed by Alan Sabel's safe space. What would life have been like if her parents hadn't been murdered? What would it have been like if Hunter kept Pia and raised her? Would she have won all the championships? Would she have become successful at everything she attempted—except destroying Roche?

It was time to change course. She liked shooting bad guys and she'd wanted to get back in the field for a long time. Why not go to Mumbai?

Pia Sabel had been the greatest to play the game because she'd thrown herself into soccer as an escape from the terrors haunting her youngest days. Now it was time to throw herself into destroying Roche. With or without anyone's help.

She'd always been alone.

"I swear," she touched the jersey's frame, "one way or another, Roche is going down."

CHAPTER 34

VERONICA HUNTER NODDED GOOD-EVENING TO the first nephew as she crossed the West Wing lobby to the Roosevelt Room. Inside, her traitorous coconspirators waited in silence. As soon as the door closed behind her, they started pleading their cases. Roche forced them. He threatened them. They had no choice.

"You came to me looking to save your careers," she crossed her arms and faced them, "and this is how you treat me? As if I cared why you weaseled out on me. You're like a bunch of mobsters jumping for the first plea agreement. First one in gets the best deal. Your problem is, he's a classic narcissist. There's no deal he won't back out of. And you guys just figured that out. Well, I don't care what you did. What I want to know is: what do you plan to do next?"

All four of them stood in a line in front of the fireplace. They looked at each other with open mouths and no ideas.

"Haven't thought that far ahead?" Hunter shook her head.

She held up the Redjacket phone and stared at Thomas. "Does this work? Is it bugged? What happens if I call the Redjackets on it?"

"Why, of course, it works." He stammered and looked at Ratched. "It can't be bugged. It's perfectly clean, you can trust it. It's a CIA phone. Not even Sabel can bug those things."

"And the Redjackets I call?" Hunter nosed in like a drill sergeant.

"I thought you done called them." The Texan shook his head. "They beat up the Sabel girl for you. Isn't that what you wanted?"

"Chuck never made that video transferring leadership from him to me. They won't listen to me."

Ratched said, "You think Chuck's dumb enough to make that video?

It would be a confession you'd use against him."

"And if he doesn't transfer leadership to me," Hunter snapped back, "I'd be a fool to give them orders. He'd use it against me."

"Whoa, now." Thomas held up a hand. "You had to be the one who set them on Sabel. After our first meeting, you asked me to have them do you a favor."

"I didn't even know she was coming to—"

Roche's voice in the hallway approached the door. Hunter shoved the phone deep in her purse and covered it with a scarf.

Together, the five watched the door handle turn. The door swung open. Roche stepped into the room. He looked them over with disgust.

Hunter faced Roche. "We have agreed, you truly are the original Zenith Man."

"Bullshit." He turned and headed back to the Oval Office. "Follow me, Veronica. The rest of you—get back to work. I want that war. NOW!"

Hunter followed him in.

"You'll never trust them again," Roche said.

"I never trusted them in the first place." Hunter crossed to his desk and started rifling through his drawers.

"Hey," Roche said. "Get out of there. What do you think you're doing?"

Hunter flashed an angry glance his way. "Is the Redjacket phone the only way to contact them?"

"Of course it is." He grabbed her arm and yanked. "We need to discuss your child."

Hunter pulled free and kept opening drawers and pawing through them before slamming them closed.

Roche said, "That stunt you pulled beating up your kid took the wind out of my war. I had all of Twitter retweeting my call to arms, but that video took over everything. By the way, she looked terrible. You should be ashamed."

"That was all your doing," Hunter looked up. She felt the heat in her face. She always kept her cool under fire. This time, she was pissed as hell and didn't care. "You had her beaten. I should tear you apart."

"Nice cover story. You're a failure, Veronica. You failed to win the election. You failed in your little coup. And you failed to control the Redjackets."

Hunter rifled the contents of the last drawer. Nothing. No second phone. Maybe he left it upstairs in the living quarters. Maybe he had it taped to the bottom of his chair.

"Pia's beating was a bad decision." Roche picked up a bag of Cheetos. "Not that your little brat didn't have it coming, I'm pleased about that part. You made me look stupid. I hate that part. You need to take her off the front page. Get her out of the area."

Hunter looked up from the desk. She wanted to kill him. She'd been angry many times in her life, but never like this. She really wanted to rip the head off his body and roll it into the Rose Garden.

"You should get her out of the country," he said. "Talk her into joining her pals in Mumbai. She would love to bring in Wilkes by herself."

Hunter came out from behind the desk. In five steps she was toe to toe with him. She batted away his Cheetos. "Mumbai? How many Redjackets did you send there? How long would she survive?"

"If you think I'm trying to kill her, use the magic phone." He looked at his Cheetos scattered on the floor. "Call them and tell them to stand down."

Hunter shoved him.

He staggered back a step.

"Don't fuck with me, Veronica." He raised his cane and came back to her. "I have her Kill-Video. The right people will put it in the daily briefing. A few days from now, I'll be asked to renew the security levels. I'll ask about the contents of that video. When it's revealed, I'll have a decision to make. Should I keep it under wraps or release it to Congress? If I release it, what do you think Congress will do? Will they vote to oust their precious vice president?"

Hunter calculated the bureaucracy's controls. She had asked Ratched to bury it when she was president. Ratched moved to State months ago. Under a new regime, legitimate reviews of things kept under lock and key happened all the time. It could easily come to light without implicating Roche in the cover up.

Roche watched her eyes like a hawk hovering high above a mouse. "What do you think the Hill will think of you covering up your daughter's crimes?"

"What do you want?"

"I want Congress to declare war on Saudi Arabia. We haven't declared war on anyone since 1941. Making history is Zenith Man's destiny. But every time I get the ball rolling, your little rug rat lands on every website in the country. Get rid of her."

"By sending her to her death?"

"She's survived worse."

"You think you outsmarted her." Hunter peered into his eyes. "I doubt that. On the other hand, given what happened a couple hours ago, she's safer there than she is here. I'll talk to her, see if she takes the bait."

"Better get moving."

"What do I get out of it?"

"Nothing."

"I want the other phone. The one that you really use to talk to the Redjackets."

"You haven't been listening, there isn't one."

Neither of them had blinked in some time. Hunter kept thinking about her options while holding his unwavering gaze. There had to be a second phone. Thomas had gone overboard convincing her the one she held was invincible. If he'd told her there was no way to be sure, she might've believed him.

Releasing the Kill-Video would end her career. There was a potential risk of jail time for both Pia and Hunter. Sending the kid off wasn't as big a risk as keeping her around. Pia would do fine in Mumbai. The main reason Hunter resisted was her hatred of doing anything Roche wanted. She could get over that if he were serious about the video.

There was one last card to play before she capitulated. It was risky in a hundred ways, especially if it worked.

She pulled out her regular phone, careful to keep the Redjacket phone from view. When Pia answered, Hunter said, "This time, I need your help. That phone I gave you with Chuck's picture on it, can your people take it apart and discover any secrets it holds?"

Hunter paused for effect because Pia was still ranting and hadn't heard a word.

Roche's face had gone crimson with fury. He shouted, "You gave a high-security phone to someone without a security clearance? I'm having you arrested!"

Hunter faced him with a finger in the air to wait. "Great, let's get together later tonight and discuss how to release your findings."

She clicked off. It was a huge bluff. One Roche couldn't afford to call. If Pia had heard Hunter at all, she would have a lot of questions. It might lead to actually turning over the Redjacket phone to Pia. Which wouldn't be such a bad idea in the grand scheme of things.

"Mutually assured destruction, Chuck." Hunter shoved her phone in her purse. "Anything happens to Pia—like that Kill-Video coming out—and she releases the phone data. I'll take your silence as your agreement. Don't worry, I'll drop a hint about her bringing Wilkes in."

Hunter headed out the door and through the lobby to the exit. Her limo awaited her.

She got in and closed the door and redialed Pia. "Calm down. I really need your help." She waited a beat. "Pia, stop shouting and listen to me. Pia! I have something on Chuck."

CHAPTER 35

RADHIKA CHOPRA LOOKED AT ME with a mixture of surprise and fear. We both knew what had happened. Her fear concerned what would happen next. For good reason. Because. For the first time in my life, I took a swing at a woman. As hard as I could. And I didn't feel bad about it. My hands broke the plasticuffs. My swing was awkward. My fist didn't land square. At least it sent her sprawling.

Jumping from the table—I fell flat on my face. I'd forgotten my ankles were zip-tied. So much for the hero-getaway.

Chopra pulled a knife and slashed at me. With a quick roll, I body slammed her and pushed her on her side. I pounded my knee into the bottom of her butt cheek. It was a nasty trick soccer players pull when the refs aren't looking. Ms. Sabel taught me. The pain incapacitated the victim for a whole second. Enough time to slam an elbow into her temple and knock her out.

I took her knife and slit the zip tie off my ankles and assessed the room. Then I grabbed her revolver. Might work as a bluff. I looked around for a bottle of water, I was still thirsty.

Mercury held the firing pin in the palm of his hand. Every firearm has a small metal pin attached to the hammer that strikes the bullet. Without it, the gun is worthless. Firing pins aren't held on with Superglue. They rarely just fall off. Even on an ancient relic like Chopra's. Over time, expansion and contraction from hot and cold environments can work the pin loose. It is one of the things you check when buying an antique. On the other hand, there could've been divine intervention involved. Mercury was implying he had somehow wrenched it off. If so, I owed a lifetime of gratitude to a certain god. But. First, I would have to believe he actually existed and wasn't part of what some psychiatrists labeled as my PTSD-induced schizophrenia. At that moment, I was leaning toward accepting divine intervention. The evidence was in the palm of his hand.

But if there's one thing I find annoying, it's a god so insecure he needs adoration while you're in the middle of making a break for it.

I said, *Which way out?*

Uh. Dude. Mercury tried to draw my gaze to the firing pin.

I get it, you saved my life. Thanks. Which way out?

Fucking mortals. Mercury tossed the firing pin over his shoulder and pointed to the window. *Wasting my time, they said. Ungrateful bastard, they said. He's never going to give thanks and praise much less make a sacrificial offering, they said. Hung like a centipede, they said.*

I didn't hang around to ask about the centipede reference. I punched out the window. Then suddenly something registered in my brain. Chopra's purse sat on a small table. I fished out her keys. Running back to the window, I slid out and crept to the edge of the building. I glanced around at the neighborhood. Nowhere near Congress. No idea where I was. Or where to go from here. But that never stopped me before.

A Redjacket stood guard near a door in the morning sunshine. He had a rifle across his chest like a pro. Not far beyond him, my favorite Tata, recovered from Coal Bunder, waited for my triumphant return. I pressed my back to the wall in the shadow of a Blue Jacaranda. Pros would have one man stand at the door while another walked the perimeter in a random pattern. If they had the numbers, they'd have three or four outside. I listened for footsteps, conversation, anything. Nothing but silence.

It was now or never. Holding the pistol by the barrel, I took three quick strides and brought it down hard. The guard faced me just as I arrived. With no time to defend himself, he collapsed under the blow but got off a warning grunt.

I snatched his rifle and pulled a Glock out of his belt.

"You OK, Jared?" A voice from around the corner.

"Hit my head on the fucking branch," I said.

I ran for the Tata, unlocking it at a distance. I jumped in and looked over my shoulder. A Redjacket was pulling up his rifle. He was untrained and scared. His hands shook from the adrenaline pumping through his muscles. Leaning against the corner of the building, he steadied himself.

"Don't do it." I fumbled the keys into the ignition.

When I checked again, he was aiming at me. I leveled my weapon and held it steady. I hesitated because he was American. He fired. The first round missed the windshield by an inch. He pulled the trigger a second time before he handled the recoil. A common mistake for someone in a hurry. The second went high. He realized what had gone wrong and took more careful aim.

"Don't do it," I called again.

His eyes lined up behind the sights.

Self-preservation. I fired. My round hit him in the aorta. The man fell to his knees as blood spurted out like an ugly fountain. He looked at me with a question.

"Because you fired first." I cradled the rifle and started up the car and dropped it in drive and hit the accelerator and flew out of the dirt lot.

I felt like a heel.

In the rearview mirror, I saw Americans pouring out of the squat building behind me. They were in shock but trained well. They prioritized in units. Three of them assessed their two compatriots. Another two took off in pursuit. Four more secured the area. One man watched my vehicle dive into a narrow lane between buildings and realized whose car it was. Which informed him about his adversaries. Rather than an attack by an unknown force, it was an escape of one person.

I rounded a corner, so I lost sight of the leader, but I knew what he would do. He would re-task everyone from securing the perimeter to giving chase. There were two close behind me in one car. There would soon be three or four cars with two each, driver and shooter.

I nearly ran over two kids walking to school. After my swerve, my foot hit the floor. The passenger mirror smacked a telephone pole. The left fender scraped a storefront. I squeezed between shanties stacked four-high and skidded sideways onto a broad boulevard. I floored it, then slammed on the brakes.

All the cars in the world were in my lane, heading straight for me at high speed.

Mercury appeared in the passenger seat. *Forget something, homeboy? Former British colonies drive on the left.*

I swerved through a median made of planters to get back on the left. Ahead of me were the gleaming glass and steel buildings of a monumental industrial complex. Something on the dashboard spoke to me in Hindi.

I turned to Mercury, *How do I get out of here. A wide street like this is a shooting gallery for them.*

He shrugged.

Traffic stopped for a light. The pursuit car flew toward me. I kept my speed up, closing on the stationary vehicles with frightening velocity. A guy stood up through the sunroof and aimed at me. I swerved a little. The driver didn't follow my jogs which kept his shooter upright. As they got close enough to ensure a clean kill, I stood on the brakes. They slammed into the back of Chopra's Tata. Their airbags deployed, their radiator blew up. The shooter flew out of the sunroof and crushed his nose on Chopra's rear window.

Her rental car company would be pissed.

I floored it into the oncoming lane. Driving on the left is just wrong.

Mercury said, *You think I'm going to save your life in traffic after you dissed me on the firing pin, dawg?*

I said, *Nah. I got this.*

Oncoming traffic swerved around me, honking, waving, and shouting. I put on my flasher to make a right turn. Someone trying to avoid me dove into the space I wanted. The Tata stopped an inch from a fruit stand. Backing up, and making the turn, I saw a car full of Americans coming from one direction and a cop car coming from the other.

I sped down the side street.

Mercury said, *Where you think you're going, anyway, homie?*

I said, *Anywhere away from them.*

Mercury said, *That's where you're wrong. You need to get back there. Pretty little Radhika tried to kill you. You gonna let that stand?*

Are you nuts? I said. *Go back there? I'll get killed.*

Mercury said, *What's that in your lap?*

I glanced down. The rifle I took from the guard was an AR-10, .308 caliber, set up with a scope for deer hunting. Not military issue, thank Jupiter. Still, anything that could kill a deer could have ended my dreams.

No way, I said. *I'm going to the nearest airport to wait for a Sabel Security extraction.*

Dude, Mercury slapped the back of my head, *when did you stop thinking in terms of god and country? Since when is it all about you?*

I did what I set out to do, I said. *Rescue Dhanpal. I plan to get home and make that pork stuffed cannelloni. That means it's time to do what I do best: flee quicker'n a rat out of an aqueduct.*

I sideswiped a parked car trying to navigate the narrow side streets.

Quit thinking like a scared little white boy and start thinking like a Caesar. Mercury popped a grape in his mouth. *Pia-Caesar-Sabel would be disappointed to see you cut and run like this. Good thing she ain't here, huh?*

I'm not running! I looked at his handful of grapes. I was still thirsty after those shocks. *OK—technically—I'm running. But what do you think is going to happen if I go back there?*

You're going to die. Mercury ate another grape and eyed me with grave concern. *But hey, at least your miserable attempt at a life will end in a blaze of glory. Oh. And you might save Sunil and Jabamani.*

I said, *Who?*

As soon as I said it, I knew who. They were Dhanpal's grandparents, and there was a good chance they were tied up in the same hovel I'd just escaped from. As soon as he found out, Dhanpal would fight hospital staff to let him out so he could come back and save them.

Mercury popped another grape. *I can help you kill Chopra before you die.*

Two blocks in front of me, a Subaru skidded to a stop in the cross street, blocking my route.

I knew a jack-in-the-box shooter would pop out any second. Driving with one knee, I leaned the AR-10 out the window. As soon as his head came up, I popped off a round with the hope it would brush him back. Shooting from an odd angle while driving on a bad-brick road isn't as easy as one might think. I took out the driver which shocked the shooter enough to fire back.

But his car jerked forward as the driver spasmed on the gas pedal. He ducked down and took the wheel and drove forward into the side of a building.

As I rolled by, I squeezed off a couple rounds at his gas tank.

Mercury said, *You need to save the world. Get the Singhs, have them lead you to Wilkes, and then go back to that weird pork thing you were making last week.*

Why can't I have a nice, quiet life like everyone else? Want to know what I care about? I care about sleeping in my bed once in a while. I care about making a dinner nice enough to make a young lady fall in love with me. You know what I don't care about? I don't care about Wilkes.

No one followed me for several blocks. I found the Mumbai version of a Circle K and drove around the block to make sure I'd lost the Redjackets. Three men stood outside the little shop looking at me like I was an alien from outer space.

Mercury was right, though. As much as I didn't want to tangle with my fellow Americans, especially a brother Ranger, I had to go back. Every time I blinked, an image of Dhanpal with gangrene played inside my eyes. Those squirmy Redjackets did that to him. I should've been there.

I said to Mercury, *I don't care about the Singhs either, except that I can't let Dhanpal come back and rescue them. I'll never hear the end of it. 'A Ranger couldn't get the job done, so a SEAL with gangrene had to do it.' Besides, I've got to find out why a nice girl like Chopra would sign on with the Redjackets.*

I pulled in front of the shop and stopped.

Nice girl, bro? Mercury ate another grape and looked at me. *She beat the crap out of you. She put a pistol to your forehead and pulled the trigger. What kind of sick, kinky shit are you into anyway?*

I got out and went inside and bought a big ass bottle of water and guzzled half while paying for it. I went outside and offered the men €500 to drive Chopra's Tata to Coal Bunder and leave it there. They jumped at the chance. I took the rifle and a rain coat to cover it and said goodbye to the Tata. It looked like hell, but it had treated me well.

I trudged up the road with my favorite god. *Which way to Chopra's crib?*

CHAPTER 36

"YOU'RE NOT DONE WITH HER, *flaca*?" Bianca Dominguez stood in Pia's home office.

"She claimed to have real dirt on Roche." Pia leaned back against her desk and crossed her arms. "I can't pass up the opportunity."

Pia's mind reeled through options and alternatives to ever seeing Hunter again. None of them resulted in bringing down Roche. She needed to keep her mind from spinning out of control. "How's married life treating you?"

"Emily wants children." Bianca had a dreamy look in her eye. "Are we ready for children? We hope we are. There are so many things to consider. Who would we pick for a donor? Would he agree? How does that work out twenty years later? Is adoption a good idea?"

Bianca choked her last question.

"Yes, I'm adopted." Pia gave her friend a disarming smile. "But I have no opinion about other people's choices."

"You're sure about that?"

"You're thinking," Pia squeezed her friend's arm, "of the many times I challenged anti-abortion advocates to adopt from foster care. That's not a recommendation to prospective parents in general. That's my challenge to those who cling to the abortion issue as proof of their personal holiness. If life does begin at conception, it doesn't end at delivery. On any given day, there are half a million un-aborted children in foster care waiting for a loving home. If people truly believe others should not have abortions, they can prove it by adopting some of those abandoned children."

"We're not the kind to tell others what to do with their reproductive systems." Bianca relaxed. "We're leaning toward a donor. Emily claims she doesn't care, but she was quick to take my name after the wedding. To me, that indicates she's hewing closer to a traditional nuclear family than she lets on."

Pia laughed. "Not something I have to worry about for a while."

"You're not getting any younger, *flaca*. Better get serious about finding true love."

"My last 'true love' ended badly when—"

The butler announced Hunter as she swept past him.

Hunter shouldered between them, ignoring Bianca, and pushed the red phone into Pia's space.

"This is the phone you tried to hack earlier today," Hunter said.

Pia watched Hunter's gaze take in her injuries. The black eye, the bruised cheek, the broken nose. Hunter said nothing about them.

Pia took the phone. The picture of Roche popped up when she touched the screen. "And?"

"I heard—from people who would know—that President Roche has committed a crime. Evidence of that might be on this phone. I also heard that he directed the Redjackets directly from this."

"Hi, Madam Vice President," Bianca grabbed Hunter's arm and turned her. "I'm Bianca Dominguez. We've never met, but you once fired me for helping Pia. Since then, I worked my way up to president of a $12 billion division of Sabel Industries." Bianca grabbed Hunter's hand and pumped it. "Thank you."

"Isn't that nice." Hunter gave her a fake smile. "You're welcome."

Hunter turned back to Pia. "Can you find out what's on there? Can you find out if there's evidence of his crimes on that phone?"

Pia's gaze rolled slowly from the phone to Hunter and back. "Me? I barely know how to turn mine on. Why don't we ask an expert in technology?" She brushed Hunter to the side. "Bianca, what do you think?"

Bianca's first glance at the phone gave her a look of utter shock. She took it as if it were a rabid animal. "Wait a minute. Is this what you were uploading to our server earlier today?"

"Yes."

"Thank god we deleted it." Bianca glanced back and forth at Pia and Hunter. "This is a CIA secure phone."

"I know," Hunter looked down her nose.

"Hacking this would be a serious crime." Bianca looked at the two. "Madam Vice President, just handing this to Pia, whose security clearance was revoked, might be a felony all by itself."

"I assure you," Hunter said, "if we find criminal conduct on it, I will pardon you."

"If you survive the impeachment." Bianca handed the phone back to Hunter. "What is the status of that phone? Who was it issued to?"

"That's what I'd like to know," Hunter said.

"Totally illegal, then." Bianca shook her head and backed up a step. "No way."

"How did you get it?" Pia asked.

"Chuck gave it to me."

"Why would he give you a phone filled with evidence of his crimes? He might seem stupid, but his evil is genius level. He had a reason."

"He wants me to get caught with it." Hunter sighed. "I'm speculating here, but I think he uses a different phone for real communications. This one could be full of texts and incriminating evidence that he can blame on me."

Pia caught Bianca's gaze. Her friend was not happy about the situation. Pia didn't mind breaking rules to get results. But she'd never ask anyone to commit a crime on her behalf. It never occurred to her that hacking this phone, with all its dark secrets, would cause Bianca to push back. Pia was not a lawyer, and her understanding of hacking was not great, but she understood the risk to her friend. Bianca loved the high security clearances she enjoyed at Sabel Technologies and previously at the NSA. She was one of the most trusted experts in the world. Falling into what could be a trap might lead to jail and a miserable future. Losing her career could end her family plans. It might even wreck her marriage.

Should she ask that much of Bianca? Could her plan work without Bianca?

"I have the best lawyers in the world. She's asked us to investigate a crime. We can—"

"You trust her why?" Bianca's usually calm voice had a desperate edge. "It would be her word against ours. This whole thing could be a set up by Hunter and Roche. And it wouldn't be the first."

Pia studied her birth mother and waited for a defense.

Hunter fidgeted. "What could I say that would make you believe me? Look at this thing. It might be the key to everything you wanted. It could bring down Roche. What assurance do you need from me?"

"I want it in writing," Bianca said.

Hunter gasped. "I … I can't do—"

"What I thought."

"Wait." Pia held up her hand. "What if Vice President Hunter asked you to help her recover lost files on the phone Chuck gave her? Would it be legal to help her?"

"Semantics, *flaca.*"

"If it were provable that she asked for help, would it be legal? As part of Sabel Technologies, could we legally fix a secure phone?"

"Technically? Yeah. But—"

"Trust me on this." Pia gave Bianca a stare then slid her gaze to the hidden security camera near her desk. Pia turned back to Hunter. "Do you want Bianca to check this phone for you?"

Hunter's gaze swept the room quickly as if looking for microphones. When she came back to Pia, she nodded. Then she turned to Bianca. "Could you help me by checking out this phone carefully and making sure everything that may have been meant for President Roche's eyes only has been carefully and securely archived for public records?"

Bianca nodded reluctantly and took the phone.

"How long will it take?" Hunter asked.

"This model is something they developed specifically to be un-hackable by Sabel Technologies. In theory, we should never get in without the encryption key. So …" Bianca frowned as she calculated an estimate, "maybe a couple hours?"

Hunter smiled. She looked at Pia as if waiting for an invitation to stay.

"How do you now it wasn't remotely wiped?" Pia referred to the security system built into nearly every secure phone.

Hunter smiled and held up the SIM card. Bianca snatched it from her.

"I'll show you out." Pia took Hunter's elbow and maneuvered her toward the door.

"Before I go," Hunter said. "How is Jacob getting along?"

"Before I answer, you owe me the name of a mole."

"Elmer Sabel," Hunter said.

The name struck like a knife. Pia staggered a step. Dad's first cousin. Her father had given him the job of caring for Pia's jets and cars. Not the brightest family member, but he was everyone's friend. A constant, pleasant and unremarkable presence. One who could ask anyone where they were going, and no one would guard their answer.

"Here's another proof of my allegiance to you," Hunter said. "Roche sent extra Redjackets to Mumbai. That shoot-to-kill tweet was an authentic instruction. That's why I asked. What's the latest news?"

"We just got word that Dhanpal is in the air, heading for a secret location to get medical attention. Jacob stayed behind. We believe he's close to finding Admiral Wilkes."

"Good news, then." Hunter stopped as Pia handed her off to the butler. She squeezed and held Pia's bicep. "You'll be going to Mumbai to help him for the final checkmate, I assume? When you do those last minute, heroic things, it always makes me so very proud of you."

"Goodbye, Veronica."

CHAPTER 37

ROCHE LOOKED AT THE NEWS feed on his phone. Congressional emergency hearings on the *USS Caine* investigation would start in the morning. Those hearings could go on forever. The Saudis could sink another ship before Congress moved. He sent a tweet to that effect.

He sent a secure text to the Joint Chiefs reminding them that he would be watching the hearings. He was doing everything in his power to protect the country. Anyone who went off script would be dealt with.

The weight of the world pressed on his shoulders. He was in the Oval Office. The most powerful room in the world. It was late at night. Everyone else had gone home. He kept working to save the country from terrorists. No one seemed to appreciate that.

Hartwell Thomas opened the door and leaned around it. "Sir, I just learned through a friend of mine at India's IB: the Redjackets failed. Stearne and his friends went and escaped."

Roche looked up slowly. "Are your boys any closer to finding Wilkes?"

"I'm afraid not, sir." Thomas backed out and closed the door quietly.

Roche pulled a Cheeto from the bag on his desk. He ate it, but it tasted no better than cardboard. All colors had faded to monotone, and all food was tasteless. He turned to the window and saw his reflection. Where was Hunter? Had she really teamed up with Sabel to take that phone apart? He'd erased everything, but the witches at Sabel could work their black magic on it and produce something. That would be his alternate story. Deepfakes. Computer generated videos. It would work as long as the Redjackets held firm and didn't turn on him. How much could he count on their loyalty?

Why did Hunter hate him so much? Why does the wind blow? Some things are just the way they are, and nothing can be done about it. But Sabel. She blamed him for killing her parents. She blamed him for telling Popov to kill Alan Sabel. That child wouldn't rest until he had been humiliated. He hated that thought more than anything.

All around him, his most loyal aides and confidants plotted against him. Everyone denounced him and denied him an easy, sweeping victory in war. Congress hampered everything he wanted to do. He might as well be a zoo animal. What good was a president who accomplished nothing between rising in the morning and going back to bed at night? Why had God given him this vast capacity to ferret out evil perpetrators if not to act? The nation would be destroyed by Muslims if not for him. Anyone could see that.

What stopped Congress from joining his call for justice against the Wahhabis who committed nearly all the terrorist attacks against the USA? Congress staggered through cowardly analysis, reviewing and reviewing and reviewing, hoping to prevent a mistake—when their sloth was the very mistake they were making.

They ridiculed him as a strutting and inexperienced president driven by naked ambition while ignoring his self-made fortune, his death-defying bravery, his indisputable leadership and his mandate from the vast majority of the American people. Yet they were the fools. They refused to act.

Roche knew how Zenith Man would gain the people's respect. Greatness is found in action.

And act he would. Zenith Man did not sit around waiting for death to find him. He went out and caused it. He would attack. Attack again and again.

First things first. The first and biggest problem Roche had was his VP. Was Hunter bluffing about the phone? Could they find anything incriminating on it? Who would care if she and her brat were both in jail?

He texted Gina Wind. "#whathappenedtoPopov?"

She texted back, "If you have something, prove it. Otherwise, Mr. President, piss off."

Roche threw his phone across the room and shouted in the empty space. "Damn her. I gave her that lead because she promised to run with it! Who does she think she is?"

Silence.

He crossed the room and found the pieces of his phone and tossed them in the trash. He went back to his desk and sat and stared at the desk phone.

He could feel his enemies closing in around him. The doubters and the liars and the investigators and all the vermin in the murky ooze surrounding the center of power. A fluke, they called him. An electoral mistake. An incompetent. He would show them. He could lead a nation better than anyone. There was no greater test of leadership than leading a country at war.

Religion was a superstition he found useful when he needed people to like him. But at times like this, they said prayer would help. He closed his eyes and tried to remember one of the prayers the religious people said in church. Something came to him though he couldn't remember where he heard it. *Most merciful God, we confess that we have sinned against you in thought, word, and deed, by what we have done, and by what we have left undone. We have not loved you with our whole heart; we have not loved our neighbors as ourselves.*

Sounded like a prayer for a bunch of losers. A prayer for people who think they're no better than anyone else. Everyone's equal? Not a prayer for Chuck Roche. Not a prayer for Zenith Man.

Then an idea came to him. One that didn't need a prayer. One that would ruin those who aided and abetted the traitorous Wilkes. With them out of the way, the Redjackets could dispose of her, and the nation could march to war. Only the true Zenith Man would have such a stroke of genius.

He smiled and sat and ate another Cheeto. The flavor had improved a good deal.

He picked up the landline and dialed Gina Wind's cellphone. "Get your ass to the Oval Office in five minutes, and I'll prove it."

"Mr. President," she hesitated, "I live in Reston. I couldn't get there that fast if I flew."

"Get here as soon as you can."

"This better not be one of your late night 'office visits.' I'm not falling for that one again."

"You wanted proof. Get here. I'll show you the video."

She didn't speak for several seconds. Then her voice came through the line in a rush. "I'm on my way."

CHAPTER 38

AFTER PICKING UP A PHONE and a pair of field glasses, I rented a shack. The inhabitants were quick to take my money and ran off to visit relatives far away. It was a hovel on par with a child's treehouse in terms of construction and safety. But it was perfect for my needs. It was perched on top of two other shacks overlooking the dirt lot that served as a parking area for the slum surrounding Chopra's torture chamber. Twenty cars were parked without any form or pattern. For drivers, there was one way in or out of the lot.

I watched them all day long. The best op is the one with thorough intel. By midday, the Redjackets had returned to base. They weren't happy about losing me. I was the guy who killed two of their pals. But they'd accepted it. From their casual body language, I figured they weren't expecting me to return.

While that was a good thing, it created a different problem. Chopra would turn to the only clue she had left to find Wilkes: the Singhs. And, little did she know, they were the only ones who knew where Wilkes was. Making my problem simple: rescue the Singhs by taking on twelve heavily armed men and one IB agent with anger-management issues crowded into a small building.

In the rooms below me, several men were gambling, fighting, laughing and drinking. The noise they made distracted me. I struggled to come up with a plan that had a happy ending.

By evening, I'd run out of ideas. So I did what desperate people always do. I prayed.

When that didn't work, I turned to Mercury. I said, *The only way to save the Singhs is to sneak inside, cut them loose and then create a diversion. In that scenario, the Singhs get away, but the odds are twelve to one against me seeing another sunrise. Why do the gods always put me in this position?*

Mercury checked out the bedding in the corner. *You lazy-assed mortals always blame the gods when you don't wanna do what you gotta do. The Singhs are in that house because you didn't want to leave your comfy life back in Bethesda. Just like the Holocaust.*

I said, *What? What's that got to do with the Singhs? I'm not responsible for the Holocaust.*

Mercury said, *Five hundred years ago, white Europeans forgot about 'Love thy neighbor' and started rampaging around the world, killing and enslaving natives everywhere they went. Dragging people out of Africa in chains, killing Incas to steal their gold, giving smallpox-blankets to Indians to steal their land. Y'all knew it was wrong. But you didn't do anything about it. When y'all grew a conscience and stopped slavery— you segregated. Where was the guy standing up and saying, 'This is wrong!', huh?*

I said, *I didn't do those things. I would've stood up.*

Mercury said, *Oh really, homie? Your people knew what Kristallnacht was all about. Anti-Semitism was rampant along with every other kind of prejudice. Your people knew the pogroms were going on— but they didn't do anything. You want to know how many people the gods tried to motivate to stop it all? Millions. How did they answer our call? Same as you, 'Not my problem.' Then Pearl Harbor put them in the war. Next thing you know, they're liberating Concentration Camps. And then everybody asks the big question, 'How could the gods let this happen?' Y'know what, bro? We didn't let it happen.* He stuck his finger in my chest. *You did.*

Mercury pointed out the window at Chopra's house of horrors. *And don't say you didn't let the Holocaust happen because it happens every freaking day. It's not always Nazis and Jews. Sometimes it's Sunnis and Shiites. Sometimes it's blacks and whites. Right now it's Redjackets and the Singhs. If you don't do something, it'll be your sister wearing chains and being dragged into slavery or having a yellow star pinned to her chest.*

There weren't a whole lot of snappy comebacks drifting through my head. There were images of Mom and Dad and Joyce hiding in an attic like Anne Frank.

After shaking those images out of my mind, I said, *There's twelve of them. At least three are veterans. I won't save the Singhs. I'll die before I get inside.*

Mercury said, *The gods don't save people because we're bored. I didn't save you from Chopra's bullet so you could sit around whining all day. I saved you so you could do this. And don't worry about dying, it's not such a big deal. Besides, you have everything you need to survive the attack within fifty yards of you.*

With that, he disappeared.

I hate divine riddles. I considered fleeing the area. I'd bought a burner phone to call Sabel HQ and get the hell out of Mumbai. I flipped it over in my hand. One call. Home safe.

With the weight of slavery, Native American genocide and the Holocaust still on my shoulders.

A wretched scream came from Chopra's house. Electric torture. An unmistakable shriek. Then another. Both the cries of a woman. Jabamani. Chopra was using Sunil's wife to get him to talk. That pissed me off.

I still wasn't ready to fight other Americans. My vow to protect citizens aside, it was like cannibalism or incest, there are some things you never even consider. But. Mercury was right about how the Singhs ended up in there. Not being Catholic, there was no point in beating myself up with guilt. I resigned myself to my duty. I would go in there and do my best or die trying. Most likely, it would be, "*and* die trying."

It was getting dark. The patrols outside the house had slowed to a minimum. I could guess the reason. The veterans inside knew they were up against a former Ranger. Rangers are famous for showing up when you're tired and groggy around three in the morning. To minimize early morning fatigue, they were getting in some sleep early. They were turning the clock around to their advantage. For me, this was the hour of maximum opportunity, a little after 10 PM.

In the gambling den below me, there was a crash and shouts. A new fight had started. And that gave me an idea.

I ran down the wooden ladder with my rifle and stepped into the gamblers hut. I held my gun across my chest in a way people find both friendly and terrifying. Five men straightened up and did their best to look sober. One guy had a bloody nose. Another had a scraped fist that he hid when I spotted it. On a table in the middle were scattered cards, a few rupees and a bottle of clear alcohol.

I picked up the bottle and sniffed. It gave off the aroma of kerosene. Homemade hooch distilled for maximum impact. Probably poisonous. I pointed to the bottle and pulled out a fifty euro note. The gamblers looked at each other.

"You want to buy it?" the bloody nosed guy said in perfect English.

I thought of Vishal and wondered if Madam Aditi was right, I had picked the only guy in Mumbai who didn't speak English.

"Got more of these?" I asked.

"*Ho*," he said. "I mean, yes."

"How many?"

"Six."

"That'll work." I looked them over. "There are good Americans and bad Americans. I'm one kind, and the guys who are in that building over there are the other. Which do you think is the good kind?"

"They are very bad men. Break my door down, steal my car." He looked me over. "I do not know about you."

After talking to Mercury, I wasn't so sure about me either.

Then we heard more screams. The electric-shock screams coming from Chopra's house. The men in the room flinched and tensed. They knew what it was. It made them angry.

"I need your help to save two Mumbaikars. I'll need all six bottles with rags stuck in the tops." I grabbed a lighter off the table and lit it up.

"Molotov cocktails?" Bloody-nose asked with a grin. He pointed outside. "For them?"

They agreed to blow up the Redjacket's cars in a timed sequence for a small fee. I put the cash on the table, and we went out into the dark. We took different routes through the narrow spaces between shacks and took up positions.

Chopra's place had two doors. My best angle gave me total coverage of one and a sliver of the other. Not ideal, but all I was going to get.

I gave the signal. A lighter flicked on. A rag flickered into a flame. A bottle flew through the air and landed on a shiny rental. It shattered beautifully. The blaze engulfed the car closest to the exit lane. Although there were ten ways out of the slums on foot, Americans would never leave a car behind. For some reason, we can't wrap our heads around the concept of walking somewhere. Which meant the Redjackets were effectively trapped.

Two guys came out of the house to assess the situation. One man on patrol joined them. It was too early to start shooting. I needed more Redjackets in the open.

I gave the second signal. Another lighter, another flaming bottle, another car in flames.

More Redjackets ran into the night. These men were armed and ready for combat. I counted seven exposed. If they were smart, that's all they would send to that side of the house. The others would be opposite, in case of a backdoor attack.

I calculated a firing sequence. I could wound at least four before I had to change positions. They would take cover wherever they could. Then it was anyone's guess as to whether I could get any more of them before they got me. That didn't get me inside to free the Singhs. But it was my best chance.

My sights lined up on the most casual Redjacket. I practiced my aim for the sequence.

Someone else fired three rounds. Two Redjackets fell.

CHAPTER 39

A THIRD FLAMING BOTTLE FLEW through the air, landed on its target and burst into flames. Pia fired another three-round burst, and another Redjacket fell. Three out of twelve. Nine more, if their reconnaissance had been accurate. The recoil from the rifle kept smacking her broken orbital rim. She wanted to reposition her face but needed to line up the sights. She resigned herself to more pain.

From his position twenty yards to her right, Cody fired a burst. One more man went down.

They both shifted positions seconds before bullets started flying toward them.

"Darts suck," Cody said in the comm link. He referred to the bullet-replacing Sabel Darts in the rifles Pia had brought with her. Filled with a nonlethal dose of Inland Taipan snake venom backed by a heavy sedative, they caused instant flaccid paralysis long enough for the sedative to put the victim to sleep. Her professional soldiers hated the unstable flight path caused by the liquid core.

"Beats facing murder charges in a foreign country," she said.

Six Redjackets fanned out in pairs, searching for the shooters. Pia noted that Jacob, only thirty yards away to her left, remained silent. He could help them out by drawing fire.

Pia reconsidered her hope. Thinking Jacob could draw fire was a manipulative expectation. One worthy of Veronica Lodge Hunter. It was a reasonable hope, one soldier supporting another by taking some of the risk for themselves. Yet, one of many reasons for coming to Mumbai was to save Jacob. Why would she want him to take a risk for her sake? Was her anticipation of him taking that risk Machiavellian? Hunter-esque?

She began to comprehend the complexity of a soldier's battlefield decisions. Self-preservation was at the bottom of the list. Teamwork stood at the top. Which meant Jacob was keeping a low profile for a reason. Was it to ambush the Redjackets? Or had their surprise attack frozen him with fear?

Not fear. Not Jacob. Maybe he was trying to figure out who was out there shooting at the Redjackets. Without comm links, she couldn't communicate with him.

"Ms. Sabel," Cody's voice, "you there?"

She realized he'd fired and moved while she remained frozen in thought. "Moving to location Charlie."

A quick peek as she crossed a walkway between shanties told her two shadowy Redjackets were chasing her into the dark passage. She squeezed off a burst. Nothing. She took a sharp turn, leaned out and fired another salvo. The lead man fell. The second man shot over his friend. Pia felt the bullets graze her body armor. Sliding behind a shanty for protection, she stuck her gun into the alleyway and fired blindly. She heard nothing. No footsteps, no body falling, no shots fired.

She squatted and leaned around the corner. The Redjacket was aiming at head level. He saw her, adjusted and fired. But she had already let loose a burst. His bullet hit the ground and ricocheted as he fell.

"My two are down. Moving to location Delta."

"Roger," Cody said. "Two down here. Eight total. Two to four remaining. Moving to location Echo."

Pia took the long route they'd mapped out in the hour they had to set up. It should bring her near Jacob's location. Seeing him in Cody's binoculars had been a pleasant surprise. She'd feared the worst when Cody reported in shortly after his arrival that morning. Cody had volunteered to rescue Jacob but arrived in time only to see Jacob flee in a stolen car. Six armed men had given chase. Which certainly fit Jacob's style.

Cody had kept tabs on the Redjackets ever since, waiting for Pia's arrival. He hadn't seen Jacob until moments ago.

Another firebomb hit a car near the Redjackets' hideout. The flames spilled over to the wall. The building caught fire on one corner. She had not seen the Singhs leaving. They must still be inside.

Pia felt the light of the car fires on her face, which meant she was visible. Before she had time to slip back into darkness, she caught a glimpse of her reflection in a piece of glass. In the flickering warm yellow light, despite her black eye, she looked like Veronica. That made her ill. She ran down the gap between buildings.

Veronica Lodge Hunter, good or bad or misguided? Who knows what decisions she faced twenty-eight years ago? Pia had the same determined outlook on life as Hunter. The same will to win. The same risk-everything attitude. What did that say about Pia's future?

She came up the pathway between shacks to where Jacob had been. The prospect of seeing him filled her with joy. The surprise would do him good—if he didn't shoot her by accident. Pia peeked around the corner.

Jacob was gone.

"Jammed." Cody sounded calm. "Can't fix it."

"Are you exposed?" she asked.

"Two coming. I can make Charlie, maybe."

"I can cover you there." Pia ran across open ground to an empty hovel with windows on all sides. She cleared it, jumped inside and checked Cody's Charlie location. Empty. She heard gunfire.

In the comm link, she could hear him cursing. His weapon clinked as he tried to clear it while running.

Out of the corner of her eye, she saw movement across the dirt lot. She moved her sights to find a figure silhouetted against the fires. Jacob, in a dead run, headed for the Redjackets' stronghold.

Two of her men needed help. She could only help one. She desperately wanted to follow Jacob into that burning building. She wanted to save the Singhs. Because she loved the glory of victory. Who would that help, the team or her ego? It was time to think through her decision. Jacob held his fire so he could attack from concealment. A good plan.

The implied contract with her teammate Cody was to cover each other at all costs. She moved her iron sights back to where Cody should be, location Charlie. He still wasn't there.

"Trapped." His one-word call chilled her.

Pia realized she wasn't like her mother at all. Veronica would never do what Pia was about to do. She ran from the safety of the shack and bolted straight for a point mid-way along Cody's path.

She popped out between shacks. The enemy would be on one side or the other. She wouldn't know which until the shooting started. She could aim left or right. An even chance of aiming in the right direction. She chose left and fired blindly.

Wrong side. Two of three bullets aimed at Pia slammed into her shoulder. The body armor protected her from lethal penetration, but the blow felt like a sledgehammer. The force threw her against a wall and knocked the wind out of her. She pivoted and fell on her butt.

Scrambling to her knees while ignoring the sharp pain in her shoulder, she fired a three-round burst before she could acquire a target. Nothing. The Redjacket had ducked behind something. Pia flipped on her NightVisor. Infrared images overlaid with heat sensors showed her nothing. Spinning around, she looked in the opposite direction. Nothing. A creepy sensation flittered up her spine like a spider.

She looked up. Swinging down from a pole that held two buildings apart came a man dressed in black. He landed on her shoulders and drove her to the ground. He jumped up, feet on either side of her and drew a pistol.

A rifle butt flew over Pia's head and landed in the man's arm. His pistol fired wild. It gave her enough time to raise her rifle and dart the man in the groin.

"Last man," Cody said.

"Get him off me."

Cody and Pia pushed the walrus-sized Redjacket to the side. She rose and checked her arm's range of motion. It was sore but workable.

"Jacob went in," she said.

Cody understood. They separated around a shack and moved to the edge of the dirt lot. Pia ran toward the door first. Cody covered her, then followed.

Police sirens screamed down the street outside the slums. They would arrive in seconds.

As Pia reached the door, Jacob stepped out. Their eyes met. They both cocked an ear toward the sirens. The Singhs stood right behind him.

"Sunil and Jabamani Singh," Pia said, "I need you to wait here for the authorities. Tell them about these people."

The scared, disheveled couple in their seventies were shocked. They held each other and looked past Pia hoping to appeal to Cody or anyone nearby. They wanted out.

"Sorry, I've no time to explain," Pia continued, "but a friend has arranged for the police to come. Good police. There will be several reporters with them. But we have to leave you."

When Jacob started to protest, she held up her hand. "Trust me."

Jacob looked over his shoulder at the Singhs. "I have friends here. They'll take care of you."

He whistled and several drunk locals appeared out of the darkness holding unused Molotov cocktails. They swarmed around the Singhs. Jacob's ideas often gave her pause. This one more than most. Pia found the arrangement as disconcerting as leaving the Singhs behind.

There was no time to discuss it. Cody took point on the exit. Jacob understood her plan and followed. Pia felt a surge of satisfaction. She was beginning to tap into the soldier's telepathy. Each of them could see the master plan and understood their part in it. They communicated by trust alone.

After sneaking through the rabbit warren of the slum's footpaths, they reached the waiting car. They piled in and sped off into the night.

"They were waiting for that fight," Jacob said.

"Reinforcements are coming from Redjacket Central," Pia said.

"What makes you think that?"

"Because Hunter wanted me to come here."

"And you walked into her trap anyway?"

Pia said, "You're welcome."

CHAPTER 40

CHUCK ROCHE GREW TIRED OF lecturing the congressional leaders Thomas had shepherded in and out of the Oval Office all afternoon. He'd threatened and cajoled and praised and berated them. Some he'd won over, and others invited his wrath. Most troubling was Senator Smith who claimed he would find proof that Roche directly controlled the Redjackets. After a couple threats about regulating healthcare in his home state, the Senator shut up.

He didn't let that kind of dissent rattle him. As his most ardent supporters reminded him, he was destined by God to lead this country. These were nagging problems, not administration killers. As long as he kept the momentum going forward, they would forget all the petty problems of the past.

It was beneath Zenith Man to get directly involved in the negotiations to bring the war to a vote. Yet, he would do what was needed. And what he needed was fast action. With the Redjackets' failure to stop Sabel in Mumbai, that little bitch could bring Wilkes out of hiding at any moment. The war had to be declared before that happened. When it did, Wilkes would disappear quicker than Iraqi Weapons of Mass Destruction. No one would care once the trumpets of war started blasting.

Even the leadership smiled when he told them, "My basic plan is to attack and to keep on attacking regardless of whether we have to go over, under, or through Mecca itself."

People rally behind that kind of leadership.

Finally, the last of the whiny representatives left—after promising to join the cause.

Then Thomas let Hunter in.

She crossed the room like a woman on a mission. "Who the hell is Gina Wind? Who let her watch the Kill-Video?"

"You need to make a decision, Veronica." Roche gestured to the facing couches and waited until she took a seat. "Are you going to side with me—or that little extension of your DNA?"

"I sent her to Mumbai, Chuck. We had a deal."

"I never made any deals. You do as I say, or you suffer."

"I'm out." Hunter rose and leaned over and shook a finger in his face. "Letting her see that video was the last straw, Chuck. I know you've been ordering the Redjackets directly. I'll go public with proof unless you denounce Gina's upcoming post."

Roche considered her threat. What could she possibly prove? It would be her word against his. He never apologized, never backed down. She was just pissed because of her little girl. She'd never cared about that kid in the first twenty-eight years, why was she getting bent out of shape now? Undoubtedly nothing.

"What's Gina's post about?" he asked.

"She called me for background and comment before she posts it."

"I've been busy. What did she tell you?"

"That she saw a video of Pia Sabel shooting Viktor Popov nine times, point blank."

"She's a good reporter then." Roche relaxed and extended his arm along the back of the couch. "You've seen the video. Isn't that exactly what your little punk did?"

"I'm not going to back down. I'll testify to Congress that you control the Redjackets."

"I'll call you a liar. So will half of Congress."

Hunter sat back, crossed her arms and scowled. "That phone you gave me wasn't issued to you. It was issued to Hartwell Thomas."

That bit of information took him by surprise. How could Hunter have known that? Sabel must have decrypted the phone. Maybe Thomas told her. In either case, it didn't matter. All they could come up with would be some texts and calls made. No content. Nothing explicit. She was bluffing.

"So?" Roche tried to look casual. He was a good actor.

"The CIA issued it as a field phone for covert operators." Hunter began to look smug. "Their operatives often get information but then get killed. So their field phones record every call for later retrieval."

Roche's heart stopped. Impossible. She was lying. Why would they record every call? He'd have to ask Ratched. Her story was plausible. But most likely a bluff.

He shrugged and flopped his hands.

"When you, the President of the United States, gave me that phone, I was concerned there may be some of your files and calls on it that should be kept as part of the public record as required by law. I asked Sabel Technologies to preserve any and all calls, texts, pictures, basically everything on that phone. I was just preserving the public record. They did. Guess what they found?"

Roche knew precisely what the traitorous witches found. If Ratched's plan had worked, they found exactly what he wanted them to find. But if Ratched failed or lied, he might have a problem. If she failed, he could explain it away. Zenith Man would win the battle before anything went public. Calling her bluff would work as long as she hadn't told anyone else about it. He got up, went to his desk, picked up the phone and paused before dialing.

"That phone belonged to Hartwell Thomas." He gave her a stern glare. "You knew that because you've been working with Hartwell for days. When you found it, you chose not to return it to the CIA. Instead, you took it to a hostile corporation and let their foreign spies see all the Top Secret files. You're a traitor to your country. I'm having you arrested for espionage."

He pretended to dial.

Hunter got up and came to him, a concerned look on her face. "That's never going to fly. Four other people saw you give it to me and tell me it was mine."

"Ratched, Thomas and company? I told you not to trust them. They'll swear it's Hartwell's phone and that you knew."

"They won't lie under sworn testimony."

"Think about it, Veronica." He gave her time to consider the partners in her failed coup. "Who will they side with, the man in power now or the woman who may or may not be in power later?"

Hunter's harsh face began to dissolve. He'd beaten many people. He could always tell by their body language. She showed all the signs of resignation to fate. Her shoulders caved in.

He'd won. Because he was Zenith Man. Ordained by divinity.

He cradled the phone.

"I'll hold off for now." He waited until she met his gaze. "But I need you to make a call on that phone. Do you have it with you?"

His heartbeat remained constant. No rise, no excitement. He was calm. Ordained.

Her heartbeat rose. Roche could see it in her flushed face and the slight quiver in her jacket sleeves. Losers always let their emotions get the better of them.

After a long pause, she patted her purse and swallowed hard. "Right here."

"Good." Roche smiled. "Here's what I want you to tell them."

CHAPTER 41

HOW DHANPAL ENDED UP IN a whorehouse became understandable after I talked to his grandfather. He'd handed the admiral off to the old man, a former cargo ship captain, before drawing the Redjackets away. Grandpa Singh came up with a brilliant plan to hide Wilkes for a week. But Dhanpal took a bullet on the far side of town. Due to the ancient symbiotic relationship between sailors and madams, Dhanpal knew he could find protection in a house of ill repute—for the right price. He counted on me showing up with my magic card to get him out of hock.

I explained all this to Ms. Sabel and Cody as we flew down city streets. She'd pulled our driver from the local office. He drove like a madman. Not an uncommon sight in Mumbai—but he took it to a competitive level. He squeezed our Jaguar XJ through traffic like a motorcycle. He piloted the six-foot wide car in and out of spaces five feet wide. He swung wide onto a boulevard and chased smaller vehicles to the shoulder.

Ms. Sabel was busy texting someone. When I asked who was more important at this hour, she said, "I've concluded that fighting and killing people is a poor way to get Roche out of office. When nothing else works, it's time to resort to the surprise attack. I've cooked up something with my attorney that will happen when I get back. If I get back."

"We're all getting back." I patted her hand, but it was too late, my voice had cracked.

Ms. Sabel had managed to get weapons and body armor and a spare phone for me through customs. I kept my pilfered AR-10 but also took an MP5SD filled with darts. We shared a laugh comparing our bruises and broken noses.

"Where are Miguel and Tania?" I asked.

"Remember your incident in Singapore?" Ms. Sabel said.

"The statute of limitations should've run out on that. It's been weeks."

Cody, riding shotgun, looked over his shoulder with one of his many WTF looks.

"We have a lawyer working on it," Ms. Sabel said. "They'll join us in no time."

Mercury appeared in the small space between us. *Saved by Pia-Caesar-Sabel herself. You da man, homie. The bets in the Dii Consentes were 11 to 1 in favor of you dying at the hand of Chopra.*

I said, *Let me guess, you were the one betting I'd make it?*

Mercury said, *Oh Orcus no. I know you. You screw up lightbulbs—and they were made to be screwed up. Juno bet on you. She always bets against Jupiter. I don't know how they keep that marriage together. But she's rolling in coin right now.*

I said, *I'm just glad it's over.*

Mercury leaned away from me. *Over? Brutha, you've just begun. Do you think Pia-Caesar-Sabel is going home right now?*

I looked at Ms. Sabel. "We're going to the airport, right?"

"Airport? You said Kamathipura." She looked at me as if I'd come down with the measles.

"I said Wilkes will be there later tonight. But we can leave that to the Indian police. We don't need…" My interest in talking waned as her frown deepened. Apparently, Ms. Sabel wasn't leaving anything to the locals.

"We have to see this through." She squeezed my hand. "Did Mr. Singh tell them anything?"

"Chopra tortured his wife. He broke down. But he didn't tell them everything. I got there in time to offer the Redjacket leader an option."

"What option?" she asked.

"He could put the phone down and walk away or take a bullet in the knee. Turns out, he's not big on skiing."

"How much info did he get over the phone?"

"Just the Orange Gate, Princess Dock parts."

Ms. Sabel opened her satellite maps and zoomed in on a half mile of rusted out docks, wharfs and ships. There were hundreds of vessels along the coast in various states of repair. Some were big and freshly painted. Most were small and barely afloat. Two were actually sunken derelicts rotting in the middle of the harbor.

"He told you which dock?" she asked.

"Kinda." I looked at the map. Nothing but treetops between the main boulevards and the docks. No street views. "He gave me directions based on buildings. I figured we could send in the cops and they can comb the district."

Mercury stuck his head in through the pass-through in the trunk. *Dawg, is that you talking? Why didn't you kill Chopra when you had the chance? Now she's gonna cook up some story about illegal aliens sneaking in the Orange Gate, and you'll never hear about what happened to Wilkes.*

"What kind of woman do you think Chopra is?" Ms. Sabel asked.

"Reminds me of that lady in Game of Thrones." I looked out the window and watched as large stationary objects passed by within a quarter inch of the glass.

Ms. Sabel looked out her window. "You've been through enough, Jacob. Our driver will take you to the airport."

Ouch. Mercury sat on the console between the two front seats, posing as Rodin's Thinker. *You are not going to let Pia-Caesar-Sabel have all the glory, are you? I mean, sure you're all going to die tonight, that's for sure. But let her die alone? That just doesn't sound like you.*

I said, *Why is she so interested in Wilkes?*

"Who me?" Ms. Sabel whipped around from the window. "Because she might be the key to stopping World War III. I don't know what she knows, but Roche wants her dead. If there's a chance she can make a difference, it's worth my life to save the world."

Cody did another glance over his shoulder at me. This time with disappointment. He was just as young and idealistic as the boss. They thought saving the world was possible—and worthwhile.

Mercury snapped his fingers in front of my face. *Look here, boy. This is you.* He held out his palm. A miniature version of me appeared in it.

And these are your connections to everyone you love and care about. Gossamer threads of blue appeared and connected me to thousands of people: Mom and Dad, Miguel, Tania, Dhanpal, Ms. Sabel, and countless others. It was a cosmic web. *And these are your connections to the gods.* Each of the miniature people had golden threads leading into the sky. *You're all part of a great and interstellar oneness. You all hear a god—of some sort—who tells you to take care of others. Sometimes you hear the voice and sometimes you don't. We don't care about that. What we don't like is when one of these guys shows up.* A miniature version of Roche appeared in the middle of all the other miniatures. He wasn't connected to anyone. No gossamer threads.

Mercury said, *This is the guy who only cares about himself. We don't worry about those guys because nobody likes them and they die alone. But. Once in a while, a guy like this grabs power somewhere. Like when the German Reichstag passed the Enabling Act of 1933 that turned a republic into Hitler's dictatorship. There were too many who mistook Hitler's tyrannical narcissism for divine inspiration. That worried us, and we started telling all these people who are connected to each other to stop the guy. They didn't listen. They didn't act. They were comfy and lazy. They sat back and watched while World War II approached.*

Mercury closed his hand, and all the little people disappeared. *Now here you are, on the eve of a great and horrible war no one can win. You can go home and wait for the end of the world. Or. You can help a Caesar bring down a future dictator. All you need to do is care about something outside your sphere. Reach a little deeper, try a little harder, and you can change the world.*

I said, *Will I die?*

Mercury said, *Of course not.*

You just said we are all going to die tonight. I pointed at Cody and Ms. Sabel and me.

Uh. Mercury looked like a five-year-old caught fibbing. *Just kidding. Would I let you die? Who brought you this far?*

I said, *The god who keeps telling me to go out in a blaze of glory. I'd rather live.*

Mercury said, *In a world where Pia-Caesar-Sabel dies?* He looked at a sundial that suddenly appeared on his wrist. *In about twenty-three minutes, give or take.*

I said, *You'll get me through this?*

Probably.

There were days when I knew I was part of a great and cosmic oneness. There were other times when I felt alone and abandoned. Being part of something for a few minutes—even if it meant hastening my death—felt like a better option than spending another fifty years feeling alone and abandoned. On the other hand, if I had to spend the next fifty years with Mercury leaning over my—

Mercury said, *I can hear you, y'know.*

The bigger problem was what Ms. Sabel said. Roche wants this war. And it will escalate. Any warrior knows the horrors and futility of war. Roche never served. He has no idea what it means to put people like me in harm's way. Everyone who served in the last decade, including all my friends and me, would be called back to fight in his self-important war. Lots of good people will die. It could escalate to 2.4 billion Christians versus 1.8 billion Muslims. No one would be safe in that conflagration.

I came to Mumbai to save Dhanpal, then his grandparents. Noble, but that was thinking only of my tribe. A long time ago, I joined the Army to save the world.

"You're right," I said to Ms. Sabel. "We need to get Wilkes back to the USA. We can't let Roche start that war. What did you say about more Redjackets coming?"

She squeezed my hand. "Hunter suggested I come here. She told me they were sending more Redjackets."

We drove to the Orange Gate. Our driver was just a driver, untrained in urban warfare. We left him on the main road with a comm link to tell us if he saw hordes of armed men swarming after us.

Whoever the Princess behind Princess Dock was, she hadn't paid the rent in a long time. The streets were broken, the buildings moldy and cracked. Here and there a shop perked up with a hopeful coat of new paint. The majority were dilapidated. We crossed a large parking lot filled with commercial trucks waiting for tomorrow's cargo. Most were built thirty years ago.

I watched Ms. Sabel and Cody sweep the area. She was a lot taller. They looked like that famous picture of Maria Sharapova and Floyd Mayweather. But they worked in a cadence as if they'd gone through Ranger School together.

We rounded an abandoned dock. The rusted hulls of two sunken cargo ships rose halfway out of the water.

Sunil Singh's directions consisted of colors. Stay to the right of the red and yellow building with blue shutters, turn left at the cream-colored building with a tin roof, things like that. The collapsed apartment building he mentioned didn't make sense until I saw it. Five stories tall, a quarter of it had collapsed into a pile of rubble. The hallways where the building had sheared off remained open to the elements. People still lived in the standing part of the building.

We arrived at an abandoned pier. Great empty structures overgrown with trees and bushes stood against the city-lit sky. A transfer station that once teamed with activity was now an empty warehouse. We crossed the vast space. It was covered by a tin roof overhead held aloft by wooden pillars and enclosed with an occasional wall. On the far end, we had a view of a permanently polluted dock just big enough to berth a super yacht but not a tramp steamer.

Ms. Sabel covered the north end. Cody covered the south. I slid behind a wall and scanned the thin concrete wharf opposite. Three Redjackets patrolled it.

They were ahead of us and nonchalant about it. Not a good sign from a tactical point of view. They controlled one of several abandoned piers. We would have to use a different one and get away quickly.

I pulled away from the edge and motioned the others deeper into the darkness. "Sunil Singh put Admiral Wilkes on a tramp cargo ship that went to the Maldives last week. It returns tonight. It should be out there in the bay right now. The captain is waiting for a Morse code signal in infrared." I handed Ms. Sabel an infrared spot light. "You go back to where all the trucks were parked. On the end of that pier, give the signal. He'll send her out in a launch. It should take fifteen minutes or so. Cody, you cover the north, I'll cover this side."

We ran back to the larger pier and made our way past the parking lot of trucks. Ms. Sabel went to the water's edge and gave the signal. Three large ships waited for dawn outside the shipping lanes. She repeated the message several times before getting a response.

A few minutes later a launch was coming toward us across the water. Visible only with our NightVisors, they approached with all the running lights turned off. It would take about three minutes for them to cross the distance. For us, those were a totally exposed three minutes. Even though it was a moonless night and a little foggy, sooner or later, the noise would lead the Redjackets to where the boat would land.

Mercury floated down from the sky and hovered above the water on my side of the wharf. *Notice something about that boat, bro? Check the angles.*

I took my eyes off my area and watched the boat. *They're off course.*

"Why do you say that," Ms. Sabel's voice in the comm link.

"I'm not a sailor, but the angle's off. Check the sights on your rifle. If they're heading to you, they should be lined up bow to stern. If they're off, you'll see the boat at an angle."

"You're right," she said. "They're going to my left. North."

She used Morse code to tell them they were off course. An infrared answer came from the main ship. It said, "Are you not holding a regular torch for them to follow?"

She went back and forth with the ship only to discover the launch had no infrared receivers and had turned off the radio to prevent the squawk from alerting anyone. A clever idea now going horribly wrong.

I started running for the pier where I'd seen the Redjackets.

Mercury flew alongside me as I ran around the dock and through the abandoned warehouse. *Dude, those Redjackets are smart. Know what I'm saying? They just hijacked your admiral. Are they going to get away with it?*

I took up a position near the land's side of the pier. I said, *Not on my watch.*

Mercury said, *You know the three on the pier are expendables.*

The three Redjackets on the end of the broken pier held a flashlight. They'd fooled the pilot into thinking they were us.

My used god was right. They looked around as if they could feel my eyes on them. They were not professionals. They did not know how to keep watch like a soldier. That could only mean there were more Redjackets in reserve.

I lined up my sights with the boat. It was less than a minute from landing. The Redjackets had a rope ready to toss to the pilot.

Backing up, I went as far out as the street before I saw two squads hiding in the shadows. They had older versions of night vision. They could see amplified light. With plenty of surrounding city-light, it was nearly daylight to them. They also used individual transponders that identified them as friendly to each other. Our patented Sabel NightVisors read that identifier, also amplified light, and added an overlay of heat signatures. We could see them a lot better than they would ever see us.

I texted the enemy information to Ms. Sabel and Cody. We set up fake transponders to make them think we were on their team. But what the Redjackets lacked in technology, they made up for in numbers. I found a third squad moving in to cover the first two.

Mercury said, *What's the military term for this situation, homie? I forget. Oh, wait. I remember: You're fucked.*

I said, *Thanks for staying upbeat. It helps my confidence and self-esteem.*

"One of us has to create a distraction," Ms. Sabel said. She raced to a position near me.

Cody stood guard a few yards away. He was trembling. PTSD from the war zone hacked at his nerves with worse results than what Chopra had done to me. I knew because I'd been there. A firefight gone wrong stayed with you a long time.

I texted Ms. Sabel individually, "Our man is freezing up. You need to send him home."

"He was upfront about his condition when he volunteered to rescue you," Ms. Sabel texted back. "Said he wanted to confront his demons—and that you'd understand."

I did. Most likely, Cody had survivors' guilt and wanted to go out in a blaze of glory like his old squad in the 101st. Couldn't deny him that. As cold as it sounds, if he went back to the office now and anything happened to Ms. Sabel or me, he'd put a bullet through his brain. He needed a win more than he needed his life.

Mercury said, *See, homie? Cody gets it. Nothing matters but honor and glory. Are you ready for this?*

"Jacob, you get Wilkes," Ms. Sabel said over the open comm link. "Cody and I will open up on these guys here."

Both options, going for Wilkes or creating the distraction, were suicide missions. Our only hope lay in making such a big noise the press would descend from all corners of the globe to identify the Redjackets as the bad guys. Maybe we'd be recognized as heroes. Posthumously.

Engaging the enemy in all out warfare was better suited to my resume than hers. I should lead the frontal assault. But I figured out her strategy and wrapped my brain around it. On the odd chance Wilkes got out alive, Roche's people would watch every passport coming into the USA. Ms. Sabel was recognizable even in small border towns. She could never sneak Wilkes in. I was anonymous. Even if I had no idea how to sneak into the USA, it was the only battle plan with any potential for winning. To make it work, I would have to switch gears. I'm a trained killer with plenty of experience. But you can't shoot your way across the border. I'd have to think of something.

Mercury said, *Think of something like Ed Guach.*

I texted her. "I get it. Tell Miguel I'll take her to Ed's house."

To her credit, she didn't ask who Ed was. I could only hope Miguel remembered the guy.

I turned to Mercury. *Why did you let me fall into this trap? Why not just let me die back at Chopra's house?*

Mercury said, *This is why the gods love you, brutha. Betting on you living through hell on Earth is better than betting on how fast a lottery winner will lose his fortune. And this time, I've got money riding on you. You can do this. Probably.*

"Identified three squads west of end of pier," I said in the comm link. "Two for immediate deployment and one in reserve."

"We take down the two, then meet the third when they come for us." Ms. Sabel sounded as determined as any vet I'd served with.

"We're going to need real bullets," I said. "They're wearing armor. Only their shoulders and legs are exposed. Too small a target for darts."

I heard Cody hiss his agreement before Ms. Sabel said, "Right. We'll take their weapons off the first ones down."

It was nice to hear her optimism—unrealistic as it was.

There was nothing left to discuss.

I said, "On three."

CHAPTER 42

WHEN PIA HEARD JACOB COUNT down, she fired three darts from her position and charged forward. A tree gave her cover. She felt the presence of Alan Sabel and the hundreds of murdered souls left in the wake of Chuck Roche. Their spirits gave her more confidence than her liquid metal armor. She peered around the tree and saw her targets with more clarity, as if her eyes could focus better. She fired three more darts. One caught a man in the face.

Her broken eye socket screamed in pain with each round.

The Redjacket squads had been focused on the crumbling concrete pier. They expected a direct assault on their Wilkes-greeting crew. She advanced at a 90-degree angle to their rifle barrels. Her attack forced them to face her. Cody had circled to her left and waited until she drew their fire. Now he unleashed an entire magazine, forcing them to turn completely around to return fire. As a result, she could launch a broadside attack.

Cody had the right idea. Hitting flesh between gaps in their armor would be more luck than aim. Therefore, more darts meant more luck. Pia charged into the squad and fired the rest of her magazine.

The Redjackets had been huddled together behind an abandoned pickup truck. They had planned to charge the pier as soon as Wilkes landed. They would secure her and make their retreat shielded by the two other squads. A good plan that failed them. Two men were down. Three others were confused by her bold attack and ran for the empty warehouse. She swapped magazines, slung her MP5SD, then grabbed one of their rifles and two magazines.

"My three down, boat approaching," Jacob reported. "I'm holding the pier."

"Three down." Cody's voice. "Five or more now in the warehouse."

The Redjackets regrouped where they would have a field of fire covering the landing pier and could fend off Pia's attack at the same time. The third squad remained behind them with the discipline of seasoned veterans.

Pia spotted a figure scaling a support pillar. He was near the top with a scoped rifle hanging from his shoulder. She aimed carefully and fired three times. All three shots pinged off the roof, slightly below the sniper.

The rifle she'd stolen was a civilian AR-15 semi-auto without the three round burst mode she was used to. It also had no sound damper. Nor did it handle the exhaust gases from the barrel. The loud snaps echoed across the wharf. The flame of her shots fired gave away her position. Just the locator the Redjackets had been waiting for.

They opened up from inside the warehouse.

Cody returned fire with a similar weapon, intentionally taking the heat off Pia. She ran from the truck to a stub wall. The whole time she felt the eyes of the third squad following her. They were waiting for her and Cody to charge the warehouse. A classic crossfire. One that she knew she would have to fall for to get Wilkes and Jacob off the pier.

Pia reacquired the sniper, compensated for the poor sights, and fired. The figure grabbed his leg in agony. He rolled onto the roof. Once the pain subsided, and he got a field patch in place—if she hadn't hit the bone or the femoral artery—he could still be a terrible threat. Pia prioritized. It would be possible to charge the warehouse before the sniper could regroup. She fired three more rounds through the corrugated tin roof. If she didn't hit him, and she would never know, it might discourage him from coming near the edge.

"Ready when you are," Cody said.

"Ten seconds," Jacob answered.

Pia tensed and counted down the seconds in her head. She felt the explosive tension all combat veterans feel in the seconds before running into a hail of gunfire. Nature forces animals to embrace self-preservation, to go in the opposite direction of danger. Humans had invented a way to do the opposite. Face down a deadly challenge, call it courage and see who can handle the pressure. Battle is unnatural. Her legs shook. Her fingers trembled. She estimated her heartrate at well over 200.

"Jumping the boat," Jacob called out.

Pia knew he would have his own problems on the launch. They weren't expecting someone to jump onboard and tell them to back out fast, go to a different pier. There would be concerns about his identity and intent. But those were his problems.

For Pia and Cody, it was time to move. Without a word, she and Cody simultaneously opened fire on the warehouse. He had a position on the far side from her. They both raced for the wide opening in front. From deep inside, they saw the flashes of muzzle fire then heard the cracks of the weapons.

She felt a bullet graze her shoulder. Another glanced off her helmet. Then one hit her center mass. Liquid body armor disperses the impact across an area the size of a dinner plate. But the violence knocked her off her feet. She landed on her back and rolled to one side before scrambling into a prone firing position.

She fired round after round at muzzle flashes deep in the warehouse. Two hit, five missed. But the hits were in armor and did no lasting damage. Cody had taken up a position behind a support pillar. It gave him better aim. He picked off one then another.

When her breathing stabilized, Pia found another pillar like Cody's. She took careful aim and lined up a man who was just as carefully aiming at her. She squeezed off three shots and watched his head fall apart inside his helmet.

"I'm hit." Cody's voice was calm.

He knelt next to the pillar and fired off two more rounds. Her thermal imaging showed a pool of blood beneath his calf. Down but not out. She aimed again and took down another Redjacket.

A bullet buzzed her ear like an angry hornet. It came from behind them. Her biggest fear was now realized. She was in a crossfire.

She turned and fired as many rounds into the dark outside as she could, then ran for Cody. Halfway across the open space, she let loose with another series. She heard a man cry out in pain.

She swapped magazines and slid in next to Cody. She looked at his wound. Exposed bone. Blood poured out at an alarming rate. She wanted to scream for a time out. The futility of battle hit her hard. There had to be a better way to stop Roche.

She looked up.

Cody was looking at her. "Proud to die in your company, ma'am. You're good people."

He aimed and fired down range. Pia fired in the opposite direction.

A swarm of bodies came near the entrance. The backup squad. Only Jacob had been wrong. There wasn't one squad in reserve. There were two.

"Bringing the boat to the warehouse, east end," Jacob said. "Get on board."

Pia watched as three men ran to the side of the warehouse and made their way toward Jacob's location.

"Ms. Sabel. Go!" Cody fired a round and hit a man. "I'll hold 'em."

Pia looked at his leg again. She couldn't carry him.

"I didn't get here alone," she told Cody, "I'm not leaving alone."

She fired off three more shots. One hit something. "Jacob, they're overwhelming our position. Get Wilkes out of here."

"I'm not leaving without—"

Gunfire cut him off.

"Get Wilkes back to the States. That's an order, Jacob. Stopping the war is down to you now. You have to make it out." Pia felt the frailty of her mortality. She had only minutes of life left. She would not go quietly. But Jacob wouldn't leave if he thought that. "Don't worry about us. We'll make it out of here. Just ask Mercury."

Cody snapped a look at her. She shrugged.

More gunfire erupted outside. Cody and Pia looked at each other.

"I play dead; cover you as long as I can," Cody said. "Get out there and cover Jacob's exit."

Over the comm link, Pia could hear the boat pilot arguing with Jacob. The launch was leaving, no matter what Jacob wanted.

She squeezed Cody's shoulder, handed him her last spare magazine, and ran across the vast space to the water's edge.

Just outside the wall, three Redjackets fired on the fleeing launch. Pia fired three rounds. The man closest to her fell, clutching his butt. His helmet rolled off. She blasted another round into his head. Her gun clicked. No more bullets.

Inside, Cody's version of playing dead didn't last. Gunfire crackled like firecrackers on Chinese New Year.

She tossed the stolen rifle aside and pulled up her MP5SD. A burst of darts sent the remaining Redjackets scrambling. One fell into the water. The last took cover behind a collapsed wall. She crawled behind a pillar. She aimed and waited for the man to pop up. Her back tingled with the sensation of someone aiming at her with a high-powered rifle.

Death slid his scythe up and down her spine.

Behind her, the gunfire crackled less. Then it stopped. A couple muffled pops from an MP5SD. Cody was out of ammo too.

That was it. Her luck had run out. The Redjackets and their zealotry were more powerful than anything she could field. She should've realized long ago that fighting them with guns would never work. She should've started the plan with her attorney earlier. Too late now. Her only regret—that she'd brought Cody to his end.

Then more of the quiet but distinct pops from an MP5SD. And a few more from a different position. Two people. Cody couldn't have moved.

"Clear!" Tania's voice.

"Clear." Miguel.

CHAPTER 43

CHUCK ROCHE WALKED INTO THE White House living room and took one look at his nephew lying on the sofa. The newest reality game show, *The Other Woman: Can You Force a Divorce?* played on the TV.

He pointed his cane at his nephew. "That better not be empty."

The young man looked up at the president, temporarily stunned. He looked down at the empty Cheetos bag on his belly. He jumped to his feet, crumpled the bag into a ball and ran for the kitchen.

Roche grabbed the remote and switched to Fuchs News. A talking head kept gasping for air in disbelief. The anchor said, "I'm not sure why she would report such a thing live, Bill. Uh. Maybe she thinks ... well ... could there actually be evidence? No way."

Whoever Bill was said something about rolling the video again. The screen cut away to Emily Dominguez, reporter for the *Post*. She stood in front of a burning shack in India. A Mumbai police official of regal bearing stood next to her. She stuck the microphone in his face.

The official enunciated slowly to minimize his accent. "We have direct evidence that these were members of the American paramilitary group known as the Redjackets. We believe they have killed and murdered citizens of Mumbai. We are working to understand if they received instructions from America. We found these."

Roche's heart collapsed. He felt a massive and invisible pair of plyers crush his chest. The Indian official held a red phone in his hand.

Exactly like Hunter's.

He knew what suspicious minds would think. That Americans were conducting secret operations in foreign countries at his direction. As if he had some control over the Redjackets. Veronica had the phone. She gave the orders. Most of them. He could prove that. Unless the phones in Mumbai hadn't been updated. He would check with Ratched on that.

But what of that damned lesbian, Bianca Dominguez? Did she dig up something? Veronica was bluffing when she said CIA phones recorded all calls. Of course, she was. If Veronica had any dirt on him, she never would have made the calls he demanded. Right? Definitely. She wanted his job. If she had one spec of dirt, she would've gone straight to the press. A bluff.

His phone rang, Gina Wind. He sent her to voice mail. Philip Haberman got the same treatment. The calls kept coming. He turned it off.

"That was the last bag." The first nephew returned empty handed. "They're all gone."

Roche just stared at him. His mind rolled through what to do next about the incident in Mumbai. Everyone told him if he were connected to the Redjackets, his career would be over. But then, they'd told him his career was over decades ago when he went bankrupt. Could he tough it out? Bluff his way through? No need, really. He could blame the whole thing on Veronica and get rid of her. That little circle of coconspirators would stop looking at him as if he were nuts. They'd go back to doing what he told them—with no more alternative ideas.

He noticed his nephew looking pale and clammy. "Did you call down to the main kitchen?"

"They laughed at me." He fidgeted his fingers. "Said I should go to a store."

Roche stared at the young man. Ten years since he graduated last in his class and he still didn't have enough smarts to tie his shoes. Velcroman.

"I could go get some." His nephew tossed a thumb over his shoulder. "Um. But…"

Roche rolled his eyes and pulled a twenty from his wallet and gave it to the boy. The young man ran down the hall.

If he could get away with giving the Redjackets one more mission, he'd send them after his sister's boy.

Thomas jogged up the stairs and into the living room. "Did you see that there?"

The Texan pointed at the TV where Emily's clip was running again.

"Terrible thing. Patriots killed while trying to take down a terrorist cell. Sad day when the terrorists win. What of it?"

"Only a couple of them died." Thomas shook his head. "And the rest were knocked clean out with Sable Darts. The Indian Department of Internal Security took them into custody."

"You mean the Sabel people are in jail?"

"No, the Redjackets, sir." Thomas motioned toward the stairs. "Several members of your cabinet want to meet with you. They're awaiting downstairs in the Cabinet Room."

Roche pushed Thomas aside and dropped down the staircase double time. He marched in to find a meeting already in progress.

Ratched, O'Brien and Rochester sat at the table facing his executive chair. Thomas joined them. Someone had taken away the maps. He eyeballed them and pushed his chair away. Standing would be fine for this crew. No one spoke.

"Well?" He slapped the table with his cane. "Out with it."

"Sir, given the news," O'Brien puffed up his chest and used his Ivy League voice, "we've decided the best thing would be for you to resign."

The Gang of Four found a backbone somewhere. No doubt they bought it cheap.

In their miserable careers, all they ever felt was shame. These civil servants who thought "serving" their country somehow made them better than everyone else were a pack of losers. How could the center of the capitalist world be entrusted to altruists? No one successful ever apologized for being successful. These kids needed to learn the basis for success. They needed a teacher, and he was the perfect one because he had reached the Zenith.

"Why?"

"Because," O'Brien glanced at his coconspirators, "the Indian government has a phone that directly connects the Redjacket operation in Mumbai to this administration. If you resign today, we can talk Veronica into giving you a pardon and—"

"You sniveling cowards." Roche gave his cane an overhead whack on the table. They jumped. "Why would I resign? Because American heroes took initiative where Congress took a recess? Because Americans had to take it upon themselves to defend this country from Saudi terrorists? Did you know that's who they were interrogating in that burning building?"

"Well, uh." Ratched stared at the table. "We don't have any intelligence on—"

"Guess why not?" Roche thundered. "Because Sabel Security agents were hired to rescue the terrorists. You ask the Indians about it. They'll tell you there were Sabel Darts all over the place. I'll bet they started the fire."

All four mouths fell open.

"You committed a crime here." Roche put his hands on the table and leaned toward them. They leaned back in their seats. "You conspired to overthrow the freely elected President of the United States of America. If I called the FBI in right now, I could have you all arrested. Where would your precious careers go after the perp walk?"

"We only suggested a course of—"

"Shut up." Roche picked up his cane and held it mid-shaft. "They were following up leads from the bombing of the *USS Caine*. They were interrupted by Sabel Security agents. Which one of you fails to believe me?" He stared at each of them. "You, Thomas?"

"No, sir." Thomas looked like he'd seen a ghost. "I believe we have intelligence on Sabel Darts at the scene. You could be right about that. I'll have to check on—"

O'Brien looked the Texan over as if he smelled gas.

"I'll ask the CIA for everything they have on the crime scene." Ratched scribbled notes. "As soon as they give me something, I'll demand the Indian ambassador call it a crime scene, sir."

O'Brien swung his gaze to her with the look of a drowning man.

"I'm on board," Rochester said, "as long as we can clear up one potential problem. What about calls to and from that phone. It looked identical to the one Veronica had. If anyone gave them instructions, it would—"

"Be grounds for her resignation." Roche stared the man down. "If you think your brilliant VP is going to save your career, think hard about that.

You saw the phone in her hand. You heard people identify her as the owner. If she did anything crazy like give them encouragement or instructions, we'll stand behind her for as long as we can. If she did do something wrong, she did it with the best of intentions."

The room was silent for a long time.

"What you pathetic worms don't understand is," Roche rolled his glare over them, "what will save your careers is fighting an all-out war."

"Yes, sir," they mumbled over each other.

"We can use this little problem to get the war on track." Roche paced behind the table as he thought. "Nora, you get our ambassador out there to visit those brave young men in the hospital. Make sure he brings the message about the terrorists they were tracking down. And get the best attorneys for the Redjackets. I don't mean defense attorneys, I mean plaintiff's lawyers. Make sure someone files a lawsuit against Sabel Security by morning. I will not stand for any vigilante group attacking and killing American patriots."

As the group filed out of the room, Roche tugged Nora Ratched's elbow and whispered in her ear. "I heard a rumor that those clandestine phones record all the calls in case something happens to the operative. That's not true, is it?"

"Yes, it's true. Why do you ask?"

<h1 style="text-align:center">CHAPTER 44</h1>

IT WAS A BIT SURREAL, to say the least. I pushed a rifle into the coxswain's ribs while Admiral Annie Wilkes held a pistol to my head. The fact that my threat used non-lethal Sabel Darts while hers used live rounds didn't come up. The coxswain hightailed it out of the area as bullets buzzed our ears. Ms. Sabel's mission priority was to save Wilkes. Which meant, my mission priority was to save Wilkes. Although, at that moment, I felt like disarming her, tossing her overboard, and going back to rescue my squad. Luckily for her, victory shouts erupted in my earbud.

I decided to let Wilkes and the boatman live. But I did disarm the old lady before she hurt someone. Navy people might be good with 16" cannons, but you never know what they'll do with a sidearm.

Ms. Sabel took her crew—and all the official police attention—to the hospital with her. There was some concern about Cody losing his leg. She was confident they could save it, if not in India then in the States.

Indian police voiced a good deal of concern about who fired first, who attacked who, and how so many Americans managed to smuggle weapons into India. The officials were officially pissed.

All of which left Admiral Wilkes and me in the hands of Mumbai's Lewis-Hamilton-wannabe. I wondered if Ms. Sabel picked our driver for his penchant for speed or if it just worked out that way. He didn't ask where we wanted to go. We got in the Jag, closed the doors, and we were rolling.

"Take me to the nearest police station," the admiral said.

Whoo-ee! Mercury twisted into the back from the passenger seat. *You got out alive, my brutha. Only one problem: I had to have someone put a pistol to your head. What is with you? Did you want me to lose a hundred thousand Aureus to Juno? Don't you trust me to send in Miguel and Tania?*

I said, *Since when do you have anything to do with Monster Slayer? I thought you were afraid of his gods.*

I ain't afraid of nobody. Mercury faced front. *I coulda had something to do with it. You don't know.*

I said, *How do I get Wilkes back to the US?*

Mercury said, *More important, how do you get out of Radhika Chopra's backyard?*

I said, *Yeah, that's tough.*

"What's tough about it?" Wilkes asked. "Take me straight to the authorities."

I choked. "This morning, one of 'the authorities' held a pistol to my forehead and pulled the trigger."

She looked me over. "You healed fast."

"I saved your life, you know. You could show a little gratitude."

"You're my fourth kidnapper in a week." She crossed her arms and pouted. "I demand you take me to the American Embassy."

Wearing a week-old torn uniform, she was clean but disheveled. The ambassador would turn her away as a homeless whacko. Then the Redjackets would show up. I tried to imagine why she had such a shitty attitude.

"Dhanpal didn't kidnap you. Mr. Singh didn't kidnap you."

"The hell they didn't. I told them I need to get to NAVCENT in Bahrain."

"Where the Redjackets will kill you before you get on base."

"I'm an admiral in the US Navy. Who the hell do you think you are?"

"I'm Jacob Stearne, former Ranger with a Distinguished Service Cross and a few Bronze Stars."

"So?"

"So?" I always knew admirals and generals thought the sun and stars orbited them, but I never expected this. "Those guys back at the docks were there to put a bullet through your head."

Mercury laughed hysterically from the front seat. *Aw, homie, tell me how it feels to deal with ungrateful mortals. You risk your life, you get electrocuted, your buddy gets his leg shot off—and she complains the pillows aren't fluffed. Sucks, huh? Welcome to the life of a divine being.*

I said, *Does she think I'm a Redjacket?*

"How do I know you're not?" The admiral looked me over like a side of moldy beef.

"Cuz I just rescued you."

"From a lecherous old captain who wouldn't let me use the sat-phone or the internet."

"I don't know about that stuff. I'm the good guys."

"You were about to shoot the coxswain if he didn't take us back to the people you claim were Redjackets." She grabbed my arm and dug in her fingernails. "Take me to the embassy, or I'll jump out at the next stop light and walk."

When I was a teenager, my sister and I had nearly-fatal fights because of her mouth. She'd say something horribly demeaning, and I'd chase her through the farmyard with murderous intent. This woman reminded me a lot of Joyce. Letting her walk through a city crawling with paramilitary commandos looking to end her life sounded like a pretty good option. I said, "Who do you think appointed the guy in the embassy?"

Something finally ticked into place for the admiral. We used to live in a world where people served their country out of selfless dedication. Now we live in a world where the ambassador was appointed for his willingness to lie when called upon.

We passed lamp posts, buildings and oncoming traffic with enough separation for a slice of buttered bread to squeeze between us. Every time we stopped, which wasn't often, I half expected Wilkes to bolt on me. I considered convincing her to do things my way. But then, I didn't know what my way was, so it would be hard to explain.

"Who are you, anyway?" I asked. "As far as I can tell, you're a spoiled brat who's a bit too old to get away with it."

She glared at me the way top brass always does when you don't recognize them. As if their likeness were sitting in a memorial as big as Lincoln's and every schoolchild would know them on sight.

I asked, "Why does everyone think you can stop World War III?"

"Because I have an SD card filled with video recordings of people plotting to blow up the *USS Caine*."

"Great, give it to me, and we'll get it to the press and Congress."

"I don't trust you." She crossed her arms, turned up her nose, and faced the window.

"Why the hell did Bobby Jenkins storm into my kitchen and demand I go save you? Why did General Thompson give me a world of grief when I told him I wouldn't?"

"Bobby?" She perked up and turned to me. "You know Bobby?"

"I had to drive him home from Sabel Gardens a few times. He's not good with Scotch."

"It never brought out his good side." She shook her head. "And Mikey? You know Mikey Thompson?"

It had never occurred to me that General Thompson had a first name. Even if he did, how well did you have to know him to put the "y" on the end? I recalled the exchange between Mikey and Bobby back at my house. A hint of youthful passions had surfaced. She was a fit woman with hard eyes and a presumption of rank and privilege. I'm sure the first entry in her personnel record read, "Thinks she graduated from Annapolis as an admiral." No doubt it was scratched out when she became one. Somewhere along the line, she and Mikey shared a moment that appears to have lingered.

"Known him for years," I said. "General Thompson saved me from the insane asylum."

Whoa. Dude. Mercury waved at me from the front seat. *Remember when we talked about whether you should tell people you were inches from a spending the rest of your life in an institution?*

I said, *Yes.*

Mercury said, *And do you remember what we decided?*

I said, *That some people might think I'm a psycho.*

Mercury said, *And what does the expression on Admiral Wilkes's face tell you?*

I glanced over at her. She was staring at me as if I'd farted in yoga class. *She thinks I'm a psycho.*

Mercury said, *And what about your driver?*

The man behind the wheel had slowed considerably as he watched me in the rearview mirror. After a second, he gave it up and put the hammer back down.

I decided to explain. "The army psychiatrists wanted me locked up. Instead, the general got me into a culinary school where I graduated with honors. But, y'know, after a while, I missed killing people too much, so I joined Sabel Security."

Bad idea. The admiral backed into the door hard as if there were something wrong with me.

Mercury said, *Your mission is about to jump out of the car and take her chances in traffic at fifty miles an hour. Maybe you should take your dad's advice about women.*

I said, *What advice?*

Then I remembered. When I came of age, my dad told me that women like a guy who has either charm, looks, money or power. Then Dad looked me over and told me my best shot was charm.

"General Thompson was right about you." I looked into her fear-widened eyes and said, "He said, and I quote, 'She's one helluva woman.'"

"Mikey said that?" The tough old admiral conjured up a little-girl voice.

"Yeah, and Bobby started asking him questions and then they left."

"They came to your house TOGETHER?" Her shriek was much more mature.

"Maybe you don't want to go back to America after all."

She didn't say anything for a long time. Whatever happened between the three of them had to have happened ages ago. Bobby had remarried and had another crop of kids. General Thompson divorced back in the Dark Ages.

Can people carry a torch for twenty years?

Not my problem. My problem was Admiral Annie Wilkes. How was I going to circumnavigate half the world with her and not kill her along the way? Dare I even ask where her SD card that can save the world is? Because if we have to stop in Tierra Del Fuego along the way to get it, that might be good to know. But she wasn't ready to tell me anything yet.

"You have to get me back right away." The admiral was back to barking orders.

"Why?"

"Because I stashed an SD card that can bring down the Roche administration and save the world from endless war."

I said, "Now you're talking my language. I hate that guy."

After seeing the Redjackets in action too many times, and seeing foreign agents co-opted into something they didn't understand, and seeing a decorated admiral pursued like a dog, I was onboard for saving the country. The actions of Roche's base were so far out of line from the constitution I swore to defend, I was ready to die for my country. Again.

Admiral Wilkes said, "Then let's get going."

"We're going. We just have to get there without going through any places monitored by the Redjackets."

"What does that leave us?"

"Bishkek, Kyrgystan."

CHAPTER 45

IN THE END, THE LAWYERS didn't get Pia and her people out of police custody, a smart move by the Major did. Pia's CEO removed the last sticking point in the contract between Sabel Satellites and the Indian Space Research Organisation, ISRO. If Pia wasn't in jail, the Major had argued to India's prime minister, her company could double ISRO's satellite launches. As a result of the Major's political prowess, they were freed. Pia left Mumbai only twelve hours after the Redjackets stopped shooting.

On the long trip home, she had time to think. She thought about how the Redjackets had penetrated every crevice in society and how they didn't care if Roche's war brought about the end of civilization. They operated on nothing more than blind faith. Because Roche was bombastic, he appeared to be a leader. No real leader was fooled by his bluster for a minute.

Pia had put her faith in Jacob and Wilkes. They were off the grid now. The only thing Pia had to go on was Jacob's last communication, they'd cleared the docks. Pia could only hope Wilkes had something on Roche. The president was no longer a target for her revenge, she had to save the world. To do that, Jacob would need time to sneak Wilkes back into the US. And the best way to do help them both was to steal headlines from Roche.

She stared at the last text from her attorney, "Are you sure you want to do this?"

She replied, "No doubt in my mind."

An odd thought occurred to her. Originally, she had cooked up the plan as a last-ditch effort aimed at revenge. Now she found herself doing it to save an admiral she barely knew.

Somewhere over Finland, Hunter called. "I need to speak to you in person. When will you be back in Sabel Gardens?"

Pia calculated her mother's possible reasons for wanting to meet. The most likely scenario made her nauseous. "After we stop in Germany to evaluate Cody's leg," she lied. "I'd say, noon tomorrow. Whatever day that is in DC."

Hunter didn't argue. She took the information and dropped the call.

Despite what she told Hunter, she landed several hours before dawn. Miguel and Tania accompanied Cody to the hospital. Pia went straight to Sabel Gardens to take care of some unfinished business. During the whole trip, the problem had taken up space in the back of her mind. She had decided how to handle it on the way home.

She walked up to Cousin Elmer's apartment in the car barn and knocked. Elmer had been a family fixture all her life. Shy and insecure, he preferred not to participate in events at the main house. Alan made a point of spending an afternoon with Elmer at least once a month. He had charged his cousin with maintaining the cars and jets about the time Pia started driving.

She'd once heard a proverb that society presents the crime, the criminal completes it. That appealed to her in this situation. She hadn't spent any time with Cousin Elmer in the year since Alan's death.

He came to the door in a robe with bed head and sleepy eyes. Average height with short, gray hair, he was the opposite personality of the big, boisterous Alan Sabel.

"May I come in?" she asked.

He backed up and waved her through the small foyer, a curious look on his face.

"I regret ignoring you since Dad died." She picked up a stack of car magazines from a chair and sat. He took the only uncluttered chair in the room, a recliner that he twisted from the TV to face her. "That was my fault. In his absence, I fear you've taken up a friendship with someone in the Roche administration. Who is it?"

"It's pronounced Row-SHAY." His gaze wandered around the room. "I voted for Roche, but we're not friends."

"Let's not debate the politics, let's discuss who you've been talking to in either the Redjackets or Chuck Roche's inner circle. I know you told someone about our travels. In particular, you told someone about Dhanpal Singh. He went to Mumbai and was met by Redjackets. They tried to kill him, Elmer."

"How dare you make accusations like that?" His eyes flashed, and his face reddened. "No way. They wouldn't kill anybody."

"We have the bodycam video. Would you like to see it?" She waited while he processed her offer. "We know you told someone when Jacob went there to rescue Dhanpal. And when I went there." She leaned forward and put a hand on his knee. "They knew when we would land. They were waiting for us. They came very close to killing me, Elmer."

"You can't blame Roche for something that happened on the other side of the—"

"Only one person knew I was going to see Hunter's speech at Wharton. I called you about the Aston Martin when I left Baltimore."

His face changed. Pale and uncertain, he fought for words to say. Pia could see his emotions cycling through different responses he might make. Each time he looked ready to say something, he thought better of it. She would never lie to him, and he knew it. His shoulders slumped.

"I didn't know he would…" Cousin Elmer's eyes filled with tears. He hung his head. "I never meant any harm, Pia. You know that. I can fix it. I'll fix it. Please don't fire—"

Pia held up a hand to silence him. "I forgive you. I won't easily forget it, but I'm partly to blame. I know I've not filled Dad's shoes. Not just with you, but the company and his old friends. I'm not the extrovert he was. I miss him."

"Me too."

"I'm going to fix that, Elmer. You and I will have an afternoon every month, just like when Dad was alive. We'll go to the Smithsonian. We'll get you a new suit. Anything you'd like."

"That would be nice, Pia." Elmer looked up with bloodshot eyes.

"I need to know who talked to you."

"You know President Roche's nephew?"

Pia bit her lip and closed her eyes. The two church mice of their respective organizations, darting about under the feet of titans. Whoever thought up the match was a genius. Her next step was the most difficult choice she'd made yet. Elmer was not chosen for his intellectual capacity. He organized cars and jets.

"I'm really sorry, Pia." He clasped his hands between his knees. "I swear I didn't know he was going to—"

"It's OK." She didn't want him going down a rabbit hole of guilt. "It actually works out. Here's what I need you to do."

She filled him in on the details until she was confident in his understanding. After reiterating her promise to spend time with him, she left.

It was time for phase two. Pia called Gina Wind. "If you can get here before sunrise, I'll let you in on a scoop that will blow you away."

"Is this a real interview?" Gina asked. "I mean, the on the record, no-preconditions kind? Or are you using me for something?"

"Both."

"At least you're honest about it. I'll be there in an hour."

True to her word, Gina met Pia in the home office an hour later. As soon as Gina walked in, before any greeting, she pointed at Pia's black eye. "Is that from Philly?"

"Good to see you too. Follow me." Pia led Gina outside to the garden as the sun rose on dew covered hydrangeas.

"You promised a big scoop." Gina pulled out a phone gimbal and snapped her phone in. She pressed video record and mounted it in a harness strapped to her chest. "I know, looks funny. They don't pay for cameramen anymore."

Gina pulled a legal pad filled with handwritten questions. "Why me, isn't Emily Dominguez your good friend?"

"She didn't want this scoop."

Gina looked up from her pad, a keen curiosity in her face. Pia met her with a reserved calm. Recomposing herself, Gina started in. "I saw the video from Attu Island. There is no doubt in my mind—"

"There is only one person who could've shown you that video," Pia said. "You're not a fan of his. I'm going to answer your question, but later, at the end. Trust me on this."

"Pia, that video is everything Roche said it was. You can't leave me in the dark. What happened out there?"

"Have you posted anything about it?" Pia asked.

"Not yet. I wanted to hear your side."

"Where we end this interview will answer all your questions about it."

"OK." Gina thought this over for a moment and watched Pia with such intensity she almost walked into a bed of begonias. "Why are you spending so much time with your old adversary, Veronica Hunter?"

"She's my birth mother."

"Wow." Gina's mouth fell open. "That's the scoop? How did you keep that a secret for so long?"

"I only discovered it a month ago. Outside of a few close friends, I've told no one. But no, that's not the scoop. Next question."

"Uh. Yeah." Gina looked over her hostess for a moment before going on. "You've been seen in her company quite a bit lately. Are you catching up on mother-daughter time?"

"She never revealed her motherhood to me. I figured it out for myself and confronted her. Ever since, she's been using me to accomplish her goals."

Gina took a moment to jot notes as they walked under a magnolia tree. A dew drop landed on her pad. "What goals could she possibly have that you would let her use you to attain?"

"I'm not going to answer questions you can figure out for yourself."

They strolled past a bed of multi-colored ranunculus. "She's waiting for Roche's impeachment to step back in? Or is she pulling a palace coup? Or, are you giving her enough rope to hang herself?"

"All of the above, maybe? It's hard to tell with slippery people. Sometimes you work with the opportunities they present." Pia brushed the dew off a flower in a raised bed of peonies. "Next question."

"The Redjackets have announced their intent to file a lawsuit against you and Sabel Security for wrongful death. How will you respond?"

"My attorneys can't wait for the Redjackets' filing—if they file." Pia smiled. "Bringing a suit will prove problematic for them. They will have to name plaintiffs and reveal the sources of their intelligence. When they do, we will make our bodycam videos public. Those recordings will prove they had malicious intent and fired first. My prediction: they will never file the lawsuit."

"What do you mean their sources of intelligence?"

"Redjackets traveled to Mumbai to ambush my agents. My attorney's first question will be, 'How did you know Dhanpal Singh would be in Dharavi?' The Redjackets will be forced to reveal their source of intel in discovery. We know that person to be a senior official in the Roche administration."

"That will let you prove the administration is deploying an extra-judicial paramilitary organization not seen since the Brownshirts." Gina scribbled furiously.

They walked on until Gina caught up her notes. They stopped in front of a large bed of dahlias in shades ranging from maroon to bright yellow. Gina asked, "How do you keep everything so perfectly in bloom?"

"I've no idea." Pia shrugged. "The staff does an amazing job, don't they?"

Gina watched her while they walked another twenty yards.

"Yes, in some respects I lead a charmed life." Pia stretched her crewneck down, revealing a bruise starting at her clavicle and stretching down her breastbone. She let the material snap back and walked away. "In other respects, not charming at all."

"That's not from Philly." Gina jotted more notes.

"Redjackets in Mumbai. Were it not for my advanced body armor, we wouldn't be having this conversation."

"That brings up my next question. Why were you in a shootout in Mumbai?"

"My team located Admiral Anne Wilkes."

Again, Gina's mouth fell open. "That's the scoop?"

"No." Pia walked past the last bed of flowers on that side of the garden, a large patch of chrysanthemums.

"Wait, you can't just drop that on me and not tell me where she is."

"I have no idea." Pia pointed to the garden behind Gina. "The staff does an amazing job, don't they?"

"You have her stashed somewhere? I mean, your staff has her—"

"I doubt they'd handle it like that, but then I leave it to them."

"You're bringing her in. You're going to make sure she testifies in public. Why? What does she know?"

"I've not communicated with the admiral in any way. I know no more than you." Pia walked along the sidelines of her soccer field. Two teams of girls from the inner-city league she sponsored warmed up. She waved to them. They shouted greetings.

Gina said, "The president called her a traitor and issued a shoot-to-kill order, which he later retracted. You took on the Redjackets in a gun battle. You got shot. Why take those risks if you don't know anything about her?"

"We know plenty about her." Pia walked through the training facility. "She's an admiral with an unblemished record. She served her country for over thirty years. Like all dedicated service members, she deserves our respect for the sacrifices she's made. Whoever sent the Redjackets to silence her is the exact opposite. Whatever she knows, whatever she did, our nation owes her a safe return and a chance to be heard."

Gina looked around the facility, out of questions for the moment. Pia considered everything Gina asked. The questions she could've asked and didn't. Her willingness to take Pia's answers at face value. Trust is hard to gain and easy to lose. Pia wanted to trust Gina because of the flattering articles she'd written as a sports reporter. Her more recent reports were less complimentary. Which Gina could she trust with her big news? The recent posts were as honest as they were inflammatory. She needed inflammatory. The more, the better to fuel her agenda. Pia could never be sure her words wouldn't be twisted into pretzels, but her instinct told her she could trust Gina with her next step. The big scoop.

They came out of the gym near the car barn. Cousin Elmer waited outside.

"What's the scoop then?" Gina asked. "It's something about Roche, isn't it? You're going to take down Roche."

"Elmer," Pia said, "what do you recommend for a nice ride downtown today?"

"You do love convertibles," he said, "but does your friend find the weather a bit chilly?"

"I don't mind cold," Gina said. "Are we going somewhere?"

"Downtown for the scoop." Pia tapped her lips as she thought. "A Lamborghini will knock our teeth out on the rough streets. What about the Porsche 918?"

"You scrubbed the tires, and the replacements haven't arrived yet," Elmer said. "How about the Pagani? You liked that suspension in street mode."

Pia nodded, and Elmer disappeared into the barn.

"You don't need to impress me," Gina said. "I don't care about your fancy car—"

"It's for the video you're going to record. I'd hate to be on all the news sites driving a Camry." Pia gave her a mischievous smile. "Some things need to be done in style."

One of the bays on the car barn rose. A low-slung Pagani Huayra Roadster rolled out looking like a prop from a science fiction movie. Elmer hopped out and opened both doors.

Pia took the wheel as Gina hesitated near the passenger door. "Is this the part where you're going to use me for something?"

"I plan to use you in a mutually beneficial project. When we get there, you'll understand how much trust I'm putting in you."

"Get where?"

"Our destination." Pia considered confiding more in the reporter but decided against it. "In an hour or two, every other news organization is going to descend on Sabel Gardens with what they think is the scoop of the year. If you record our next hour together—and you don't post it until the other sites have committed—you'll put them all to shame."

CHAPTER 46

HUNTER PUSHED PAST HARTWELL THOMAS and entered the Oval Office. President Roche lounged on the couch watching the endless news. She said, "What's this I hear about you releasing the video from Attu Island?"

Roche got up and turned off the TV. "I'm not releasing the video to the public. But I've reviewed it. Shocking stuff. Naturally, as soon as I knew what it was, I turned it over to the FBI. For now, I didn't say anything about your involvement in the coverup."

"You can't release that video." Hunter clenched her fists. "You saw it live. You've known about it for over a year. If I go down, I'm taking you with me."

"Why, Veronica, what on Earth are you talking about?" He grinned. "I never saw this thing before, or I would've reported it straight away. Like I said, there has been no mention of a coverup—yet."

"Your tweets connect you to the Redjackets. You'll go down for that no matter what you do to Pia. So stop the steamroller. It won't do you any good."

"My tweets simply cheer them on."

Hunter realized the man was diabolically clever when it came to saving himself.

"You're doing this to Pia because the red phones connects you to the Redjackets." Hunter never hated the man as much as she did at that moment. She felt her fists ball up and considered decking him. "What did you ask the FBI to do about Pia?"

"To get rid of a problem." Roche stamped his cane. "Everyone wants to know what happened in Mumbai. No one is asking what happened to the *USS Caine!* That's your fault. You keep helping her grab new headlines. Now we're going to silence her."

His nephew ran in unannounced carrying a 3-kilogram bag of Cheetos as big as a sack of flour in his outstretched hands. "Here ya go, Uncle Chuck."

"That was two days ago." Roche frowned at the young man. "Where the hell have you been?"

His nephew shrugged. "They only make the monster bags in Mexico. Had to get the State Department to fly me down there."

The three of them looked at each other, twice.

The young man sagged. "I thought it would make you happy."

Hunter said, "Two hundred fifty thousand tax-payer dollars a year to fetch Cheetos?"

"Hey," the first nephew said, "that guy told me Pia's going to be at Sabel Gardens early. Like within the hour." He handed over the Cheetos and backed away two steps, out of the cane's swinging range.

"Get out of here," Roche said to his nephew. The boy ran off. Roche struggled to open the bag.

Hunter snatched it from him and pulled it open and handed it back. "You had me find out when she was getting in. Then you had him doublecheck, why? What are you doing, Chuck?"

"All of a sudden, you think of her as your darling daughter. She despises you. She lies to you. She told you noon. She landed already. She's there right now."

"What do you think you're doing?" Hunter's voice betrayed her anxiety.

"What happened with that red phone you turned over to the lesbian?"

"I don't know."

"You're lying," Roche said.

"I learned from the master."

Roche picked up his desk phone. "Get me George at the FBI." He cradled the handset under his chin while he waited, "Tell me what she found on the phone."

"She told me it would take two hours. That was two days ago. She hasn't called me, and she hasn't taken my calls."

Hunter watched him. She knew what he was doing, and the thought enraged her. He'd gone from using the Redjackets for his personal attacks to using the FBI.

"You failed." He shifted the phone under his chin. Roche pointed out the window where aides were setting up a podium. "We're going to have a little Rose Garden conference in a few minutes. You'll stand next to me, or I release that video to the public. When they see it, Congress will vote to remove you. Don't think they'll be afraid of you once they find out you protected your murderous daughter."

Hunter felt herself break out in cold sweat. She paced the room. Anger crashed through her. How dare he threaten her like that? Fear of the video kept her from leaping on the man. If she had a gun, she'd shoot him.

"George," Roche said into the phone. "You ready? I believe she'll be there any minute. Go ahead with the plan. Did you leak it to the news outlets? Good. Don't forget, there are usually several heavily armed agents on the premises. Don't count on them using darts. They could have live ammo."

He slammed the phone down. Outside, TV cameras and high-powered lights went up.

"You're sending a SWAT team for her?" Hunter heard herself hit a shrill note. "Encouraging a gunfight? You're despicable."

"How did you phrase it? I learned from the master."

"The Indian Intelligence Bureau has your people and their red phones. They'll decrypt those communications and publicize them."

"You gave all the commands."

"India will know the difference between the phone you gave me and the one you're using to order them around." Hunter tried to keep calm when Roche grinned like a kid getting away with something. "You alienated India a long time ago. They'd love to blow you up."

"Indians are downright bastards." Roche pointed his cane at her. "The prime minister called me an asshole this morning. He made all kinds of threats. Seems he's chosen to side with Sabel. I'll be counting on you—and your desire not to do time for covering up for your homicidal mini-me—to smooth things over with them."

"You cut aid to India by half and called the prime minister a fat slob. What can I tell him that will smooth anything?"

"I'm sure you'll figure something out." Roche pointed to the door with his cane. "Your freedom depends on it."

Hunter considered her options. She should warn Pia. Refuse to walk out to the Rose Garden. Run. Anything. Those options fueled her hatred for the scheming bastard. She had the idea to grab his cane from him and beat him to death with it. Her teeth clenched so hard her jaw hurt.

Then her long-game beckoned. Roche would never survive the fallout of whatever happened next. As long as she survived the next few days, he would be out. She would be in. The red phones would save her. Pia's people must've found Roche's voice on it by now. She could ensure their release to the public. Surely Pia would do that much for her.

Roche opened the door and held it for her.

She eyed him as she walked out and took her place behind him at the lectern. She took a deep breath and tried not to let her revulsion for the president color her expression.

Roche held up his hands. "Thank you, before I make my big announcement, I'd like to point out to all the fake reporters that my vice president and I have a fine relationship. She's here today to support my agenda."

Cameras clicked and whirred. Reporters scribbled notes.

"This morning," Roche looked directly into the cameras, "I learned the FBI has reviewed a Top-Secret video taken on Attu Island last year. In it, Pia Sabel fired nine bullets into Russian diplomat, Viktor Popov, killing him. The act is brazen, premeditated, and cold blooded. The FBI determined that Ms. Sabel is a flight risk, heavily armed, and known to resort to violence. For that reason, I've authorized the use of force to apprehend her and bring her to justice."

CHAPTER 47

OUR MARIO ANDRETTI IMPERSONATOR GOT us to Nashik, about three hours northeast of Mumbai, in half the time Google maps predicted. From there we flew commercial airlines to Ashgabat, Turkmenistan and caught a connecting flight to Bishkek, Kyrgyzstan. There, I planned to look up an old friend.

During the trip, I let the admiral stream some news from home on my phone. She was not pleased about how the president had presented her case. She took issue with being accused of treason. But she didn't want to talk about it.

Snow covered Bishkek's imposing mountains when we arrived. We took in the view as we waited for Rick. He pulled up in a beaten Toyota Estima. We passed several Soviet monuments that the Kyrgyz appeared to honor as the "good old days." Bishkek is not as backward a town as you might think, though. They have a Hyatt Regency. We didn't stay there. Rick took us to his place, a moderately upright warehouse in a sketchy part of town.

Mercury wandered around the empty space. *Rick's been busy, y'know what I'm saying, bro? If you fail to save the world, cockroaches like him will always survive.*

I said, *Don't be talking about my man like that. He did alright in the Waziristan operation.*

Mercury said, *OK.*

When Rick told Admiral Wilkes to put on the outfit he provided, she balked. "I'm not wearing that. I'd look like the third wife of a village chieftain."

Rick looked at me.

"That's the idea," I said. "We're traveling through some backwater countries who don't care about you and Roche. The less you look like a beautiful American admiral, the better."

She sneered. My charm offensive had worn off somewhere over Tajikistan. Then Rick held up the headscarf. She said, "No way."

"You need to look less American."

"What am I supposed to be?"

"Third wife of a village chieftain works." I looked at Rick. He shrugged and nodded.

She said, "I need a phone."

It was her fifty-eighth request.

"Passport first," I said.

Wilkes grabbed the hijab out of Rick's hands and went behind the blanket he used to segregate his living quarters from his photography studio.

Mercury wandered the far end of the place. *Y'know who the admiral reminds me of, homie? Livia Drusilla. You remember her? Mother of Tiberius. She and Augustus were married to different people when she seduced him. Livia made him divorce his wife the day the poor girl gave birth to his daughter. Then she talked the Emperor into adopting her son as heir to the Julio-Claudian Dynasty.*

I said, *So?*

Livia was a clever girl. Mercury kicked an open duffel bag. *She put poison on the figs in Augustus' garden to kill him. I know it's popular these days to say her detractors made the story up, but I was there, homie. I watched her. No one knows what determined means like Livia Drusilla. She had so much power, her boy Tiberius moved to Capri rather than be ridiculed as the Emperor who was neutered by his mommy.*

I said, *So?*

I told you the admiral reminds me of Drusilla. Mercury threw his hands up. *Think about what a woman like that is gonna do to you after she figures out where you brung her.*

I looked around the sparse space.

"Hey, Rick," my eyes wandered over a large pile of sheets in the corner, "what've you been doing since you left the Army?"

"Doing my photography thing," he smiled. "Wildlife videos, mostly. There's a big demand for exotic Eurasians in unique situations."

A stack of thin mattresses leaned against a wall. Four duffle bags with plastic tubing sticking out of them waited in the corner. Enough lights on tripods rested in the corner to light a stadium. I did a doubletake on the plastic tubing. My heart stopped.

If Admiral Wilkes figured out what Rick did for a living, she'd beat us both to death and take her chances on a direct flight to Dulles. I crossed to the duffle bags and zipped them closed.

The admiral rejoined us as I kicked a stray phallus under a table. She looked like a middleclass vaguely-white Kenyan. She stood in front of the screen. Rick snapped four photos. Then took some of me. Then he sat down at a computer and started doing his artwork.

"Kenya is converting to the EAC digital passport. These old blue ones will only work until September."

"We only need them for a couple days." I kept an eye on the admiral who stared at me as if she were stabbing me with her gaze. "What's EAC?"

"East African Community, Africa's version of the EU."

His printer clicked and buzzed. Two beautiful, probably authentic passports churned out. Realistic stamps from several countries covered the back pages.

Wilkes grabbed hers and tried to shove it in a non-existent pocket. "I need a purse."

Rick tossed her a Gucci-knockoff from a pile of props.

"And a phone," she said.

Rick looked at me for a yay or nay.

I considered her request. "Who do you want to call that won't tip the Redjackets?"

"None of your business."

Not the answer I was looking for. Maybe she'd call Bobby Jenkins? He couldn't help her. General Thompson? Nah, she'd sound too eager. Besides, she'd tell me if she wanted to call him. No other option came to mind.

"Then no." I gave her my soldier stare. Rick backed me up.

Guess the Navy boys have the same stare. She'd seen it and wasn't impressed.

"I need to get a message to someone," she said.

"I can make a video and share it anywhere you want," Rick said.

"Who is it going to?" I asked.

"Media," she said.

I gave Rick the go-ahead. He lined up a camera and gave her a chair.

She ripped off the hijab, finger-combed her hair, and looked to the camera. "There has been a lot of misinformation about the bombing of the *USS Caine*. Paramilitary operators have been trying to kill me for days to keep me from going public. But I will find a way back to the US. I will testify to the truth. I will prove everything I say."

When she stopped talking, Rick and I shared a glance. It seemed kind of short and non-specific but if that's what the admiral wanted, I didn't have a problem with it. It sounded right up my I-hate-Roche alley.

"We're out of time." I tugged Rick. "Can you buy us those tickets now?"

Rick went online and bought ten tickets to ten different destinations on several airlines using our real names and my American Excess card. If someone monitored my spending habits, it should slow them down a bit. Then he bought a pair using his credit card on Air Astana to Baku, Azerbaijan under our new passport names. He charged me an inflated price for his services. He charged it to my card.

We grabbed our tickets and got in his car. Bishkek doesn't have traffic like most cities. A line of cars stops for the stop signs on every freaking block, but otherwise, it's as quiet as a midwestern American city.

Mercury leaned over him. *Your expense report is going to raise a lot of questions 'bout your morals, dude. 'Eurasian Modeling Studios' ain't fooling anybody.*

I said, *How was I supposed to know? Rick used to forge passes when you wanted to get off base for a drink.*

Mercury said, *That's not your biggest problem. You need to start thinking about how Romulus defeated the Fidenae in 800 BCE. Y'know what else you need to think about? How did the Fidenae find you?*

Something ticked off in my memory. One of Mercury's many lectures about Roman history that I usually slept through. He told me the Fidenae story after I drank a pot of coffee. Romulus fooled the Fidenates into thinking the Romans were undisciplined warriors, then ambushed them. But who would be playing the part of Fidenates in Bishkek?

On the drive back to the airport, we were followed. A clean, recent model sedan with five men in it. Redjackets favored the five-man squad. And they had an uncanny ability to find us in the most obscure places. In the movies, some sinister clandestine agency pinpoints heroes on the lam using omniscient artificial intelligence. Anyone who's worked for the government can tell you that's impossible in real life. There is no department efficient enough to make it happen. The Redjackets had been tipped off.

"Rick, do you have any friends who could help us out?" I asked.

He caught my meaning and made a call. A minute later he diverted our route to a bar. We bailed out in the alley, switched to a Toyota Prius and drove off while Rick picked up a couple drunks and drove off in the opposite direction.

When we were clear of Rick, Wilkes turned to me with a somber voice. "You ever take me to a porn studio again, and I'll have you court martialed."

"Show some gratitude, lady. We're getting out of here alive because of him. For what it's worth, last I heard he was an expert photographer of lynx and wapiti, Asian elk."

Five miles down the road, when I was pretty sure the enemy had missed our switch, I asked my favorite admiral. "Did you borrow anyone's phone when you used the ladies' room at the airport?"

She looked out the window.

CHAPTER 48

PIA WAVED GOODBYE TO GINA and followed her monumental-sized attorney. He led her into a small meeting room decorated with walls of suicidal-beige, a matching blah-table, acoustic-tile ceiling panels and fluorescent lights. They took chairs to wait. His compressed with a mechanical groan.

"They've agreed to terms." Her attorney assured her. "Something's going on upstairs, so we might be here a while."

"Understandable." She smiled and patted his hand. "Mind if I catch up on this morning's news?"

He shrugged and thumbed out emails to his office.

Before she could bring up the *Post*, the Major texted her. "Just heard from Emily. What the hell are you doing?"

She texted back. "Stealing Roche's thunder."

The Major texted, "Is this Veronica's idea?"

Pia replied, "Mine. 100%. Trust me."

"There must be another way," the Major texted back. "You should talk to me before you do these rash things."

That was true, she should talk to the Major more, but she would've said no. Pia felt this was the right track. It would not be long before Roche came tumbling down.

An email dinged in from the eBay memorabilia vendor Pia had contacted. The woman wrote two paragraphs about her fascination with Pia's career and how she couldn't believe she was exchanging emails with the greatest soccer player of all time. Then the vendor confirmed that she had indeed sold a state championship bracelet to Vice President Hunter. She included Hunter's invoice. Shipped straight to the Naval

Observatory three weeks ago. Pia recalled seeing the bracelet prominently displayed on Hunter's handbag. It fit with the text exchange she'd had with her old boxing coach, the VP had inquired about her training three weeks ago. An incredible attention to detail on Hunter's part that Pia had to admire. Still, it left her depressed. No matter how much she wanted to believe Veronica cared about her, the evidence proved otherwise.

She brought up the *Post's* site. A big red BREAKING NEWS banner flashed across the screen. A live video feed was in progress.

Emily Dominguez stood in front of Sabel Garden's gates with a cameraman and a microphone. The camera took in the scene. The gates stood wide open. All the staff were lined up along the brick driveway as if waiting for a parade. The guards held their empty hands in front of them, weapons on the ground, disassembled and out of reach.

The camera panned to the road leading up to the premises. A caravan of FBI SWAT teams in heavily armored personnel carriers drove up the street. Immediately behind them, a horde of news crews. Two drones whirred over their heads. One marked FBI and the other NEWS.

Pia's attorney scooted closer and looked over her shoulder. She turned her phone to better share the screen.

Emily reported from the scene, but her audio was immediately drowned out by loudspeakers from the armored cars. They instructed everyone on the property to get on the ground, face down. The Sabel Gardens' staff complied right away. The vehicles disgorged a swarm of agents carrying automatic weapons and battlefield armor. They knocked Emily down as they stormed the grounds.

Handcuffs clicked onto every wrist. Pia winced when she saw Chef and Maria jerked to a sitting position. Agents yelled in their faces. The women's defiant looks gave her some solace. Her guards, led by Tania, received doubly harsh treatment. Ankle cuffs snapped onto belly chains. The handcuffs were attached as well, preventing any free movement. All the weapons were gathered up. Agents were posted to keep an eye on the presumably dangerous maids and cooks. The rest of the agents fanned out.

No one asked anything of the Sabel employees.

Emily stuck her microphone out, trying to reach a man who waved and motioned as if he were in charge. "Do you know she's not here? Sir? Sir? Are you aware that she left an hour ago?"

The man ignored her. From there on, the video followed the FBI doing a tedious search of an empty mansion. Pia found her interest waning.

Changing to the related story, she watched President Roche's statement from the Rose Garden. She paused the video. Standing behind Roche, Veronica had the same blank, emotionless look on her face she'd had at Wharton while watching Pia get beaten to a pulp.

Hunter chose that moment to text her.

"I couldn't stop him," Veronica's text read. "You have to believe me."

Pia replied, "You asked when I would return to Sabel Gardens. I lied because I knew why you were asking. Watch Gina Wind later this morning."

Hunter didn't respond.

Pia felt the closure. She was, once again, a motherless child.

Gina sent a text. "Edited and online now. Are you sure this is a good idea?"

Pia didn't reply. She wasn't sure. What she was doing was risky. There were facets she could only hope she had right. The smart move would've been to check with her attorney, but he, like the Major, would've said no. Everyone was risk averse. Maybe they were right. It seemed like a great idea until she sat in this depressing meeting room and had time to face the reality of it. But then, she thought, play your game not Roche's.

Pia switched to *Politica's* site.

Standing outside the FBI's J. Edgar Hoover Building, Gina announced, "Hours before the FBI mounted an unnecessary raid on her home, Pia Sabel drove to FBI headquarters to turn herself in for last year's killing of Viktor Popov."

In the video, Pia's Pagani pulled up to the curb. She got out, met her attorney on the sidewalk, and walked in. The camera focused on the FBI seal as the door closed behind her.

Gina's voice-over continued, "Long before President Roche made his announcement in the Rose Garden, Ms. Sabel felt it was time to clear up what conspiracy theorists and the administration have been leaking for days." Gina's video cut to the Hoover Building lobby where a smartly dressed Senior Agent in Charge answered questions.

The SAC said, "Yes, we set this up days ago. Apparently, certain agents did not read the internal memo and did not follow proper procedure. There may have been some political pressure for a photo op. I'm not sure. There will be an investigation. We apologize for any inconvenience to Ms. Sabel's staff."

Pia's attorney squeezed her arm and giggled with unbridled glee. "You did this on purpose?"

"I did the right thing." She gazed out the window at the bright sunshine. "Others did what was in their nature. They made and fell into their own trap."

Gina's report continued with her earlier interview at home. Pia liked how Gina saved the exchange about Wilkes deserving to be heard for the end. It would help her image in the coming days.

White puffy clouds sailed above the city outside her window. She wondered how long it would be before her freedom was restored. The women in prison she didn't worry about. Playing competitive soccer was a cutthroat world in which she had excelled. With her height, she intimidated most women by merely standing up. But the enclosed space was depressing. For someone who'd spent a lifetime outdoors on the pitch, running, playing, swimming and biking all over the world, the concept of prison was inconceivable. It felt as if a blender were stirring her innards into soup. Days without rain or sun or fog or snow were unimaginable. And it was a risky plan at best.

"Second thoughts?" Her attorney put his hand on top of hers to get her attention. When she looked at him, he said, "You sure you want to go through with this? You can run right now."

"Better to get it over with and move on."

Suddenly, she remembered something. She thumbed out a text to Gina. "Thanks for returning the car to Sabel Gardens for me. I forgot to mention: there is a tennis ball under the gas pedal. Yes, seriously. Do not take it out! Enjoy the drive." She added a smiley emoji.

Gina texted back. "Thanks for the scoop. It was a tough assignment. I can see why your friend turned it down."

Within minutes, her phone blew up with texts. Friends, old coaches, acquaintances, teammates, everyone wishing her support and offering help.

Three men entered the room. One Pia recognized as the SAC from Gina's report. They took seats and introduced themselves. The mood was somber as the SAC explained what would happen next. The US Marshal Service would send someone to pick her up. She would be booked, fingerprinted, and processed through the federal system. They had arranged for her to be released pending trial. There would be an arraignment at some point in the coming days. She would surrender her passport, promise not to leave the region, and so on.

A Deputy Attorney General would be assigned to the case. They would be in touch with her attorney. If there were any interest in a plea deal, that would be discussed with Justice.

They gave her some papers to sign. The tactile feel of the documents brought home her plan. It was a significant risk. A calculated risk. One she had given a lot of thought. Nonetheless, risking her freedom was scary. Suddenly, she felt nauseous as the reality of prison came ever closer. The surreal situation dissolved her comprehension. The words on the paper were meaningless. Her eyes glazed over. Since her attorney had already read and approved it, she had no need to read it.

The whole reason for risking her freedom and her future was to give Jacob a couple days to bring in Wilkes. This was a huge risk for just a couple days. Pia took a deep breath.

She signed.

CHAPTER 49

HUNTER TRIED UNSUCCESSFULLY TO GET his attention before Thomas ushered the interested parties into the Oval Office. It was time for the signing of the National Gingersnap Day Proclamation. Thomas lined up the cookie executives, parents, children and other assorted cookie-nerds behind the desk. The press photographers were in position opposite them. Hunter looked over the crowd's shoulders but couldn't see Chuck Roche. Thomas pushed people into place and ordered them—like dogs—to stay. He came back toward her.

"Hartwell," she said as he approached, "has he seen the video?"

"Of Wilkes? He's in there watching it now."

"No, Pia's interview from this morning." Hunter stepped in his path. "What Wilkes video?"

"Facebook, Twitter, take your pick." He pushed her out of his way and left.

Hunter brought up a feed on her phone and watched the tousled admiral promise to substantiate her impending testimony with irrefutable facts. For a moment, Hunter was glad Roche had kept her in the dark about Wilkes and the *USS Caine*. On the other hand, whatever he'd done might take her down with him.

Roche appeared and touched her elbow. "Veronica, I need to talk to you after this charade in here. The Wilkes problem is going critical, you need to find a solution."

He slid around her and marched into the Oval Office with an outstretched arm, his cane twirling. He boomed his greeting. "Hello, gingersnap lovers. Is there a better cookie in the world? Let's make this official, shall we?"

Hunter couldn't believe his ignorance of Pia's moves that morning. Had he heard, the last thing he'd be worried about was Wilkes. Within hours, Pia would once again move the Saudi war off the front pages. Wilkes would be old news by noon. By dinner time, everyone would be talking about the nation's darling admitting to murdering a Russian diplomat. Hunter had been unable to figure out Pia's plan. But the girl wouldn't have taken such a risk without a strategy. If Pia wins, Hunter realized, she had to be firmly in the young billionaire's camp, or she'd never raise enough for a second term in office. After appearing in the Rose Garden press conference, the only way Hunter could get back in Pia's good graces was to get the girl pardoned by Roche. No easy task.

Hunter watched through the open door as Roche did the whole feel-good thing that she had once enjoyed. There was nothing like a harmless proclamation to take you away from the pressures of the day. National Day sponsors are advocates, not critics.

All the observers wanted was a stage on which to say something special about the all-important gingersnap. They talked. And they talked. The snack was the backbone of American ingenuity. Eating them brought prosperity. Roche noted that it was the red-headed stepchild of the cookie industry. No one laughed. Someone stepped in and recited a list of famous gingersnap lovers.

A voice from the press shouted over one of the cookie pontificators. "Mr. President, was Admiral Wilkes referring to the Redjackets when she claimed paramilitary operators were trying to kill her?"

"Where did you get that crazy idea?" Roche snapped. "Who knows what Riyadh Rose is talking about? Does anyone know when she recorded it?"

"What misinformation was she referring to?" another reporter asked.

"Riyadh Rose is not on the agenda today, folks."

"She said she will find a way back to the US to testify, will you rescind your shoot-to-kill order?"

"I never gave any shoot-to…" Roche's face grew crimson. "GET OUT! All of you. Get the fuck out of my office. I'm the president, and you're not, so shut up."

He slammed his cane down on the desk an inch from a scared child.

After a moment of shock, everyone ran from the room as if fleeing an erupting volcano.

"HARTWELL!" Roche paced the room batting lamps and knickknacks with his cane. "Goddamn it, Hartwell!"

Hunter crossed the room to him. "Wilkes is on her way back here. When she testifies, your house of bullshit is going to come tumbling down."

"Like hell," he glared at her.

The phone rang. Roche rounded the desk and picked it up. "Shut up, Krueger. What could she possibly have? The Saudi's did it, and she helped them. If she has evidence, she made it up. Everyone knows she's a liar. I've got a new name for her. I want you and everyone else to start…" Roche looked at the phone as if it had turned into a snake. Then he put it back to his ear. "I don't care if she served her country. They're all cowards and idiots in the military. I'm smarter than any of them. Riyadh Rose fits fine, and I'm using it."

He slammed the phone down and fisted his hips and turned to the window.

Hunter said, "You need to pardon Pia."

He spun around to face her. "Why the hell would I do that?"

"Because she's up to something." Hunter parked a hip on the desk. "I haven't figured it out yet, but she's got something. Did you see her interview from this morning?"

"Watched her walk into jail where she belongs."

"After that." Hunter crossed her arms. "At the end, what she said about Wilkes, '…our nation owes her a safe return and a chance to be heard.'"

Roche grabbed his cane and tapped it on the floor and turned back to the window. "You're right. Wilkes must have something. My people said she never connected with Pia. That Jacob-guy took off with Wilkes and disappeared into the night. How could they have communicated?"

"So, you are in touch with the Redjackets directly."

"No, you are."

Hunter grabbed his arm and twisted him to face her. "What are you talking about?"

"You know how they can take the sound a violin makes, sample it, and put it into a computer and make a whole new song? No one actually plays instruments anymore. It's all synthesized. Well, they can do the same thing with voices. When I call the Redjacket generals, every word I say into this phone," he pointed his cane at his desk phone, "is synthesized into your voice and put on that phone." He moved his cane to the purse hanging from her shoulder.

Hunter gasped. "I haven't touched this phone except to give it to Bianca."

"Tell that to the Senate Intelligence Committee. Tell it to the FBI."

"You misappropriated my identity! You can't do that." Hunter tried to calm her shrieking voice. "One of the people involved in your little scheme is going to get hauled in front of Congress, and they'll squeal. You're going to get caught."

"A little trick I learned from you," he smiled on one side of his mouth. "Undated, blanket pardons given in advance. They can lie like hell then turn it in after they testify."

"You can't do this. It would ruin me. I'm a politician. That's all I've ever been. I don't have a second career to fall back on. No husband to support me. No trust fund to bail me out of bankruptcy like you. This is all I have." Hunter waived her arms around the Oval Office.

"And you don't even have that." Roche walked away. "Quit whining and do what you're told."

Hunter felt her world slipping away from her. Everything she'd fought so hard to make happen was falling apart because of some slimy little asshole who didn't know a thing about governance. She laughed out loud. It was funny. She'd been screwed by a fool. The man was a blithering idiot, yet he knew how to survive better than anyone in history. And he was about to survive the Wilkes fiasco. But it was going to cost Veronica Lodge Hunter dearly. She could feel that in her bones.

He stepped up, nose to nose. "I want you to call Pia and make her tell you where Wilkes is. Don't let her pull that 'I dunno' crap. If she doesn't know, she sure as hell can find out."

How dare he treat her like that? After all she'd done for him. Hunter had never felt the urge to kill someone so strongly before. If she had a weapon, she'd bludgeon him to death. But he had her in a vise and was squeezing hard. "I want her pardoned."

"Ha!" Roche stuck the silver handle of his cane under her chin and lifted it. "From now on, you're my dog. You come when you're called. You sit when you're told. You heel when I snap my fingers."

They stood still for a moment; Hunter's chin stretched uncomfortably upward. Then he snatched the cane away and went back to the window. "Call her. Promise her a pardon if you have to."

"Will you do it? The pardon?"

"Call her."

Hunter thought about their last contact. Pia's text burned in her mind. "I lied because I knew why you were asking." The memory made her wince. The girl was two steps ahead of her. Could a pardon come close to patching things up between them?

Roche eyed her from across the room. "You know what's interesting, Veronica? You memorized her little interview where Wilkes was concerned, but you didn't notice she went public with the mother-daughter thing. She hates you so much, she just mentioned it as if you were a busker she gave a dollar to. Don't think you can hold your relationship together. You burned that bridge. Years ago. Call her. Threaten her with the death penalty."

Hunter covered her shock with her hand. "I won't. I can't..."

"Quit pretending you care." Roche crossed back to her. "You never wanted kids in the first place. They all turn out like that idiot nephew of mine."

At that moment, they sensed the young man's presence. In unison, they turned to the door and found the first nephew with one hand on the handle, half in and half out. His face fell and he turned away and pulled the door closed behind him.

It was over for her. There was nothing more she could use to resist Roche's blackmail. It made her feel like throwing up. Hunter pulled her phone out and dialed Pia. Her call went straight to voice mail.

CHAPTER 50

WE HAD REACHED THE END. It was over. We made it from Bishkek to Baku and from there to Tripoli and on to the western-most spit of land on Africa without a hitch. That's where our luck ran out. At each stop, we spent a few hours in an airport lounge, then I found a connecting flight to somewhere. But Dakar is where the streak ended. Senegal is not as big a travel destination as the other places. The next plane to anywhere wouldn't happen until dawn. And it was midday.

Mercury stood behind the clerk at the counter. *You look like Publius Quinctilius Varus at the battle of Teutoburg Forest. Smell like him too.*

I said, *Varus? Was he the guy that got slaughtered by the Germans? He fell on his sword for losing that battle.*

And they let his body rot. Mercury said. *You're using the same cologne. That's why they won't let you hire a private jet to Suriname.*

I said, *They have a private jet around here? I'm renting it.*

Mercury said, *Slow down, dawg. I'm just playing with you. The only private jet belongs to Sadio Konate, the ecommerce king of West Africa.*

The clerk shrugged. I thanked her and asked about the best hotel in town. Mercury was right. The admiral and I stank after being on the run for days. I still had on the clothes I wore to Mumbai.

Since we hadn't seen a Redjacket in four thousand miles, I chose the best hotel in town based on price. The cabbie was impressed when I told him the Radisson Blu, then he did a doubletake on our well-worn attire. But he took us there anyway.

Senegal has two socioeconomic spectrums, a small, close-knit community of wealthy Africans and the rest who struggle to make $4,000 a year. That meant the hotel and mall were enclosed in a compound surrounded by a fence and guards in dapper uniforms carrying automatic weapons. I had to prove myself a man of means before entering the grounds.

As always, the magic card worked wonders. As soon as the hotel clerk saw black titanium, he had only one room left, the Royal Suite. It had two bedrooms and a view of the Atlantic—and it didn't cost as much as the Holiday Inn in Manhattan—so I took it. Before going up, we went to the Sea Plaza Mall for fresh clothes and sundries. After cleaning up and changing, we ate lunch at an upscale restaurant overlooking the ocean.

And that's when she changed her tactics. "I would appreciate it if you would let me use your phone."

It almost worked. After sitting side-by-side for more than a day, listening to her unending demands, the word "appreciate" sounded like music. I looked her over as the waiter served our margaritas. She had admitted the Redjackets traced us because of a call she made, but she refused to consider them the enemy.

I asked, "Who do you want to call?"

She crossed her arms and stared at the waves. "I could tell people I'm a victim of human trafficking."

"How did that work in Baku?"

"I cannot believe you told them I had dementia." She huffed and kept her gaze out to sea. After a long think, she turned back to me. "I want to call Bobby."

"Now you're talking someone reasonable," I said. "When you get him, ask him if the Redjackets are good for your health."

She sneered. An act she must have developed in high school and worked hard to perfect since then. Although, I didn't see it working for her as a flag rank officer. Maybe she honed it all those years just for me.

I dialed Bobby's number for her and handed her the phone. She tried to look shocked that I didn't trust her. I didn't.

She took the phone and listened then handed it back. "Voice mail."

She drummed her fingers on the table.

I tried to think of an alternate mode of transportation. I didn't mind sleeping in a bed for the first time in a week, but I wasn't too keen on sitting still. It felt risky.

"Can I call Mikey?" she asked.

Mercury swept by the table like a waiter. *Can't say no to that, huh, homie? You're dying to know what's up between Mikey and Annie, right? I'll bet those two talk dirty to each other. Or maybe they're like Marc Antony and Cleopatra, they like to wager on who sacrificed more soldiers than the other.*

I said, *Generals don't wager on losses.*

Mercury said, *Oh. OK.*

I dialed General Thompson and handed her the phone. To be honest, I did want to eavesdrop on them.

Wilkes took the phone and greeted him. Then she got up and walked away far enough that I couldn't hear. Which pissed me off. Not enough to do anything about it, though. I was tired.

I sipped my margarita and enjoyed the warm, humid breeze—with one eye on my impudent admiral. Eventually, she ended the call and headed back for her drink.

Two feet away, my phone, still in her hand, started ringing. She held up a finger and answered the phone. "Bobby."

She walked away again.

What secret could a woman her age need to keep from the guy who saved her life—twice? This time, I strained to hear. I couldn't make out the words. The tone of voice didn't sound like ex-spouses working out what's best for the kids. It seemed more like an admiral talking to a cadet. Sharp, short commands. Was Bobby Jenkins, billionaire owner of Jenkins Pharmaceuticals, into a dominatrix vibe from his women?

Wilkes looked over her shoulder as if she could read my mind and moved down wind. It took me a minute to figure out why. The old admiral had spent many hours talking on windswept decks. Even a small breeze carried your words away from prying ears. Clever.

She came back, handed my phone over, and chugged her drink like a sailor. "Bobby says I should trust you."

"That twenty bucks I slipped him worked?"

There was a difference in her composure. Somehow lighter as if talking to Bobby made all her troubles evaporate. I would've asked her about it, but my fatigue from jet lag, being electrocuted by the lovely Radhika Chopra, and shot at by Wilkes's rescue squad was setting in hard.

Wilkes was feeling much the same. The tension might be gone, but the exhaustion remained. We agreed it was time for an afternoon nap. Upstairs, she went to her room. I barred the front door by putting a chair against it. I balanced the entire tea service on a stack of books on the chair. She was not going to escape on my watch. Even if Bobby had vouched for me.

I hit the sack with my pistol and phone tucked under my pillow.

IT WAS DARK WHEN MERCURY shook me. *O sleep, O gentle sleep, Nature's soft nurse, how have I frighted thee, That thou no more wilt weigh my eyelids down, And steep my senses in forgetfulness?* Mercury shook me again. *Did I ever tell you about how I made Shakespeare famous? Notice how he wrote all those plays about Rome? Yeah. He was an ingrate just like you, dawg.*

I opened one eye. The clock said midnight. Seven hours before the first flight out of town. *Did I ask?*

Wakey, wakey, Mercury said. *D'you remember how we lost to the Germans at Teutoburg?*

I said, *Not right now—because I'm sleeping.*

Mercury pulled the sheets back and yanked my arm. *Arminius, he was the German dude, knew Varus would try to escape at night, so his tribes built a wall in Varus' path.*

I said, *I need six more hours of sleep and another shower to feel human again.*

Mercury slapped my cheek gently. *Now, you will recall that this hotel compound has a single, guarded entrance and exit.*

Suddenly, I had an urge to look out the east window. I ran wearing nothing more than my tidy whiteys through the dining room to the window that overlooked the entrance. Three uniformed guards lay sprawled on the ground in unnatural positions. Four locals were in the process of stealing their weapons. The locals looked left and right before sneaking across the lawn. Only two more guards stood between the assassins and our elevators.

I crossed the dining room, heading to my room when I heard the tea service rattle. I backed up and flipped on the hall light. Admiral Annie Wilkes stood at the front door, fully dressed. The backpack holding her uniform hung from her shoulder. She held the tea service in her hands.

"Yeah. So." She looked to the ceiling. "I was hungry. Thought I'd go downstairs and grab a sandwich."

I watched her and wondered why she thought I would believe a lie like that. I said, "Assassins are here to kill you."

"I was afraid room service would wake—"

"And the backpack?"

"Um."

Admirals don't lie enough to develop a deep skill set. I let her twist for a second.

She changed tack. "I didn't want them shooting you by accident?"

"Thanks for the consideration." I aimed the pistol at her. "Get into my room—now."

She obeyed. I had her sit in the corner while I slammed my body into some clothes and grabbed my pack. Then I took her to the window and pointed out the dead guards on the ground. The pools of blood seeping from their bodies brought it home to her—finally.

We fled. I opened the door to the stairwell and listened. No footsteps were coming up. Lucky for us, they were lazy assassins who rode elevators. We ran down.

A guy with a radio patrolled the lobby. He yelled something. I didn't wait to discuss it. Gunfire snapped and echoed. We ran outside as the glass entrance crashed into small shards around us. The bullets went over our heads. We turned, crouch-running along the side of the building where the cabs had been. They were gone. Dakar is not known for its energetic nightlife.

The only vehicle around was a motorcycle. I knelt behind it to make my last stand.

Wilkes said, "The keys are in it."

"So?"

"Let's get on the bike and get out of here."

I looked at her, then at the bike, then re-aimed at the front door. There is an unspoken belief held by many people that all virile young men are expert motorcyclists. It's emasculating to face that presumption when you've never been on anything huskier than a pedaled two-wheeler.

One of the assassins poked his head around the corner. I brushed him back with a warning shot.

"You don't ride?" she whispered.

"I'm from Iowa."

"What's that got to do with it?"

"If it can't pull a plow—it's useless."

"Get on, then." She hopped on like a life-long biker chick and kicked over the motor.

Another gunman rolled out across the broken glass, sat up and fired at us. I fired back as two more came outside, shooting. I sensed their fourth man coming around the bushes behind me.

There's no better motivation for taking your first ride than fleeing a crossfire.

I got on. Wilkes clunked it in gear and popped the clutch. She leaned over the handlebars, her face just over the headlamp. We tore out of the parking lot, weaving through the flying lead.

"Hold on tight," she yelled over the noise. "Keep close to me."

My arms wrapped around a solid core. The girl might be my mom's age, but she still did her sit ups.

We heard the scream of two-stroke bikes giving pursuit.

There was no way to obscure our exit. There was one broad, flower-lined driveway. As Mercury predicted, the assassins had closed the gate. Being in a hurry, they left an arm-wide space on one side of the guardhouse. Wilkes shot us through the gap before I could scream. We turned on to a four-lane boulevard with walled shoulders. The assassins were within visual range quickly. They were as fast as Wilkes and had the advantage of knowing the city.

She revved it down the boulevard before making a sudden turn up a side street. It was littered with cars parked in haphazard fashion. With masterful precision, she leaned us between potholes and cargo trucks.

We swerved down an alley and found ourselves back on the four-lane road with nowhere to hide.

Wilkes cranked the throttle. "I can hold it straight for half a mile. Can you shoot one of them?"

When I turned to look behind us, I felt the weight shift the bike offline. "No. Turn around. Run straight at them."

"Like jousting?"

"Exactly."

"You must be damn good with a pistol."

"I am."

"I like it." She slammed on the brakes, popped the clutch, burned rubber, and spun us around on a manhole cover. She leaned over the headlamp again, twisted the throttle all the way down and held it there.

I used her shoulder as a firing platform. It wasn't great, but it could work. The first bike had been close behind us and flew three hundred yards past us when we turned around. The second bike was on us in a flash. I waited until I could see the surprise in the rider's face. He didn't expect our maneuver. He went down.

It was hard to tell if I'd hit him. He might've freaked and crashed. It didn't matter. I took aim at the third. He'd been far enough behind the others to figure out what was going on. He aimed a rifle.

Wilkes swerved. I wasn't expecting it and didn't lean. The bike wobbled. We lost a lot of speed.

The other guy shot past us. He turned around and gave chase.

We weren't moving away as fast this time. Two bikes were gaining on us.

"We're losing a tire." Wilkes did her best to keep it rolling.

She cranked it up anyway. I could feel my teeth rattling.

Mercury flew alongside us. *Hey, homie! Does this beat watching Orange is the New Black or what?*

I said, *A little help?*

Mercury laughed. *I gotcha, bro. Take a left at the next street, turn into the third driveway.*

I relayed the instructions to Wilkes.

"What the ... How do you know ...?" she asked.

"I get messages. Trust me."

Gunfire opened up behind us. The admiral resumed the serpentine weaving to throw off the killers. When we came to the turn, she took it. It wasn't clear if she was following my directions or trying to get out of the line of fire.

We were in the rich people's neighborhood. I could tell by the razor wire on top of the walled homes. Big houses with guarded gates lined both sides. Everything was closed. Except the third driveway. Headlights bathed the road from inside a compound.

"Tire's gone," she yelled. "We're going down."

The bike hit the rim as our friendly, neighborhood assassins turned onto the street behind us. Bullets flew by. Wilkes cranked the throttle. Sparks flew from the rim.

The bike lurched forward at speed. She leaned it to one side and lay the bike down, sliding into the driveway. The bike slid under the car that lit the street. We skimmed across a polished concrete entry on our butts. We came to rest in front of the bumper. Scorched but not broken.

A man in uniform jumped from the passenger seat with an automatic weapon leveled at us. *"Arrêt!"*

We raised our hands.

Our pursuers stopped on the street just a few yards away. The guard raised his rifle at them. They sped away.

The guard returned his attention to us. Then he slowly lowered his weapon. "Mr. Stearne?"

I nodded. "Do I know you?"

"Sir, it is me, Victor Ndidi. Sabel Security, Lagos."

"Oh, right."

Mercury said, *Don't lie to my man, dawg. You forgot all about that trip with Ms. Sabel to inspire the oil-rig security teams in West Africa.*

I said, *Nah, I remember that. Probably.*

It had been a couple years, but the last I heard the Nigerian branch was doing well and growing as West Africa's must-have security company.

Victor said, "It is an honor to see you again, sir. Are you all right?"

"Flat tire," I rose and helped the admiral to her feet.

"Qui sont ils connards?" A big man, black as the night with a voice that boomed like James Earl Jones stood behind Victor in the most expensive suit I'd seen since Alan Sabel was still alive.

Victor apologized and introduced us to Sadio Konate.

"You are knowing Pia Sabel?" Mr. Konate said with a thick French accent.

"Head of personal security, sir. It's a pleasure to meet the ecommerce king of Africa."

Wilkes looked at me as if I'd grown wings.

Konate nodded with a solemn air, his gaze on me while he thought. Then his smile broadened, and he stepped around his bodyguard. "Alan Sabel, the greatest of men. Never would we have launched all satellites in time without him. We are in his debt for all eternity. Please, be giving of my condolences to his lovely *fille*, ehm, daughter."

"I will, sir. Thank you."

"Would I stay to welcome but," he spread his empty hands wide, "alas, I hurry now to Suriname. You are welcome to stay in my home as my guest. My driver will be at your command."

"You know," I grinned, "I was just telling my mother that we've never been to Suriname." I leaned conspiratorially close to him and pointed at Wilkes. "Dementia, this is our last adventure."

"Ah!" He reared back with a welcoming roar. "Then you must be my guest on this journey!"

CHAPTER 51

Processed and released, the FBI had told Pia. She had expected it would take an hour, maybe two. They took her DNA, fingerprints and mugshot. They put her in a concrete holding cell that had a steel picnic table bolted to the floor, six steel bunks without mattresses bolted to the walls, and a one-piece, stainless steel sink and toilet bolted in the corner. No privacy.

The morning guard didn't know anything. The woman who brought lunch didn't know anything. The afternoon guard didn't know anything.

Hours later they brought in two women who whispered to each other about making a deal, turning on a third person. The two were engrossed in their conversation and paid no attention to Pia.

A guard came to escort Pia to the phone. A call had come in for her. It wasn't her attorney. In a dead-end hallway, a payphone waited for her. She said, "Hello?"

"Pia," Hunter said, "I'm working to get you out of there."

"Don't."

"Believe me, you need my help. This is going to get a lot worse before it gets better. He's talking about the death penalty."

"Of course he is."

"You have to take this seriously." Hunter raised her plaintive wail a notch. "He has the entire Justice Department at his disposal. No one can afford to fight such a powerful and permanently funded machine. He can win this. And he will be merciless. I don't want that for you."

"Of course you don't." Pia waited while Hunter left a long silence. "I know what you're trying to do. You're riding two horses with one foot on each saddle. This horse is turning left. Here's the deal: I don't know where Wilkes is. I can't contact Jacob. He's working autonomously. Give it up." She waited a beat. "Mom."

"You could find out. His credit cards. His phone. You could call him."

Pia marveled at her mother's transparency. How had voters not seen through her? Other politicians? If it had been a desperate attempt to save Pia, it might have been understandable. But it was a desperate attempt to save Roche from Wilkes. She said, "It sounds like you and Chuck figured out the NSA won't trace a Sabel phone without a court order."

"There's no need to be rude. I'm trying to help you. It could help with a plea bargain."

"There won't be a plea bargain. I have a plan. And it's solid."

"What is it?" Hunter asked. When Pia didn't answer, Hunter filled the silence. "If you won't let me help you, how about helping me? Did you find anything on that red phone?"

"We did. Many recorded instructions."

"They synthesized my voice. It wasn't me giving—"

"Goodbye. Mom."

"Wait! I could arrange a pardon for you. Give me something, and I'll work him. I can do this for you, Pia."

Pia weighed what she wanted out of all this. When she'd started out, she thought humiliating Roche into resigning would satisfy her. The fact that he'd forced her mother to debase herself like this changed her mind. Humiliation was still her goal—as long as he died as well. But what fate should Hunter suffer?

"I refuse any pardon from the Roche administration or any empty promise of a pardon." Pia hung up and nodded to the guard.

She went back to her cell where her cellmates had been talking in normal voices. They dropped back to whispers.

Pia had no idea of time. There were no windows, no television, no books, no radios. Clanging steel doors, indistinguishable shouts, distant conversations were all she could hear. Sharp, hard noises that jangled nerves without being terribly loud.

A woman came for her, put handcuffs on her wrists, then led her down a concrete corridor to a small room. Her attorney rose when she entered and asked to have the cuffs removed. Her jailer gave it some thought, then obliged. They sat at a laminated desk on stackable steel chairs.

Her attorney said, "They backed out of the deal."

"They can do that?"

"Not really. But they did."

"What next?"

"The FBI people we dealt with have been reassigned. The Justice people we dealt with have been reassigned. They're changing the charges."

"Roche." Pia bit her lip and nodded. A move she should have expected. "No wonder Hunter called me for a deal."

"She called you? That's illegal. That's tampering—"

"She'll say she called as a concerned mother."

"That was a shocker." Her attorney shook his head in disbelief. "How could she have seen you in the news all those years and not reached out?"

"What happens next?"

"A judge is hearing motions in an hour."

"What time is it?" Pia asked.

"Coming up on six. Our session ends when they serve dinner here." He paused and looked at her with concern. "You don't seem worried."

"They want to wrap it in national security blankets." Pia thought for a moment. "Even if the court and proceedings are sealed, I still get to request evidence in the discovery phase, right?"

"Only evidence relevant to the charges they bring."

That sounded bad. They had to bring murder charges. It had to be about the killing of Viktor Popov. That's what Roche said it was. But Roche was not a prosecutor. He might appoint the Attorney General, but he didn't direct operations. The Feds could bring any kind of interstate charges they wanted. Could they bring charges that precluded her evidence?

"If they change the terms, can I back out of the deal?" Pia asked.

"They had a warrant this morning." He shook his head solemnly. "You should tell me which ace you have up your sleeve. I can maneuver better in the hearings if I know where you're going."

A sick feeling crept into Pia's stomach. Hunter warned her about Roche's tricks. Thousands of attorneys were at his disposal. Telling her attorney the plan was definitely a smart move. Getting out of jail would be nice. But playing it too quickly would allow Roche to change the discussion on the next news cycle.

"Not yet."

CHAPTER 52

IT OCCURRED TO PRESIDENT ROCHE that he'd not seen his nephew all evening. Not since the kid walked in on his conversation without knocking. At least he had the Cheetos all to himself for once. He popped another one in, munched and watched the Fuchs News Channel. They were the only ones who cared about saving the nation from Radical Islam.

Hunter called on the landline. She must've figured out he blocked her calls on his cell. He considered sending her to voice mail but figured it was better to get it over with. "What."

"Pia refused the pardon."

"What'd you expect?" He munched another Cheeto.

"When facing a death penalty and clear evidence of guilt? I expected an emphatic YES. There are only two reasons she would refuse a pardon. The first is that she's suicidal."

"OK." He wondered if he should say something about what an awful option that would be, but he thought suicide would work out better for everyone involved. No sense pretending he didn't. "What's the other one?"

"She has something. Some kind of evidence she'll bring up at trial."

"Since it happened on your watch, you'd better find out."

"That's where I need your help." Hunter exhaled. "This is tricky. You need to call the Attorney General and tell him to have me review any and all document requests from her defense attorney. I'll determine if we need to pull executive privilege or national security concerns. I can't stop whatever she's up to, but I can get ahead of it."

"Fine." Roche wondered why he should care about Hunter's

problems. "Good luck." He clicked off.

A banner ran across the news screen. The pundits who were in the middle of extolling the virtues of Zenith Man stopped midsentence. One of them held her hand to her blondness. "I'm being told we have breaking news. Over to you, Diane."

Another blond stood in front of a courthouse. "*Politica* is reporting this evening that President Roche's chief of staff Hartwell Thomas has been arrested. No official announcement has been made at this hour. We're standing by at the courthouse in case they make a statement."

"The *New York Times*," the blond anchor said, "is reporting the man arrested for vandalizing the *Miami Herald* has reached a plea bargain. Their report says that he named Hartwell Thomas as the ring leader of the Redjackets. Do you have anything on that?"

"No," the courthouse-blond said. "I'm an outrage-reporter, not investigative."

"I'm sure we'll find this is another deep-state attack on the administration," the blond anchor said.

Roche clicked off the TV. If the bastards in Congress would just give him that war, none of this would matter. The nation would pull together as it always does in a time of crisis and rally around the flag and the administration. The same way they did for Abraham Lincoln and FDR. In three or four years, after the next election, he could declare victory, and all these insignificant distractions would float away on the tide. Who cares about Redjackets?

He dialed the Attorney General. "You have to get Hartwell out of jail."

"I can't do that, sir," the Attorney General said.

"What good are you if you won't take care of problems?"

"It's a state case, sir. We do not have any control over state cases."

"Well make a federal case out of it, then. Yank it out of state court. Then kill it."

The Attorney General blew out a breath as if he were exhausted. "I'll look into it, sir. Goodnight."

"Wait. Hunter wants to work with you on the Sabel case."

"I heard she's the girl's birth mother."

"So?"

"That would violate just about every … Look. She'd compromise our case. We'd be thrown out of court day one. If the defense team wants her help, she can work with them."

"Great." He clicked off.

Roche wondered why everything had to be so difficult in the government. He should make it mandatory for his employees to do what he told them. That's how it worked at his company. Everyone did what they were told. The government was so slow and dull. Why were they always whining about checks and balances?

His next call came from the Redjacket general who'd lost Stearne and Wilkes in Baku. The Redjackets simply had to find the fugitives.

The man said, "They escaped Senegal."

"After all I did to find out where they were, YOU FAILED?" Roche left his shout hanging. "Did you lose any more of you useless morons this time? Do I have to send an ambassador out in the middle of the night to spring someone from jail again?"

"No, sir." The man hesitated. "We outsourced this one."

Roche hung up on him. "Surrounded by idiots."

He thumbed out some tweets about his arch enemy, a long dead senator. He sent more tweets about a lame representative who dared to request documents on the *USS Caine* investigation. He tweeted about Saudi terrorists sneaking into the country with illegal immigrants from Mexico. He stared at the ceiling while he tried to think up another one that would keep people from talking about Wilkes and Thomas and Sabel and the Redjackets.

The White House was quiet. He felt bored. Day after day, all these annoying problems kept creeping up on him. Ridiculous stuff like arresting an American patriot like Hartwell Thomas. Spending one's life on such trivial and tedious crap could drive a man insane.

The CIA Director called. He planned to track the movements of Miguel and Tania and thought that would lead to Jacob Stearne and Wilkes. It sounded to Roche as if the man wanted a medal. Stearne and Wilkes would never make the headlines if he could start that war. He clicked off after spitting out a "good job."

Why care about anything if everything's going to hell? Thomas in jail. Sabel plotting something. Senegal operation in flames. One quick call to Hunter about resigning and all his problems would become hers. She could handle all the investigations, the subpoenas, the questions. God, the questions were endless. Why are there dead Redjackets in Mumbai? What happened on the *Caine*? Why did Pia Sabel refuse a pardon? Why is your campaign manager in jail? Why is your chief of staff in jail?

He took a selfie and posted it with the caption, "Your President, Zenith Man, on the job!"

Right away, his post got hundreds of likes from his base.

He watched the numbers rise like a spinning dial. A smile spread across his face. They loved him. They really loved him. He shouldn't be moping around getting depressed about this crap. God didn't create Zenith Man with such great intellect and divine authority to sit still. He'd been overthinking, that's all. This evening's thoughts had been one-quarter wisdom and three-quarters cowardice. He always relied on his gut instincts. Why should he say, "let's do this" when he should be saying, "it's done."

What was obvious was the need for war. Look at the Saudi prince's pretend army. It was American made and led by a man who had everything handed to him, who never accomplished anything. And he thinks he's God's gift to military strategy.

The prince's open invitation to all nations allowing fly-over inspections was intended to prove he wasn't building up military men and machines. What a blunder. Without realizing it, the prince had exposed his tender underbelly to American might for no other reason than pride. One big airstrike and the prince would surrender. They're soft. The time is now.

He called his National Security Director. "Get me a reason to bomb a Saudi air base right now. I want bombs going off by dawn."

"We've found nothing out of the—"

"Don't give me that shit!" Roche felt his anger rising. Zenith Man had no more time for slackers and fools. "You found WMDs for Bush, goddamn it, find me something!"

CHAPTER 53

THE ADMIRAL AND I WEREN'T on speaking terms during the flight to Suriname. The whole trip I talked to Sadio Konate. Fascinating guy. She sat in the back and stewed about being called a dementia victim again. I told him our story. He verified my credentials by calling the Major. She knew him well. They had a few good laughs in French which meant the jokes were about me. In the end, he got off in Suriname where he had business over the next couple days. He let me borrow his jet and pilots to reach my final destination.

We landed in Hermosillo, Mexico at ten that evening. I sent the jet back with a bottle of mescal and a thank-you card. I think that's what rich people do when they borrow jets. I'm never sure about the etiquette.

I rented a car and drove north toward Nogales, then turned left at Santa Ana. We were in the middle of nowhere and going deeper. Several times, the admiral had undermined the mission. With a long day ahead of us, it was time to figure out why.

"Want to tell me who you called?" I asked for the ninetieth time.

"I told you," Admiral Wilkes said, "it was a mistake. Someone lied to me."

"Since that someone who lied to you almost got me killed, I'd like to know who and why. I deserve that much."

"When this is over." She chopped the air with her hand as if giving a final command and another word would be insubordination.

Tough.

"You've been leading them straight to us. Before I get into a territory where there's a good chance the Redjackets will find us and kill us, I'd like to know why."

"Life sucks, soldier."

"I might leave you in the desert."

She reached in the backseat, pulled her backpack up front, yanked the medals on her uniform out far enough to see them and pointed. "Commendation and Arctic Service medals. Comms and nav went dark north side of Greenland. I got us out navigating by the stars."

I grumbled and drove on.

It was a good thing it was night. The scenery was nothing but creosote and cactus as far as the eye could reach. We stayed on that road for an hour or so, then turned up a rutted dirt track for a couple more hours.

Mercury sat on the console between us. *Wilkes doesn't like you much, does she, homie?*

I said, *I don't care. I'm ready to leave her in the desert and let her die.*

Mercury said, *Hey, now. Go easy on the ol' gal. She's been through some tough times, ya feel me? Look at her. Notice what's going on with her? The closer you get to the border, the more anxious she gets. Like everything you did up till now was just pre-game. She's hearing the lions roaring in their cages. She's hearing the crowd chanting for her blood. Any minute, the gates'll swing open, and she'll be forced into the middle of the Coliseum with a stick to fend off the beasts. The Emperor has his thumb down. Don't you want to know what she's thinking?*

I said, *I wanna know who the hell she called and why.*

Mercury said, *You could learn a thing or two from her. Why not try talking to her?*

"How'd you learn to ride a motorcycle like that?" I asked Wilkes.

She looked at me for a long time. "I set my sights on the admiralty when I was a kid. My mom told me to forget it, the Navy is a man's world. So, I set out to learn the ways of men." She looked me over with contempt. "Can't say I was impressed."

"What do you mean, the ways of men?"

"Aggressive attitude, win at all costs, competitive as hell, take whatever you want, assume no one is better than you until he can prove it."

"Aggressive attitudes and competitive nature got us to the moon before the Soviets."

"Women did the math."

I said to Mercury, *Where is this getting me? She hates men. Big deal. She probably gets off on shouting orders at cadets and captains.*

Mercury said, *Keep listening.*

"And in all that, the motorcycles come in where?" I asked.

"Part of learning to cope in a man's world. I couldn't compete with men in a boxing ring, but a motorcycle leveled the playing field. Raced 'em back in high school. It had that wind in your face feeling like the sea. The bikes impressed the academy more than my sailing trophies."

She sighed and rifled through our road snacks out of boredom. She stopped cold and dragged out one bag. "Cheetos? Really? You don't eat these do you? You know what these things are made of?"

"I just grabbed stuff off the shelf. They were all out of organic broccoli."

We rode along in silence. Mercury was right, she was keyed up and getting worse. She sighed every third breath. Kept her gaze out the window even though she couldn't see anything.

"What else did you do to make it in the man's world?" I asked.

"Learned to do shots. Played poker. Memorized the NFL. Knife fights. When I got to Annapolis, I could challenge the guys to just about anything." She laughed. "First guy I dated at the academy dumped me because he said it was too much like dating a guy with boobs. That loser never even made commander."

"Is that when you met Bobby?"

"We're not talking about Bobby."

And that was the end of that conversation.

I had no idea how to figure out what her game was. She had a different agenda from what Ms. Sabel and I expected, that much was for sure. What I could do about it was eluding me.

I found a station that played Ranchero. It was my only company for the next hour.

First light was still in the future when we turned onto the last dirt road. A few more miles of bumps and dips and we parked it. We got out the hydration packs. It was hot already. The ice had melted. We started hiking by moonlight.

About three miles down the dry stream bed, we began to see fresh tracks. Thirty people in five separate groups were following the same arroyo. They were not far ahead of us.

When I planned our route on the satellite map, it didn't look traveled. It would take people fifty miles across barren desert to the nearest road. I couldn't imagine smugglers using it. Desperation makes people do extraordinary things.

The admiral understood the situation without any explanation. We continued quietly, keeping to the sandy side of the wash and away from their tracks. The sandy side of an empty stream bed is where the water flows. If it rains twenty miles upstream, a flashflood could sweep down without warning and drown everyone. They were hiking the higher ground about twenty yards to our left for safety. With any luck, we could pass them unnoticed.

But our luck ran out. We heard what sounded like a fight. But not a fight. We came near a small group of people, a stand of sycamores between us. Some were yelling and screaming. Others were shouting warnings. We went wide to avoid them.

Our world was turning to a predawn pale blue. The dark silhouette of a man stood out. We moved slowly, working our way around the people. We carefully planted our steps to avoid stumbling over a river rock.

Wilkes grabbed my arm and squeezed hard. She pointed into the darkness.

In the half-light, I could make out one man standing with a rifle aimed at a huddled group of five. There were two people on the ground. Entwined.

I felt Wilkes let go of me and stride across the sandy stream bed.

"What the hell do you think you're doing?" she bellowed in her admiral-voice. "Get off her."

I turned to Mercury. *What is wrong with that woman? She could get us all killed. There could be fifty more of these armed guys.*

Mercury said, *Did I tell you she's a complex person? Did I tell you to learn more about her? She has her reasons.*

The man with the gun turned to Wilkes. He raised his rifle and aimed at her.

I put a bullet through his left shoulder.

His rifle went off as his barrel flew up, the bullet tracking skyward. He shouted and cursed and tried to level his weapon at me. I was on him, grabbing the gun and slamming it into the bridge of his nose. He fell across his companion.

The rapist scrambled to his feet and tried to reach for something. I shot him in the left femur. It was a miss, five inches lower than planned.

The two of them howled. One of them cursed me in all-American English. I took a closer look. American cowboys.

Admiral Wilkes pulled the victim off the ground and said something in Spanish with a terrible accent. The five huddled figures drew the victim into their midst. The admiral hushed them and tried to reassure them.

I put my pistol in the face of one guy and tossed his weapons. Then did the other guy. Knives, a revolver, brass knuckles—nice guys. They growled and hissed and threatened and clutched their bleeding wounds.

Boots kicked their way down the wash, surrounding us. The rest of the expedition pulled back branches and stepped into the clearing with us. They were all Mexican. Only the two cowboys were Americans.

Someone turned on a flashlight and surveyed the scene. The Mexicans were very concerned.

When the light crossed the admiral, a very different woman appeared. Wilkes was sick. Drained of color yet filled with rage.

After a moment, everyone talked at once. The men asking questions, the women crying. Then the admiral raised her hands and shouted like an admiral. Everyone shut up. She started talking in Spanish. She determined the rapists were the coyotes, the guides for the group trying to cross the border illegally. They had insisted on breaking the groups up, taking personal care of the women. They had been hiking since noon the day before.

The sun rose by the time we had the group calmed and sorted out.

"We have to take them with us." The admiral looked at the sky.

"No way." I grabbed her arm. "The last thing we need to do is get caught by Border Patrol. They'll turn you over to the Redjackets before they process these people."

"I can navigate just as well if not better than you. If you won't take them, I will."

"You? An admiral in the US Navy, is going to lead a bunch of illegal aliens across the border? C'mon."

"I'm serious." She looked it too. "I'm not going to leave them out here to get raped by the next asshole who comes along."

"Because you know the 'world of men' so well, you just assume we're all rapists?"

"No." She looked away.

Something struck me inside. "Because you were a victim?"

"No."

She crossed the wash back to the huddled women. They looked up as she approached, their eyes filled with equal parts of hope and fear.

Mercury said, *Complex. Did I mention she's a complex woman? Did I mention she's going to get her way? Did I mention the high in these parts is going to reach 113F? That's 45C, dawg.*

I watched her talking to the women. Despite the culture, language, and socio-economic canyons between them, she connected with them in a way I doubt many other women could. She exuded some form of compassion that transcended pity. She wasn't giving them a pep talk. She wasn't commiserating with them. And she wasn't badmouthing men. She was talking them up and out of the well of despair and getting them ready to accomplish their goal. Even if that goal was illegal. She didn't care about the law at that moment, she cared only about giving them one minor victory toward empowerment.

As honorable as it might have been, it was an act that undermined the mission. Again.

I looked around at the rest of the group. Every male stared at a different part of the ground. None of us knew how to respond. One guy bandaged the rapists. He did a half-assed job before he lost interest. The rest of us were fine with letting them bleed out in the dirt.

"Admiral," I called out, "going to be a scorcher today. We need to get moving."

She translated this. Everyone got up and trudged up the wash.

I made sure the rapists had some water. If they were lucky, another group of crossers might come along and take pity on them. Maybe not.

The illegals had split into squads again. It helped make them less noticeable to drones. I sidled up to a group of men.

Admiral Wilkes moved over to my squad.

She walked alongside me. "When I called Bobby, it was a prearranged signal. He called President Roche, and they conference called me. We were making a deal to get a pardon for our daughter."

I stopped in my tracks.

She stopped about ten feet away. "She killed the officer who raped her after her CO tossed the rape kit into the Sea of Japan and told her to forget about it."

Mercury stepped between me and the sun. *Yo, brutha. You dizzy or something? You look sick.*

I said, *You knew all this?*

Mercury pulled his toga tighter. *Of course. I get the 4-1-1 on all y'all, I'm a god.*

I said, *And you didn't think I needed to know she was selling out my life for a pardon?*

Not really, no. Mercury looked at me as if the question was a dumb one. *First, you're just a mortal, and we don't care about you. Second, you don't believe anything I tell you.*

I said, *How do you expect me to believe in you when you tell me stuff like this?*

"Because it's true." Wilkes had her head tilted to the side as if she were deciding whether or not to tell me I had a tarantula on my neck.

"You sold me out? I'm the guy who's rescuing you. You were going to let them kill me in Dakar?"

"Bobby said you could survive anything. And Mikey said you had god on your side—whatever that means."

"Mikey? General Thompson was in on this? You … and Bobby … and Mikey just decided to let me take my chances with four assassins armed with automatic weapons?"

"It was a mistake."

"Ya think?"

Mercury put his hands out like he was stopping a bus. *Hold on, homie. No need to get salty with an admiral. They're like almost-Caesars. Show some respect. You should be honored to die for a woman of her caliber.*

I said, *Have I lost it completely? Are you—my personal god and savior—telling me my life is worthless?*

Duh. Mercury shrugged. *But don't take it so hard.*

"Don't worry," Wilkes started following the others, "I can take it from here. You don't owe me anything. And for what it's worth, you're a decent guy. Army and all."

I watched her walk around a palo verde tree and become a wraith in the shimmering heat. I considered shooting her. A jury would give me a medal after hearing my story. Or. Maybe not. She was trying to save her daughter. Who was in jail for justifiable homicide. That had to sting for a family who had otherwise done well in life.

I started walking.

Mercury appeared with a walking stick. *You owe it to Pia-Caesar-Sabel to bring the admiral back. You can't let her wander around.*

I said, *She claimed to be a brilliant navigator.*

Mercury said, *She doesn't know Ed Guach, yo. Or how to get to his house. She'll just hike up this wash until the lot of them hit Sells, Arizona. ICE will pick them up and deport them. They'll start all over again tomorrow. But they'll turn the admiral over to Roche. You're not going to let him win this one, are you? The president who disrespects war heroes every time he turns around?*

I said, *She was trying to make a deal with that devil. Why would I help her?*

Mercury said, *Because, my man, you know how to beatdown on a coward like Roche.*

As much as I hate to admit it, once in a while god is right. For that matter, so was Ms. Sabel. None of this shooting people was getting us anywhere close to stopping the war. I'd been playing Roche's game by Roche's rules. That's never a good idea. I needed a strategy. One that would fool everyone.

Mercury said, *And you're the biggest fool of them all. Don't worry, bro, we gotcha covered.*

I caught up with Wilkes. "I can get you that pardon."

CHAPTER 54

PIA'S ATTORNEY WAS LAST TO join the meeting. He waddled in, sat with a grunt along the broad side of the expansive mahogany table and looked at the documents laid out in front of him. He nodded at Pia, then at each of her assembled experts: former FBI Director, Daniel Shikowitz; former Attorney General, Derrick Holden; former CIA Director, John Brandon; and Sabel Technologies President, Bianca Dominguez. Other staff and associates lined up behind their respective bosses.

"Thanks again," Pia said to her attorney, "for getting me out of jail this morning. Last night was not the greatest experience of my life."

"Pia," he said, "you're lucky. The only reason you're free is because you landed the only judge in town who has a daughter in soccer." He waved at the assembled experts. "And you're damn lucky to have so many important people willing to drop everything for this meeting."

Pia nodded.

He picked up a meeting agenda. "Let me recap the defense you want to present here. This is what we call the Texas Defense, you can kill a man as long as you can prove he needed killing. I get that part. The evidence you provided is insurmountable for the prosecution. They can't argue this guy Viktor Popov was misunderstood." He waited for the chuckles to subside. "A quick recap: Popov started his career by supplying the bomb that Hezbollah used to blow up the Marine barracks in Beirut in 1983; he supplied al Qaida with the explosives used to bomb the US Embassy in Nairobi." The attorney fanned through his Popov brief and set it down. "I'll leave the rest for the jury."

Pia pointed to the stack as the attorney moved it to the side. "Don't forget, we have physical evidence and testimony that he was involved in the airline disaster that propelled Roche into office. If we go to trial, that has to be brought in."

"National security issues on that last one." The attorney sighed. "Let me think. They're charging you, Title 18, Part 1, Chapter 51, Section 1116, Murder or manslaughter of foreign officials." He shrugged. "They might get it suppressed. Depends on the judge."

The attorney picked up the next stack of documents. "Let's start with this discovery request. You want Executive Order 15388, Enemy Belligerents in the War on Terror." He pointed at Holden. "EO's went through you in your day, what is this one?"

"It's what the last three administrations used to justify targeted strikes," Holden sat up, "which most people think of as drone strikes but can be applied broadly. You have my affidavit that the EO exists and that the official one online is not complete. You'll need the full version. It includes the exception from *jus ad bellum* analysis for targeted strikes in general." Holden looked at Pia. "Jus ad bellum is the right to wage war. The basis for the next step in targeted strikes. In this EO, the jus ad bellum is automatic whenever the president wants it to be."

"Nice." The attorney inhaled. "OK. What is the next step in targeting a person? Mr. Brandon, how did you proceed when you were head of the CIA?"

"Same as my predecessor, I relied on that same document because it also contains the *jus in bello* rules."

Her attorney held up a hand. "I'm not familiar with that one, but my Latin tells me that means right *in* war. Does it spell out the right to do x, y or z in a warzone?"

Brandon pointed at him. "Exactly. The four rules gave us the right to target a specific person for a specific reason. We would love to see the current version brought out in court because we believe the Roche administration has suspended the rules. They are now targeting whomever they want, wherever they want, whenever they want— regardless of citizenship or country involved."

"What are—or were—the rules?" the attorney asked. "That's what will apply to Pia."

"The first one is that you have to provide a legal basis for resorting to an instant death penalty. Second, you will only target this person because of an imminent threat to an American citizen. Third, that you minimize collateral damage and have no other way to resolve the issue. And lastly, that the local government cannot or will not solve the problem for us."

The attorney frowned. "Those rules don't help us. If Popov is on this list as Ms. Dominguez claimed in her deposition, he wasn't an imminent threat after, Ms. Sabel disarmed him. And we can't say Alaska was unwilling or unable to solve the problem."

The former FBI director raised a finger before he began speaking. "Alaska is not the local government in this case, the US is. Therefore, we were willing to target this terrorist and Ms. Sabel did so. As for imminent threat, he had a weapon on his person."

"Weak." The attorney ran his hand over the stack of documents.

He took a long deep breath and leaned back in his chair. Resembling an anachronism from a pre-war era, Pia half expected him to light a cigar and smoke while he thought. After a long time, his eyes came back to survey the group before settling on Pia.

"Take the pardon, Ms. Sabel." He patted the papers. "This is great stuff. This is the stuff of legal thrillers. I'm sure the judge and jury would be shocked to find out several presidents have targeted foreign diplomats for aiding our enemies. It's disconcerting that they've found a loophole to extend the warzone to American soil. The imagination conjures up all manner of problems. Democrats targeting Republicans. Republicans targeting Democrats. The administration targeting editors and reporters. But, and this is a big but, they're never going to cough up the documents."

"We know they exist," Shikowitz said. "We've sworn out—"

"Sure." The attorney held up his hand. "They'll take it to the Supreme Court, drag it out thirty, forty years. They'll lose. You and your grandchildren, Ms. Sabel, will celebrate your pyrrhic victory. By then, your company will have been in ashes for decades. There's even a chance they could win a couple motions, try you without your discovery request, and you wind up spending all your years waiting for your victory on death row."

Everyone exhaled and rocked back in their chairs, knowing he was right.

Pia chafed and squirmed and ground her teeth. A pardon would put everything behind her. She and Sabel Industries could move forward. The Major would be happy. Forty thousand employees would be happy.

Who else would be happy? Hunter.

Who would be unhappy? Pia. Who would lie awake every night plotting revenge? Pia. Who would have to start over in her quest for vengeance? Pia.

She needed Jacob to bring Wilkes in. If he failed, Pia could spend a lifetime facing these charges. Even if Jacob made it, she wasn't sure what Wilkes would say. She'd been confident the admiral had evidence that would bring down the administration. After spending a day in jail, she wasn't so confident. Was Roche smart enough to play her for Wilkes? Pia felt a sinkhole in her stomach. Her attorney was right, the safe bet, the smart move, was to take the pardon.

Doing so would take Pia out of the headlines and leave Roche an opening to push his war. Once the war started, nothing Wilkes could say would stop it. It came down to risking her life on a possibly-mad soldier and an enigmatic admiral. A big risk. And the upside? She goes to jail but saves the world.

"No pardons," she said. "I already have the documents in question, no need to wait for discovery." Pia pulled a stack of papers from her bag and tossed them on the table. "Send the request for discovery. Then immediately send a thank you note for prompt service. Copy Veronica Hunter on the note."

CHAPTER 55

President Roche sat alone in the Oval Office picking away at his giant bag of Cheetos. The TV news anchors wailed about things that no longer seemed important to him. Stock market swings, tariff complications, cabinet secretaries abusing their positions, people he barely knew going to jail, it was all so tiresome. Who cared about any of it?

"Word is," a reporter said from outside the White House, "that he sits alone all day because no one wants to go near him. He's that toxic."

Roche threw a handful of Cheetos at the screen. "I'll show you toxic, asshole. I don't need to see anyone. I'm sick of all the failures like you, whining about everything I do. You make me sick."

Wondering if his outburst could have been overheard by his secretary, he crept to the door, peeked around the edge. Her chair was empty, her computer screen dark.

Back at the TV, a breaking news banner flashed. The anchor announced a live broadcast from the Pentagon. Roche turned it up. It had to be about the bombing he ordered. Maybe they would show video footage from drones. Boom! A house vaporized. The swing set and the bikes outside tossed like trash in the wind. Everybody loved those videos.

An Air Force general took the podium. "Today, for the first time in my thirty-two-year career, I felt compelled to refuse a direct order from our commander in chief. I firmly believe the order to destroy a Saudi Air Force base was illegal. Rather than refuse the order, I have resigned."

Roche turned it off. The bastard. A press conference? He would have to show that rat what a mistake he'd made. He thumbed a text to the chairman of the Joint Chiefs of Staff demanding the man be fired for insubordination. Any of his relatives who may be in the military should also be fired.

But he couldn't remember the man's name before he finished the text.

Roche turned the TV back on. Instead of reporting about the general, the anchors were talking about something else entirely.

"You heard that right, Diane," one blond said to the other, "The *Herald* is reporting that Hartwell Thomas has entered into a plea agreement with the State of Florida in exchange for information about other people who have directed the Redjackets to perform acts of violence. Rumor has it that President Roche may be named."

Roche threw his cane at the TV. It crashed into the surface and stuck in the middle. He wondered if TVs spilled blood. The cane sticking out of the broken set looked like it should be dripping blood.

He pulled his phone and sent a series of tweets. Hartwell Thomas was a nobody, barely knew him. Generals are dumb as socks. Immigrants are pouring into the country looking to rob your homes.

Hunter stormed in with enough anger in her eyes to slay him.

"I just got a thank you note from Pia's lawyers. Guess why." She tapped her toe impatiently. "Your idiot staff turned over Executive Order 15388—unredacted—for Pia's discovery. Her lawyer already has it logged and entered into evidence."

Roche grabbed a couple Cheetos and stared at her while he ate them. He never understood why women got so emotional.

Hunter crossed her arms and paced as if she were agitated. "Where the hell is your secretary? I walked in here unchallenged."

He shrugged and popped a couple more Cheetos.

She stopped pacing. "Don't you get the problem?"

"It's Top Secret," he said. "They can't publish it."

"Shouldn't have published it, you mean." She hissed. "They did. It's now part of the public record in court. You can look it up online. Anyone can look it up online. The only reason it hasn't dominated the news is because the reporters are too lazy to read through the first fifty pages of legal jargon while Thomas and Cooperman are the headlines. But trust me, by this time tomorrow—"

"Who's Cooperman?"

"General Cooperman. He just outed you for an illegal order to bomb the Saudis."

Roche picked up his text to the chairman about firing Cooperman and any relatives. "He's dead meat. I never gave any order to bomb the Saudis."

"They'll have it in writing, Chuck. You can't say you didn't give the order."

"I'll deny it."

"For Christ's sake," Hunter waved him off. "Cooperman is the least of your problems. EO 15388 will have even Senator Krueger calling for the Mayan solution."

"The what?"

"They'll cut your heart out on a high altar in front of everyone."

Roche didn't care for her girl-drama. He also didn't care for hearing about people publishing Top Secret documents. "Why? What's the big deal? That order came from Bush, four administrations ago."

Hunter grabbed his shoulders with both hands. "Each president stretched the rules. Congress abandoned their duty to declare war and let president after president invade, kill, bomb, strafe, whatever they wanted, from Korea to Yemen. The War Powers Act limited 'police actions' after Vietnam and so on. But when drones became effective, we all started bending the rules. Obama included American citizens fighting for foreign adversaries. I included American terrorists wherever they might be, even inside the USA. Publishing it will destroy the legacy of every president since Nixon."

"They set precedent." Roche shooed her away. "I'm just doing what everyone else did."

"No. You went overboard. You broadened the definition of terrorist to include anyone who disagreed with you. Then you named names. One of those names is a prominent news editor. Another is the Speaker of the House. And the one that could become a problem in the next few hours is Admiral Annie Wilkes."

That could definitely be a problem since the CIA Director tracked the Sabel operatives, Miguel and Tania to Brownsville, Texas. He'd sent all the Redjackets he could muster to cover the coast, the border crossings and the river crossings for miles in any direction. They were to kill Wilkes and anyone with her.

He said, "I never put any names on that list."

"Then Hartwell did it for you. Who added them doesn't matter. You signed the document, and they're on there for anyone to see."

"Then I'll pardon Pia, and her case goes away."

"She already refused the pardon."

"Can she do that?"

"Yes, Supreme Court, US versus Wilson, 1833."

He said, "I'll have the Attorney General dismiss the charges."

"You can't," she said. "That would be obstruction. The Justice Department prosecutes when they believe there is a crime. Telling them not to after they've filed charges means you're directing them for political reasons. They need legal reasons why the charges should not have been brought in the first place. I can make that happen, but it takes time. We can get the NSA director to redact the EO on security grounds, but that also takes time. We need to keep Pia off the front pages before the Cooperman and Thomas headlines get stale. We need her to keep her mouth shut for three days so we can get everything done and make it go away."

How she knew all this stuff made him wonder if she were making it up. She could be making it up. He ate more Cheetos while he thought.

"Are you going to offer me some of those?" Hunter asked.

He turned away, holding the hefty bag far from her. People were always trying to take his stuff. If he gave her some, everyone would put their hand out. Everyone around him was a filthy beggar.

"What do you recommend we do?" he asked.

"Get her in here and make a deal."

"What kind of a deal?"

"I have no idea," Hunter said, "but she wants something. Kids do things like this, ruin your life and your legacy because they want something. They're always trying to get your attention. We bring her in here and make any deal she wants. It only has to buy us two or three days."

That hadn't gone well last time he got together with Sabel as he recalled. But Hunter was right, if he didn't get the EO taken down before Wilkes was killed, that list would get his name scratched off every building in the world. People would scoff at the term Zenith Man. The Russians would call in his loans. He'd be the laughing stock of the business world.

He looked up Sabel in his contacts and thumbed out a text. "We need to talk. I'm open to any idea you might have. Get to the Oval Office as soon as possible."

Pia's reply was immediate. "OK."

Hunter looked over his shoulder. "Too easy."

CHAPTER 56

ED GUACH SERVED IN THE Rangers with Miguel and me. He and Miguel were both Native Americans and stuck together like glue for a tour. When Ed's uncle died and left him a ranch in the Tohono O'odham Nation, he left the killing fields behind. Ed sent us an email about the only downside being the illegal aliens running amok in the region. Then he mentioned there were a bunch of Mexicans coming through too.

Miguel had to explain to me that to natives, *illegal aliens* are those of non-native descent. He said, "We didn't give your ancestors visas, green cards, citizenship or anything. Y'all are a bunch of anchor babies—with attitudes."

We arrived at Ed's place in the afternoon. We were sunburnt, thirsty, dirty, and tired. Ed gave our Mexican companions directions on how to find their destination. We waved goodbye. Ed caught me up on the plan to keep Wilkes and me under the radar. Miguel had told him to expect us by relaying the request through a third friend who lived in Brownsville, Texas. Miguel and Tania had gone there to throw off the Redjackets looking for Wilkes.

The admiral called General Thompson while Ed drove us to somewhere with high speed Wi-Fi for a video call. He figured the old Spanish mission, San Xavier del Bac fit my plan best. It was a somewhat popular tourist destination so Redjackets couldn't open fire if they found us. And he knew the priest.

When I wondered why Ed would know a priest, Mercury appeared, scaring the daylights out of me. *He's a just-in-case Catholic, yo. A couple hundred years ago, the Catholics offered to save the Tohono O'odham from the conquistadors, all they had to do was convert.*

I said, *Catholicism or slavery? The Spanish were so thoughtful.*

Mercury scowled. *Don't go acting all superior, bro. In 1960, the US Government built a dam that flooded 10,000 acres of the Tohono O'odham Nation. To say 'sorry' the Feds gave the tribe 40 acres somewhere else. After a thirty-six-year lawsuit, the Feds lost all their appeals and finally coughed up another $30 million in cash.*

I said, *What's that got to do with Ed being a whatever-you-said Catholic?*

Mercury said, *These days, the Nation teaches the O'odham language and spiritual ways in school, but some people like Ed go to mass every so often just-in-case.*

I considered going to a Christian church just-in-case their gods were any funnier than mine.

When we arrived at the ancient mission, the priest and Ed gave us some privacy in a parish office. We gave a pre-arranged signal to General Thompson to start proceedings on his end. Wilkes went to the lady's room to change into her crumpled and torn uniform. She came out with an admiral's bearing and a homeless look. She sat down next to me. We had a long wait.

"I need that SD card now," I said. She'd claimed to have evidence on it that would back up her testimony. Turning it over was part of our deal.

She still hadn't told me about her testimony or the evidence, but her hatred of Roche was matched only by her distrust of the man. She said, "Not yet. It's my last bargaining chip."

"Tell me what's on it, then."

"You promised me that pardon. When it's in Mikey's hands, you get what you asked for. Not until then."

An hour later, General Thompson used Skype to connect from the Oval Office to a laptop the parish priest let us borrow.

Before he could get out half a greeting, President Roche grabbed his hand and stuck his face in the lens. "Where's that boss of yours, Stearne? She was supposed to be here a long time ago."

"We've not communicated—to prevent you from finding me."

"We're going to trace this call, and have you arrested, you know that?"

"Then the deal's off." I clicked off.

Wilkes nearly exploded in anger at me. "You said this would work. You—"

With a smug grin, I pointed to the laptop as they rang me back from the White House. She realized my intent to establish the upper hand. She nodded and backed off. I turned the camera to her.

"I'm here, Annie," Thompson said. "I told you Jacob can walk through hell."

"You're right." She gave me a nod that was as close to a thank-you as I was going to get.

"The president has agreed to our deal." Thompson held up a piece of paper. "He's going to file this pardon while you do your part."

"Are you sure he can't back out of it?" she asked.

"Once it's filed, it's in the hands of the Justice Department and part of the public record. It will be a done deal."

"I want it filed first. Then I make my statement."

"You get nothing!" Roche shouted in the background.

I leaned into the camera angle. "Then we're going back to blank screens, and this time I won't be accepting any more call backs."

"Fine. Here, you happy?" Roche signed the document in the background. An intern ran in the room, took the folder, and left.

"It's done, Annie," General Thompson said. "You sure you want to do this?"

Mercury massaged the admiral's shoulders. For the first time since we met—when she pressed a pistol to my head—she looked relaxed.

My used god said, *You don't have any idea what she's going to say, do you, homeboy? You put all that blood, sweat and tears into getting her here and you didn't even notice that Roche seems to be fine with this. Why would he be fine with this?*

I said, *Because we have a deal. At some point, we have to trust the lying scumbag.*

Mercury said, *You still won't listen? Check the news back home.*

Slipping out my phone, I checked the *Post*. My heart stopped like a bear was squeezing it in his paw. Pia Sabel in jail for murder? She was taking one for the team. Just like on the docks in Mumbai. I had to come through for her.

Mercury said, *Which means you need some insurance about what*

Wilkes is gonna say. Remember those blue threads that connect you to people? One of those threads connects you to Pia-Caesar-Sabel and she's tugging on it. She's counting on you to make this work. Good thing you didn't leave Wilkes back in the desert, huh homeboy?

I said, *Yeah, she has to say something that'll bring down the Roche administration to save Ms. Sabel.*

"Hang on a second," I grabbed the laptop from Wilkes and stabbed the pause button. "Why is Roche so happy about this?"

She stared at me. It was a cold, hard stare that most likely reduced ensigns to puddles onboard a navy ship.

But I'm not an ensign. "I'm pulling the plug on this right now unless you tell me what you're going to say."

"At some point, you have to trust me. Don't worry, I've got this." She pulled an SD card out of her medals. It had been sandwiched between two, looking like a riflery ribbon. She handed it to me. "But you can have this. You've earned it."

It was a halfway measure. I could live with it or drop the whole project and walk away. I was leaning toward walking.

Mercury said, *Yo, homie, this is the big question: who do you trust? The admiral has never lied to you. She's withheld information but never lied. She has an unblemished record, she's accomplished a good deal despite a hostile working environment throughout her career. Are you going to let a rich guy who wormed his way into the presidency win? Or Annie Wilkes? I'm telling you, it's time to let her do her thing.*

Sometimes, when god speaks to you, you go with it. Except for the times when he tells you to pillage and plunder. Some of his ideas are a bit dated. This time, I decided to go with it.

I repositioned the laptop, so she took up the frame and looked as much the admiral as possible after our flight halfway round the world. I told Roche, "You can begin recording now."

Wilkes straightened up, took a deep breath and fought back tears. "I am Admiral Anne E. Wilkes. I conspired with Saudi nationals to set charges in the magazine of the *USS Caine* with the intent of blowing up the ship. They gave me money and promises of safe passage to and resettlement in Riyadh."

CHAPTER 57

PIA WAITED IN THE COFFEE shop two blocks from the West Wing for General Mike Thompson. He came in and sat across from her with a big grin.

"Thank you, Pia." He patted her arm. "Your father would be quite proud of you."

"Just doing my part." Pia finished her orange juice. "Jacob will get Ms. Wilkes back here after midnight. Who's picking her up?"

"Bobby's wife is the jealous type." He nodded. "We thought it best if I met her. Thanks again."

He squeezed her hand and pushed back and walked out.

A little while later, Jacob sent her a text. "All set."

Pia rose, shouldered her bag and walked to the West Wing entrance. At this late hour, it was eerily quiet. There were no reporters. Few Secret Service agents patrolled the grounds. She checked in at the gate and stopped in the lobby when she saw two familiar faces. Hunter's detail lingered outside the Oval Office.

"Dan, Catherine," she waved, "how are you?"

"Tired and overworked. The principals are such jerks, no one accepts this assignment anymore. Nothing but overtime, no replacements." Catherine rolled her eyes. "How about you?"

"Optimistic." Pia smiled.

Catherine opened the door for her. Roche and Hunter stood in the middle of the room, sharing a folder of papers.

Roche looked up, angry. "How dare you let her in here without asking, Catherine? What the hell is wrong with you? Are you stupid? You have to be the two dumbest agents in the service."

"OK, that's it." Catherine burst around Pia. She crossed to face Roche. She took off her gun belt and badge and slammed them on the Resolute Desk. "I'm not stupid enough to work for either of you. I quit."

Dan was right behind her. He slammed his things down on the desk next to Catherine's. The two of them stormed out and slammed the door.

Pia turned to Roche. "Nicely done, Mr. President."

"You're back to wearing those ninja outfits?" Hunter crinkled her nose. Then shook an attitude change through her face and body. "Good to see you, Pia."

"You're working with Chuck Roche after you promised to help me destroy him?" Pia asked.

"What?" Roche's gaze bounced back and forth between the two.

"Association of necessity." Hunter lifted her chin and dropped a disdainful glance on the president. "I'm doing this for you."

"I can't wait to hear all about it."

Hunter waved the folder in her hands. "We worked things out with the Justice Department. We can get them to drop the charges."

"You said that would be obstruction of justice," Pia said.

Hunter frowned. "What makes you think I said that?"

Pia shrugged.

Hunter held the folder out for Pia. "The executive order you requested reminded me of the US position on Popov. He aided terrorists for decades. We pointed out the executive order to the attorneys who filed the charges. After a little research, we discovered there was a $10,000 reward issued for him dead or alive during the Iraq War. You've actually done your country a service."

Pia observed Hunter and wondered if they shared any personality traits. Or flaws, as the case may be. The woman's calculated thinking was remarkable. But it was always calculated to help Veronica. And it was cold. Icy cold. Pia felt a chill in her veins.

She wondered if her DNA meant she could do the things Veronica had done. Whipping campaign crowds into a fervor using hate and division. Finding assassins to kill Lloyd Aston and Sandra Velocitane, her adopted parents. Capitalizing on Viktor Popov's crimes while ordering him targeted for destruction.

"The last time we met," Pia faced Roche, "you wanted me to back your war because the Saudis bombed our ship."

"Now that your murder is swept under the rug, you're feeling pretty cocky, aren't you?" Chuck Roche tapped his cane on the floor and squinted at her. After an uncomfortable span of time, he said, "The country needs you on board, Pia. You can join me and help rally the people. You're the perfect person to wave the flag and lead the charge against those damn Saudis."

Pia checked out the pistols the agents left behind. She pulled one out, a SIG Sauer P229, fully loaded. She slipped it back in the holster and leaned her butt against the desk and folded her arms.

"You still pushing that lie?" Pia asked.

"I never lie." Roche shook his cane at her. "You should get on board before we track down whoever leaked the copy of Executive Order 15388 to you. You can still go to jail for espionage, you know."

"We've restored your security clearance." Hunter stepped in front of Roche. "But how did you know I said anything about obstruction?"

"You know who bombed the *USS Caine*." Pia leaned around Hunter to glare at Roche.

"Answer me." Hunter pressed into Pia's space.

"Did you know?" Pia asked Hunter. "Are you aware that your president orchestrated the bombing of the *USS Caine*?"

"We have the full confession from Admiral Wilkes." Hunter pursed her lips while trying to figure Pia's angle. "We've released it to the press. She backed up everything Chuck's been saying."

Pia tried to suppress her smirk.

"What?" Hunter asked. "What is it? Is it something you found on that red phone?"

"We found your synthesized voice," Pia said. "Lots of orders going to Redjacket generals. We know it wasn't your real voice, but we can't prove who actually gave the orders."

The both slowly turned to Roche.

Hunter faced Pia. "What else? How did you know what I said?"

"Bianca made a mistake." Pia pushed off the desk. "When she scrubbed your red phone of all previous calls, she left the mic open. All your conversations were inadvertently recorded. Unfortunately, you take it with you everywhere you go—so I've heard everything you said for the last few days. You've been quite duplicitous—Mom."

"You idiot!" Roche shouted at Hunter. "Had to take that phone to your little girl, didn't you? You're a freaking moron."

"How could you do this to your mother?" Hunter's eyes narrowed and her mouth zipped tight. "You evil little viper."

"You're thinking it's nature over nurture then?" Pia asked. "That's my biggest fear. Consider the eavesdropping a form of payback for calling my boxing coach and ordering memorabilia online to fool me into thinking you cared."

"I just wanted…" Hunter looked away. "You'd grown up so fast. I'd been busy. I wanted to see…"

"Wait, this might work out," Roche smacked a couch with his cane to get their attention. "I'm sure there's evidence of Veronica's failed coup attempt on there. Give me those recordings. I can get rid of her."

"Is that what you want?" Pia asked him. "You don't need her in office to pardon you after Wilkes's second video?"

"Why would I need a pardon?" Roche asked. "I've been exonerated. Wilkes confessed to everything." He shook his head in disgust. "That's it, I'm done with you, little girl. I'm calling for a full investigation into how you wound up with that executive order."

"First, you'll want to see part two of the Wilkes interview." Pia waved her phone. "When Jacob finished recording the video you demanded, he and the admiral recorded a second video. In the second one, she explains that she made the first one under duress. Then she clarifies some other things, like how you approached her to scuttle her own ship in exchange for a pardon. Would you like to see it?"

Roche and Hunter froze like deer on a lonesome moonlit road. Pia relished the moment.

"We made a deal." Roche's face grew red. "A deal, damn it. She confessed, and her daughter went free. We had A DEAL!"

"She did what you asked," Pia said. "You forgot she promised to release evidence to back up her claims. She and Jacob uploaded that evidence to the *Post's* website half an hour ago."

Hunter covered her face with her hands, peering between her fingers and leaned back against the desk. "What is it?"

"The evidence backs up her second video, not the first." Pia left a dramatic pause. "It turns out US Navy ships are concerned about security. Sailors are not allowed to bring phones onboard. But it's good for morale to have phones available. So, the navy has internet-based phones connected via satellites for the sailors to use. Of course, they monitor those phones to make sure no one is giving away secrets."

"Damn it!" Roche slammed his cane into the coffee table.

Pia moved sideways, out of the cane's reach.

"After a few suspicious phone calls from Nora Ratched," Pia continued, "one of the security officers brought some recordings to the admiral's attention. Admiral Wilkes discovered Nora supplied explosives to some Redjackets onboard. Several other members of the administration were complicit as well."

"O'Brien, Rochester, and Thomas." Hunter leaned in and barked at Roche. "You blithering idiot. You're the President of the United States, and you let your people get involved in sabotaging an American ship?"

"SHUT UP!" Roche smacked Hunter in the ribs with his cane. "Why didn't Wilkes stop it?"

Pia grabbed him by the collar and lifted him off the ground. "Don't ever hit her again."

"If Wilkes knew about it," Roche yelled in her face, "why didn't she stop it?"

"Because you called and moved the time line up while she was in Mumbai." She dropped him and backed up.

"YOU?" Hunter bent in pain, one hand on her ribs. "You picked up an unsecure line and called the Redjacket on the ship? You stupid fool. Why would you make a call like that on an unsecured line?"

Roche picked up his cane to swing like a bat. Pia sprang forward and yanked it out of his hands.

Hunter reached for one of the pistols on the desk. She aimed it at Roche. Then at Pia. Then back at Roche.

Shocked, Pia considered her options. She'd moved too far from her mother to lunge for the weapon. Talking Hunter down was her best option.

"Hey," Roche's voice broke. "Wait a second, Veronica. Hang on." He held his hands out in front of him as if they could stop bullets. "Don't hurt me."

Hunter stepped forward, aiming with one eye.

"Not a good idea, Veronica." Pia nodded at the pistol. "Send him to jail, not the graveyard."

"The legal process takes too long," Hunter thumbed the safety off without taking her eyes off Roche. "Besides, he'll find a way to weasel out of it."

"Are you forgetting the basis of American government is the rule of law?" Pia asked.

"All for it," Hunter replied. "Until it doesn't work."

"We have the red phone data. We can prove he synthesized your voice."

"I've been victim long enough." Hunter glanced at her for a second. "Want to know why I gave you up for adoption? He said he'd never marry a woman with someone else's baby." Hunter scoffed. "He never married anyone."

"Please, please, please," Roche broke into tears. "I'll marry you. Put the gun down."

"You dumb motherfucker." She jacked a round into the chamber. "You just had to be president. Wasn't enough to be a billionaire. Don't know shit about governing or economics or politics, but you had to be president."

"You're not going to shoot." Roche regained his arrogant look. "You're just a dumb cunt."

Hunter squeezed off a round that grazed his ear. They were all silent while the sound reverberated, and their hearts raced.

"Please, don't hurt me." Roche turned to Pia. "Help me. Please."

Pia felt the pressure of a moral question weighing on her. When she'd started out, she wanted him humiliated. Then she wanted him dead. Now that he pleaded for help, part of her felt compelled as a caring person to do something. The other part of her wanted to stop a war that would spiral into a world-wide conflagration. Roche's life for millions of lives.

But could she live with herself after witnessing Roche's cold-blooded murder?

She turned to Hunter. "Don't do something you'll regret. Jacob told me I'd see Popov's death over and over again in my head. He was right."

"I'd love to see him die over and over again." Hunter kept her aim on Roche. "Do you have any idea how many humiliations I've suffered at his hand?"

"Take the gun from her," Roche's wide eyes pleaded with Pia.

How many assassins had he paid? How many sailors died to provoke his war? How much hate had he inspired among the people? What were the chances for his redemption? Was his life worth saving?

"When you cross to the other side," Pia crossed her arms, "say hey to Alan Sabel for me. And Lloyd Aston and Sandra Velocitane—and all the others whose deaths you negotiated."

"I never meant to hurt anyone…" Tears streamed down the president's face.

"You talk big," Hunter sneered. "Now you're just another sniveling coward. Can't you even die like a man?"

"Don't hurt me, please," Roche fell to his knees. "I didn't do anything."

"Still can't take responsibility?" Hunter took another step forward. "I had everything under control, cruising to a second term. No problems. No scandals. But you thought you were smarter than everyone else. You thought everyone would adore you. You've got nothing but a string of scandals, the government lurching from one disaster to the next, because you don't have a clue how to run a government. Finally, your gross incompetence came to light. I could've fixed it for you. But you couldn't take help from a woman, could you? You hatched a plan to cover up your negligence with a war. And that required a little sabotage. SO YOU CALLED IT IN FROM A DESK PHONE? You're the dumb cunt. Fuck you."

Hunter fired. The bullet hit just below his right eye. She fired again, a miss. She fired a third, that hit above his left eye. She fired a fourth that ripped open his neck.

President Chuck Roche hit the floor with a dead thud. Blood and brains spilled over the presidential seal on the carpet.

Hunter stood still, the smoke wafting from her barrel. She slowly looked up at Pia.

"A hundred and twenty-five Americans dead," Pia said, "and your only concern was that Roche used an unsecured line? With hope, help and therapy, maybe I can overcome your genes."

A Secret Service agent opened the door. His eyes swept from Hunter to her smoking gun, to the president's corpse.

Hunter turned to Pia, "Help me."

CHAPTER 58

Miguel was joking with Cody when I visited his hospital room. A sling held his leg above the bed. Toes stuck out of the sling, which answered my question about whether he lost the leg. A titanium rail ran above his tibia with titanium screws rising from inside his bone through his skin to the rail. Seeing it made me wince.

Miguel was on his way out. We bumped fists and made quick plans to meet up later for dinner.

"I gotta apologize," Cody said after the initial greetings. "First time we met, I thought you were just a washed-up white boy."

Mercury sat on the edge of his bed. *Hey, homie, don't let him talk atcha like that, smack his injured leg.*

I said, *Ima let it go, see where he's heading.*

"You didn't seem to care about nobody but yourself and nothing but fine food." He picked up his bed's remote control and raised his head up. "I saw a different guy in Mumbai. Someone who cared about people. Cared about his country."

"Nah. I only care about great recipes."

"Serious, man," he closed his eyes. "How do you do that?"

"Pretty much just look up dishes on the internet."

"I mean, how do you go making some strange cannelloni-thing, then pick up a rifle and ice guys in the streets of a city halfway 'round the world—then come back home like it ain't no big thing?"

Mercury said, *Ah, now we're getting somewhere, ya feel me, dawg? This guy is ready to hear the good news about the whole Roman Pantheon.*

I said, *I think he's more interested in Hozho.*

Mercury said, *Don't you be bringing that Navajo heresy in here now. Who brought you home safe and sound? Was that Monster Slayer? Did Changing Woman tell you where the bad guys were waiting to ambush you? I don't think so, homie. You gotta dance with the god that brung ya.*

Cody was looking at me funny.

"It happens to me too," I said. "Sometimes, in a battle, I freeze up. Call it what you want, but when the bullets start flying, and people start dying, sometimes, I just can't move." I pushed the funny-looking hospital chair closer to the bed and sat. "Tell me about Somalia."

"Yeah. I froze." Cody looked away for a while. I kept quiet. Then he took a deep breath. "We was on a routine mission to protect some local guys. They moved ops from one town to another. Intel was clean, no rebels in the hood. Then outta nowhere, they rain down on us. Jose and Paul were outside. I could've gone for 'em. I didn't."

He took another deep breath. When he started up again, his voice was quaking. "They died right there at my feet. That's when I un-froze. I went nuts and mowed down six rebels. Two of 'em tried to surrender. I blew their brains out. Where was my fury when I needed it?"

I waited while he composed himself, then I picked up his hand as if we were going to arm wrestle. I closed my other hand over his. "If they knew what I was thinking when I earned that Distinguished Cross, they'd have thrown me in jail instead. Courage isn't something you pull out of your pocket, it's what comes up when you're so scared you don't care about dying anymore. Nothing matters because—in your head—you're already dead. You transcend life and do what needs doing. But that's not what bothers you, huh, Cody?"

He met my gaze.

"The hard part," I squeezed his hand and let go, "is coming home— after that monster burst out of your soul in Somalia."

Mercury said, *Now tell him about doing a feriae imperativae for him.*

I said, *We're not going to hold a victory parade for him, or festival, or whatever that means.*

Mercury said, *Cheering crowds, showing off your captured slaves, throwing gold to your adoring fans, what's better'n that?*

"I never thought I could get like that," Cody said. "Primal and violent.

I can't stop seeing it. The blood, the bodies, the smell of the dead. I got home and thought I put it away but then, in Mumbai…"

We sat and stared in different directions, thinking about our demons.

When I didn't want to think about them anymore, I said, "I'll talk to Miguel about doing an Enemy Way ceremony for you. He did one for me after our last deployment. It worked wonders. It helped me let go of the monster inside of me, make him a separate person, pull him out when I need him, put him away when I get home."

Mercury leapt to his feet. *Wazzat? I'm the reason you can kill a man one day and cook a mighty fine dinner for his surviving kin the next. Tell him, homeboy. Tell him Jupiter's honest truth.*

Cody looked confused. "I come from a Christian family. I don't know about doing any—"

"They don't do it for outsiders, so you're not doing anything just yet. If Miguel agrees, and I think he will because you were a great asset in India, then he'll explain it to you. It's about getting your Hozho back, the balance in life. I swear to you, it made my nightmares go away."

Mercury said, *Say what? I make your nightmares go away.*

I said, *You are my nightmare.*

Cody looked skeptical, but he didn't have to commit, so he nodded.

I got up and headed out. I stopped by the door. "You did well, kid. You didn't freeze. You saved me. You saved the boss. You're in the Sabel family now."

He teared up, so I turned away. Men don't like other men watching them cry.

"Wait," he said. "I been hearing this voice. Kinda weird, like some old guy trying to talk street. Will this Navajo thing make it go away?"

"One can only hope," I said. I left.

Mercury waited in the hall and put hand out to stop me. *You heard him, homie! He can hear me. That's the first step. Now go back in there and tell him to forget all that crazy-Indian crap. Tell him you're going to hold a victory parade with pretty girls throwing rose petals on him and—*

I said, *If I'm not totally insane, go in there and tell him yourself.*

The drive home was relaxing. I stopped at the grocery store and picked up ingredients to make that dish I was working on before I was so rudely interrupted. But the idea of my nice soft bed, and getting my dog back from the neighbor, and taking a long nap took root in my mind.

When I saw the car in my driveway, it was something of a letdown. Since it was blocking my garage, it became more of an annoyance. I parked behind it, kind of a right-back-atcha thing. I grabbed the groceries and headed for the front door.

A woman held a bouquet of flowers as big as she was and a basket full of jams. She peered through the foliage. "Are you Jacob?"

"Depends."

"These are for you." She thrust the flowers at me and blushed. "I wanted to thank you for what you did."

I dropped the grocery bag while trying not to fumble the blossoms.

We bent down to get the bag at the same time. We bumped heads. We laughed. "Sorry."

"And you are?" I asked.

"Oh," she blushed. "Jenny Jenkins. Jaz Jenkins is my brother, Bobby, well, um. You saved my mother's life, though she'll never admit it, and you …"

Her voice trailed into the background while I looked her over. Jenkins was not the right name. She was a Thompson. She had the general's tough-as-nails build in a distinctly feminine package. She had Annie Wilkes's pretty face. She also had her mother's poise—after she started her prepared speech.

Mercury held up the flowers. *Hey dawg, you falling for a murderer? She was in jail until my brilliant little plan paid off.*

I said, *What's wrong with a little murder now and then? The guy needed killing.*

Mercury looked her over, head to toe. *You think Bobby knows? I mean, he's got to suspect, right? His boy Jaz, supposedly this young lady's brother, is like a wet slice of bread compared to her.*

There was a lot to like about the admiral. General Thompson was right, she was one helluva woman. Her daughter didn't appear to fall far from the tree.

Mercury said, *You've been wanting to find the right woman, settle down, start a family—is she the one you're thinking about? I mean, her mom didn't seem to take those marital vows all that seriously and we know Jenny has a temper. You hearing me, bro?*

"Have you ever had pork stuffed cannelloni?" I asked.

She hesitated, looked at her car.

I had the flowers in one hand, the groceries in the other. I turned sideways so she could see the holster on the back of my belt. "You can hold the gun on me, make sure I'm as nice a guy as General Thompson said I was."

"What makes you think Mikey said anything about you being—"

"You could've had the flowers delivered."

CHAPTER 59

PIA SWISHED HER GOWN AS she surveyed the guests gathered in the living room at Sabel Gardens. She half expected her dad to come in, his booming voice drawing everyone's attention with his customary witty welcome. She should take that role and make a short speech.

Maybe next time.

The crowd was bigger than she expected. After hours of poring over the guest list and memorizing the backgrounds of all her top executives, employees and customers, she felt she knew them better than ever. She knew why her father was so gregarious in a group like this, they were all remarkable people. They were people who made the world a better place.

"General Thompson, so good to see you again," she said. "It was an honor to work with you on this mission."

He responded with effusive thanks before another guest interrupted.

"Allow me to present my grandparents." Dhanpal grinned despite the sling holding his arm and the large bandage beneath his suit. "Sunil and Jabamani Singh."

"We've met actually," Pia said while shaking hands, "but we didn't have time for formal introductions."

They exchanged pleasantries and discussed Dhanpal's bravery until the Major politely drew her away.

"The Prime Minister of India is arriving," the Major said. "You will recall—"

"That he saved my life and we committed to developing a new generation of Indian satellites? His wife's name is Ranjita, their children are—"

"OK, you did your homework." The Major smiled. "I'm proud of you."

"Are you sure?" Pia asked. "No reservations?"

"In the end, what you were doing became clear to me. I still disagree on the necessity. But I understand. You did what you needed to do. One thing still bothers me. She's not strong, and she's not quick. You could've taken the gun away from Hunter."

"That would've been one way to handle it." Pia took a glass of water from a passing waiter. "It felt like an out of body experience. I didn't feel compelled to intervene. I felt like a cold, dispassionate observer watching someone fulfill her destiny. Tell me the truth, does that make me as evil as she?"

The Major met her gaze and breathed several times before forming her reply. That worried Pia.

"Did the end bring what you wanted?" the Major asked.

"What did I want?" Pia looked in her glass for an answer that wasn't there. Many fears rose in her mind about being her mother's daughter. Did she want to elucidate all that for the Major? "Vengeance, maybe? You told me; revenge brings nothing but remorse. You're right. So, I'm looking on the bright side. Between the two of them, they were destroying the country. I let them destroy each other instead."

"You sound like Brutus justifying his killing of Caesar, 'not that I loved Caesar less, but that I loved Rome more.'" The Major touched her arm to draw her eyes. "Did you get what you needed from Veronica?"

The question circulated through Pia's mind like ice water. Letting the woman self-destruct left Pia back where she started, motherless. Was she, like Brutus, making an excuse for calculated treachery? Or had she sacrificed her long-lost mother for the good of the country?

Pia wrapped her arms around the Major and hugged her tight. "I never really needed anything from Veronica. I know that now. While I'll visit her in prison, she meant nothing to me. It took me a long time, but I figured it out. Some people have a loving birth mother. Others are blessed with a surrogate. Every time I'm in trouble, you're there. Every time I hoist a trophy, you're there. I am blessed with you. I realize that now."

The Major patted her eye with a cocktail napkin.

"You were right from the beginning," Pia said. "I was using Hunter until I could find an opportunity to destroy her. I hope you'll forgive me for fighting with you. I hated that part."

The Major gave her an understanding, reserved smile.

Sensing someone behind her, Pia turned around.

"Admiral Wilkes," Pia said, "it is an honor to meet you in person. I've felt such strong admiration for you these past few days."

"Thank you for believing in me in my hour of need." Wilkes teared up. "I felt terribly alone until Dhanpal showed up. Your faith in me saved the country, Pia. You saved the world from a horrific and endless conflagration. You know, the Navy needs leaders like you. Have you considered serving?"

The Major burst out laughing. "Pia? Take orders? I'd love to see that happen."

The Major excused herself to check on the evening's special guest.

The party swirled her in circles. Never more than thirty seconds with one person before moving on. She began to understand why her father started the party with a hearty welcome, it saved time and covered the bases.

From across the room, the Major gave Pia the sign. Pia held her up her wineglass by the stem and tapped the bowl with an hors d'oeuvre fork until she had everyone's attention.

"As you are painfully aware," she said, "Veronica Hunter refused to resign after her arrest. Congress came back from recess to impeach her. Moments ago, the Senate convicted her. Shortly thereafter, Speaker of the House, Charles Williams was sworn in as president."

A round of applause went up. Cheers and toasts began but Pia cut them off. She said, "President Williams has chosen this dinner party as his first appearance. He needs to recruit several people in this room to join his administration. Admiral Wilkes, if you have no interest in being our next vice president, now would be a good time to tour our kitchen."

More applause followed by laughter. This time, Pia let her guests toast to their hearts' content.

Before the toasts died down, dinner was announced, and the group moved to the dining room. Pia hadn't set foot in it since Alan's last big party. Everyone took their places. The staff brought a round of Pia's favorite tequila for each guest. It was time to start a tradition of her own. She stood at the head of the table and picked up her shot glass. An aide rang a chime.

Everyone's attention turned to her.

"Here's to starting a new life," she raised her glass, "in the corporate office. From now on, I will dedicate my life to changing the world through conscious capitalism. No more bullets, no more fights. I'm going to stay home so I can get fat and sassy."

She threw back her shot.

Everyone hurrahed and downed theirs.

The Major looked up at her. "I don't believe that for a minute."

THANK YOU!

Thank you for choosing my book. I hope you enjoyed reading it as much as I enjoyed writing it. As an independent writer, I am dependent on word-of-mouth referrals and book reviews. If you liked this book, please tell everyone, and leave reviews all over the place. I will be eternally grateful.

When you do write a review, send me a link to it and I'll put you in the next drawing for an autographed book. I run at least three or four drawings a year.

If you can't get enough of Pia, Tania, Miguel and Jacob*, checkout the series at SeeleyJames.com/books. While you're there, join my newsletter to get discounts, drawings, fun, news, outtakes, and more about the Sabel Agents club on Facebook! Every week (or so, sometimes I'm lazy), I'll let you know about the book in progress, personal triumphs & tragedies, what I'm reading and other fun stuff. I even had one person write to me to say, "I don't like your books, but I love your newsletters." To which I replied, "Thanks, Mom." Yeah … whatcha gonna do?

I'd love to hear from you. Please write, message me on Facebook, let me know what you think.

*I like you already.

NOW THAT YOU'VE READ THIS BOOK, WHICH ONE SHOULD YOU READ NEXT?
HTTPS://SEELEYJAMES.COM/BOOKS

ACKNOWLEDGMENTS

My heartfelt thanks to the beta readers and supporters who made this book the best book possible. Alphabetically: Miguel Rodriguez, Pam Safinuk, and Gloria Shirley.

- Certified StoryGrid Editor Leslie Watts whose brilliant coaching and critical diagnosis turned this book from my usual greatness to a masterpiece. Visit her website https://writership.com/
- Extraordinary Editor and Idea man: Lance Charnes, author of the highly acclaimed *Doha 12, SOUTH, THE COLLLECTION, and STEALING GHOSTS.* http://wombatgroup.com
- Medical Advisor and Character Diviner: Louis Kirby, famed neurologist and author of *Shadow of Eden.* http://louiskirby.com
- Amazing Editor: Mary Maddox, horror and dark fantasy novelist, and author of the Daemon World Series and the fantastic thriller, DARK ROOM. http://marymaddox.com

A special thanks to my wife whose support, despite being reluctant to say the least, has been above and beyond the call of duty. Last but not least, my children, Nicole, Amelia, and Christopher, ranging from age nineteen to forty-five, who have kept my imagination fresh and full of ideas.

ABOUT THE AUTHOR

His near-death experiences range from talking a jealous husband into putting the gun down to spinning out on an icy freeway in heavy traffic without touching anything. His resume ranges from washing dishes to global technology management. His personal life stretches from homeless at 17, adopting a 3-year-old at 19, getting married at 37, fathering his last child at 43, hiking the Grand Canyon Rim-to-Rim several times a year, and taking the occasional nap.

His writing career ranges from humble beginnings with short stories in The Battered Suitcase, to being awarded a Medallion from the Book Readers Appreciation Group. Seeley is best known for his Sabel Security series of thrillers featuring athlete and heiress Pia Sabel and her bodyguard, unhinged veteran Jacob Stearne. One of them kicks ass and the other talks to the wrong god.

His love of creativity began at an early age, growing up at Frank Lloyd Wright's School of Architecture in Arizona and Wisconsin. He carried his imagination first into a successful career in sales and marketing, and then to his real love: fiction.

For more books featuring Pia Sabel and Jacob Stearne, visit: SeeleyJames.com.

facebook.com/seeleyjamesauthor

instagram.com/seeleyjamesauth

bookbub.com/authors/seeley-james